THE
FIRST
RING

A Novel

Robert Anthony

Also from Robert Anthony

Mark Roberts travels to southern Transylvania in search of a renowned doctor to help his ailing wife. A string of recent murders has the loving husband wondering if the deaths are connected to the doctor and his clinic while the local police suspect Mark. With lies coming from all directions, and not knowing who to trust, Mark must unravel the secrets in the small village before it's too late.

Copernicus Paradox is the codename for a top-secret multi-agency mission. Charlie Poole is a 40 year aeronautical engineer with NASA who is forced into retirement and now working as a low-level employee with an environmental organization at a remote site in Antarctica. Charlie discovers a signal from space and becomes entangled with a mysterious Chinese woman who may be the key to knowing who to trust…if he can trust her.

Contents

"It is easy to go down into Hell; night and day, the gates of dark Death stand wide; but to climb back again, to retrace one's steps to the upper air – there's the rub, the task."

- Virgil

PART I

Two to Barbados

"Please…" the young woman begged, "please…don't…make me." She stuttered as she drew in a deep breath, and a single tear ran down her reddened cheek. She dropped her head and wiped away a tear with the back of her hand, as her sandy blond bangs fell over her face.

"Keep moving," said the man standing beside her in a dry and unsympathetic tone. He nudged her forward with his right hand while holding a gray sports jacket draped over his left arm. He was five feet eleven and wore khaki pants and a blue collared shirt with unbuttoned sleeves rolled halfway up his forearms. His black hair had grayed around the temples, but he still moved easily with a lean, fit frame.

"I don't want to die," the young woman sobbed. She shuffled her feet and moved in the direction the man pushed her.

"Drowning is what you should really be worried about," said a tall, thin man standing behind the shorter man in khakis. The second man was easily six feet four and wore a pair of black, large-framed glasses that were pushed far up the bridge of his nose, making his eyes appear larger than normal and accentuating their pale blue color. His curly hair was thick, black, and disheveled, making it appear he had just rolled out of bed. He wore a blue and white, plaid-patterned, button-up shirt with a navy-blue sweater vest. His blue jeans were wrinkled, and his black high-top sneakers were faded and worn with a few small holes around the toes.

"Statistically speaking, you're ten times more likely to die from drowning after crashing into the ocean than from the plane crash itself," the tall man continued. He pushed his glasses with his right index finger but withdrew it immediately when he realized they were already resting against his brow. "People don't realize that most plane accidents are survivable…" he paused, "still, you'd probably pass out before the plane hit the water and then drown in your seatbelt as the plane sank to the bottom of the ocean."

The young woman covered her ears with both hands, closed her eyes, and started singing a song she heard in the cab on the way to the airport.

"You're not helping, Ethan," the man in Khakis said while turning to face his taller companion.

"I know a thing or two about communicating with teenagers, Brendan," Ethan said, dropping his head to look at the shorter man over the rim of his glasses. "Modern theory suggests that you're supposed to remain calm, be honest, and reason with them." He lifted one hand and pointed his finger to emphasize his point. "The 'Do It Because I Said So' days of parenting died with the rotary phone." He put his finger to his lips and added, "She's a lot like her mother."

Brendan Clark rolled his dark brown eyes and turned to face his daughter. He placed his hand on her shoulder, took a deep breath, and spoke calmly to reassure her.

"We've been through this, Ash; nobody is going to die. I know this is your first time flying, but you're not a child, you're sixteen years old. It's going to be fine; I promise."

Ashley Clark grabbed the plastic handle of her pink carry-on suitcase and reluctantly shuffled forward until she stood behind the last person in line. "Where's Mom? I thought she was meeting us here," she said as she scanned the long line of passengers waiting to check in. The idea of a one-hundred-thousand-pound hunk of steel floating in the air didn't sound natural to Ashley. She knew thousands of people flew safely every day, but heights terrified her, especially when there wasn't anything to hold onto that was anchored to the ground. She even refused to get onto elevators that were going higher than five floors. She wasn't sure when she developed a fear of heights, but at the age of eleven, on a family vacation from Texas to California, she had refused to get out of the car when they stopped at the Grand Canyon.

"She's meeting us at the departure gate," Brendan said. He checked his watch and then looked up at the flight information board hanging above the information desk in Terminal 1, Hartsfield-Jackson Atlanta International Airport.   "Amsterdam, Argentina, Aruba…there, Barbados…gate B13," he thought as he scanned to the right for departure time.

DL flight 713 to Barbados, Delayed read the green digital letters. Brendan groaned and wished they hadn't arrived for the international flight three hours early. He scanned the adjacent board for arrivals and found the flight Julia, his wife, would be arriving on. *DL flight 77 from Chicago, arriving at 19:32, on time.* Read the information.

Brendan closed his eyes and tried to remember the last time he had seen his wife. It had been nearly four weeks since she packed a bag and left to stay with her mother. He remembered the fight they had had the day before she left and regretted the way things had ended. No, that's not quite right. He didn't regret how things ended; he regretted that things had reached a point where an ending was inevitable. It hurt to even think about seeing her again, and he wasn't sure he was ready. He couldn't forgive her; he wished he could, but every time he saw her, he pictured her with the other man. He twisted the thin silver band on his left hand and wondered why he still wore it.

"Rip off the band-aid, right? Isn't that what they say?" He thought to himself as he recalled a conversation from work. A group of women stood in the breakroom comforting a younger woman who stood crying after telling the group she was getting a divorce.

"Rip off the band-aid, girl," said a tall black-haired woman wearing a tan colored pencil skirt and matching blazer. "The quicker you get over him and on to the next, the better off you'll be," she continued as the other women stood around the young woman and nodded in agreement.

"How would that look? Showing up with the family to your best friend's wedding and not even wearing your own wedding ring," Brendan thought. He sighed and shook his head.

"Next!" The short attendant behind the counter stood on her toes, peered over the high counter, and called to the next travelers waiting in line.

An older woman wearing a white pair of wide-leg pants with a high waist, a gray blouse, and a long black shawl pulled her carry-on bag to the counter in one hand while holding her four-year-old grandson in the other. She wore an oversized pair of sunglasses that held back her short-cropped, black bangs and exposed the gray roots underneath. A short, middle-aged man wearing cargo shorts and a tropical, short-sleeved button-down shirt carried their two suitcases to the counter, along with a carry-on backpack over each shoulder. The smaller backpack was red and white, with blue straps, and featured pictures of three cartoon dogs in police and firefighter outfits on the front. A yellow nametag marked *KEVIN* hung from a plastic strap attached to the front of the bag.

"Going on vacation?" The attendant asked the little boy on his grandmother's arm.

"I'm taking my son to Barbados for his birthday," the older woman answered when the shy little boy hid his face in her shoulder. "This will be his first time flying," she added as she raised her grandson and tried to get him to look at the attendant.

Brendan lifted the black duffle bag next to him and swung it forward one spot as the line inched forward. "Maybe you should send your mom a text and ask her to call you when she lands," he told Ashley when he saw her white knuckles clenching the suitcase handle. He realized his attempts at comforting her weren't working.

Ashley slowly removed her cell phone from her jeans pocket and texted her mom. She looked up and noticed the tall man staring at her.

"What?" she asked. She looked down at her clothes and held her arms out to the side.

Ethan wrinkled his brow and stepped back to get a better view. "Did anyone ever tell you that you look like that famous actress?" He snapped his fingers repeatedly, trying to remember her name.

"I look like a movie star?" Ashley asked. The corner of her mouth lifted slightly in a near smile.

"Yeah, yeah, the blond-haired girl that was in that movie that came out on Netflix this month. It was about some weird monsters in the woods," Ethan said. He shook his finger as if trying to point to the show's name.

Ashley shook her head and then shrugged her shoulders.

"I can't ever remember her name…" Ethan said, "It's one of those names like a city…or a state. No?" he asked, hoping that would jog Ashley's memory.

Ashley shook her head again. "What else was she in?" she asked.

"She was in that movie about the end of the world…the one with Tom Cruise."

Ashley continued to stare at him blankly.

"She was also in that TV show about the criminal psychologist who solves crimes in New York City in like, the nineteen-hundreds…she was the secretary who went on to open her own detective agency."

"The Alienist?" Brendan interrupted after hearing their conversation.

"Yeah, that's it," Ethan said as he pointed his finger at Brendan. "What was the secretary's name?" he asked.

Brendan was quiet for a moment before shrugging his shoulders.

"It'll come to me," Ethan said. "People say I look like Jeff Goldblum, you know," he added when he realized they were stumped on the name of the blond actress.

"Who says that?" Brendan said it more as a statement than a question.

"Who?" Ashley asked.

"Jeff Goldblum...you know, the guy who played the scientist in Jurassic Park," Ethan answered Ashley's question and then turned to Brendan, "lots of people tell me that."

Ashley studied his face for a moment before responding. "Yeah, I guess. I think you look more like Kramer, though...the guy from Seinfeld," she added when Ethan stood there with a confused look on his face.

"Oh...Really?" Ethan asked.

Brendan nodded in agreement.

"No one has ever told me that," Ethan said skeptically.

"I think it's the hair," Ashley added.

Ethan turned his attention to Brendan after attempting to pat down his hair. "I think you look like Bradley Cooper," Ethan said after studying Brendan's face.

"Ewww," Ashley commented.

"You think he's ugly?" Ethan looked surprised as he turned to Ashley.

"No way, he's hot...my dad's not," Ashley said. She wrinkled her nose and stuck out her tongue.

"Thanks," Brendan said dryly. "Doesn't he have a beard and blue eyes?" He asked, turning back to Ethan.

"Yeah, I mean aside from that," Ethan replied. "Maybe if you squint a little," he added. He squinted as if trying to read the small print on a menu and continued to look Brendan up and down.

"I think Uncle Myles looks like the guy from Thor and The Suicide Squad," Ashley interrupted.

Ethan and Brendan stood still momentarily, thinking about the movies.

"Idris Elba?" Ethan asked, trying to recall the black actors from the movies.

"Yeah, he kind of does, doesn't he…where is he by the way?" Brendan asked.

"He sent me a message about an hour ago," Ethan said. He retrieved his phone from his backpack, which he used as a carry-on bag, and checked his messages. "Yeah, he and Shanice are running late, but they're on the way."

"Next!" the short attendant announced again.

Brendan lifted his duffle bag over his right shoulder and stepped to the counter. He turned and waved for Ashley to join him and then placed his sports coat on the counter as he searched the pockets for their passports.

"Two to Barbados," he said to the woman behind the counter as he handed her the passports.

The woman opened the passports to the picture page and verified the information before typing on the keyboard in front of her. She glanced under the counter and then smiled.

"No bags today?" she asked, peering around the counter.

"Just carry-ons…" Brendan answered, "It's just a short trip for my friend Thomas' wedding."

"Sorry, the printers are a bit slow today," she said as they waited for the tickets to print.

Brendan smiled. "I understand," he said. "Gotta love technology."

"You picked a nice time to visit," the woman commented out of the blue. "Make sure you try the fish cakes while you're there," she added after glancing under the counter again. Still no boarding passes.

"Is the plane full?" Brendan asked. He hated flying with babies, small children, and pushy tourists, especially on crowded flights.

"Not this one," the woman replied. "The earlier flight was packed, but most of the tourists try to get there earlier in the day."

"That flight was already sold out by the time we searched for tickets," Brendan explained.

A faint whir came from under the counter, and the woman leaned over and retrieved two boarding passes. "Here you go, gate B13," she said while reading the information on the ticket. "Enjoy your flight."

"Thank you."

Brendan checked the names on the boarding passes and handed Ashley hers. He placed the duffle bag strap over his shoulder, and he and Ashley moved to the edge of the counter to wait for Ethan to check in. Ashley lowered the handle of her pink carry-on suitcase and sat on the edge as she watched Ethan empty the contents of his backpack onto the counter in search of his passport. A young man waiting in line behind Ethan tilted his head back in frustration at the long wait and then lay his head on the shoulder of the young woman standing next to him. A sticker on the young couple's luggage read *JUST MARRIED* and contained a QR code to scan if you wanted to donate to their honeymoon. The thin young man wore blue jeans, a black t-shirt, and an old pair of cowboy boots while his new bride was dressed in a floral-patterned sundress with spaghetti straps that tied in back. Both had the same sandy blond hair as Ashley and Brendan didn't think the two could be much older than his daughter.

"Didn't you once say that Uncle Ethan was the smartest kid in school?" Ashley asked her father. One of her eyebrows was raised higher than the other as she watched her uncle out of the corner of her eye.

Brendan turned his attention from the young couple to the counter and watched the woman behind the desk frown as Ethan removed his passport from a pair of folded underwear.

"He's a genius with the social skills of a ten-year-old," Brendan said, shaking his head.

After Ethan received his boarding pass, the three zig-zagged through the crowd on their way to the security line on the opposite side of the terminal. Ethan tugged at a black cord around his neck until he retrieved the attached pouch from the front of his shirt. He unzipped the small black zipper, folded the boarding pass, and slipped it into the black pouch. He opened the front of his shirt again and returned the pouch to its hiding place.

"You keep your boarding pass close to your chest, but hide your passport in your underwear?" Ashley asked as she watched the tall man straighten his sweater vest to try to conceal the large bulge under his shirt.

"You can never be too careful…" Ethan started, "Did I ever tell you about the time I was on a plane that was being hijacked?"

"Please don't," Brendan said after watching Ashley's face go pale. He gave Ethan a disapproving glare and tilted his head toward Ashley.

"Right…" Ethan said, catching the hint, "Did I ever tell you about the time we won the state basketball championship?"

"Only about a million times," Ashley groaned.

"There was less than a minute left in the game…" Ethan began to tell the story…again.

"I think I should go to the bathroom before getting in the security line," Ashley said as she took a sharp right turn and headed to the far wall with the terminal bathrooms. Her suitcase bounced over a man's shoes as she darted quickly across the terminal.

"Maybe you should just ask others about themselves and let them do the talking," Brendan advised Ethan as they paused in the middle of the busy terminal to await Ashley's return.

Ethan nodded as he watched Ashley race towards the bathroom. Brendan sometimes wondered if he shouldn't be so direct with Ethan, but also felt it was his duty as Ethan's best friend to try to help him, especially when dealing socially with other people; that wasn't Ethan's strong suit. With an IQ of 154, he was even on the high end of genius-level intelligence. Still, his social intelligence quotient of 10 meant he had problems understanding social situations and was unable to act wisely or be effective in most social situations. Ethan fit in perfectly as an engineer working as a contractor for the National Aeronautics and Space Administration, where he worked alone, testing rocket navigation systems.

"So, how are you and Julia doing?" Ethan asked.

Brendan shuffled his feet and pretended to look for someone through the crowd. "Never mind, maybe you should just let others ask the questions."

Ethan shrugged. He could never understand people. Sometimes they wanted him to talk and be more friendly, and at other times, they just wanted him to be quiet. He never knew which way to go, so he often flipped a mental coin in his head and went with the result.

Ashley returned from the bathroom, and they followed the signs pointing to the security lines for all *B* gates. They arrived at the security line just as Brendan finished putting the contents of his pants pockets into the inside pocket of his blazer. As they snaked slowly through the security line, Brendan removed his keys, wedding ring, and wallet and placed them all in the already over-filled blazer pocket. It had been a while since he traveled through Atlanta, and he didn't remember the security procedures. Still, he found it easier to remove everything and put it in one location, making it easier to find once he got to the other side.

He removed the silver Garmin Fenix 7 smartwatch from his right wrist and held it up to Ethan.

"Still got yours?" He asked.

"Of course," Ethan replied, holding up his left hand in a fist, revealing his Garmin smartwatch around his wrist.

Each of the four boys had the same watch. It was a gift from Myles, after his father had passed away, to remind them that their time in this life was short and to enjoy every minute.

Brendan tried watching the people arriving at the conveyor belt to see if he needed to be ready to remove his shoes, but he was still too far back in line to see their feet. They moved through the line in silence, making Brendan wonder if he had hurt Ethan's feelings when he told him he should wait for others to speak to him before talking. He glanced back at Ethan but couldn't tell what he was thinking. The thought that he should just tell his friends about the situation between him and Julia crossed his mind, but quickly faded. He wasn't sure why, but he just wasn't ready to share that information.

"Laptop and electronics out of their cases", the security guard behind the conveyor belt said as Brendan approached. He was a tall middle-aged man with short-cropped black hair. He wore a large black belt with a radio, a Billy Club, and handcuffs, and stood with his arms crossed over his chest.

Brendan watched the two men in front of him as they waited to go through the metal detector and noticed they were still wearing their shoes. "Good," he thought. He liked things that made the process move along quicker. The two men wore colorful swim shorts and matching tank tops that exposed their muscular arms and shoulders. Brendan thought they should spend a little more time on their legs, but they appeared fit nonetheless. The white tank tops with red lettering on the back indicated they belonged to the Pi Kappa Alpha fraternity at the University of Arkansas. Both men had close-shaven crew cuts with a tapered fade and a flat top. The first man entering the metal detector was sent back in line to remove his brown sandals because he had a bottle opener on the sole.

His friend removed his sandals before going through the metal detector, then stuck out his tongue and gave a *Hang Loose* hand signal to his friend waiting in line to be re-scanned.

Brendan placed his bag on the moving belt and put his blazer in a plastic bin before taking his place in line for the metal detector. He stepped forward, one step at a time, until he passed through the arch, and a guard on the other side waved him through. He waited next to the conveyor belt on the other side and watched as Ashley was chosen for screening in the X-ray machine between the security lines.

"Step in, face to the right, and place your hands over your head like the picture," the security guard standing next to him said to Ashley.

Ashley entered the X-ray machine and lifted both hands over her head. Brendan heard a man yelling from the other side of the X-ray machine and hoped there wasn't some emergency that would slow them down. He stepped to the left, peered through the metal detector, and then put his hand to his forehead when he saw Ethan yelling and waving at Ashley in the x-ray machine.

"Dakota," Ethan yelled from the rear of the line of people waiting for the metal detector.

"Wha…?" Ashley started to ask. She wasn't sure what was happening.

"Dakota Fanning…" Ethan yelled again, "The secretary in the Alienist." Ethan stepped out of line and smiled in Ashley's direction. His hands were held out in front of him as if he had just revealed a magic trick.

A heavy-set, middle-aged woman standing in line looked around excitedly.

"Is Dakota Fanning at the airport?" she asked the bald man standing in line in front of her.

The entire security line was abuzz with people looking around, hoping to catch a glimpse of Dakota Fanning.

"Do you know that man?" the security guard asked Ashley.

"Not really," Ashley answered. She waited for the gesture to exit the x-ray machine and then ducked her head as she walked to the rear of the conveyor belt to wait for her bag.

Brendan and Ashley waited in the small seating area next to the security station as Ethan was escorted through the line, frisked, questioned, and then released to continue to his gate.

"I knew I'd remember her name," Ethan said as he approached Brendan and Ashley, still threading his belt through the pant loops.

"You know you're crazy, right?" Brendan asked. The look on Ethan's face told Brendan that Ethan had no idea why yelling from the rear of the security line might be considered crazy.

The three continued their conversation about who looked like which movie star as they made their way to gate B13.

"Now we know what the kid would look like if Bradley Cooper had a baby with Drew Barrymore," Ethan told Ashley. Ashley pulled up a picture of the actress on her phone and scrolled through several pictures before responding.

"You think my mom looks like Drew Barrymore?" she asked as she held up the picture for Ethan to see.

"Oh yeah, don't you?" Ethan asked.

"A little…what do you think, Dad?" Ashley asked her father, walking in front of them and scanning the area for a store with something to read on the plane.

Brendan paused and started to turn to see what his daughter wanted when a loud voice came from somewhere up ahead.

"TROJANS FIGHT!" came the booming voice of a man standing at attention. His deep voice echoed on the tiled terminal walls. The others in the terminal quieted and made room for the loud man as they watched and waited to see what was happening.

Brendan and Ethan both froze and immediately came to the position of attention. In unison, the three men began to sing...

"P...H...S...our Alma Mater, ever loyal will we be. P...H...S...our Alma Mater..."

Ashley stood dumbfounded, and her disbelief turned to embarrassment as her father bent over with both hands on his knees and started to chant while Ethan and Myles continued singing at the position of attention.

"Trojans Fight...Trojans Fight...Fight, Fight, Fight," Brendan chanted. His chest heaved each time he said the word fight.

Ashley felt an arm around her shoulders and heard a familiar voice: "Don't worry. It's been my experience with this group that you can't actually die from embarrassment."

"Aunt Shanice!" Ashley said as she hugged the tall, light-skinned African American woman.

The three men wrapped up their song with all three standing at attention. They yelled "Trojan's Fight" one final time and thrust a fist in the air when they said the word fight. Passengers in the terminal weren't quite sure what had just happened. A few clapped quietly as the group dispersed and the three singing men began to high-five each other and clap each other on the back. The two fraternity brothers from the University of Arkansas shouted "Wooo!" as they passed by on their way to their gate.

"It's good to see you, man," Brendan said as he gave Myles a one-arm hug.

"You too, old man," Myles said, brushing Brendan's graying sideburns with his finger.

"Uncle Myles!" Ashley yelled as she ran to the men and leaped to reach her arms around Myles' neck.

"Wow, look at you, kiddo," Myles said as he placed Ashley back on the ground. "You're a grown woman."

"Uncle Ethan says I look like Dakota Fanning, the movie star," Ashley said proudly.

"I don't know who that is, but I'm sure you're way prettier," Myles answered.

"She played the secretary in the Alienist…" Ethan said from behind the group, "as well as…" he stopped mid-sentence when he realized no one was listening and the group had started to walk away. He ran to catch up with them and stepped between Brendan and Myles, putting his arms around their shoulders as they walked. Shanice and Ashley held hands and followed behind the three men.

"It's hard to believe they all met when they were my age," Ashley said. "And that they actually won a basketball championship," she added when Ethan lifted his legs, and the three men nearly fell trying to carry his weight.

"So, you've heard that story, huh?" Shanice asked. "Well, it's true. You should have seen your dad and Uncle Myles when they were younger…girl, they had moves. Your dad made it on the varsity track team when he was only a freshman…he was so fast! And your Uncle Myles…could have made it to the pros if he hadn't hurt his leg."

"And Uncle Ethan?" Ashley asked. She looked up and gave Shanice a skeptical glance.

"When you're six-foot-four in the 9th grade, you don't have to do much other than stand there and catch the ball," Shanice said, looking down at Ashley and giving her a wink.

"Did you know them in high school?" Ashley asked.

"No, I met your dad, mom, and Uncle Myles when they got to college," Shanice answered. "But over the past twenty years, I've heard all the stories about the Rat Pack."

"The rat pack?" Ashley asked. She had heard many of her dad's stories, but never any mention of a Rat Pack.

"That's what they called themselves in school; your dad, Uncle Myles, Uncle Ethan, and Uncle Thomas…the Rat Pack."

The Rat Pack

In the spring of 1987, four years after the death of her first husband, Shelly Stevens remarried and moved her eleven-year-old daughter, Trisha, and eight-year-old son, Brendan, to the suburbs of Dallas, Texas. Her new husband, Edward Clark, was a fifty-one-year-old widower with no kids of his own, working in a major bank's accounts receivable department. Their new home was more spacious than their previous home and rested in a quiet cul-de-sac of a middle-class suburb. The neighborhood was teeming with children of all ages, and the kids quickly made new friends. Three other houses in the cul-de-sac also had boys the same age and grade as Brendan, and the four quickly became inseparable.

The four boys competed against kids in the surrounding neighborhoods in soccer, football, baseball, basketball, and just about every other competitive team sport imaginable. It was a time when kids played in the streets until the streetlights came on and their mothers called them home for dinner—a time when kids fought in the streets one day and then had ice cream together the next. Kids jumped bikes, drank from the water hose, and spent hours hanging out and listening to the boom-box with friends. It was the year the public service announcement on TV asked the question, "It's ten o'clock, do you know where your children are?"

In the summer of 1992, just before their 8th-grade year, the boys discovered a new interest and met once a week to play the popular board game Dungeons & Dragons. If it was a Saturday afternoon, their parents knew exactly where they were…in the basement of Brendan's house on Greenwood Circle.

"Who dares enter the caves of Neroth?" said a tall, lanky young boy with disheveled black hair. He slurped when he spoke, and his braces made his lips stretch thin over his mouth. He pushed his black framed glasses higher on his nose as he leaned over the square table cluttered with small plastic monsters and colorful manuals with various dragons on the cover.

"I do, Sir Brendan the Brave," said a skinny pimply faced kid with black hair that grew over his ears and began to curl on the ends.

"I do, Sir Myles the Strong," said a young African American boy with a close-cut afro. Even at age twelve, he displayed a stocky, muscular frame.

"I do, Sir Thomas the Cool," said a short, chubby boy with thick, dark hair.

"The cool?" asked Brendan and Myles in unison.

"Knights can be cool," replied Thomas defensively. His Hispanic heritage showed in his thick black brows and coarse hair that grew on his arms and legs. It wouldn't be until the end of the ninth grade that Thomas hit a six-inch growth spurt and grew lean and muscular. Still, at five feet four and 150 pounds, he made the perfect baseball catcher, football lineman, and soccer goalie for their sports competition with the other kids in the neighborhood.

"Wait…" Ethan announced, "As the Dungeon Master, I'll allow it…knights are pretty cool."

"I don't think he's taking this seriously," Myles announced with his arms folded over his chest.

The four boys stood in the dusty, dimly lit basement of 1753 Greenwood Circle, their medieval weapons and armor at the ready. Their shiny metal suits of armor were marked with their family crests, adorned in feathers and gold cords, while long swords hung from the studded leather belts around their waist…at least that's what it looked like to the twelve-year-old boy's imagination. In reality, Thomas wore the brown plastic lid of his mom's clothes hamper tied around his chest with a piece of rope, his father's oversized fishing waders, and carried a cardboard tube from last year's gift wrapping as his sword. Myles wore his school football helmet and shoulder pads, carried a metal trashcan lid as a shield, and carried a bent branch with the bottom wrapped in duct tape. Brendan wore his soccer shin guards, elbow pads for skating, and a cardboard box wrapped around his torso with duct tape while carrying a plastic butter knife in the waistband of his shorts and an aluminum baseball bat in his left hand. Ethan had a faded blue bed sheet draped over his shoulders and carried a gold floor lamp that was missing its base. The lightbulb hung from the top, connected to a cord that ran through the lamp pole and was tied in a knot at the bottom.

"There is a trap at the cave entrance, " Ethan announced in his mysterious Dungeon Master's voice. "Each of you must roll a twenty-sided die. A roll of twelve or lower means you avoid the trap," he read from the manual before him.

Brendan searched a purple cloth bag filled with dice for the roundish one with twenty sides. "It's not here," he said as he dumped the bag's contents onto the table.

Thomas bent down and then went to his knees, searching for the dice underneath the table. He poked his head up over the tabletop and shook it left to right after a minute of searching.

"Maybe we can just roll the six-sided dice multiple times," Myles said. He removed his football helmet, wiped his forehead with the back of his hand, and then stood there with his helmet tucked under his left arm.

"If we roll it three times, it won't be enough…" Thomas said, "But if we roll it four times, it will be too many." He counted with his fingers as he explained the issue with using the six-sided dice.

"Twelve is sixty percent of twenty…" Ethan said, "And seven is fifty-eight percent of twelve…so if we roll the six-sided dice twice and use seven as the target number, it will approximate the same chances."

"If I wanted to do math work, I would have invited Mr. Tillman," Brendan said, referring to their 7th-grade math and science teacher.

"Yeah, I didn't give up my Saturday to do homework," Myles added.

"Well, what's your bright idea?" Thomas asked Myles. He slapped Myles' shoulder pads, making a loud clacking sound.

"Don't touch my armor…Sir Drool," Myles said as he tapped his tree branch against the hamper lid tied to Thomas' chest.

The boys began to bicker and fight over whether to use different dice when a voice interrupted them from the top of the basement stairs.

"What are you retards doing?"

Sixteen-year-old Trisha Clark had long blond hair like her mother and had matured physically over the past year. She wore a tight pair of faded blue jeans and a white t-shirt with the picture of a pale man with unkempt black hair and the words *The Cure* written underneath. The shirt was tied in a small knot just above the waist of the jeans. She stood bent over the stair rails with one foot on a lower step than the other.

"Hi Trish," Ethan said. His smile spread from ear to ear, showing his silver-braced teeth.

"Why are you guys wearing trash cans?" Trisha asked.

"We're the Knights of Greenwood," Thomas said from underneath Myles.

"And I'm the Dungeon Master," Ethan added, holding up his broken lamp. He was very proud of his title.

"Whatever." Trisha rolled her eyes. "You look more like a bunch of pack rats hoarding trash," she added.

"Shut up and go away," Brendan said. He pulled the knife from his waistband and pointed the plastic utensil in her direction.

"Or what?" Trisha asked, "You'll make me a peanut butter and jelly sandwich?"

"MOM!" Brendan yelled.

"Oh, stop crying…" Trisha said, "Mom says to put away your dolls and come get ready for dinner."

"They're not dolls…" Brendan started to protest, "MOM!" he called again.

Trisha turned and ran up the stairs as the boys began collecting their things and putting away the game.

"We can try again tomorrow. I'll bring my dice," Myles said.

"I need a new sword anyway," Thomas said as he held up the smashed cardboard tube.

The boys collected their things and walked up the creaky wooden stairs, heading out of the basement.

"Here comes the trash master and his pack of rats," Trisha said to her mom as the boys crossed the living room and headed for the front door.

"Shut up," Brendan said. He sulked as he walked by, not even bothering to try to argue what knights look like with a stupid girl.

"Honey, why are you dressed like a hobo?" Mrs. Clark asked when Brendan passed the couch.

"Because they're the pack rats of Greenwood," Trisha laughed.

For the next week, Trisha took great pleasure in teasing her brother and his friends about being a pack of rats. It seemed very fitting since they wore trash cans and crawled around in the basement. But as funny as it all seemed, she enjoyed it mainly because it made her little brother mad. By the second week, the effect of the teasing seemed to be wearing off, so she shortened the joke to simply refer to the boys as the Rat Pack. This was the first time the actual title was used for the boys, and over the next few months, Brendan's mother and father also started referring to the boys as the rat pack, and the title stuck. It wasn't that his parents were joining in on the joke, but rather that it was easier to refer to the collective group as the Rat Pack instead of naming each boy individually.

"Is the Rat Pack coming to dinner?" was much easier than "Are Myles, Thomas, and Ethan coming to dinner?"

The name Rat Pack soon spread to the neighbors and then to the school, where it was easier to identify the four specific boys when they were in a group of other boys.

"Mrs. Jones, can you send the rat pack to my office?" was clearer over the intercom than "Mrs. Jones, will you send the boys to my office?" Mrs. Jones knew exactly which boys to send to the principal's office when a group of 9th graders skipped gym class to play Dungeons and Dragons.

The title really took off once the boys learned the original Rat Pack was a group of famous, wealthy men who enjoyed drinking, smoking, chasing women, and just having fun in general. There was a brief period of time in the tenth grade when Myles stopped using the title after he realized that the actual Rat Pack was a group of white guys and one black guy. He had always wondered why people referred to him as Sammy Davis Jr. when addressing the group. By the end of the year, the title was restored, and the four boys proudly referred to themselves as the Rat Pack. After a basketball game, a school reporter had taken a picture of the four boys with their arms around each other's necks, and the title in the school paper the next day read, *The Rat Pack Win Again*. Brendan kept the framed picture on his desk in the bedroom, next to the only picture of his biological father. The picture of his father showed a young man with brown hair and a brown mustache wearing a white jumpsuit with red and blue stripes running down the sides. He held a white helmet under his left arm and stood in front of an orange sports car. Brendan was almost five years old when his dad had left, but he still remembered standing in the front yard of a small one-bedroom house in Flagstaff, Arizona, as his dad dipped a large yellow sponge into a bucket of water and washed the car.

"She was made to fly, Champ," Brendan remembered his father saying of the shiny 1971 Chevrolet Camaro Z28. His father had begun calling him champ when he was old enough to throw a ball.

The orange muscle car had a thick black stripe running across the top of the hood, silver-chromed spoked rims, and a five-inch tail fin also painted black. The 4.1-liter, six-cylinder engine produced a whopping 330 horsepower, which made it one of the top racing cars of the 1970s. His father had even upgraded the front and rear suspensions to enable the car to race and jump as a stunt performer in carnivals, circuses, and other road shows throughout the Southwestern United States.

***

"Come on, you're going to be late," Mrs. Clark called to Brendan from the bottom of the stairs.

"I'm coming," Came the response from the upstairs bathroom.

Mrs. Clark checked the time on her watch for the third time in the past minute and shook her head.

"You're going to be late for the first day of school," she shouted.

The bathroom door opened, and Brendan appeared in a new pair of blue jeans, a long-sleeved T-shirt with the word *GUESS* written on the front, and wearing one Puma sneaker while carrying the other in his right hand. His hair was partially wet and neatly combed, but much longer than his mom would have liked.

"You're getting a haircut this weekend," Mrs. Clark said as he passed her on the last step on his way to the front door.

Brendan mumbled something inaudible while holding his sneaker clenched in his teeth. He grabbed his faded blue-jean jacket from a hanger by the front door and threw a red backpack over his left shoulder.

"Why can't I get my driver's license?!" Brendan asked as he hopped on one foot, trying to put on his last shoe.

"You don't need a driver's license…" Mrs. Clark answered as she fetched her car keys and purse from a small table by the door, "What are you going to drive? Your bicycle?"

"Thomas has his learner's permit and his family only has one car," Brendan argued. "And Myles is allowed to drive when his mom doesn't need the car."

"Well, I need the car, now drop it and get in before I make you take the bus."

"Aww, mom," Brendan groaned as he walked to the other side of the family car and threw his backpack into the back seat. He was careful not to push his luck because he knew his mother was serious. The last time he asked her to turn down her embarrassing disco music, on the ride home from school, she kicked him out of the car and made him walk the rest of the way home. The only thing worse than being dropped off at school by your mom was riding the bus with the new freshmen.

Brendan lifted the 1984 Ford LTD chrome door handle and swung the heavy door wide enough to climb inside and sit on the padded red cushion of the front bench seat. The massive family sedan had a red exterior, red cloth seats, and a red cloth roof lining that was sagging in the middle between the front and rear passengers. Big Red, as it was affectionately called, was a gas-guzzling metal monster with a V8 engine that could seat Brendan's parents, sister, and all three friends in a pinch. There were three seat belts in the front bench seat and three in the rear, but seat belts in 1986 rural Texas weren't a major concern, and even less so for those sitting in the back seat. Brendan felt small as he sank into the cushioned seat with his head just above the massive red dashboard. As much as he hated the car, he would be more than happy if he could drive on his own.

Even at a smaller 3A high school, most eleventh-graders already had their driver's licenses or were in the process of obtaining them. Brendan had asked his mom and dad several times, starting when he turned sixteen, but his mom always had a reason why it wasn't a good time. He had once heard his parents arguing about it and realized that it was actually his mom who was dead set against the idea. His stepdad thought he was old enough to learn to drive and tried unsuccessfully to persuade his mother. It was difficult to make out the entire discussion from his bedroom, but he was sure his mom's reluctance had something to do with his biological father.

"Maybe she's afraid I'll run away too," Brendan thought as he lay in bed listening to the argument.

"I can get out here," Brendan said as Big Red turned right from Main Avenue into the Piedmont High School parking lot.

The first school bell rang as Brendan opened the rear door and retrieved his backpack from the back seat. He placed his right arm through the black strap, closed the door, and sprinted to the school entrance.

"Bye, love you," Mrs. Clark leaned across the bench seat and yelled through the passenger window.

Brendan raised his right hand and waved while holding the backpack strap with his left hand. He raced up the front steps to the glass entrance and waited his turn as other students filed into the school. Piedmont High School was a two-story building made of pale-yellow bricks with modern high glass windows at the front and rear entrances. Classrooms lined both sides of the locker-filled hallway, and the administration offices were located on the first level, on the far left side. A tall Roman Trojan statue, wearing gold armor and a helmet with a red plume running from front to back, stood just outside the administration offices. The building was connected to an auditorium on the right side with stadium-style seating used for school plays and assemblies. The basketball court and athletic building were a separate facility behind the school, and the sports fields with bleacher stands were across the rear parking lot.

Brendan entered the school and removed a folded paper from his backpack. A127 indicated his locker on the top of the paper.

"Good, first floor," Brendan thought as he searched the numbers of the blue metal lockers on the first floor.

After finding it at the end of the hallway, he placed his backpack in the locker. He stood there momentarily reading the paper with his class schedule as the sounds of the first day of school filled the hall. Metal lockers clanked and banged as students practiced their new combinations. Students greeted old friends they hadn't seen since spring semester, showed off their new school clothes, and huddled in their cliques in front of the lockers. As a Junior, Brendan was already familiar with the school layout, and after verifying his class schedule, he wrote the names of his friends next to each class they had in common.

Homeroom	room 100	
1st period - History	room 119	**Myles**
2nd period - Algebra I	room 130	
3rd period - Spanish II	room 215	**Thomas**
Lunch		
4th period - Physics	room 220	**Ethan & Myles**
5th period - Lab	room 220	**Ethan & Myles**
6th period - Athletics	Sports Complex	**Ethan, Myles, Thomas**

Every year, the four boys tried to coordinate their schedules to get the same classes, but each year, the only class they ever all had in common was Athletics. They played both football and basketball for the fall and early spring semesters; in late spring, they all transitioned to baseball. In his freshman year, Thomas played soccer instead of baseball, but switched his sophomore year when he grew six inches and found that his newly developed hand-eye coordination made him a natural pitcher.

Brendan decided to learn Spanish when he was forced to choose between a language course and home economics. He wasn't particularly interested in learning Spanish, but with Thomas' parents being from Colombia, he was fluent in Spanish, and Brendan knew he could get help if he needed it. At home, Thomas's family pronounced his name (TO-MAS) while his friends used the English version, Thomas. It was rare for any of the boys to share a class with Ethan since Ethan had begun taking high school classes in the 7th grade. The four boys typically rode to school with Myles, ate lunch together, and then spent the afternoon together in sports.

Brendan closed his locker, folded his class schedule, and made his way through the crowded hall towards room #100 for homeroom, where students would get all the school rules for the first day of class.

"Brendan!" someone yelled from the other end of the hall.

Brendan heard his name and stood on his toes trying to find the person who had called him. He saw Thomas at the end of the hall and turned to wave. "See you in…" he started before being knocked off his toes by a student looking in the opposite direction.

"Oh, I'm sorry," said a young woman with long brown hair. Her bangs were thickly gelled and stood six inches up in bouncy curls while her curly locks were combed outward and stretched to mid-back. "I was just trying to find my classroom."

Brendan stared at the young woman, wondering why he had never seen her before. The high school had only 320 students, with half of them being freshmen and sophomores. He was pretty sure this young woman wasn't a freshman, and no girl this pretty went unnoticed by the rat pack. They had ditched Dungeons and Dragons in the 9th grade when they realized most girls weren't into it and instead spent their Saturdays hanging out at Dillard's and JCPenney in the mall, where the girls liked shopping for new clothes.

The young woman returned to searching for door numbers when Brendan just stood there with his mouth open.

"Wait!" Brendan yelled. "What room are you looking for?" he asked.

"Room 100," The young woman said after double-checking her schedule.

Brendan smiled. "That's where I'm headed."

"Great…I hate being new. Do you mind if I tag along?" The young woman asked.

"Yeah, sure…my name's Brendan by the way."

"I'm Julia," Julia said as the two turned and she followed Brendan to the side doors.

"Room 100 is the only classroom not in the main building," Brendan explained as he held the door open, and Julia walked through.

They crossed a small courtyard and followed the walkway into the adjacent auditorium.

"Where'd you come from?" Brendan asked. They strolled through the auditorium and stopped in front of a door labeled 100.

"California," Julia answered. "My dad retired as a cop, and we moved to Texas to be closer to my mom's family."

"Cool," Brendan replied.

They both stood awkwardly in front of the door, trying to think of something further to talk about when the second school bell rang.

"Are you two lovebirds coming in, or are you standing out there all period?" Asked a short, middle-aged woman wearing glasses that slid to the end of her nose.

"Oh…err…no, we're not…" Brendan began stammering. His cheeks blushed red, and he felt warm when he saw Julia waiting to hear what he would say.

"There's a seat available up front, and one towards the back," the homeroom teacher said, pointing to the seats.

Brendan took the seat at the rear, and Julia sat up front, placing her notebooks on the desk. The teacher began taking attendance, and the students raised their hands when their names were called.

"Neal French," the teacher called.

"Here," said a young man with his hair combed over his eyes and wearing a t-shirt with a skeleton riding a skateboard. He raised his hand, placed his head on the desk, and closed his eyes.

"Julia Connley," the teacher called.

Julia raised her hand and then quickly lowered it when the teacher nodded in her direction.

"Brendan Clark," said the teacher.

"Here," Brendan said as he raised his hand from the back of the room.

"Romeo…gotcha," the teacher said as she pointed the end of her pen at him.

The class giggled, and Neal lifted his head off the desk long enough to look back at Brendan and whistle.

"Whewwt, whewww.".

The other students burst out laughing and began making their own romantic noises. A tall young man sitting next to Brendan puckered his lips and started making smooching sounds. Brendan sat beet red as Julia turned around and smiled.

"Okay, calm down," the teacher said as she completed roll call.

The teacher handed out a packet containing the school rules and regulations and then reviewed each line, ensuring the students understood the information.

"Make sure your parents sign the last page and turn it back in by the end of the week," the teacher said, just as the school bell rang.

Students gathered their belongings, double-checked their schedules to determine which class they had next, and began filing out of the room. Brendan watched Julia file the rules and regulations into her organizing file and then organize her books as she prepared to leave. He looked away quickly when she looked in his direction and decided not to risk the embarrassment of restarting their conversation. The teacher smiled as she watched Brendan leave class, head down, with Julia right behind him.

"Hey, would you mind pointing me to my next class?" Brendan heard Julia ask when they had both left the classroom.

Brendan turned and saw Julia with her arm outstretched, holding her class schedule. He took the paper and read the information next to 1st period.

"Sure, you're going to…no way," Brendan started and then stopped with a look of surprise. He looked up at Julia and then back at the piece of paper.

Julia wasn't sure what the issue was, but she waited for Brendan to continue.

"You're going to History in room 119…" Brendan said after a moment of silence, "That's where I'm going."

"Really?" Julia asked. She smiled and waited for Brendan to return her schedule, but instead, he retrieved his own folded schedule from his pocket and compared the two side by side.

"History 119…Algebra 130…Spanish 215…lunch…" Brendan said as he read back and forth between the two schedules.

He handed Julia her schedule and smiled.

"We have the same first three periods and then lunch," he said.

"That's great," Julia beamed. "At least I know one other person in school."

"Four," Brendan added. Julia gave him a puzzled look.

"I'll introduce you to my friends at lunch…" Brendan started to tell her about the Rat Pack, "that is, if you don't already have lunch plans," he quickly added.

"No, just a ham and cheese sandwich," Julia replied.

"You're going to like the guys…Myles knows everyone in school, Ethan is the smartest kid you'll ever meet, and Thomas is good at everything he's ever tried."

They walked slowly to history class at the other end of the building while Brendan filled her in on the school, the town, and his friends. He didn't realize it that day, but Brendan had a fourth best friend by the time they had reached room 130. Over the semester, the two spent a lot of time walking to and from class, meeting at each other's house to help with homework, and eating lunch together on the bleachers next to the football field. The two weren't dating at first; they were more like good friends who had known each other for a long time. Julia was also into sports and made the varsity team in volleyball, soccer, and track by the start of her senior year. The Rat Pack was always seen in the bleachers during her matches and cheered the loudest when she scored. In turn, Julia was always at their football, baseball, and basketball games and had even traveled over 200 miles to watch the boys' basketball tournament the year PHS won the state championship.

***

"I hear there's going to be college scouts at the game tonight," Brendan said to Myles as the two walked across the school parking lot in their gold and red basketball uniforms.

"They're here to see Myles," Thomas said from behind the two. Thomas and Ethan followed behind Brendan and Myles, also dressed in their basketball uniforms.

The four boys wore their high school letter jackets and carried a gym bag over their shoulders as they followed the basketball team across the parking lot to board the yellow school bus taking them to the game. The varsity jackets were red with yellow sleeves, representing the school colors, and featured numerous sports patches and school years sewn onto each sleeve. Large letters on the back spelled out TROJANS, and the head of a Trojan wearing a helmet with a red plume was underneath the letters.

A large group of students and parents stood next to the school bus, cheering the team as they crossed the parking lot and loaded onto the bus. Some students carried homemade signs that read *Go Trojans, State Champs,* and *To Victory,* along with other inspirational quotes, while parents held homemade signs with their kids' names and jersey numbers.

"Where's Julia? Is she going to the game?" Ethan called to Brendan from behind.

"She's riding with the cheerleaders," Brendan replied. He scanned the parking lot for the large red cheerleader van but turned his attention to the bus when he couldn't find it.

"Stay fresh," a man standing in front of the bus door said. "It's a long drive to San Antonio, and we don't want anything stupid to happen on the way down."

"Alright, coach," a tall boy in a basketball uniform said as he passed the man and climbed up the stairs into the bus.

Coach Williams was a large, blond-haired man with a brown mustache and a large, bulbous nose. He was balding on the crown of his head and wore a red baseball cap to cover the hair loss. He wore red athletic shorts that were just a tad too small and a white polo shirt with the Trojan logo on the breast pocket. A black whistle hung around his neck, and his white tube socks had two red bands around the top. He high-fived each player when they entered the bus.

"We're counting on you, Myles," the coach said as the four reached the bus doors.

Undoubtedly, the team wouldn't have made it to the championship without Myles. He was by far the best player on the team, and they were going to need him against the Roosevelt High Wildcats, the defending 3A basketball champions.

"Trojans Fight!" Myles yelled and raised his fist in the air.

The rest of the team shouted "Trojans Fight" from their seats on the bus.

Myles and Brendan sat together in an empty seat halfway to the back of the bus while Ethan and Thomas took the seat in front of them. Several players put on headphones and lay their heads against the windows and seats, while others tried to get a good stretch in the aisle. Coach Williams was the last to board the bus and took a quick headcount before sitting in the first-row seat and giving the bus driver a thumbs up. He picked up a clipboard lying on the seat next to him and spent the rest of the two-hour ride reviewing the team's playbook.

Myles placed his elbows on the seat in front of him and tapped Thomas on the shoulder. Thomas finished his prayer by crossing his hand from head to chest and then to his right and left shoulder.

"Yeah?" Thomas asked as he turned in his seat to face Myles.

"So, are you going to college next year? My mom said your mom told her you got a scholarship offer," Myles said.

"I don't know…" Thomas looked down when he answered, "It's only a partial scholarship for baseball to SFA, and I don't think my parents can afford the rest."

"You could get student loans," Myles said.

"Or you could apply for a grant," Brendan added. "Trisha got a grant her first year at Texas Tech…it didn't pay for everything, but she didn't have to take loans that year."

"I don't know, maybe," Thomas said quietly. "I might get a job to help around the house until my sisters are older…" Thomas's words grew softer as he spoke, as if he didn't like the sound of the words.

"What about you, Myles? Which school are you choosing?" Brendan asked.

"I haven't decided," Myles replied. "My mom wants me to pick Notre Dame, but I'd rather stay closer to home. Maybe you should come with me to LSU."

"I wish," Brendan replied. "Out-of-state tuition is too expensive. I can't afford it, and I don't have all the scholarship offers you do."

"Think you'll follow Trisha to Tech?" Ethan asked.

"I don't know…my stepdad says I need to figure out what I want to be in life and then choose a school that offers that degree," Brendan said as he sat back in the bench seat. "He thinks maybe I should join the Army and give myself time to figure it out."

"Wish I had a choice," Ethan said. He frowned and sat back in his seat. "I've been told I'm going to Yale ever since I was eight years old."

"Your dad went there, right?" asked Myles.

"And his mom," Brendan added. Ethan simply nodded his head.

"We're always going to be best friends, though, right?" Thomas asked.

The four boys were quiet for a moment, each looking at the others and waiting for someone else to answer the question.

"Rat Pack forever," Brendan said. He placed his right hand on Ethan's shoulder, sitting in front of him, and his left hand on Myles' shoulder, seated to the left.

The other boys followed suit and placed their hands on the boy's shoulder next to them.

"Rat Pack forever," the four said in unison.

After another hour of riding in silence, the school bus lurched when the rear tire hit the curb as it turned into the Alamodome parking lot in San Antonio, Texas. All the boys went to the right side of the bus and peered out the windows at the massive stadium with tall pillars in each corner and cables that ran down each side, anchoring it to the stadium. The large digital sign in front read, *Welcome to San Antonio and the 3A State Championship.*

The basketball team exited the bus and followed their coach through the front glass doors and into the stadium's main hall. The Alamodome was the home arena of the San Antonio Spurs until 2002, with a seating capacity of thirty-five thousand fans, and it also hosted the Texas high school basketball championships.

The team walked across the large concrete flooring halls to their locker room on the east end visitor section and marveled at the size of the venue. This was the first time the team had played in anything other than a small 3A high school gymnasium. Before today, they had only seen venues like this on TV.

"Can you believe we're playing where the Spurs play?" said a tall, skinny African American young man, peering into the basketball court at the Hall of Fame jerseys hanging from the rafters.

"Don't get star-struck, boys," Coach Williams said from behind the group of boys. "It's the same size court we have back home."

The team unloaded their gear in the lockers and then went through stretching drills before taking a knee in front of a whiteboard and going over plays with Coach Williams. At 6:45 pm, Coach Williams gathered the team at the locker room exit and prepared to enter the arena. The cheering, music, and other fan noises grew louder as the team approached the entrance to the court.

"This is it, boys, the opportunity of a lifetime…just remember that no matter what happens, win or lose, I'm proud of you for having made it this far." He raised his right hand in the air and then placed it in the middle of the group of boys gathered around him. "On three…one…two…three," he said, and then the team yelled, "TROJANS!" in unison and raised their fists into the air before they ran into the arena.

It was hard for the boys not to be overwhelmed by the size and volume of the crowd. Thousands of fans cheered as they entered the court, and the Trojan band began to play the school fight song. Brendan glanced around and easily found Julia in the cheerleader's section. She jumped up and down and waved when she saw the four boys cross the court and take their seats on the visitor side benches.

"They look like college players," a young man with short-cropped blond hair said as the other team entered the arena.

"Dang, they're taller than Ethan," a couple of Trojan players said in awe.

"They're tall, but we're fast," said Coach Williams. "We're going to beat them to the ball and wear out those long legs." He patted Myles on the back, pulling his clipboard up to mid-chest. "Brendan, Thomas, Myles, Charles, and Mike…that's the starting lineup," Coach Williams said to the gathered team.

Charles Hill was the lone tall player on the starting lineup, with the rest being much shorter, but also the fastest players on the team. Typically, Brendan and Thomas weren't starters, but both were still pretty good players and saw a good amount of playing time each game. Thomas had one of the best fast breaks on the team, and Brendan was a decent three-point shooter. Myles wasn't tall but was the best all-around player and rarely left the court once the game started. Ethan was taller than most students on the other 3A teams, but was an average basketball player at best. It wasn't uncommon for him to spend the entire game on the bench. The game plan was simple: play at a high tempo, sprint on change of possessions, and rotate players frequently to keep their legs fresh.

Brendan felt his heart race as he took the court and sized up the competition up close.

"Relax," Myles said as he came from behind and patted Brendan on the back. "Just like we do it at home."

Myles was referring to the many hours the boys spent playing basketball in the driveway at Myles' house on Greenwood Circle. They always had fun playing the game, even when playing against some of the older kids in the neighborhood. Brendan smiled, feeling much better knowing his friends were with him, and then tensed and waited for the starting whistle.

The game would go down as one of the best basketball games in tournament history. Both teams took turns with the lead, and the score was never more than a six-point difference. Coach Williams was familiar with the opposing team and had done a good job devising a game plan to counter their height advantage. Towards the end of the first half, the opposing team already had three players with more than two fouls each as they resorted to fouling the smaller, faster opponents. Brendan and Thomas each scored seven points by the end of the first half, and Myles, being Myles, led the team with twenty-six points as the clock wound down in the final minutes of the half. On the last drive of the half, a Wildcat defender was given a warning when he tripped Myles and sent him careening into the stands during a fast break. Myles gripped his leg and was carted to the locker room by the team staff as Brendan made the two free throw penalty shots and increased the Trojans' lead to five by the time the halftime buzzer sounded.

"You okay?" Brendan asked Myles as he, Thomas, and Ethan gathered around Myles in the evaluation bay of the visitor locker room.

"Ungh," Myles grunted. It was apparent he was in pain.

"It's not broken, is it?" Ethan asked.

"That was a dirty play," Thomas added.

One of the school athletic trainers came in, knelt before Myles, and began palpating his ankle.

"The X-rays are negative, and it looks like it's just a little swelling," the trainer said to Myles. "I can wrap it for you, and you should be able to return to the game if you're up to it."

"Of course he's up to it...tell 'em, Myles," came the voice of Coach Williams from behind the boys.

Myles was quiet for a moment, then looked at the trainer and said, "Go ahead and wrap it."

"That a boy," Coach Williams said as he walked over to Myles and clapped him on the back. "You boys get back to the locker room and wait for us there," he said, pointing to Brendan, Thomas, and Ethan.

Coach Williams emerged from the evaluation bay with Myles walking behind him. Myles walked with a limp, and it was apparent he was in pain. The entire basketball team applauded when they saw Myles and were relieved that he was still able to play.

"Listen up, Trojans," Coach Williams shouted to get the team's attention. "We're twenty minutes away from making history...the first state championship for Piedmont High..."

The team erupted in cheers, and several boys gave each other high-fives.

"It's not over yet..." Coach Williams continued, "But we have a five-point lead..." The team cheered again, "Half their team is in foul trouble..." More cheering, "and Myles will be there to lead us to victory!" The team erupted in cheers. Coach Williams had used the injury to motivate the team and lead them back into the arena for the second half, but the decision for Myles to return to the game would be the biggest mistake of his athletic career.

It wasn't that Myles would further injure his ankle during the game, but rather that continuing to play on the weakened and stretched tendons and ligaments would delay the healing process and leave the joint vulnerable to injury during the grueling football camps that Myles had scheduled to show off his skills to college coaches. With just two months between the basketball game and the first camp, the pain may have been gone, but the joint was nowhere near ready for that level of stress.

The second-half game plan was the same as the first half: keep the fast-paced tempo and wear down the opposing team. It was evident from the start of the second half that Myles was moving more slowly and wasn't as aggressive as he had been in the first half. He couldn't cut as sharply and had difficulty maintaining balance during his outside shots. Still, Myles was the leading scorer through the third quarter and the biggest threat to the opposing team.

"Are you sure you're okay?" Brendan asked Myles when the team went to the sideline for a two-minute timeout. Myles had been quiet since coming out of the locker room, and his face winced with pain after each step.

The game whistle sounded announcing the end of the break, and the teams took the court with just over two minutes left in the game. The Trojan's lead had eroded midway through the 4th quarter, with Myles barely able to put pressure on his left ankle. The Wildcats now had a four-point advantage and had adopted a defensive game plan to kill the clock and force the Trojans to expend energy chasing the ball. Scoring went back and forth, but the Trojans were unable to close the gap.

The Wildcats made a critical mistake underestimating Thomas' speed when they attempted a long pass across the court. Thomas intercepted the ball, charged the inside lane, and then dumped the ball off to Myles outside the three-point line, where he had plenty of time to make the shot. The Wildcat lead was cut to only one point with twenty-four seconds left in the game, and they were in possession of the ball. The Trojan defenders played tight defense and baited a Wildcat player into taking an open shot from just outside the free-throw line. The gamble had paid off. Charles Hill leaped between two defenders and came away with the ball after a brief struggle on the ground, and the Trojans now had possession with just seconds to go.

"Time," Coach Williams shouted from the visitor bench, using the team's last time out.

With seven seconds left on the clock, the Trojans huddled around their coach.

"We have time for one more play," Coach Williams said to the gathered team. He looked around at the tired faces of the boys and continued. "We are going to run a piston elevator and set up Myles for the three-pointer."

The boys looked uneasily at Myles, who was kneeling on his left knee.

"Go in with a one-four high formation and get the ball to Brendan." Coach Williams drew an air diagram with his index finger and pointed at each player for their part in the play. "Ethan...you're going in for Thomas," Coach Williams said. "We'll have two big guys for the elevator pick," he explained. "Brendan, drive to the opposite side from Myles and then quick pass to Charles or Ethan, who will fake the inside layup and dump the ball outside to Myles."

Coach Williams was quiet for a second to let the play sink in. He glanced at Myles and continued, "It's up to you, Myles. No quick cuts, no running, nothing hard on the ankle, just slowly post up outside and shoot the ball when you get it.

The rest of the team looked nervously at one another, but no one was willing to point out the obvious: Myles was in pain and had missed three of his last four three-point attempts. The whistle sounded, and five boys took the court.

"I have an idea," Brendan whispered to Ethan and Myles. The two boys looked at Brendan as they continued to walk back to their positions on the court.

"Everyone knows we're going to try to get it to Myles for the last shot," Brendan said. Ethan nodded his head while Myles continued to walk quietly.

"I'll pass the ball to you, Ethan…" Brendan said while nodding to Ethan, "You fake the pass to Myles and then send it right back to me." Brendan finished and then looked at Ethan and Myles to gauge their acceptance of his plan.

"Coach would kill me," Ethan said.

Myles continued to walk quietly, considering the play.

"They won't expect me to take the shot," Brendan said. "Half their team will run to Myles when you fake the pass."

"I don't know," Myles said to Brendan. Ethan continued to shake his head as he walked, mumbling something about being murdered by Coach Williams.

"You have to trust me," Brendan said. He stopped walking and stared at Myles and Ethan. "Do you trust me?" he asked.

"Okay," Myles said, slowly nodding his head.

"Rat Pack forever," Ethan said. "Don't miss…or forever might be today," he added.

The play started with Mike Thompson passing the ball inbounds to Brendan. Brendan's legs were tired, but the adrenaline of taking a huge chance with his play sped him past half court with the ball. He knew only seconds were left on the clock, but he slowed his pace, allowing Myles to take his spot on the right outside boundary line. Brendan immediately sprinted to the left when he saw Myles reach his spot. The ball moved rhythmically to the floor and back as he dribbled to the far-right three-point line, where he pivoted and faked a pass back to Mike in the center of the court. He lobbed the ball over a defender and watched as Ethan easily leapt up and caught it. Everything was going as planned. The Wildcats had decided to double-team Myles with their two tallest players and dare Ethan to take a shot from free-throw range. Ethan pivoted towards Myles with the ball held in both hands high over his head as the entire Wildcat team moved towards Myles on the right of the court.

"What are you doing!?" Coach Williams yelled at Ethan from the sideline. "Fake the inside layup!" He yelled and then threw his clipboard to the ground.

Ethan faked a pass two times, pretending to look for a hole in the defenders. As the referee began to count the final seconds on the clock, Ethan faked a third pass with the ball in his right hand. Instead of releasing it as his hand came down, he followed through with the arm motion and released the ball behind him. The crowd gasped. Everyone, including the Wildcat defenders, thought Ethan had lost control of the ball, but then went silent as they watched the ball bounce once and then into Brendan's hands.

Brendan had an odd sensation as he watched the ball bounce towards him. He felt like everything was moving in slow motion as he gripped the ball and looked at the disbelief in the eyes of the Wildcat players who were all bunched around Myles. He saw the referee's fingers slowly count down from three to two…

Brendan took a deep breath, bent his knees, and then slowly exhaled as he lifted the ball and released it toward the hoop. Every eye in the arena watched the ball float towards the net. It bounced once on the metal rim and then into the net as the buzzer signaled the end of the game. The crowd erupted in cheers, and the Trojan players raced onto the court, screaming and jumping in celebration. Ethan placed his hands together in prayer and looked upwards, mouthing the words "thank you" before joining the celebration.

Brendan was nearly knocked to the ground as a player jumped on his back while several others patted his back and tried to hug him. He pushed the other players aside and tried to make his way towards the cheerleaders when the crowd in the stands stormed the court, cutting off any possibility of finding Julia. He was slapped, pushed, hugged, and washed away in the crowd before finding himself face to face with her. Her body felt soft against him as the swarming crowd pushed them together. In the middle of the chaos, in a bubble of human bodies, Julia pressed her lips against his and kissed him passionately. It was the first time he remembered feeling like a champion that day.

***

The coming months brought big changes for the four boys. They graduated from high school and began the next chapter of their lives. While they saw each other several times throughout the years, they rarely saw each other at the same time.

Ethan graduated Cum Laude and gave a commencement speech that compared his participation in the championship game to every student's opportunity to succeed at the things they put their minds to.

"I may have sat the bench for four quarters, but I was ready at the end when my name was called," Ethan said to the gathered students. "In just a few minutes, each of your names will be called when you walk the stage to receive your diploma…will you be ready?" He asked as he concluded his speech.

Just one month later, he moved to Connecticut and began his studies at Yale University. He would spend the next eight years in school earning a master's degree, a PhD, and completing an internship at NASA before moving to Huntsville, Alabama, to take a position with the US Space Flight Center. Since he was an only child, his parents had relocated to Connecticut once he began school. Ethan only returned to the neighborhood if he was traveling through Dallas for work or on special occasions.

Brendan turned down a partial track scholarship to Oklahoma State University and chose instead to stay in state and closer to Julia. Julia was accepted to Texas A&M University in College Station, Texas, and majored in Business Administration, where she was also a preferred walk-on for the women's softball team. Brendan started his education at the junior college across town when he wasn't initially accepted into Texas A&M. After his freshman year, he was accepted into the Texas A&M School of Business, where he and Julia would share many classes. The two would often make the three-hour drive back home in Julia's 1987 Honda Civic to visit friends and family. Brendan took a job as a waiter at the local Outback Steakhouse to help pay for school, and Julia joined him a month later, working as a hostess.

Myles participated in a summer football camp at the University of Texas, a month after graduating from high school, where he would sustain a career-ending injury. The injured ankle, from the high school basketball game, was rolled during drills in which Myles was required to perform multiple direction changes at high speed. A loud pop heard during his fall immediately indicated to the trainers that he had torn the ligaments. Further x-rays would also reveal a bimalleolar ankle fracture in which both lateral malleolus bones were broken. Broken blood vessels and stress fractures of the talus bone would be added to the list of injuries after being seen by a specialist back home in Dallas. The University of Houston was the only Division I school to honor their scholarship in hopes that Myles would recover after only one year of rehab. He ended up switching schools during his sophomore year and began attending Texas A&M with Brendan and Julia after three surgeries and having metal rods placed in his ankle. Myles became interested in sports medicine due to the ankle injury and chose Sports Technology as his new major. During biology lab in his second semester at Texas A&M, he met and fell in love with a first-year student named Shanice Johnson.

Thomas remained local after graduating and took a job at a car wash to help his family make ends meet. Over the next ten years, he became a minor town celebrity, as he was the only member of the state championship basketball team who did not move away after graduation. He was invited to serve as a guest speaker at school pep rallies, varsity luncheons, and school reunions. He was asked to be the honorary king at a class prom, threw the first pitch during home baseball games, and even had a newspaper article written about his experience winning the state championship when the school made it to the finals six years later. Thomas rose through the car wash industry to become a site manager and eventually owned several of his own car wash sites. Due to his popularity, he spent two terms on the city council and even ran for mayor before dropping out of politics entirely and opening another car wash in the next town over. He was always available when the others came to town and had more contact with his friends than any of the others had with each other.

The unexpected death and subsequent funeral of Myles' father in the Spring of 2016 was the last time the four boys had all come together. After a long fight with cancer, his father passed just after his 80th birthday. Myles' family had moved to the south side of Dallas eight years after Myles graduated from high school, where his father was diagnosed with cancer shortly after the move. After the funeral, the boys took a trip to the old neighborhood and spent the day shooting hoops at the park where Myles' dad had taught them some of their best plays.

Thomas' wedding would be the first time the whole gang had been back together in over eight years. The wedding invitation surprised Brendan, Myles, and Ethan, as they had never heard Thomas talk seriously about a girl before. They were all looking forward to meeting the woman Thomas had met online and seeing each other again after such a long time. None of them knew much about Camila, and they wondered what she was doing with Thomas after seeing her picture.

Betrayed

"I still can't believe it," Myles said, returning the wedding invitation to Brendan.

Brendan turned the piece of paper over in his hand, rereading the card for the fourth time and letting the information sink in. The card was made of heavy stock paper and had the postage markings of an overseas letter around the borders. There was a picture of a stamp in the upper right corner, along with a mark next to it, making it appear as if the postmaster had stamped it. A large watermark in the shape of the island of Barbados covered the page, and there were two palm trees over the words YOU'RE INVITED, centered at the top.

Thomas & Camila

12th September 2024

Yellow Bird Spa and Resort, Barbados

The back of the card had all the details of the ceremony and celebration taking place over the long weekend stay.

"Did you ever think he might be gay?" Brendan asked.

Myles shook his head. "No way," he replied. "He used to chase the girls all over school."

"But he never really caught them, did he?" Brendan said, giving Myles a questioning look.

"Hard to catch something when you don't know what you're looking for," Myles said. "I think he just didn't know what he wanted from himself or from someone else."

"I'm happy for him." Brendan smiled and placed the card back into his blazer pocket.

"Shanice spoke to Camila on the phone and says she really likes her," Myles said when Shanice and Ashley returned from a trip to the bathroom.

Shanice walked between Brendan and Myles, sitting across from one another, and sat next to Myles. Ashley sat in a seat behind her dad and reached for an oversized set of black headphones in her bag.

"Are you talking about Camila?" Shanice asked. "She's so nice…I talked with her for over an hour after I made Thomas give me her number," Shanice explained after Brendan and Myles nodded at the question. "Her Spanish accent is so sexy, and you can tell she is a very smart woman," She added.

"Does she really have a three-year-old kid?" Ashley asked after overhearing the conversation.

"Ashley!" Brendan said suddenly.

"What?" Ashley quipped. She raised both hands in defense.

"It's okay…" Shanice said, "They both talk openly about the little girl. I think her name is Lita, and she is so cute."

Shanice suddenly stopped talking, and a serious look fell over her and Myles' faces. Brendan sat quietly for a moment and was about to ask if something was wrong when Shanice stood and asked Ashley if she would help her look for something in the small airport store further down the corridor.

"I think I need to use the bathroom," Myles said as he rose with Shanice and Ashley.

Brendan sat, puzzled, wondering what had caused the two to stop talking suddenly. He was about to ask when he heard Ashley shout.

"Mom!" Ashley shouted from behind Brendan. She waved and called to her mother again when she looked in her direction. "Over here!"

Brendan turned and realized why everyone had suddenly gone awkwardly silent. He was surprised and a little embarrassed that Myles and Shanice had realized there was something wrong between him and Julia, but hadn't said anything about it. Julia dropped her brown leather travel bag and hugged her daughter while Myles and Shanice walked over to say hello.

"You look great, girl!" Shanice said to Julia as she wrapped both of her arms around her and wiggled her body back and forth in a friendly hug.

"Hi Julia, it's good to see you again," Myles said. After Shanice released her from her embrace, he leaned in and kissed Julia on the cheek.

Julia's smile looked forced as she returned the greetings and then glanced towards the gate where Brendan stood pretending to check something on his phone.

Shanice glanced knowingly back and forth between Julia and Brendan and then tugged at Ashley's arm. "We were just about to go to the newsstand," she said.

Ashley pulled back from Shanice and tried to turn back to her mom. "But I want…" she started to protest.

"You said you would help," Shanice insisted before Ashley could finish. She put her arm around Ashley and escorted her down the hallway.

"I'll be back in a minute," Ashley called back over her shoulder.

Myles watched the exchange between Shanice and Ashley and then remembered his own excuse for leaving. "Oh, eh, yeah…I was just on my way to the bathroom," he said nervously. He turned and followed Shanice and Ashley down the hallway after giving Julia a sheepish grin.

"Where is everyone going?" Ethan asked when Shanice and Ashley rushed by. He was carrying a large Italian meatball sandwich in one hand and a supersized cup of soda in the other.

"There you are," Myles said as he caught up to Ethan and grabbed him by the arm. "Why don't you show me where you got that sandwich?"

"It's just up the hall, on the left," Ethan replied. He had told them where he was going just before he left to find something to eat. "Hey, is that Julia?" he said when he spotted Julia near their gate. He raised his meatball sandwich with his right hand and waved it back and forth. "Hey Julia!"

"Show me," Myles said as he pulled Ethan's arm down and practically dragged him down the hall.

"What is wrong with you people?" Ethan complained. He struggled briefly before giving in and following Myles back the way he had just come. He figured it must be one of those weird things people did around him that he just didn't understand.

Julia lifted her brown bag and walked slowly towards Brendan. She pulled a light blue carry-on suitcase behind her and held her boarding pass in the other hand. Her hair was newly cut into a shoulder-length, classic bob that accentuated her light brown eyes and cheekbones. Blond colored highlights and platinum lowlights were added to make her hair shine in the hot Caribbean sun. She wore a faded pair of jeans, and the front of her white and orange blouse was tucked under the front button, exposing a brown leather belt that matched her flat brown ankle boots. She stopped two feet in front of Brendan and the two stared at each other, waiting for the other to speak first.

Brendan broke the silence, "How was your flight?" He looked her in the eyes and then quickly looked away when he felt his stomach lurch. He had an overwhelming urge to turn and walk away, but he had promised himself he wouldn't.

"Long and boring," Julia answered. "You look good," she added after guessing it must have been difficult for him to initiate the conversation. She wanted desperately to talk with him, to begin a healing process that they both needed, but the last time she tried talking to him, he was so angry that he could only yell.

"Did you tell the guys?" she asked when Brendan didn't respond. She looked in the direction the group had left when she arrived.

Brendan stood silent for a moment, looking down at the floor. "No," he said finally. "I think they sense something, though."

Julia nodded her head, knowing how perceptive Myles and Shanice were. "And Ashley?"

"Same..." Brendan replied, looking up from the ground, "She hasn't said anything but knows something is wrong."

Brendan dropped his eyes to the floor again, and the two stood in awkward silence. Both felt like they had a lot to say, but neither knew where to begin.

"Is this the way it's going to be the whole trip?" Julia asked, referring to the awkward silence. "It's okay if you want to go without me..." she started.

"He's your friend, too," Brendan interrupted.

Julia nodded in silence; she felt defeated and didn't know how to move the conversation forward. "What happened to us?" she asked.

"You mean besides you sleeping with your boss?" Brendan spat back coldly. He knew it wasn't the time or place for the conversation, but the anger felt good. It filled a void that once belonged to the love he felt for her. His words were hurtful, and he hated himself for finding comfort in her pain.

Julia stood silent and fought back the tears welling in her eyes. "I don't know how many times I can say I'm sorry," she said. "You deserve to be angry, but we can't move forward if all you want to do is keep punishing me."

"I just want to know why," Brendan said. "Was I not good enough? Did you no longer care about me and Ash?"

"It's not that," Julia said, shaking her head slowly. "It wasn't you; it was me…somewhere along the way I forgot…" Her words trailed off into silence.

"Forgot?" Brendan asked. "Forgot what?" He said in a louder voice than he intended. The two moved closer to the large window overlooking the busy flightline when they noticed their conversation made others in the waiting area uncomfortable.

"Everything…" Julia responded. She looked him in the eyes before continuing, "who I was, who we used to be, why we were together, why you made me feel special, the…" She took a deep breath, "everything."

"Why couldn't you just tell me?" Brendan asked. "Why couldn't you talk to me and tell me you were unhappy?"

"I don't know…" Julia started, "That's my fault, and I take responsibility for that, but you can't say you were happy with the way things were, that you didn't notice what had become of us."

"So, it's my fault!?" Brendan said through clenched teeth.

"That's not what I said," Julia countered.

Brendan considered her words as he stared out of the tall glass window. He knew Ashley and the others would likely be on their way back soon.

"You're right," he said. "I knew things had changed, but I thought that's just what happened when two people had been together for so long."

"I'm not blaming you…" Julia began.

"No, I know you're not, I just can't help it. I've been angry for so long that it feels like the only emotion I know," Brendan said as he held up his hand to stop her. "I told myself that I wouldn't let it get the better of me…that I could be an adult, and we could be cordial and be happy for Thomas." He took a deep breath, turned to face Julia, and smiled. "Can we start over?" he asked. "How is your mother doing?"

Julia returned his forced smile. "She's fine," she replied. "She keeps forgetting that she already fed Rodger, and the poor dog is now as round as a pumpkin."

Brendan chuckled, "Poor thing." He remembered the last time he saw the overweight beagle when they visited Julia's mom over Easter. The dog was wearing a red knit sweater and would stand on his rear legs wanting to be lifted and put onto the couch.

"It's actually good to see you," Brendan said quietly. "I like what you've done with your hair."

Julia smiled and turned her head quickly back and forth, making her hair swing over her shoulders. "I thought it would look nice out on the beach."

"I know Ashley is happy to see you. She misses you and is still scared about flying," Brendan said.

"I can't believe you got her to come this far."

The two walked slowly back into the main seating area and found an area that would accommodate all six of their group.

"I don't know if I can…" Brendan started to explain his silence.

"I know," Julia said. She placed her hand on his and was happy that he didn't pull away. "I just want you to know that I remember…I remember why I fell in love with you, and I know I need to give you the opportunity to remember on your own terms."

As much as it hurt, and as angry as he was, Brendan still believed what she said. "I guess taking time and going to your mother's helped you figure things out."

"No, I figured it out the day before I left for my mother's...the day before our fight," Julia said. "I made the decision that I wanted to be with you...that's why I had to tell you about Eric." She saw Brendan flinch at the name and knew how much it must hurt. She continued, "I knew we could never reclaim what we once had unless we had honesty. It was a big risk, but one worth taking."

Brendan changed the subject when he saw Ashley and the group returning to the waiting area, "Can you believe Thomas is having a destination wedding in the Caribbean?"

"I can't believe he's getting married...I actually thought he might be gay," Julia replied.

Brendan burst into laughter while Julia looked around, wondering what was so funny.

"Julia!" Ethan shouted from behind the group. He handed Myles his supersized soda cup and spread his arms as he walked towards her.

"Hi Ethan," Julia said as she stood and was engulfed by Ethan's long arms.

Ethan took a step back and placed both hands on her shoulders. "Wow, have you gained weight?" He asked. It was one of those coin flip questions in his head; based on Brendan's earlier response, he figured it would be safer to stick to questions that only pertained to her. From the current look on Brendan's face, he felt like he probably got it wrong again.

"What?" Julia asked. "I don't think so." She frowned and looked down at her blouse and blue jeans, wondering if the outfit made her look fat.

"Don't listen to him," Shanice said. She slapped Ethan on the back of his head and then sat beside Brendan. "You gotta tell me who did your hair," she said, turning back to Julia.

Ethan rubbed the back of his head. "I knew I should have gone with the hair," he said, thinking of his choice to ask about her weight instead.

Ashley and Julia sat next to Shanice and began a serious conversation about which hairstyles worked best for beach vacations. They then switched to the very important topic of proper bathing suits for women their age.

"Do you two have a minute?" Brendan asked Ethan and Myles. "I'd like to talk to you about something."

The three men found a quiet spot, and Brendan reluctantly explained how he and Julia were having problems in their relationship but were trying to work it out. He didn't tell them about Julia cheating because he thought that was a bit too personal, even for his best friends, and he didn't want them to think badly of her.

"I'm sorry that I didn't confide in you earlier," Brendan told the two men.

"Nothing to apologize for," Myles said. "I'm happy to hear you two are working on it and still willing to try and make it work." He patted his friend on the back as he spoke. "Lord knows it's not easy."

"That's good news," Ethan said. His two friends gave him one of those looks again. "I mean, I'm glad it's not me…I thought you were mad at me about something I said. I'm relieved to hear it's just a problem between you and Julia."

"Shut up, Ethan," Myles said.

"What?" Ethan asked defensively. "You know what I mean."

Brendan smiled. He was relieved to have finally told his friends about the situation, and he knew they would be supportive, even Ethan…in his own way.

The three men walked back to the waiting area just in time to catch the last part of the conversation about Thomas marrying a woman who already had a child. Julia thought Brendan looked a little more relaxed and guessed he had probably told his friends about their situation. She wasn't happy about them knowing their personal business, but was happy Brendan was at least beginning to open up about his feelings.

Ashley sat in the next row over and swayed her head listening to a man sing softly while plucking a small ukulele. The dark-skinned man's accent sounded Jamaican, and he used the word *mon* at the end of each verse. His long, cut-off camouflaged shorts and Hawaiian shirt hung loosely on his thin frame as he bounced to his tune. He was bald, with a thin, dark black beard that made his teeth look exceptionally white when he opened his mouth to sing. He winked at Ashley when he noticed her watching.

Shanice stood when she saw the men returning from their talk and moved into the chair on her right, leaving an empty space between her and Julia. "Ethan," she called to get his attention, "why don't you come have a seat and tell us about the women in Huntsville, Alabama?" She stuck out her index finger and then curled it back and forth, beckoning Ethan to come sit next to her.

"The women in Alabama?" Ethan asked. "I don't know…I think they are kind of like the women everywhere else," he said as he took a seat between the two women. "I would say they're predominantly brown haired and twenty-seven percent heavier than the US average."

"Are there any pretty ones?" Julia asked.

"Pretty ones?" Ethan asked quietly as if he wasn't sure how to quantify the measurable.

"Ones that a smart, handsome scientist might want to ask out?" Shanice clarified from the other side.

"Oh…oh, I see," Ethan said as he looked to Myles and Brendan for help.

"Don't look at me," Myles mumbled. "I'm going to sit over here and eat my sandwich."

"I need to go find something to read during the flight," Brendan added when Ethan looked to him for help.

Ashley returned to her seat when the man finished singing and leaned over Ethan's shoulder from behind, "Come on, Uncle Ethan, there must be someone you've met since you've been there."

"Good luck," Brendan called over his shoulder as he left the waiting area to go find something to read.

Brendan walked the entire B and C terminals, looking for a bookstore with a better variety of reading material, but returned to the small gift shop next to their gate when he couldn't find a better store. He picked up and read the back cover of a hardcover book with a picture of a large moon over a dark castle on a small table labeled best sellers.

"No Cure for Darkness…Nah," he muttered as he returned the book to the table.

After reading several more book covers and deciding against them all, he ended up with one of the magazines in the rack next to the cash register. He folded the magazine under his left arm as he retrieved his wallet, stepped in line behind the young married couple he had seen earlier, and waited for them to complete their purchase.

"Do you have your credit card?" The young woman asked her husband.

"I bought the pizza for lunch," the young man replied. "I'm not sure how much money it has left on it."

"Urgh," the woman groaned as she opened her purse and pulled out an envelope marked *HONEYMOON FUND*.

Brendan returned to the waiting area twenty minutes later with the magazine and a shareable-sized bag of M&M's. While he was gone, two airline staff members opened the gate and began assisting passengers with seat changes and connecting flights. He glanced over their heads at the flight information board for recent updates.

DL 13 to Barbados 11:05 pm - boarding 10:35 pm, read the green digital information. He pulled the folded boarding pass from his pocket and held it up to compare with the flight information. DL 713 departs 11:05, GRP 5, Seat 17D was printed on the folded paper. He was about to get in line to verify the flight number with the attendant when the green numeral 7 flickered on the information board, indicating the correct flight number…713.

"It was just a typo," came a voice from behind Brendan.

Brendan turned and saw the two muscle-bound fraternity brothers looking over their boarding passes.

"I don't think you know what a typo is," said the man on the right. He was about an inch taller than his fraternity brother and had a more squared face and larger ears. "That's just a technical malfunction."

"Okay, Doctor Spock. I say it's bad luck," replied the shorter man. "I'm just glad today's not Friday."

Brendan turned his attention back to the information on the ticket and then twisted his arm to check his watch. 9:42 pm read the digital numbers above the Garmin name.

"What'd you find, Dad?" Ashley asked when her father took a seat across the aisle.

"Magazine." Brendan pulled the magazine from the small bag with the store's logo and showed it to her, revealing the cover.

"Science and Technology…boring," Ashley replied after reading the title.

"And I got these for you." He pulled the M&Ms from the bag and tossed them to Ashley.

"Thank you!" Ashley smiled as the bag landed on her lap. She immediately opened the bag and began sorting the round candies by color. It was something she and her friends always did when she was younger, when she believed the different colors had different flavors.

"Is that the September issue?" Ethan asked about the magazine in Brendan's hand.

"I think so," Brendan replied. He flipped the magazine over and looked for the edition information on the cover. "I wanted to read the article about batteries for electric vehicles."

"That's a good one, it says that…" Ethan started to tell Brendan about the article.

"Stop!" Brendan shouted. "Don't tell me, I want to read it on the plane."

"Oh, right," replied Ethan. "We can discuss it when we land in Barbados."

"Sure," Brendan said as he slid back in the chair and made himself comfortable. He pressed the small round dot at the top of his smartwatch, set a reminder for twenty minutes, and then leaned his head back and closed his eyes. He felt tired but relaxed as he listened to the various conversations of the people sitting around him.

"They're never going to give that promotion to a woman…" Shanice was telling Julia.

"You should have put the medication in your carry-on…" a woman in the next row of seats was scolding her husband.

"Hmmm-hmmm…hmmm-hmmm-hmmm-hmmm-hmmm…" a man hummed a popular tune as he lightly picked at his ukulele.

Brendan's head was heavy, and his eyes blinked slowly as he began to fall asleep.

"Throw me the ball, Champ…" the man taking a birthday trip with his mother said to his son a few rows over.

Brendan remembered playing in the yard with his own father, recalling a hazy memory of their time together.

"…come here, Champ…" a faint voice in his head called to a four-year-old boy with a bowl cut wearing a pair of suspenders over a white t-shirt.

"...Champ…" said a smiling young man with blond hair and a mustache.

When We Dream

"Come here, Champ," the blond-haired young man said as he waved to a four-year-old boy. It had been a long time since Brendan dreamed of his dad.

Brendan rarely ever remembered his dreams. He didn't dream a lot, but when he did, it was often of the time before his father left his mother to raise him and his sister alone. During his undergraduate studies, he took advantage of the free therapy sessions offered by graduate psychology students. He was told his dreams were likely due to a mixture of his own guilt and separation anxieties. They told him dreams were often just the brain sorting out recent memories, but that his recurring dreams were likely tied to some deeper, unresolved feelings. He wasn't sure he trusted the opinions of the inexperienced college kids his own age, but he couldn't shake the feeling that his dreams had a deeper meaning.

His two recurring dreams were those of his father and his orange sports car, as well as the one in which he was dressed up for a formal event and holding his mother's hand. He appeared to be about five years old in both sets of dreams. He had once told his mother about a dream in which he was racing with his father in his orange car as they both laughed hysterically. His father was smoking a cigarette in one hand and driving with the other. His mother thought he must be mixing up his dreams since his father would never smoke in his car and almost never let anyone ride in the front seat. Many of Brendan's dreams had strange details, like the one in which his family had gone to the beach and his father was flying his orange car like a kite. He could never be sure if his dreams were something he was remembering, something he was hoping for, or just a mix of random thoughts. Not even the grad students knew how to interpret the dream in which his father was flying his car. "Maybe because he had said the car was made to fly," he had offered the idea to the therapists.

Brendan had once told Myles about his dreams when he visited Myles in Austin while Julia and Shanice took Ashley to see Wicked in Las Vegas. He and Myles had spent the afternoon grilling on the back porch of Myles' new home and were halfway through their second case of beer when the topic of dreams came up. Brendan picked through the last crumbs in a bag of Lays potato chips as he finished telling Myles about a dream of him and his dad riding in the orange car. He was wearing a red pair of swim shorts, a gray tank top with the letters ATM on the front, and a pair of sunglasses as he reclined in one of the Adirondack chairs in the yard.

"Do you think they mean anything?" Brendan asked after telling Myles about the recurring dreams.

Myles finished the remaining beer in his dark brown bottle of Shiner Bock and shook his head. He sat back in the wooden Adirondak chair next to the fire pit and studied the yellow label on the front of the beer bottle before answering.

"You know…" He started and then tossed the empty beer bottle in the grassy area next to the firepit, "If you had asked me that three years ago, I would have told you they don't mean anything at all, that it's just a bunch of random thoughts." He opened the white lid of a red-colored ice chest, sitting between him and Brendan, and retrieved another beer before sitting back in his chair.

"And now?" Brendan asked, thinking maybe he had had too many beers and had forgotten what he was saying.

Myles' eyes looked glossy as he turned to Brendan and continued.

"Now…I think there just might be something in those dreams." Myles twisted the bottle with his right hand while holding the bottle cap in his left, and then tossed the cap into the fire when it came off.

"You mean like repressed feelings?" Brendan asked.

Myles tipped his beer bottle towards Brendan, "You've been watching too many Lifetime movies with Julia and Ashley." He sat back in his wooden chair and closed his eyes.

They sat in silence for a minute, listening to the crackling fire, before Myles spoke again.

"After my dad died, I started having a strange dream. At first, it occurred about once a week, but over time, it became less frequent. It was just like one of those recurring dreams you've been talking about."

"It was about your dad?" Brendan asked.

"Yeah," Myles said. He sat up and came to the end of his chair, where he took a drink from his beer and then stared into the fire. He sat with his legs spread wide, resting his elbows on his knees.

"You know I used to love going fishing with my dad when I was small," Myles stated. "Back before you moved to Greenwood Circle…It would just be the two of us out on the lake. That used to be my favorite thing to do…go fishing with my dad."

Brendan could see the smile on Myles' lips and knew it still saddened Myles to talk about his father.

"I remember you told me about going fishing with him," Brendan said softly.

"After he died, I started having this dream…" he took a long sip of his beer before starting again, "we were going fishing, just me and him. It wasn't like a flashback; we were both the age we are right now…or were when he died." Myles leaned over and placed his forehead on the beer bottle that he was holding with both hands between his legs.

"We were riding in the old Volkswagen van we used to have." Myles lifted his head and glanced over at Brendan. "It was such a vivid dream…know what I mean?" He asked.

"Yeah, mine are the same way sometimes," Brendan replied.

"We got to the place where we were going to fish," Myles restarted the story. "We stopped at a parking lot that was at the edge of a deep ravine. We were the only ones there. The water level was low, so there was a steep bank and a wooded area on the bank before you got down to the riverbed. The river was only about ten feet wide, with about twenty feet of dry riverbed on each side of the river." Myles took another sip of his beer. "There was a train track that ran across the river from one bank to the other. The kind of train track you see in old movies…just the steel tracks laid on wooden ties and a wooden frame holding up the bridge."

Brendan thought it was a good description and reminded him of a scene from the movie they had seen together about four boys going to see a dead body.

"I don't know why," Myles was saying as he shook his head. "Why did I want to cross the bridge and fish on the other side? I was so happy to be out fishing with my dad…I just took off across the bridge, hopping easily from one wooden beam to the next. It wasn't until I was halfway across the bridge that I realized this might not be a good idea for my old man…"

Brendan noticed a change in Myles's tone and guessed correctly that the dream was about the death of Myles's father.

"I looked back just in time to see him stumble and then trip on a beam as he lost his footing and fell…" Myles stopped for a minute and took a deep breath. "Why didn't I wait for him? He was 80 years old…trying to follow me over that stupid bridge."

"It was just a dream, Myles." Brendan tried reassuring his friend.

"I don't think so," Myles stated. "It's crazy, but I watched him fall in slow motion…I saw the look on his face plainly, and you know what? He wasn't scared. He just looked at me like he was confused, it was some weird look like he didn't know what was happening." Myles' eyes were wide, and he was staring at Brendan, but Brendan didn't think he saw him; he felt like Myles was looking right through him.

"I watched him fall all the way to the rocks below…no one could have survived that fall. He just lay there at the bottom of the ravine."

Myles became animated as he began telling the next part of the dream.

"I yelled for him…DAD! DAD!" He was actually yelling as he told the story, and Brendan worried the neighbors might come to check to see if everything was okay.

"I ran back across the bridge and tried to cut through the woods to get to the riverbed…the bushes were so thick…I couldn't get through them. I kept calling for him…DAD!" Myles appeared a bit frantic at this part of the story.

"When I got onto the riverbed, I couldn't find him," Myles said calmly as he sat back in his chair. "He wasn't there…I went to the exact spot I saw him fall…and he wasn't there."

"That's weird," Brendan said. He was happy Myles had calmed down and was speaking normally again.

"Yeah," Myles said. "I thought maybe he somehow survived the fall and had tried to drag himself back up the riverbank…maybe he was stuck in the bushes like I was. I started to call to him again and tried going back into the bushes to look for him."

"Where was he?" Brendan asked. He sensed the dread in Myles' voice.

"When I made it back to the top of the riverbank, I caught a glimpse of a man sitting on a bench by the parking lot. I yelled to him several times, but it was like he couldn't hear me. As I got closer, I realized it was my dad…he didn't appear hurt, he just sat there like he was waiting for the bus."

"He wasn't hurt at all?" Brendan sounded puzzled.

"And that's not even the weirdest part," Myles said as he shook his head. "He wasn't an old man anymore."

"What? How old was he?" Brendan asked.

"He was about my age. He looked so young. I felt so tired after searching for him up and down that riverbank. He didn't say anything to me…just looked at me and smiled. I told him we should get to the van and go get some help - go to the emergency room. He just sat there and looked at me, smiling the whole time…"

Myles sat there shaking his head as he recalled the dream.

"I was so tired and decided to take a seat next to him on the bench. I sat there with my head down, trying to catch my breath."

Brendan had finished his beer but didn't want to interrupt the story to get another.

"Why wouldn't he talk to you?" Brendan asked.

"I was still looking down when I heard him…someone…say, it's time to go. I was tired. I told him I would be there in a minute, I just needed to rest for a second. He got up and started walking away…I didn't see him; I was still looking down…but I heard his footsteps walking away on the gravel path. When I looked up, he was gone."

Myles stood up and walked over to the fire. He picked up a stick next to the pit and stuck it into the burning logs to stoke the fire.

"Wait," Brendan said. "He was just gone? Where'd he go?"

Myles simply shrugged.

"And you think that dream means something?" Brendan asked.

Myles stopped stoking the fire and pointed the stick at Brendan.

"I used to be like you," he said. "I used to think the dream was about me feeling guilty, about running so fast in my own life that I never looked back to see how he was doing. I used to think the dream was just feelings of regret."

"You spent plenty of time with your dad," Brendan said. "You shouldn't feel guilty about that."

Myles laughed. "That's what Shanice always said." He walked back to the ice chest and took out two beers. He opened one and handed it to Brendan, and then opened the other for himself.

"You're going to need this," he said. He raised his beer in a toast and took a large gulp.

"Do you remember that year I broke my ankle and couldn't play ball anymore?" Myles asked after wiping foam from his lips with the back of his hands.

"Of course," Brendan said. "That was terrible."

"I kept hoping I would get better, even after everyone was telling me that my ankle would never be the same. I prayed that I could overcome the injury and still have a career in football."

"Everyone was hoping you'd recover...especially the University of Houston," Brendan joked. He smiled, trying to lighten the mood that had gone eerily somber.

"I knew it was over long before they put the hardware in my ankle. I didn't want to admit it because I didn't know what else to do. Sports were all I knew."

"What? You had plenty going for you," Brendan said as he placed his hand on Myles' shoulder.

"Sports was my whole identity...it's why I was popular, why the girls liked me...it was my future. Can you imagine feeling like your identity, your future, your life has been ripped from you?" Myles asked.

"That's not…" Brendan started to answer.

"I know," Myles said, cutting him off before he could finish. "But at the time I thought my life was over…I…" his voice faltered, and he stopped talking long enough to take another long drink from his beer.

"I went back home and got one of the guns my dad keeps in a case in his closet." Myles stopped again and stared blankly at Brendan. "I almost did it, I almost pulled the trigger…"

"Why would you…I never knew," Brendan said softly as he released the breath he was holding.

"No one knew…except maybe my dad," Myles said. "I think he realized I had gone into his gun case and that I had been depressed…but he never said anything."

"You think your dream has something to do with that?" Brendan asked.

"My dad wasn't the touchy-feely type," Myles said. "We never talked like that, or shared emotions."

They sat back down in the wooden chairs and opened another beer.

"I think my dad didn't know how to talk to me, or how to help me, but I do think he was trying to tell me something," Myles said.

"Like what?" Brendan asked.

"First, I think he wanted to say goodbye…to let me know that it was his time. I think he was worried about me, though…that look in his eyes when he fell…he wasn't worried about himself, he was worried about me."

Myles looked up into the air, making Brendan assume he was looking up at his father in heaven. In reality, looking up was the best way Myles knew to keep the tears from rolling down his face. After a minute of scanning the stars or letting the tears dry, Myles returned to the conversation.

"Two…" he said, "I don't think he was ever on that bench."

"I thought you said you saw him sitting there looking younger,' Brendan said.

"I think that younger man was me," Myles said. "Every time I go back home, my mom and sisters are always telling me how I look just like him."

Brendan nodded his head. "You do look just like him."

"I think he was trying to tell me that everything I admired and saw in him was also in myself. For a long time, I couldn't see that; I was all tangled up and lost in the bushes. I felt tired for a long time because I didn't know who I was…he wanted to show me."

"That's great, man," Brendan said softly. "How'd you figure out that's what the dream meant?" He asked.

"First of all, you have to stop trying to figure it out and just let it come to you," Myles said. "I don't know about religion…" he said as he put his index finger to Brendan's forehead, "but your dad's up here trying to tell you something…try to pay attention."

Brendan sat in silence for a few minutes, digesting the news Myles had just told him about attempting suicide.

"I know it sounds crazy," Myles said. "But after I realized that the dreams were some kind of message from my father, they stopped."

The two finished their beers, and Brendan began cleaning up the pile of beer bottles as Myles put out the fire and then covered the pit. When they finished cleaning around the patio, they decided to call it a night and left the pile of dishes in the sink for the next day.

Myles paused on the second step of the staircase and looked back at Brendan lying on the couch, "I haven't told the others about…" his words tapered off.

"No worries…as far as I'm concerned, it never happened," Brendan said before his friend could continue. He was happy Myles had confided in him, but felt terrible about not being there when Myles needed him. He should have known. He should have been there to see the pain his friend was in and to try to help. He had always seen Myles as the strong one of the group and was pretty sure the others did as well, but now he wasn't sure he would ever see him the same way again.

A horn honked somewhere in the distance as Brendan stared at the ceiling, trying to fall asleep. A soft orange glow from the power button behind the TV made the wall clock visible as the minute hand slowly ticked past 4:00 am. The last thing he remembered before falling asleep was a quote he had seen from a man named Bryant McGill: "Be careful fighting someone else's demons – it may awaken your own."

He slept soundly on the large gray leather couch except for the few times his right hand shot up in mid-air reaching for his mother's hand. Unlike the recurring dream with his father, the recurring dream with his mother was not vivid and did not feel real. The scene was hazy, as if he were looking at an old Polaroid picture that had faded, making it difficult to see any details. It was also one of those dreams that didn't make much sense.

Four-year-old Brendan stood dressed in a white button shirt that he refused to keep tucked in his black pants with a stretchy waistband. The shirt was wrinkled and had a purple stain on the front where he had spilled his juice at the church social two months ago. A black wool tie was tied loosely around his collar, and he wore a black pair of slip-on Hush Puppies. He couldn't see his mother's face, but he sensed that she was sad. He heard other people around him but couldn't recognize who they were or what they were doing. He tugged at his mother's grasp, trying to find a place to go and sit to play with the matchbox car he carried in his right pants pocket, but his mother's grip was too tight. She tugged on his arm when he tried to find someplace to go, someplace that wasn't so stuffy, somewhere where he didn't have to stand in uncomfortable clothes.

"Why was he here..." he wondered, "and who were these other people?" Brendan felt weary as he tried to focus on the faces of the other people standing around the room. No use. The more he tried to focus on the people's faces, the more tired he became.

The First Ring

The Other Strangers

"Bzzzzt, bzzzzt…bzzzzt, bzzzzt…" Brendan felt the alarm more than he heard it, but it was enough to snap him out of the short nap he had taken while waiting to board.

He held his left hand over his mouth to cover a long yawn and then glanced at his watch. 10:30, read the digital number on the Garmin Fenix 7. Glancing around the waiting area, he found things just as he had left them before the nap. Julia and Shanice were still deep in conversation, Ethan had found a book to read, Myles had taken Brendan's cue and was napping in the next aisle, while Ashley flipped through her smartphone wearing her oversized headphones. A few passengers had already begun to congregate around the boarding lines, hoping to board early and find the best overhead space for their bags. A thin man wearing a blue suit stood impatiently in the priority boarding line, checking his watch every two minutes. He had gray hair, a white beard, and wore square wire-framed glasses that also appeared to be oversized for his head. Brendan figured he was impatient to get to his first-class seat so he could start working on the laptop he carried in his leather carry-on briefcase.

"Dad." Brendan returned his attention to the waiting area when he heard Ashley calling. Ashley sat across the aisle and was gesturing to him by wiping her hand and arm across her face. She removed her headphones when her dad gave her a puzzled look.

"Your mouth," she said while repeating the wiping gesture.

Brendan wiped his hand across his chin and felt the wet area Ashley was referring to.

"You were drooling. Mom said I should just let you sleep," Ashley explained.

"Thanks," Brendan replied. "I'm going to the bathroom before we board," he added and then got up and disappeared in the crowd on his way to the bathrooms.

"Good evening, ladies and gentlemen..." the announcement started just as Brendan returned to the waiting area. "We apologize for the delay...Delta flight 713 will begin boarding procedures in two minutes. We ask that passengers in wheelchairs, small children, and anyone needing extra time for boarding please proceed to gate B13 for early boarding."

The man with the leather briefcase rolled his eyes as a young woman pushing a baby stroller approached the gate and handed the attendant her boarding pass. She wore a large, pink colored diaper bag over her right shoulder and dragged a carry-on suitcase with a missing wheel with the same arm she used to hand the attendant her ticket.

"Probably had an economy ticket," the man sneered in a voice just loud enough for the surrounding passengers to hear.

Brendan checked his ticket. Economy class, seat 17D, Boarding Group 5, read the information on the ticket. "Good..." he thought, "no chance I'll be sitting near that jerk." He folded his ticket and joined the others collecting their bags in the seating area.

"What seat are you in?" Ethan asked when he saw Brendan return to the waiting area.

"17D, I got the aisle, Julia has the window, and Ashley's in the middle," Brendan replied. "And you?" He asked.

"21A, window seat," Ethan answered. "I think Myles and Shanice are behind me," he added.

"22 B and C," Myles confirmed.

"We'll now begin boarding our world medallion and first-class passengers," the attendant announced over the intercom.

Brendan glanced back at the boarding line and watched the thin man in a blue suit rush to the attendant to get in line before an old woman approaching the gate pushing a two-wheeled walker with tennis balls on the rear legs.

"Got everything?" Brendan asked Ashley as she passed by, dragging her pink carry-on bag on the way to wait in line with the other passengers. Ashley simply grunted as she passed, keeping her attention on the phone she carried in her left hand.

Myles walked past carrying his and Shanice's bags while the two women rose from their seats and followed behind without missing a beat in their conversation. Brendan retrieved his black duffle bag from his seat and called to Ethan, who was staring out the large window.

"Ethan…you coming?"

Ethan turned to his friend and nodded his head before taking one last glance out of the window. He retrieved his boarding pass from the black pouch hanging on his neck and then went to retrieve his backpack from his seat.

"Get back here…" Brendan heard a woman yell. He turned and saw the woman traveling with her son chasing the little boy around the bench seats. The boy had removed his socks and shoes and was resisting all attempts to put them back on.

Brendan scooped the little boy in one arm as he ran by the last row of seats on his way to freedom.

"Gotcha," Brendan said. He dropped his bag to catch the little boy with both hands as the grandmother approached with the boy's shoes.

"Got him," Brendan said as he handed the boy back to his grandmother.

"Thank you," said the woman. She took the little boy in both hands and then sat in the nearest seat, holding the boy in one arm while trying to put on his socks.

Brendan searched the waiting area for the boy's father before finding him in the boarding line with the carry-on bags. The man's shoulders drooped from the weight of the bags, and Brendan guessed the bags under his eyes were a weariness from caring for the young boy.

"Can I help?" Brendan asked the woman as the boy squirmed out of her grasp, and she barely held on by one ankle. "Please," the woman replied. "I can hold him in my lap if you think you can put on his socks and shoes."

The boy quit kicking when he realized it was useless to try to free himself from the firm grip on his ankle. "Cool shoes," Brendan said as he tied a bow knot in the first shoe.

"Better do a second knot," the woman said. "He doesn't like wearing shoes and will take them off if he can."

Brendan tied a second knot over the first. "There," he said. "He's probably just eager to get to the beach." Brendan smiled and tickled the boy's other foot as he held his ankle. The boy giggled and squirmed while clenching his toes, trying to escape Brendan's grasp.

"I wish," the woman said. "He just doesn't have manners. He spends half the month with my son, and the other half with his mother…neither wants to be the bad parent after the divorce, so they let him do whatever he wants." The woman breathed out heavily and glanced over to her son, standing in line. "I'm sorry, I shouldn't be venting…thank you for your help…" she paused.

"Brendan," Brendan offered his name. He tied a double knot in the last shoe and then tested them to see how easily they might come off.

"Thank you, Brendan, you're a good man. My name is Helen." Helen held the boy's hand and placed him on the floor. "And this here is my grandson, Kevin…and that's his dad over there in line, Paul."

"Nice to meet you, Helen, and don't worry about the venting. Sorry to hear about the divorce."

Helen walked slowly with the boy and stopped when Brendan reached down to retrieve his bag. "You have a beautiful family," she said, looking over to Julia and Ashley, who stood in line waiting for their group to be called.

"Thanks," Brendan replied. He thought there was something else Helen wanted to say by the way she stood there, just staring at him. He didn't know she was sitting in the waiting area when Julia arrived and had overheard the conversation between the two. He couldn't know that her own marriage and the marriage of her son had both ended in divorce due to infidelity.

Rain began to pelt the windows, and beads of water ran down the large glass panes as lightning flashed in the distance. Brendan and Helen stood and watched the weather front blow in before turning and continuing to the boarding area.

"Looks like a storm is coming," Helen said as they approached the boarding line.

Brendan glanced back at the window. "Doesn't look like a bad one."

"Everyone is a bad one if the house doesn't have a sturdy foundation," Helen replied. "That's me," she said when the overhead speakers announced the boarding for group three.

"Good point," Brendan said. "I'll remember that." He waved as Helen and Kevin turned to leave.

"I hope you do, Brendan...I really hope you do," Helen said before leaving and joining her son at the front of the line.

"What was that about?" Myles asked after overhearing the conversation.

Brendan shrugged.

"I think she was referring to the danger of homes with weak foundations during storms," came Ethan's voice from behind. "She probably lives in Florida or one of the southern Gulf states where homes are built over clay foundations and are prone to shifting."

Brendan and Myles turned and stared at Ethan, wondering if he was serious.

Shanice wrapped her right arm around Myles's waist and moved closer to him, "I hate flying during storms...all that turbulence."

"This one's only a minor front," Ethan said as he gestured with his thumb towards the window. "The one that delayed our flight is much larger...looks like the wind speeds are already reaching sustained speeds of 70 miles per hour...that's hurricane weather." Ethan almost appeared giddy as he unlocked his phone and began scrolling through the information on his screen.

"How do you know that?" Brendan asked.

"Is it safe to fly with winds at that speed?" Shanice asked at the same time.

Ethan pointed his phone at Brendan, "I get alerts for storms and weather events on my work phone. NASA monitors and records all weather data for future launch and return missions." He then pointed the phone at Shanice, "and no, it's not safe to fly during a hurricane, but it looks like it's been moving north out of our flight path."

"I'm sure the airline wouldn't be boarding the plane if they thought it was dangerous," Myles added to comfort Shanice.

"These types of weather patterns pop up over the northern Atlantic all the time," Ethan stated matter-of-factly. "Most of the time, the evaporating vapors don't release enough heat into the air to increase the wind speeds, and the system just dies out."

"Can we not use the word dies," Brendan said while scowling at his tall friend. He leaned his head around the group in front of him to look for Ashley and Julia, who were just a few feet ahead of them in line. He breathed a sigh of relief when he found Ashley still wearing her headphones and not paying attention to their conversation. Ashley removed the large earphone over her right ear and mouthed the word "me?" when she saw her father's head peek around the corner. Brendan smiled, shook his head, and then returned to his place in line.

"Group five is now free to board the plane," came the announcement over the overhead speakers. Most of the people congregated in the boarding area collected their belongings and began shuffling their way into a single line, merging where a red rope marked the lane for economy class passengers.

Brendan waited until he entered the roped area before retrieving his boarding pass and placing it in his passport, between the page with his picture and the page with the American eagle. He handed the attendant his documents and then walked slowly into the narrow ramp to board the plane after receiving the green indicator light. A middle-aged, overweight woman was in the middle of the line, speaking loudly into the speaker of the phone she held almost a foot in front of her. Everyone in the gangway knew she was talking with her sister in Memphis, Tennessee, about meeting and befriending Dakota Fanning while waiting in the security line at the Hartsfield-Jackson Atlanta International Airport.

"Welcome aboard," a tall African American flight attendant said as Brendan stepped onto the plane. The man smiled as he continued loading a circular tray with coffee and water for the first-class passengers. He wore a white button-down shirt, a red tie, and a gray vest that matched his cotton trousers. The man waved for Brendan to pass before lifting the tray and following behind.

Brendan saw a clear aisle all the way to row 17, where Ashley and Julia had already taken their seats, and then lifted his bag over the seat armrests to move quickly without bumping into the other passengers. Just as he began moving, the man sitting in the next row rose out of his seat to remove his blue suit jacket and place it in the overhead bin. Brendan waited for a moment before returning his carry-on bag to the floor when it became apparent that the man was in no hurry and took his time ensuring his jacket was neatly folded and would not be next to the other bags in the overhead bin.

"Need some help?" Brendan asked when he saw the man struggling to reach the smaller bags higher in the overhead bin.

The man looked at Brendan out of the corner of his eye without speaking. He continued to fumble with the overhead bags before finally placing his jacket on top, stretching, and then adjusting his seatbelt. He took his seat and let Brendan pass. Kevin, the little boy who hated shoes, sat in his grandmother's lap and waved to the man who tickled his feet as Brendan passed by row 14. Rows of empty overhead bins of the half-empty flight remained open and unoccupied as he lifted his bag and placed it in the bin over row 16. A cold, hard lump on his lower back reminded Brendan that he was sitting on the seatbelt that would be part of the crew safety checks before the plane departed. The two ends made a loud metallic *click* when he was finally able to find the matching ends behind his back and connect the belt over his lap.

"How are you doing?" Brendan asked Ashley after noticing her tight grip on her mother's hand, sitting next to the window. Ashley gave a slight nod of her head but never opened her eyes or took off the headphones. Brendan thought she appeared a little better when he placed his hand on her arm and gave it a gentle squeeze, letting her know he was there for her.

The Jamaican man with the small ukulele was the last to board the plane. He sauntered with a slow pace as he glanced back and forth between his boarding pass and the numbers over the seat rows. Brendan watched as he passed by and then turned to watch him pass Ethan in row 21, before the man lifted his arm and pointed at the middle seat between the young married couple in seats 25D and F.

"Dat be me mon," the man said in a thick island's accent. The young couple both moaned before the young man offered to sit in the middle seat to be next to his wife.

"Nuh worries," the Jamaican said happily. He placed his ukulele in the overhead bin and then stretched his legs into the center aisle from his new seat.

Ethan waved to Brendan when he saw him turn to watch the Jamaican find his seat. Brendan lifted his hand in a semi-return wave, which then caused Myles and Shanice to return their own half-hearted gesture, believing Brendan was waving to them.

An electronic crackle from the overhead speakers was followed by an announcement from the captain as he announced their departure. "Ladies and gentlemen, we want to welcome you to Delta Flight..." There was a pause as the pilot verified the flight number, "713, to Barbados. We apologize for the delay, but some weather was developing over our flight path that we needed to let pass before getting underway. The storm has now moved far enough north that it shouldn't affect our travel, and we expect a smooth ride of about..." The pilot paused again to check his information, "four and a half hours. We'll try to make up a little time once we're airborne, so sit back and enjoy your flight."

The plane slowly taxied onto the flight line as an automated message began playing on the small screens behind each headrest. "In the event of an emergency..." the message announced. Ashley groaned from the near-fetal position in her seat.

The plane's engines whirred louder as it taxied to the runway and then gained speed before the wing flaps dropped, and the plane began to lift into the air. Brendan felt his stomach drop as the aircraft rose steeply to reach its cruising altitude of thirty-five thousand feet. The plane gave a slight jerk as it passed through an air pocket at around 20,000 feet and then steadied before leveling off at cruising altitude. Brendan glanced at Ashley, who was now sitting up straight in her seat, and watched as her nostrils flared with deep breaths in and out while her eyes remained closed.

"The worst parts over, honey." Brendan squeezed Ashley's hand while he spoke to her.

Julia leaned forward in her seat and peered around Ashley. "I don't think she can hear you," she said to Brendan. "That's probably a good thing…she won't realize you lied about the worst part about flying when we have to land."

Brendan felt Ashley's grip tighten on his hand and watched as her nostrils flared even wider with each breath.

"No, I'm pretty sure she can hear me," Brendan said to Julia.

"Can you two just…please stop talking!" Ashley jerked her hand away from Brendan and turned up the volume on her phone.

"You do have your phone on airplane mode, don't you?" Brendan asked when he saw Ashley retrieve her phone. "You're not supposed to…"

"Argh," Ashley groaned as she returned to sitting with her head in her lap. She twitched her shoulder away when Brendan tried to apologize and began humming along to the song on her playlist.

"Sorry," Julia said sheepishly with a frown.

A flight attendant announced that a light beverage would be served soon and then went on to list available complimentary beverage options as well as those that were available for purchase. A slight *ding* after the announcement indicated that passengers were now allowed to remove their seatbelts and move around the cabin. This caused a flurry of activity as several passengers rose from their seats to use the bathroom and retrieve items from the overhead bins. Brendan opened the magazine he had purchased in the terminal and thumbed through the pages while Julia scrolled through the available movies on the headrest screen in front of her.

"Anything to drink?" asked a light-skinned African American woman wearing the same gray and white uniform as the male attendant serving the first-class cabin. She wore a red silk scarf around her neck and had her hair pulled tightly back behind her head. She spoke with a similar accent to the Jamaican passenger with the ukulele.

Brendan's nose was buried in his magazine, and he looked up in surprise when the woman stopped next to his seat and asked about a drink. He paused for a second, collecting his thoughts, and then responded as if he had just remembered the answer on a test.

"Yes, right…I'll have a coffee, please…cream and two sugars."

"Water, please," Julia said from the window seat when the stewardess looked over to her. "Oh, and an apple juice for her," she said, pointing at Ashley. "In case she wakes up," she added.

The stewardess handed Julia a small bottle of water and a bottle of apple juice before pouring Brendan's coffee. She handed Brendan the coffee and then searched her cart for the sugar and cream packets. "Enjoy," she said as she pushed the beverage cart past row 17 and onto the next passengers. "Anything to drink?" Brendan heard her ask the young woman sitting behind him.

Brendan stirred the cream and sugar into the small Styrofoam cup sitting on his tray and then pressed the top right button on his watch to illuminate the time…12:44. "Only three and a half more hours," he thought to himself. The *Science and Technology* magazine lay folded in half on the right side of his seat tray, open to the article he had been looking forward to reading. Electric Vehicle Batteries: The Shocking Truth, read the headline. He stretched his legs under the seat in front of him and pressed the small button on the left of the seat to recline just enough to get comfortable. "How many more people have to die?" he mouthed the words as he began reading about the dangers of EV batteries. The cabin lights dimmed around him, and the passenger noise grew to a low murmur as people made themselves comfortable for the flight. The arrival time was 5:30 am local time, and everyone wanted to be fresh for their first day on the island.

Brendan finished reading the article on EV batteries and then flipped through the pages to the front to determine what article he would read next. "May I take that?" he heard a woman ask. He looked up to see the stewardess with the red scarf pointing at the empty coffee cup on his tray.

"Oh, yes, thank you," Brendan replied, handing her the cup. She continued quietly down the aisle after placing the cup in a small white bag.

He stood up and stretched with his arms touching the roof of the airplane before opening the overhead bin and retrieving the small pillow he had placed there during boarding. He glanced up and down the aisle and noticed most of the passengers were either sleeping or trying to sleep. Only a few monitor screens remained on, casting a soft glow from various spots around the plane. The clicking of computer keys from a man sitting in 19E, and the snoring of a man coming from somewhere near the front of the aircraft, were all that was heard over the rushing wind outside the airplane. Julia lay against the airplane wall and turned often enough that Brendan knew she wasn't really sleeping.

"I'm trying to remember…" Brendan whispered as he watched Julia try to fluff the thin airline pillow. Julia's eyes blinked open for a second, making Brendan think maybe she might have heard him.

Ethan, on the other hand, looked almost dead with his head hanging awkwardly and bouncing when the plane occasionally hit light turbulence. His glasses were pushed to the right side of his face, and only the sleeve of his jacket could be seen next to the headrest where he was using it as a pillow. Shanice lay her head against Myles, who had reclined as far back in his seat as possible. Brendan rechecked his watch, 1:51 am, before returning to his seat to read the following article. He flipped through the magazine after checking the contents page…page 34…36…there, page 37, The Theory of Wormholes and the fourth spatial dimension.

Brendan heard the first pelting raindrops before he was halfway through the first paragraph. The heavy *plank* *plank* *plank* soon became a steady drone that mixed with the increased thrust of the plane's jet engines. The plane began to bounce and jerk soon after the first raindrops. The increasing turbulence was too much for Brendan's equilibrium, and he decided to put the magazine away before the motion sickness took hold. He reached up and turned off his reading light and then closed his eyes as he rested his head back against the seat. Just as he was about to get up and head to the bathroom, he felt the plane descend and bank to the right. The increased gravitational force of the plane's turn, as well as the decrease in cabin pressure, made him wonder if the plane was preparing to land. A quick check of his watch revealed they were still two hours from their destination.

Ding the overhead signal for fasten seatbelts illuminated and began to blink rhythmically.

Brendan leaned his head into the aisle and watched the stewardess shaking her head as she spoke into the plane's internal phone. She made her way hastily down the aisle after hanging up and stopped occasionally to check passengers' seatbelts. Two flashing attendant call signs flashed over the first-class cabin and went unattended as the male attendant with the red tie sat strapped in his attendant's chair facing the cabin. He adjusted the two crossing belts that connected over his shoulder and then stared intently out the small window on the plane door.

"Excuse me," Brendan called to the stewardess checking seatbelts when she drew near. He raised his hand to get her attention before she could hurry by. "Is something wrong? I noticed the plane appears to be landing."

The stewardess smiled, "No, everything is fine, the captain is making a slight detour around some weather that has popped up. No need to worry," she said and then quickly returned to her task of checking seatbelts for the remaining aisles.

"Is everything okay?" Julia asked after being awakened by the conversation.

"Yeah, I think so. It looks like we flew into a storm, and the captain is taking a detour."

Julia checked her watch before responding, "I hope this doesn't delay us even more." She quickly grabbed the seat arm rails when the plane suddenly jerked to the left and then swayed side to side before regaining control.

"Lift the shade," Brendan said as he pointed to the window next to Julia.

Rain pelted the window, and the air speed made the streaks of water move sideways across the reinforced plastic. Although it was dark outside, the occasional burst of lightning illuminated the thick clouds that made it impossible to see anything past the blinking red light on the tip of the plane's wing. A few other passengers had opened their shades, and the plane's interior was now eerily illuminated by the outside lightning.

"It looks…" Julia's words were cut short when the plane hit an air current and suddenly dropped. She had the sensation that her stomach had lurched into her throat, and she couldn't breathe for several seconds.

The plane lurched forward as the automatic controls revved the jet engines, returning the aircraft to its original altitude after an almost eighty-foot drop. The plane's interior was now abuzz with the chatter of passengers waking from their sleep and coming to the realization that the aircraft was experiencing rough weather. The overhead speakers crackled as the pilot keyed the mic to make an announcement.

chhht *chhhhhtt* "Ladies and gentlemen, this is the captain speaking. The seatbelt sign is…" *chhht…chhhhht* "and we ask that you remain seated with seatbelts…" *chhhht* *chht* "we are…weather…" a loud crash and flash of light sent the plane into darkness and cut the power to the overhead speakers ending the captains announcement. Several passengers screamed as the plane banked suddenly to the right, and the emergency lights along the floor illuminated the dark cabin.

"What's happening!?" Ashley screamed as the plane tried to regain control and the cabin lights flickered.

Brendan watched as a burst of flames engulfed the engine just outside the window. The plane wobbled back and forth as it tried to compensate for the loss of power and stability. His mind was racing, but he couldn't think straight; everything seemed to be happening at once. The emergency system restored power to the overhead speakers, allowing passengers to hear the panicked conversation in the cockpit.

chhht "loss of power...number one and two..." *chht...chhhht* "unable to..." *chht* "MAYDAY, MAYDAY..." the speakers once again went dead and the cabin was plunged into darkness as the plane lurched into a nosedive and began a rapid descent. The sudden change in altitude caused the oxygen masks to drop from the ceiling, causing further panic among the passengers.

Brendan's mind raced with adrenaline. Oxygen masks...put on yours before attempting to help others. It felt like a slow-motion dream as he reached for the oxygen mask that seemed to purposely bounce away from his grasp. He heard Ashley screaming, but felt unable to turn his head due to the increased gravitational force of the free fall. The pressure in his hand from the death grip he held on the seat in front of him was immense as everything spun out of control. It felt like a descent into madness. What do you hold onto when the whole world is falling!?

A sudden memory flashed in his head of the airport check-in line, "People don't realize that most plane crashes are survivable..." he remembered Ethan saying.

Darkness...

Alive

"Who are these people?" four-year-old Brendan wondered as he looked at the strangers standing around his mother.

He wished his mother would release his hand so he could go find a place to play with his favorite toy. The orange-colored 1971 Plymouth GTX Hot Wheels was the closest his mother could find to his father's actual sports car. The toy wouldn't roll very well in the grass...he needed a better spot to play. A woman began to cry as he stretched to look behind him for a better spot. It was the first time he ever remembered hearing crying during the dream.

"Mom?"

Brendan recalled the dream vividly; his mother always appeared sad when she looked down at him, but she never cried. The crying intensified and now seemed to be coming from more than one direction.

"Who's crying?" Brendan thought as he continued to look at the strangers.

The crying grew louder, and his back began to hurt. Brendan rubbed his lower back with his free hand and tried to turn around to see what had injured him. He felt a firm grip on his arm as he turned.

"It's my hand… Mom is gripping my hand." Brendan was remembering the dream, but this sensation was definitely on his upper arm. The dream was all wrong. Who was crying? Why does my back hurt? And…that smell?

"I think he's coming to," Brendan heard a voice say.

His vision began as a small pinhole and gradually expanded. A black man was staring at him from a foot away and was shaking his left arm.

"Come on, wake up," the man said again.

Brendan blinked a few times as his vision returned to normal. The sunlight was blinding, washing everything out in a hazy blur. His head hurt when he tried to look around and figure out where he was. A sudden surge of panic came through him as he recalled the plane falling. His muscles tensed as he acted on his last memory and tried to brace for the crash.

"Whoa, whoa…it's okay…you're okay, calm down," the man held his hand against Brendan's chest to keep him from moving.

"Where…" Brendan started to ask where he was, "Ashley!" He yelled as his memory improved. He tensed his muscles once again and fought against the man holding him down.

"Hey, hey!" Myles said forcefully. "She's okay, she's lying right over there." He pointed to a woman lying a few feet away. "She's fine," he said again after seeing the worried look on Brendan's face when the woman didn't move. "She's been crying for hours and finally fell asleep about twenty minutes ago. Let her sleep."

Brendan stopped struggling and slowly lifted onto his elbows to survey the situation. He was currently in one of the plane's eight-sided yellow life rafts with six other passengers. He could see another life raft to the left, about ten feet away from his position, and wondered how many more might be floating nearby.

Myles was leaning over him with his left arm in a makeshift sling that was tied around the back of his neck. His nose looked swollen, and a small trace of blood ran from each nostril. His cheeks and right arm were also dark red from the constant wiping of his bleeding nose. Ethan sat against the wall of the life raft next to Ashley. His hair was matted with blood coming from a gash on the left side of his head, and his left eye was also black, blue, and a pale-yellow color from some impact during the crash. His right hand rested on Ashley's back, where he occasionally stroked her hair as she slept. A woman sat across the raft from Brendan with wet hair hanging over her face. He could see dark trails of mascara running down from her eyes and would never have guessed it was Helen except for the small boy she cradled in her arms. The boy lay motionless, his arms hanging to the side, with an odd blue tint to his skin. Brendan couldn't remember the boy's name, but he recalled that he didn't like wearing shoes. To his right was the young married couple who were headed to Barbados for their honeymoon. The young woman sobbed as she rested her head against her husband. The young man's right arm was bruised from the elbow all the way to his wrist. His pants were torn around a long cut over his left thigh, and the once white bandage was now bright red.

"Drink this," Myles said as he handed Brendan a bottle of water with a red Delta Airlines triangle on the cap.

Brendan drank the water and realized for the first time how dry his mouth was. He sat for a moment, swishing the water in his mouth, when he suddenly bolted upright, "Where's Julia!" he yelled.

Myles didn't immediately answer, making Brendan grab him by the arm. "Is she…gone?" Brendan asked in a near whisper.

Myles placed his hand over Brendan's and shook his head. "We don't know," he said after a moment of silence.

"What do you mean?" Brendan asked. "What does that mean, you don't know?" he asked again when Myles didn't answer.

"It means I don't know. I haven't seen her since we boarded," Myles replied calmly, even though Brendan appeared to be getting worked up.

"Is she on another raft? We need to go back…" Brendan tried raising himself, but immediately fell back down when a sharp pain shot across his lower back.

"Take it easy," Ethan called to Brendan. "You might have a broken back."

"We have to go back," Brendan turned his plea to Ethan when Myles wouldn't answer. "Please…" he begged, "you don't understand."

"I do," Myles said, placing his hand on Brendan's shoulder to keep him still. "Shanice is missing also."

Brendan felt guilty for not considering Shanice. "We have to do something." His voice was soft and low like a mere whimper.

"The plane had four life rafts," Ethan said, and then waited for Brendan to acknowledge his statement. "Two on each side…" he continued, "two of them are here, which means there are another two floating around out there somewhere." Ethan noticed a change in his friend's demeanor. He continued, "Julia and Shanice are in good health, and are both good swimmers…there's a good chance they are safe and sound on one of the other rafts."

"Yeah, they are good swimmers," Brendan said softly to himself.

"They may already be rescued by now and sipping coffee in a Coast Guard ship," Ethan said when he realized his words were making his friend feel better.

Brendan looked down at his watch; 4:47 pm. "Have we really been adrift for fourteen hours?" he asked in disbelief. Myles and Ethan both nodded. "Shouldn't they have found us by now? I mean with modern technology…satellites and all…"

"It's a big ocean," Myles said as he took a seat next to Brendan.

"Plus, the pilot went off course trying to get around the storm…and the currents have been all over the place," Ethan offered. "There's no telling where we are."

"I don't suppose anyone has a cell phone?" Brendan asked.

"Nope…well, not a working one anyway," Myles answered.

"We even checked some of the people we found…" he paused, "you know…in the water."

"So, what do we do now?" Brendan asked.

"The only thing we can do," Ethan answered. "We wait."

Brendan crawled over to where Ashley lay and placed his head against her shoulder. He closed his eyes and thought about Julia. He recalled the semester in college when they both enrolled in a swimming class, and midway through the semester, the instructor had invited Julia to try out for the university swim team. She really was a good swimmer.

***

Brendan felt fingers comb through his hair and thought, just for a moment, that he was back home in bed with Julia. He stirred and looked up into the hazel eyes of his daughter. Her eyes were red, bloodshot, and heavy with fear. The kind of look a person gets when they have cried so long that they just can't cry anymore. A weariness that extends beyond mere tiredness. Despite all that, she smiled when she saw him looking up at her.

"Are you okay? Ashley asked.

"I'm fine, kitten," Brendan replied as he pulled himself to a sitting position, wincing from the pain in his lower back. He looked at the sky and then at his watch. He had been asleep for almost three hours. The sky was orange from the setting sun, and the first stars were already visible in the partially cloudy sky. "How about you? How are you doing?" he asked Ashley.

Ashley sat quietly, not answering his question. Brendan stroked her hair that had become matted with seawater.

"I thought…" Ashley started, "You wouldn't wake up…for a long time." She would have started crying again if there were any tears left.

"Oh, honey." Brendan wrapped his arms around his daughter and held her tightly despite the intense pain in his back.

"You said…" Ashley began, "We would be safe. That flying wasn't dangerous."

"I'm sorry," Brendan said. "I don't know what happened…"

"We flew right into a storm, that's what happened," Ethan said.

"I thought we waited at the terminal until the storm had passed," came the voice from the young man on the other side of the raft. He had been listening to the conversation between Brendan and Ashley and didn't want to interrupt, but decided to do so after the tall man with glasses did.

Ethan was surprised to hear the young man speak. "Different storm," he explained. "The first one was further north, but the heated air helped fuel another in its wake."

The young man stared at Ethan and simply nodded his head. "Are you some kind of Einstein?" asked the young woman lying against the man. "Yeah, how do you know all that?" the young man asked.

"Einstein? Oh no, no no no," Ethan protested. "Einstein was a genius with an IQ of around 160," he added.

"Ethan's IQ is only a mere 154," Myles said in a sarcastic tone as he nodded towards Ethan.

"That's not the same," Ethan argued. "That's comparing apples to oranges since…"

"Never mind that, how did you know about the storm?" Brendan interjected.

"Oh, right...I received about four successive alerts from NASA just as we were taking off," Ethan began explaining. "I had forgotten to put my phone on airplane mode when I saw they had a television series on the Hubble telescope and..."

"The alerts!" Brendan interjected again.

"I was getting to that," Ethan said defensively. "The alerts warned about another warm air cell that was quickly accelerating behind the first storm...so we flew right into a newly developing storm."

"Why wouldn't our pilots have gotten the same messages?" The young woman asked.

"They would..." Ethan said, "Eventually. NASA has its own meteorologists and typically gets its information an hour or so sooner than commercial agencies."

"So, Ethan, is it? Why does NASA send you..." The man started to ask, "No, never mind."

"He works for NASA," Ashley answered the question.

"I figured as much," the man said. "And you're Ashley, right? Or kitten?" The man smiled.

"Ashley, and he's my dad," Ashley said, pointing to Brendan.

"Brendan." Brendan waved as he said his name.

"And I'm Myles," Myles introduced himself.

"Cool," replied the young man, "I'm Spencer...Spence to my friends, and this is my girlfrien..." the man stopped mid-word and corrected himself, "my wife, Madison."

"Newlyweds," Madison said as she held up her left hand and showed her new ring.

"Hell of a way to spend your honeymoon," Myles joked. The atmosphere remained serious, but at least it no longer felt like a somber funeral.

Everyone's gaze shifted to the woman on the other side of the raft, who hadn't said a word since getting in the life raft. Like Ashley, she had cried for the first several hours after the crash and finally cried herself to sleep. She occasionally stroked the little boy's head and attempted to wake him, letting the others know she was awake.

"What's your name?" Spencer called to the woman.

The woman didn't respond. She didn't even look up but just continued to sit still with the little boy in her lap.

"Her name's Helen, and that's her grandson," Brendan said after the woman didn't respond. "I met them in the waiting area…she was taking her son to Barbados for vacation."

"Is the little boy still…" Ashley started to ask.

"No," Myles answered before Ashley could finish the question. "I'm pretty sure he was gone when your dad pulled him out of the water."

"What?" Brendan asked. "I pulled him out of the water?"

"You don't remember?" Myles asked.

"No, I just remember the plane going down, and everything went black. Next thing I know, you were kneeling over me, shaking my arm."

"The plane hit the water and bounced a few times before the wing came off…" Myles began telling the events of the crash.

"The wing came off?" Brendan's mouth was wide in astonishment.

"You helped get the door open and pulled a few people from their seatbelts to get them to the door before getting in the raft when the plane started to sink. You pulled me into the boat, and a few minutes later we drifted by the woman, and we pulled her into the boat…she wouldn't let go of the boy, so we brought them both in."

"I don't remember any of that," Brendan said, shaking his head.

"That's not uncommon," Ethan remarked. "People who suffer from high altitude hypoxia often pass out and can't remember anything that happened prior to them passing out. It has to do with low fractional inspired oxygen tension…"

"Does he always do that?" Madison asked.

"Yes," Myles and Ashley said in unison.

"Wait, what about the people in the other boat?" Spencer asked when he noticed them erecting a canopy that was attached to their raft.

Myles, Brendan, and Ethan all shrugged.

"I know there used to be more of them," Myles offered. "I remember seeing another raft next to ours just after the plane sank. I don't know how many there were, but I would say at least as many as we have in this raft. The male flight attendant from first class was barking orders and trying to keep everyone calm."

"What happened to him?" Spencer asked.

"I don't know," Myles answered matter-of-factly. "It was dark out when we started drifting, but when the sun rose, there were only four left on the raft."

"It must have capsized in the rough waters," Spencer said.

"Are these rafts safe?" Madison asked. "How long can they even stay afloat?" Everyone began inspecting the raft, trying to determine its seaworthiness, but eventually stopped and stared at Ethan when they realized they had no idea what they were looking for.

"Oh, now you want me to talk?" Ethan said as he looked back at the faces waiting for an answer.

"Come on, it's not like you don't know," Myles stated.

"Fine," Ethan said after a moment of stubbornness. "We're in one of the newer ocean-going raft models…a Zodiac ISAF model by the looks of it…" Ethan paused for a second as he ran his hand across the inflated nylon tube as if he were admiring the craftsmanship, "It's a very sturdy raft that is designed to stay afloat with ten passengers for at least 30 days. It even has a self-righting feature in case the raft capsizes."

The other passengers in the raft all began running their hands along the yellow nylon walls as if inspecting a car they were considering purchasing.

"What about sharks? And other creatures?" Madison asked as she peered over the side of the raft. The sea had calmed considerably since the crash, and the water rose and fell in gentle waves.

"Good question…" Ethan answered, "and they thought about that…the raft is designed with a double hull…" he pointed to the indentation in the raft where it looked like two innertubes were stacked on top of each other, "the bottom one is a bit thicker and designed to withstand the occasional nudge from interested animals."

Ashley breathed a sigh of relief.

"Does ours have one of those?" Spencer asked. He lifted his injured hand and pointed over Ethan's shoulder to the fully erected canopy on the other raft.

"It did," Ethan answered. He placed his hand on top of the raft and lifted a black canopy and a thin black pole that was broken in two. Brendan thought the canopy looked like the small tent he had purchased for Ashley on her 13th birthday. They used to set the tent up in the backyard and spend the night pretending to be camping in the wilderness.

The sky darkened as the sun set below the horizon, causing the temperature to drop by several degrees. Ethan opened the raft's plastic storage bin and removed a handful of plastic pouches. He tossed one to the married couple, one to Myles, one to Ashley and Brendan, and then one to Helen. Helen didn't move when the pouch landed next to her leg and never even looked up or acknowledged the gesture. The married couple was the first to inspect the pouch and then remove the thin two-sided foil blanket. One side was yellow, and the other was a shiny silver color that resembled tin foil. Spencer unfolded the blanket and covered himself and Madison with it to keep warm.

"The silver side goes face up," Ethan said after watching the couple get comfortable.

"Does it really matter?" Myles asked as he unfolded his and inspected both sides.

"The yellow side is designed to retain heat," Ethan answered. "The shiny side is supposed to be used to reflect sunlight during the day, so you don't get sunburned.

Ashley flipped her blanket over after hearing the explanation and held her arm open, inviting her father to join her under the foil blanket. She dropped her arm and wrapped the blanket around her when her father didn't join her. Brendan sat still, watching Helen intently.

"You should put the blanket on, Helen," Brendan called to the woman sitting on the other side of the raft. Helen sat quietly with her head hanging over her chest and didn't respond. Brendan looked at Ethan and then Myles before trying again. Both men simply returned Brendan's stare, wondering where this was going.

"Helen…" Brendan called again. "Helen!" He said louder. Helen never flinched a muscle.

Brendan crawled across the raft, picked up the plastic pouch, and knelt next to Helen.

"Helen…why don't you let me take the boy and…" Brendan reached his hands out to put them under the boy's legs and back as he spoke.

"DON'T TOUCH HIM!" Helen screamed as Brendan reached for the boy. It was the first time the others in the raft had heard Helen speak, and they were horrified at the heartbreak and pain they heard in her voice.

Brendan quickly withdrew his hands, "Okay, okay," he said calmly.

"Everything okay over there?" came a voice from the other raft floating ten feet away.

Brendan glanced over and saw a man standing in the raft and peering in his direction. The sun had set, but he could still make out the tall, muscular frame of the man wearing a white tank top and red shorts. He wondered if it was one of the fraternity brothers he had seen at the airport before raising his hand and waving.

"We're good, thanks," Brendan yelled towards the man. He returned his attention to Helen and then looked back over his shoulder at Ethan. "This can't be healthy," he said, knowing Ethan would know what he was referring to.

"Psychologically, it's devastating," Ethan answered. "But it's not a substantial health risk until the body starts to decompose…with this humidity and temperature, I'd say we have another 12 to 16 hours before it starts to bloat."

"That's her grandson," Madison scolded Ethan, "don't you have any compassion?"

"Welcome to my world," Ashley said from inside her blanket.

"Let her be," Myles called to Brendan. "Hopefully we'll be rescued by then…I'm sure they'll find us any time now."

"And if they don't?" Ethan asked.

"We can deal with it then," Myles answered.

Brendan returned his attention to Helen. He unfolded the foil blanket and began to place it slowly over Helen's shoulders. "It's going to get cold tonight," he said gently as he tucked the ends of the blanket between Helen's shoulders and the raft wall. Helen didn't fight the gesture and just sat staring at the dead little boy. She lifted her right hand to spread the blanket over the boy's torso in case he got cold, and then looked up at Brendan, almost daring him to say otherwise. Brendan looked her in the eyes and nodded his head. She had lost her grandson and most likely her son as well; he wouldn't take her hope, not yet.

Brendan returned to his spot next to Ashley and tapped his finger on her head to indicate he was ready to share the blanket. He stared around the boat at the desperate group of travelers and wondered at Ethan's last words. "And if they don't?" What then? How long could they survive lost at sea? He stared up into the starry night and whispered a prayer to a God he had cursed after the infidelity. It had been a long day; his body and mind were exhausted. The rhythmic rocking of the raft and the soothing sound of the waves soon put him to sleep.

Science Can't Explain

Pain and stiffness in his lower back reminded Brendan that he was still lying uncomfortably in a raft adrift at sea. He heard voices speaking softly and slowly opened one eye to try to determine the time. Billowing cumulus clouds drifted overhead, appearing gray against the early morning sky. The moon hung low on the horizon, and the faint trace of stars still peeked through the morning's first rays. Myles lay on his side and snored while the young married couple and Helen also appeared to be fast asleep. Ashley leaned on her left elbow and whispered in Ethan's direction. Ethan sat with his back to the raft and rested his head on the raft wall. Brendan closed his eyes to try and get a little more rest, but couldn't help overhearing the conversation.

"Do you think she's still alive?" Ashley whispered.

Ethan turned his head and looked up into the sky before answering, "I don't know, maybe," he said softly. "Considering the number of life rafts versus the number of passengers…I'd say chances are good…" his voice trailed off into silence.

The two sat quietly for a moment before Ethan spoke again, "What do you think?"

"Me? I don't know...I've never been good with math, or probabilities...all that predicting outcomes stuff," Ashley answered.

"What's your gut feeling?" Ethan rolled his head onto his right ear to see Ashley's reaction.

"I don't know...I mean, I want her to be okay," Ashley said. She stared at the raft floor when she answered the question, but then suddenly looked up towards Ethan. "I thought scientist types didn't believe in gut feelings."

Ethan smiled and then rolled his head back to look up into the sky again. "Did I ever tell you I had a sister?"

"What? You have a sister? No, you never told me that." Ashley pushed up off her elbow and tried to sit upright to see Ethan's face.

Brendan opened his eyes and rolled his head so that his left ear pointed directly in Ethan's direction. He wanted to make sure he could hear Ethan's reply, as he was also unaware that Ethan had ever had a sister.

Ethan rolled his head back to face Ashley again before speaking, "had..." he emphasized, "she died when I was seven."

"Oh my God," Ashley breathed a little louder than she intended. "I didn't know, I'm so sorry."

"It's okay," Ethan responded. He lifted his head off the raft wall, came to an upright seated position, and turned to face Ashley. "She was my older sister..." he continued, "she was fourteen when she was diagnosed with Leukemia." Ethan paused as if remembering something before starting again, "She was in and out of the hospital for months at a time before she finally passed away at the age of seventeen."

"That's terrible," Ashley said so softly that even Brendan, lying right next to her, barely heard her. "I bet she was pretty...and smart like you," she said a little louder.

Ethan smiled broadly. "She was beautiful, but she hated school..." he almost laughed, "it drove my parents crazy." He paused for several minutes, making Ashley wonder if he was going to finish the story. It was the first time she could recall him ever speaking with this type of emotion, and she didn't want to interrupt.

"She was a genius, though…" Ethan finally started speaking again, "It was just a different kind. She could play any instrument with just a small amount of practice. Her music was so beautiful." He paused again, slowly nodding as if listening to a tune in his head. "She used to play the guitar and sing to me for hours; it was so wonderful…my parents hated it."

"Why?" Ashley asked.

"I don't know, I was seven. I didn't even know how sick she was. She would just go away for months at a time and then show back up out of the blue. My parents never really talked to me about it, but my sister said I shouldn't be worried about her. It was hard not to; she lost so much weight…I think she was only about seventy-five pounds when she turned seventeen. Chemotherapy…you know…" Ethan choked up for a second, and Ashley could tell it was a very painful memory.

"What was her name?" Ashley asked to take him away from the painful memory.

Ethan smiled again, "Amelia…she was named after my grandmother."

"Amelia," Ashley repeated the name. "That's pretty."

"Anyway…" Ethan's voice grew louder, "She went to the hospital one day and never came back. My parents never even told me that she passed away, but I knew…one day, while she was gone, I woke up and felt different; I just knew something had happened. I knew…the music just stopped."

"Your parents didn't even tell you that your sister had died?"

"Nope," Ethan shook his head. "Not right away. They mentioned it several months later after they cleared out her room."

"I think that might be the saddest story I have ever heard," Ashley said. She wiped a tear that was forming in her right eye.

"The point is…" Ethan returned to leaning against the raft wall, "Sometimes a gut feeling is better than any math or probability formula. There are things that science just can't explain."

Brendan turned his head and pretended to sleep for another fifteen minutes before finally sitting upright and stretching. He peered over all sides of the raft but could see nothing but water for as far as the eye could see. The second raft had drifted about twenty feet away but was still tied to their raft with a yellow nylon rope. He thought the people in the other raft must be lying down since he couldn't see anyone. He feared for a second that the other raft might have capsized overnight, but then figured that was unlikely since it would have caused a ruckus.

"Can someone turn on the coffee?" Myles joked as he stirred from his sleep. He crawled to the center of the raft and then stood to survey the area once he had gained his balance.

"Anything?" Brendan asked when Myles returned to sitting against the raft.

"Lots of water," Myles answered.

"Cream and two sugars," Spencer joked as he lowered the foil blanket that was covering him and Madison.

"Ungh," Madison moaned at the morning light. "I was hoping this was all a bad dream."

Myles checked the time on his watch and then ran his hand over his head. "27 hours since the crash. I would have thought they'd find us by now."

"I'm sure they're still looking." Brendan patted Ashley's leg to comfort her as he scanned the sky, pretending to look for a rescue plane.

"Does anyone even know where we are?" Spencer said as he looked from Brendan to Myles and then to Ethan.

"Somewhere in the Atlantic Ocean…that's all I got," Myles said as he shook his head.

"Somewhere around the middle of the triangle between the 25th and 30th parallel, I'd say," Ethan offered his guess. "Based on a rough estimate of the time and speed we traveled before the plane went down."

"What triangle?" Madison asked.

"The Bermuda triangle," Ethan stated matter-of-factly. "An imaginary triangle between Bermuda, Puerto Rico, and Miami," he used his index finger to draw a triangle in the air as he spoke. "You never heard of the Bermuda triangle?"

"The Devil's triangle," Helen interjected from across the raft. Her voice surprised everyone since they had forgotten about her, covered in the foil blanket.

"Exactly," Ethan said. "I mean not exactly that it's the Devil's triangle, but that it's the same triangle…you know what I mean."

"The Devil has taken hundreds of lives in these waters," Helen shot back. "He came for them…he came for my son…came for my grandson…and he is coming for us all."

"That's a load of crap!" Brendan yelled. "That's just a bunch of superstitious mumbo jumbo."

"He'll take your daughter next," Helen spat.

"Is that a threat!" Brendan started to get to his feet before being restrained by Myles. "You threatening me!?" Brendan continued as he struggled to get free from Myles' grasp.

"Calm down, man, she's been through a lot," Myles said as he tried to calm his friend.

"Ha-ha-haaaaa…haaaaa-ha-haaaaa…" Helen laughed hysterically. Ashley thought the scene seemed eerily ominous since the woman still held the dead child in her lap.

"Is it true?" Madison asked. Her eyes were wide with fear and looked a bit cartoonish, outlined in dark mascara that had smudged around both eyes.

"I saw a movie called the Devil's graveyard..." Spencer said suddenly, "It was about the Bermuda triangle and..." he was cut short by Ethan.

"Stop, stop, STOP!" Ethan yelled as he rose to his feet and held out both hands. "Those are all just ghost stories, there is no Devil here...science has debunked all those myths. Yes, there were a lot of planes and ships that crashed in this area of the North Atlantic, but it has all been explained by natural weather phenomena, shallow water reefs, and active weather caused by the Gulf Stream."

"We have enough troubles without being at each other's throats," Myles added.

Brendan stopped struggling to free himself and returned to his seat next to Ashley. Helen stopped laughing, and the raft once again fell silent except for the constant sound of waves lapping against the raft. Time passed slowly as the raft drifted further and further out to sea.

"I've been meaning to ask about the new glasses," Brendan said, breaking the long silence. He pointed to the thin, wire-framed glasses Ethan wore instead of his usual plastic-framed black ones.

Ethan turned to face his friend, and Brendan could see the effect the constant sun and salt water were having on his skin. Ethan's lips were chapped, and his cheeks and forehead were bright red and starting to peel.

"You don't want to know," Ethan replied. "Let's just say I found them when we were looking for a cell phone."

"Oh!" Brendan exclaimed when he finally realized Ethan was telling him they came from one of the dead bodies they found drifting in the water after the crash. "And the prescriptions are the same?"

"Close," Ethan said as he removed the glasses and studied them as if he had just seen them for the first time. "Better than no glasses at all, though," he added before putting them back on.

"I'm hungry, Dad," Ashley said from under the foil blanket that she had covered herself in for protection from the sun.

"Me too," Madison whined.

Brendan lifted the yellow waterproof sack in the middle of the raft that contained the food they had been eating since the crash. He pulled out two small items and held them up. "Peanuts or cookies?" he asked. He moved his hand back and forth between Ashley and Madison for both to see the items.

"Peanuts," Ashley said with a frown.

"No more fruit?" Madison asked after a moment's consideration between the two options.

Brendan emptied the contents onto the raft floor for everyone to see the dwindling amount of food left in the bag. "Sorry," he said while shaking his head. "Where did we even get this stuff?"

"Stewardess' food cart...or at least one of the bins," Myles said. "Another one of the things we found floating after the crash. The guys in the other raft have the rest." Myles pointed to the other raft still tethered to theirs.

"I think we need to start thinking about rationing the food, and what else we might be able to eat and drink in case we're out here for a while," Brendan said.

"That reminds me of this show I just saw, Society in the Snow..." Spencer said. "Their plane crashed in the mountains, and they had to eat each other..."

"Shut up, Spence!" Brendan shouted.

"Eww, gross," Ashley added.

Madison elbowed her husband under their foil blanket, and Spencer immediately quit telling the story.

"It's actually…" Ethan started, but then changed his mind after seeing Brendan's glare, "No, never mind."

Myles sorted the peanuts and cookies, counting as he pushed each to its respective pile. "Three, four…three, four, five." He stopped counting and looked up at the group. "Four bags of cookies, six bags of peanuts…and two small bottles of water."

"That'll last less than one day," Ethan said. "Considering the average adult needs about one thousand calories per day before the body starts to starve."

"So, you're saying we'll die in a couple of days unless we get more food?" Madison asked. She eyed the small piles on the raft and then returned her gaze to Ethan.

"Oh no, that's not what I'm saying," Ethan pushed the new glasses higher onto his nose before sitting up to explain. "A person can live twenty to thirty days without food, so we would have a long time before anyone actually died of starvation."

"So, we have about a month to be rescued…that's not bad," Spencer said.

"Well…no…" Ethan said. Brendan thought Ethan looked happy to be having a debate. "I said a person would starve in thirty days…" Ethan continued, "but you'd be dead in about three days without water."

Spencer looked at the two small bottles of water and then back up to Ethan, "Okay, that's bad."

"Told you…Devils coming." Helen's voice sounded creepy. Her dried lips spread thinly across her face in a sinister grin.

"Ignore her," Myles said. He placed his hand on Brendan's shoulder to prevent him from getting up. "The other raft still has the food cart, and

I'm sure they have a lot more than we do. We just need to see how much they have."

Myles walked to the other side of the raft and placed both hands on top of the nylon tube, leaning forward to call to the other raft. "Hey!" he yelled. He called again when there was no response. "Hey, you guys in the other raft!" A head poked out from behind the canopy on the other raft, and Myles began waving his arms overhead.

"Yeah?" the head called back from the other raft.

"We're running out of food and water," Myles held his hands around his mouth as he shouted. "Can we get some more?"

The man's head disappeared back behind the canopy and didn't return. After several minutes, Myles called again, "Hey! Hey!" The man's head reappeared. "I said, can we get some more food and water…from the food cart," he added to remind the man that they had already shared some of the food, and they knew there was plenty more.

"We don't have any more," the man shouted back.

"What?!" Myles shouted back at the man. He wanted to make sure he understood him correctly.

"I said, we don't have any more," the man shouted back again.

"You have a full bin," Myles argued. "We helped you lift it from the water…remember?"

The man's head disappeared once again behind the canopy, and Myles turned and looked at the others in the raft.

"They're lying," Ethan said. Brendan didn't remember any of it and simply stood, shrugging his shoulders.

"Hey!" Myles yelled to the other raft. This time, there was no response, not even the head that had poked around the side of the canopy the last two times.

"Give me a hand," Myles said as he gestured for Brendan to come closer.

Myles grabbed the yellow nylon rope connecting the two rafts and started to pull. He handed the rope behind him to Brendan, who also began to help pull the other raft closer. Myles and Brendan watched the men in the other raft suddenly poke their heads around when they felt themselves being pulled closer to the other raft.

"Hey, stop that," a thin man with gray hair called to Myles and Brendan.

As the other raft grew closer, Brendan thought he recognized the men in the boat. The thin man with gray hair was the impatient passenger who cut in front of the old woman with the stroller to board the plane first. The two tall, muscle-bound men with short, cropped hair were the men in the security line wearing matching fraternity shirts from the University of Arkansas. The last man in the raft was the Jamaican who played his ukulele for Ashley in the waiting area. He sat at the rear of the raft and appeared uninterested in what was happening around him.

"I order you to stop what you're doing?" The thin man yelled. He pointed his finger back and forth between the two men pulling the rope. Myles looked back at Brendan and gave him a puzzled look, but kept pulling on the rope.

One of the fraternity brothers grabbed the other end of the rope and started to pull. He immediately dropped it when he realized he was only pulling them faster towards the other raft. Myles could see the men's raft was littered with empty water bottles, food wrappers, and a browning apple core when the two rafts came within feet of each other.

"Did you eat all of our food!?" Myles yelled as he pointed to the litter on the floor of the raft.

"Our food?" the thin man asked as if surprised by the question.

"We've been here for days, what were we supposed to do?" said one of the fraternity brothers.

The bigger of the two fraternity brothers put his hand on the other's shoulder and pulled him back as he stepped forward to talk for the group. "The captain said we already gave you your half of the food."

"Our half?" Myles exclaimed in exasperation. "There were three full bins in that cart." Myles stopped pulling on the rope, and the men stood only two to three feet apart.

"We pulled it from the water while you wasted time searching the bodies," the large man said, crossing his arms across his chest. "The captain has made his decision."

"We were looking for a phone to call for help…to save us all," Myles argued.

"Wait, where's the captain?" Brendan asked from behind Myles.

"Captain Kleinman," the smaller of the two fraternity brothers called from behind his larger friend. He gestured with his thumb to the thin man standing behind him.

"That's not the pilot. He's just another passenger," Brendan argued. "I saw him sitting in first class when I boarded the plane."

"He's a Navy Officer, from Joint Base Charleston," replied the smaller brother. "And we elected him as our leader."

Brendan eyed the thin man standing behind the two larger men. He appeared thin and frail, making it hard for Brendan to believe he was an actual senior Naval Officer. "What ship did you captain?" Brendan asked. He wasn't an expert on Navy service, but something about the thin man just didn't add up. The two fraternity brothers turned to look at Captain Kleinman and waited for his response.

Captain Kleinman looked back and forth from the brothers to the two men in the other boat before answering, "That's none of your business," he snorted.

"There are no ships at Joint Base Charleston," Ethan chimed in. He had come to a kneeling position with his arms resting on top of the raft wall and was listening to the men argue. "It's a weapons station where they build the missiles and other ordnance for the navy ships." Everyone turned and looked at Ethan. "NASA has a research program in Charleston that I've visited a couple of times," he said to explain how he knew about Joint Base Charleston.

The fraternity brothers turned to Captain Kleinman, waiting for his response.

"I never said I was a ship captain," Captain Kleinman sneered.

"I thought you said…" the smaller fraternity brother started to ask before being cut off by Captain Kleinman.

"I said I was a Navy Officer," Captain Kleinman growled. "In ROTC," he whispered under his breath so that not even the fraternity brothers could hear. It was more of a half-truth than a lie since Captain Kleinman did receive a Navy ROTC scholarship and would have been commissioned as a Naval Officer if it hadn't been for the heart condition that was discovered during the commissioning physical in his senior year.

"You're lying," Brendan yelled. "You don't have any more experience than any of us."

"I'm not going to stand here and have my integrity questioned by the likes of you," Captain Kleinman yelled back as he wagged his finger at Brendan. "We already gave you your half, so let the rope go."

"Maybe I'll just come aboard and take our half," Myles threatened.

"I wouldn't recommend that," the larger of the two brothers cautioned Myles. He crossed his arms across his broad chest and widened his stance on the raft.

"Gentlemen, gentlemen," Spencer called as he rose from his seated position on the other side of the raft. "We're all adults here, and I'm sure we can work this out without resorting to violence."

The men looked across the raft at one another, and no one spoke for several moments.

"He's right," stated Brendan. "We need to work together if we're going to make it out of this alive. Let's just start by figuring out how much water we have, and then we can discuss how to divide it."

"We have two bottles." Spencer held up two fingers.

Everyone in the raft looked to the men in the other raft and waited to see what they would do. The two fraternity brothers looked at each other and then at Captain Kleinman for guidance. Captain Kleinman was silent as he weighed his options. The way he saw it, he had the upper hand, more food and water on his raft, fewer people, and two large men willing to follow his orders. A slight grin spread across his lips as he considered his advantage.

"Six," came a heavy-accented voice from behind the captain. "Six bottle wata…two fruit and some peanuts, dat be all, mon," said the Jamaican. He held up a six-pack of water by the plastic carrier holding the water bottles.

"You!" Captain Kleinman said as he turned to face the Jamaican. He grabbed the water and then sneered at the man. Brendan thought he would have hit the man if he thought he could get away with it. Brendan would take the Jamaican in a one-on-one match.

"Okay, so we have eight bottles of water…now let's talk about how we might divide them to be fair," Brendan said quickly to try and help the man who was about to be attacked.

Captain Kleinman turned back to face the men in the other raft. "Fine," he spat. "We'll give you two bottles, and then both sides will have the same amount of water."

"Sounds fair," one of the brothers said while nodding his head.

"Oh no, no, no, no, no," Myles said, shaking his head. "We have seven people on this side," he explained. "We should get more bottles."

"An even split would be five bottles for us, seven, and three bottles for the four of you," Ethan said.

"Yeah," said Spencer in agreement.

"You're not in much of a position to bargain," Captain Kleinman said coldly to Spencer.

"Is that how you want to be remembered when we're saved? As the man who withheld water from the women and children?" Brendan asked. He waved his hand across the raft to emphasize the three women huddled nearby.

Captain Kleinman's eyes narrowed. For a second, Brendan thought he might have persuaded the man to give them more water.

"Never let it be said that Captain Richard Kleinman is not a fair and compassionate leader," Captain Kleinman said with his chest puffed out.

Myles rolled his eyes at the announcement.

"As well as the two bottles of water…" Captain Kleinman continued. "We will also give you some fruit and a new pole so that you can erect your canopy and be protected from the sun." He reached behind him and retrieved a banana and a thin, black canopy pole that was lying on the other side of the raft.

"Hey, that was my banana," the smaller fraternity brother complained.

"So, you're offering a rotten banana and a pole that you don't need anyway?" Brendan scoffed.

"Listen, I'm trying to help you," Captain Kleinman sneered at Brendan. "By tomorrow that banana will look like a steak dinner, and by the looks of you, you'll be dead in less than that if you don't get out of the sun."

Brendan looked at Myles and then at Ethan. He wasn't going to risk a physical altercation over an extra bottle of water, and the captain didn't appear eager to negotiate any further. "Okay, we'll take it…two bottles of water, the banana, and the pole."

The captain tossed the items across the water and into the raft by Brendan's feet. "Now let go," he ordered Myles. The rope made a small splash as Myles tossed the slack line into the water.

"I can't believe they ate all the food," Ashley commented while she watched her father return the food items to the waterproof sack.

Brendan grunted in agreement before adding, "I'll be a monkey's uncle if that little weasel is a naval officer."

Myles stood staring as the other raft drifted until the rope connecting the two went taut. "I say we wait until it gets dark and then take the food they owe us."

"I don't know," Ethan began before turning to look towards the other raft. "Those two meatheads look pretty formidable," he said, referring to the fraternity brothers in their matching tank tops.

"For what?" Brendan asked Myles. "An extra bottle of water?"

"I'm with him," Spencer said, nodding to Myles. "That extra bottle of water could mean the difference between life and death."

Brendan rose to his feet and placed his hand on Myles' shoulder. He waited until his friend acknowledged him before speaking, "It's too risky, you know it is," he said, slowly shaking his head. "Do we really want to risk capsizing the raft, or making holes and having to be in the water?" He turned his gaze to the others in the raft. "Do you want to risk putting them in the water?"

Myles looked around the raft and relaxed his posture before agreeing, "No," he said. "But how long is this going to last?" He asked as he took the food sack from Brendan's hand and held it up to emphasize the emptiness.

"I know," Brendan reassured his friend. "But let's first focus on the things that we can control." He turned and lifted the thin black pole they had received from the captain, handing it to Myles. "Do you think you can put this together so we can at least think in the shade?"

"Ethan's the one who knows about this thing," Myles said while testing the flexibility of the thin fiberglass pole.

"I need Ethan for another task," Brendan replied and then turned and knelt next to Ethan. Ethan pushed the wire glasses further up the bridge of his nose out of habit and faced Brendan. "Do you know anything about capturing moisture for drinking water?" Brendan asked. Ethan covered his mouth with his right hand and squeezed his cheeks while he considered the question.

"In theory," Ethan replied. "It's a matter of the relative humidity versus the dew point." He made himself comfortable as he began to explain the process, "On one hand, the air holds a certain amount of moisture." He held out his right palm as if lecturing young students and then held out his left palm and continued, "On the other hand is the temperature at which that moisture condenses onto a surface." He was bringing his hands together to emphasize the process when Brendan grabbed his hands.

"I don't need to know the process," Brendan said to interrupt the lecture. "I just need to know if you can do it?"

Ethan stared at his friend and wished he had a better answer than the one forming on his lips. "It's not that easy...yes, the temperatures are right for the formation of dew, but there are a lot of other factors that don't make it ideal..." Ethan was about to explain the factors when he was cut off again.

"So no," Brendan interjected.

"Maybe a little," Ethan corrected him. "I would estimate an ounce a day at best, which wouldn't..."

"Better than nothing," Brendan interrupted again. "Get to work on it and let me know if there is anything you need."

Ethan joined Myles on the side of the raft with the canopy, and the two quickly erected the canopy using the new fiberglass pole. When fully erect, the canopy stood three feet over the raft floor and provided shade for half of the vessel. Ethan ran his hand from top to bottom along the black nylon canopy and then began trying to punch a hole in the nylon fabric using the pointed end of the broken fiberglass pole.

"Wait, what are you doing?" Myles asked. Ethan had the broken pole under his shoulder and was attempting to use his weight to drive the pole through the thick nylon.

"Making a water capture point," Ethan replied. "When dew forms on the canopy wall, it will run down the sides and into this hole." He leaned his weight into the pole once again, trying to pierce the fabric. "An empty bottle on the underside will capture the water, giving us a little more to drink."

"That'll work?" Ashley asked when she overheard the conversation.

"In theory," Ethan answered. He grunted again, trying to pierce the nylon fabric. "I'm a scientist, not a Boy Scout," he added.

"Give me that," Myles said. He took the broken pole from Ethan's hand and took Ethan's spot next to the place where he was trying to make a hole in the fabric. He grunted as he twisted the pole back and forth with his hands and put his weight behind the pole. In seconds, a small hole in the fabric stretched to allow the entire width of the pole.

"Yay!" Ashley clapped.

Ethan removed a small strand of yellow string he had pulled from the rope and used it to tie the fabric around the top of an empty water bottle on the underside of the canopy. He leaned over the raft and scooped a small handful of water into the cup of his hand and then emptied it on the canopy wall. The water ran quickly down the nylon fabric, into the small hole made by Myles, and then into the water bottle inside the canopy.

"Voila," Ethan said as the others watched on.

"Woo hoo!" Spencer cheered as Madison and Ashley clapped.

Ethan bowed with his left hand on his stomach and made a small circular gesture with his right hand in his bent position.

"Good job," Brendan said. "We'll take turns under the canopy during the day when the sun is out and use our blankets at night."

"I'm first!" Madison said as she crawled across the raft and into the new shaded area. "Ahhhh," she added as she reclined against the shaded raft wall.

"One more thing I'd like to accomplish today," Brendan said. He looked Myles and Ethan in the eyes and then turned his gaze to the dead little boy still resting in his grandmother's lap. He returned his gaze to his two friends and waited for their reaction. Both men nodded their concurrence. Brendan took a deep breath and released it before crawling to a position next to Helen. He brought along a bottle of water in his left hand and a bag of peanuts in the other.

"Helen…" Brendan started. Helen didn't respond and appeared asleep with her head hanging over her chest. "I wonder if she's…" Brendan thought as he raised the water bottle to poke her. He jumped back with his eyes wide as Helen raised her head and glared at him. He felt like he was looking into the eyes of a person who had died a long time ago.

"I brought you some water and nuts," he said as he placed the items next to her. Helen continued to stare at him, giving him a very uneasy feeling in the pit of his stomach. "I thought maybe we could talk about the boy," he continued. Helen's eyes narrowed and her brow furrowed at the mention of her grandson. "I know, I know…" Brendan said before continuing, "But it's been days, Helen, and it's not healthy for the rest of us in the raft." He looked back over his shoulder for encouragement from Myles and Ethan. Both men simply nodded their heads in support and encouraged him to continue.

"I…" Brendan started again, "I mean we…" he corrected himself, "think we've been fair and given you the time you need to mourn…but…" he was interrupted in the speech he had prepared when he saw the edge of Helen's mouth rise in a half sneer, half grin. The look on her face made him wonder if the woman might have lost her mind.

"So…" Helen said through chapped lips, her voice was low and raspy, "you finally found a pair."

"What?" Brendan asked. He pulled his head back slightly as he asked the question.

"You let those men in the other boat take our food and water and then tucked your tail and ran when they confronted you about it…but now you're a big man again when it comes to bullying an old woman."

"That's not…" Brendan started to argue, but then regained his composure, "Look, we talked about it…"

"We?" Helen interrupted. "I don't remember anyone coming over here to ask my opinion."

"Well, yes, but…" Brendan felt his confidence slipping away.

"You're no better than that greedy, self-serving captain," Helen spat.

Brendan sat quietly for a moment before speaking again, "Okay, why should we let you continue to hold onto the boy?" he asked. As much as he thought it was a bad idea, he agreed that she should be allowed to speak her mind.

"Because he's my grandson!" Helen shouted. The others in the raft now sat up to listen to the conversation. "I won't let you just throw him into the ocean like a discarded banana peel."

Brendan took another deep breath to calm himself, knowing the others were watching. He decided to try a different angle: "This is just a dead bloating body, Helen, your grandson has moved on."

"You can't have it both ways, you arrogant as-," Helen cursed. "If the Devil isn't real, then neither is God…and if there is no God, then there is nowhere to move on to."

"I never said the Devil wasn't real," Brendan shot back, pointing his finger at Helen. "The idea that the Bermuda triangle is cursed is just superstitious nonsense."

"Because you say so?" Helen taunted. "Arrogant as-," she added when Brendan was silent, considering how to respond.

"Okay," Brendan said after a moment. "Here's what we'll do...we'll take a vote; that's the fairest way to settle this."

Helen glared at the others in the boat as if seeing them for the first time. The others felt uncomfortable and shifted their gaze when Helen's eyes met theirs.

"Everyone in favor of health and sanitation...of disposing of the corpse, raise your hand," Brendan announced to everyone in the raft. He turned and looked at the others to count their votes.

"I can't...I'm not going to do this," Ashley announced.

"Ash...honey, you have to. Everyone in this raft gets an equal say," Brendan said.

"I can't." Ashley hung her head and shook it back and forth.

"Technically, she doesn't have to," Ethan chimed in. "A citizen has the right not to vote in a free society."

"Fine," Brendan said. "Those in favor, raise your hand." Ethan and Myles both raised their hands immediately while Spencer looked back and forth between them and his wife.

"I don't know," Madison said. "What if that was me with our grandson?" she asked Spencer.

"We don't have a grandson," Spencer said. "We don't even have a son." He added.

"You know what I mean," Madison said with a frown.

"Okay, raise your hand if you are in favor of letting the body stay on board," Brendan announced.

Everyone watched Madison as she slowly raised her right hand. "Does it really matter if we let her hold onto her grandson? I mean, are we really going to die of disease before we run out of water?" she asked. With her right hand still in the air, she turned and looked at her husband. Spencer looked back and forth between Brendan and his wife before slowly raising his hand as well.

"Fine," Brendan said as he rolled his eyes. "I guess I'm the tiebreaker, and I vote for health and sanitation."

"Wait!" Helen shouted. "You haven't taken my vote."

"What? But you're the one on trial," Brendan said.

"You said everyone on the raft gets a vote," Helen argued.

"Mmm hmm, she's right," Madison said with her hand still raised over her head.

Ethan and Myles reluctantly nodded in agreement.

"So, it appears we have a tie," Helen said with a wry smile.

"No, we don't," came a voice from behind Brendan. "I vote for the health of all of us," Ashley said. Tears welled in her eyes as she turned her gaze to Helen and the dead boy. "I'm so sorry," she said to Helen.

"She can't change her vote; she already abstained," Helen argued.

Brendan looked back and forth between his daughter and Helen, pondering the situation.

"That's not accurate," Ethan chimed in. "She said she can't vote, not that she wouldn't vote," he said. He looked at Ashley to confirm her words, and Ashley nodded in agreement. "She isn't changing her vote; she simply decided she now has the ability."

"That's true," Spencer joined the debate. "She did say she couldn't, not that she wouldn't. Everyone has the right to be heard."

Helen looked back and forth between Ethan and Spencer before speaking. "So now the scientist is a lawyer, and the little boy thinks he's a man." Helen nodded her head. "Well, go on…throw him away like trash," she snarled at Brendan.

"It's not like that," Brendan said as he moved closer to Helen and tucked the ends of the blanket under the dead boy. He lifted the body off Helen's lap and paused as he felt the unnatural tightness of the bloating corpse under the blanket. Myles knelt next to him and helped lift the body onto the side of the raft. Everything was eerily silent as the two men slid the dead boy into the water, and everyone watched the corpse drift away before eventually sinking below the rolling waves. Madison held her hands over her face and sobbed lightly.

"That's how he comes." Helen's voice broke the silence. Everyone turned their attention to the grieving grandmother. "The Devil…" she continued, "he comes under false pretense…in the form of doing good and looking wonderful." She paused and stared at the long faces of the others. "He hides his true form, but in the end, he is always revealed." She stared at Brendan as she said the last words.

Brendan shifted uncomfortably seated against the raft wall and looked around at the others staring back at him. For the next several hours, only the lapsing waves against the raft wall were heard as everyone processed the events of what had just happened in their own way. The sweltering sun dipped in the horizon as the first faint stars indicated the coming nightfall.

Brendan, Myles, and Ethan huddled in the center of the raft, and Ethan pointed out various constellations in the night sky. He was explaining how early travelers tracked their way across the ocean using only the sun and stars while Brendan and Myles listened out of pure boredom. Madison, Spencer, and Ashley lay under the canopy and slept while Helen remained at her spot on the opposite side of the raft. Ashley tossed and turned and then finally lay on her back with her eyes open, listening to the three men outside the canopy.

"The North Star doesn't appear to move because it's situated within one degree of the North Pole…" Ethan was explaining to the men, and

Ashley could imagine her uncle pushing his glasses higher on the bridge of his nose as he spoke.

"Are you okay?" Spencer whispered from his spot next to Ashley.

Ashley turned her head to the left and saw Spencer lying on his side and facing her, only inches away. Madison slept on the other side of him with her back against his. Ashley turned to face Spencer.

"Can't sleep," Ashley whispered back. "I feel terrible," she added.

Spencer knew what she was referring to. "You shouldn't," he said.

"It was my vote that got the boy…" her light whisper trailed off to nothing.

"You didn't cause the plane to crash, or that little boy to drown," Spencer reassured her. "We all voted on what we thought was right…I actually thought you were brave." He placed his right hand on Ashley's.

"Yeah?" Ashley asked. Spencer nodded.

"I wish I would have been brave," Spencer said. He continued when he saw the puzzled look on Ashley's face. "I only voted with the woman because Madison did…I didn't think it was a good idea to keep the body on the raft. I'm glad you had the courage to speak up."

Ashley smiled. "Thanks," she whispered. "And I think you're brave also…for being able to admit you were wrong."

On the other side of Spencer, with her back turned to him, Madison lay awake and listened to her husband's confession to the young girl.

PART II

That's How He Comes

At the end of the fifth day at sea, the last remaining food and water were gone. The few drops of water captured by the morning dew were little relief to the sunburned passengers on the inflatable rescue raft. Around noon, the men on the other raft had called to inquire if there was any water left from the supplies they had "shared". It was all Myles could do not to release the rope and let the four men fend for their own. Hunger gnawed at the bones of the seven survivors, and hollowed eye sockets showed the depth of their despair. There was little talk of rescue and, in fact, little talk at all. They spent the day avoiding the sun and trying to ignore the emptiness in their stomachs. The morbid thought of who would die first had begun to play on Brendan's mind as he sat against the raft and watched the others. He wondered if today might be the day.

"The first thing I'm going to do when we're rescued is order a meat-lovers pizza," Spencer said and then looked around the raft at the others. His voice was cracked and raspy. He was trying to take his mind off his suffering, but returned to the shade under the blanket when no one returned his conversation.

They waited and drifted.

On the morning of the seventh day, Brendan leaned against the raft with his right arm resting on the raft wall and his head on his arm. He watched Helen's head bob as it hung from her shoulders and wondered if she might have passed during the night. He was too tired to get up and check and figured it was probably better if he didn't know. He hadn't heard any of the others move either, and wondered if he might be alone. The memory of seeing Julia in the airport after weeks apart came to him, and he smiled. He wished he hadn't been so stubborn and that he had tried harder to listen before she packed her bags and left. He closed his eyes and tried to picture her face when they met. "So beautiful," he thought of the image of her from high school.

"Champ," the word came faintly to Brendan across the water.

"Dad?" Brendan whispered.

"Come here, boy." His father's voice sounded distant, like a ghost haunting his memory. Brendan opened his eyes and was blinded by the hot Caribbean sun hanging overhead.

"Dad…" Brendan croaked. "Don't leave me, Dad," he whispered when he no longer heard his father's voice.

Across the raft, Myles opened his eyes and lifted his head to see what was happening. "Is he okay?" The question barely escaped his parched lips.

"I think he might be delusional," Ethan said from his seated position next to Myles. He lifted the plastic water bottle they were using to capture dew and shook his head when not even a drop registered at the bottom. The silver frames of his glasses stood in stark contrast to the dark, burned skin around his face.

"Dad," Brendan moaned again. He leaned his chest against the raft and held his right hand out over the water. "Wait for me…"

Heat waves radiated from the ground, distorting the image in the distance. Brendan saw his father in his white racing suit with blue and red stripes. He was so far away that Brendan barely recognized the white baseball cap he waved back and forth over his head. "Let's go, Champ," his father's voice came like an echo over the water.

"I'm coming," Brendan whispered as he came to his knees.

In the hazy distance, Brendan saw his father open the door to his orange sports car and sit inside. He thought he heard the engine rev as his father waved out the window for him to follow. The orange sports car spun in circles as dirt and dust flew from the ground under the tires. The engine screamed as the car darted forward and up an incline that Brendan thought looked like a steep stone hill.

"Wait for me…please…" Brendan pleaded as the car sped away.

The car reached the top of the hill and was thrust into the air by its powerful engine. It flew towards a large, dark circle on the side of a small mountain and then disappeared into the hole.

"NOOO!" Brendan screamed with his hand thrust out towards the dark hole. Myles and Ethan exchanged a worried look.

Brendan knelt and watched the scene before him become clearer. A small island, no more than a mile long, appeared in the distance. Half of the island was barren with only rock and sand, while the other half looked like a tropical paradise. The island was cut in half by the steep stone hill his father had raced up, and a short volcanic mountain on the other side, with the dark hole his father's car had jumped into. Brendan couldn't ever remember the dream taking place in this location. He rubbed his eyes and then slapped himself, trying to awaken from the dream. When he looked back across the water, the island was still there…closer in fact. The rafts were drifting slowly towards the small island.

"LAND!" Brendan yelled. He began to wave his arms and yelled again, "LAND!"

Myles and Ethan stared at their friend, thinking the sun must have finally gotten to him.

"Ha-ha-ha-ha," Brendan began to laugh hysterically. "Ha-ha-ha-ha-ha…ha-ha…ha," he laughed so hard his weakened lungs barely managed to keep up, at which point he just started pointing with both hands towards the island.

Myles knelt on one knee and peered in the distance. "LAND!" He yelled after placing his right hand on his head.

Ashley, Madison, and Spencer emerged from the canopy at the commotion and stared in disbelief at the island in the distance.

"AYYYHHHH!" Not knowing what else to do, Madison began screaming in delight.

"Land!" Everyone in the boat started to yell. Helen stared at the island across the water, placed her hands over her face, and began to sob.

"Hey, what's going on over there?" Came the nasally voice of Captain Kleinman from the other raft, trailing twenty feet behind.

"Land," Brendan yelled back and pointed towards the island.

Captain Kleinman squinted and stared in the direction Brendan pointed for several moments before placing his right hand over his mouth and turning to his other raft-mates under the canopy. He pointed wide-eyed to the other side of the raft, making the others rush from under the canopy to see what was happening.

"YES! We're saved!" Yelled the taller fraternity brother. He turned and hugged his smaller friend as Captain Kleinman and the Jamaican knelt next to the raft wall and began paddling with their hands. After their embrace, the brothers joined the other two, trying to propel the raft.

"This is going to take forever," the larger brother said as he stood in the raft and removed his shirt. "It can't be more than a mile away."

"I wouldn't do that!" Ethan yelled from the other raft.

The man with his shirt off stopped and turned towards Ethan. "Why not?" he asked. "I'm a pretty good swimmer."

"These tropical islands are often surrounded by a coral reef," Ethan answered.

"And?" Replied the man, not understanding the issue.

"Where there is a coral reef, there are small fish…" Ethan began, "And where there are small fish, there are bigger fish…and where there are bigger fish…"

"There are sharks," Captain Kleinman finished the sentence.

Ethan nodded his head and lifted his right hand, giving the captain a thumbs-up. "Not to mention the currents would rip you apart against the reef."

"So we just sit here and wait?" the man with no shirt asked.

"At least until we're two to three hundred feet away," Ethan replied. He returned his attention to his own raft when he heard Spencer yell.

"Look!" Spencer pointed towards the left side of the island's small mountain.

Brendan squinted, trying to discern what Spencer was pointing at when he saw the small black dots moving through the air. "Birds!" he yelled.

"Where there are birds, there are eggs," Myles said.

"Forget the eggs," Spencer said. "I'm going to eat about a dozen of those birds!"

Spencer and Myles began discussing what else might be edible up there when Brendan turned to Ethan.

"Do you think that could be one of the Bahamas?" Brendan asked.

Ethan was shaking his head before he answered, "Doubt it. Those would be on the southernmost side of the triangle, and according to the stars, we've been drifting northeast."

"Bermuda, maybe?" Brendan asked after trying to remember his Atlantic Ocean geography.

"Not likely…but possible, I guess," Ethan offered. "From the area we crashed, it would be at least a month's journey in this boat to Bermuda."

"So, some uncharted island in the middle of nowhere?" Brendan asked. He looked around and noticed the others had become interested in the conversation.

"That would be the most likely scenario," Ethan agreed while nodding his head.

"With all the boats and planes crossing the world every day, you wouldn't think there would be any undiscovered locations left in the world," Spencer said.

"It's not at all uncommon," Ethan replied. "Volcanic activity on the ocean floor and organic matter, like coral, often form small islands all over the Atlantic and Pacific Oceans." He pointed to the small mountain on the left of the island as everyone turned to follow his finger. "That small mountain makes me believe it was likely an underwater volcanic eruption that caused this island to form."

"Do people live on these islands?" Madison asked. Everyone turned their attention back to Ethan for the answer.

"Not usually," Ethan answered. "Typically, they don't have enough fresh water to sustain more than a handful of small animals."

"Oh man, I can't wait to eat some of those small animals." Spencer's stomach growled as he commented, causing the others to laugh.

"Might as well sit back and enjoy the view," Brendan said to the group. "At this rate, it'll be another hour or so before we reach the island."

The seven passengers on the rescue raft sat back and began to discuss all the things they hoped to find on the island. Myles and Spencer listed a dozen small creatures they thought might be indigenous to the island and whether they were edible. Madison made a gagging sound when Spencer wondered if lizards, worms, and other insects might make an edible stew. The rhythmic splash coming from the other raft indicated that Captain Kleinman and his crew were still trying to hasten their arrival to the island by paddling with their hands. Brendan laid his head against the inflated nylon and tried to rest in case they needed to swim once they were closer to the island. The earlier rush of adrenaline was wearing off, and he felt the stiffness in his legs from standing and balancing in the raft. He was about to try stretching exercises to relieve the tension when he was interrupted by Myles.

"You had another dream about your dad, didn't you?" Myles asked.

Brendan closed his eyes and tried to remember the dream he was having before spotting the island. "Yeah, it was strange," he replied. "I've never had a dream like that one before," he added.

Myles placed his hand on Brendan's shoulder. "I was worried about you," he said softly. "I thought you had lost it when you started calling for your old man."

"In my dream, he was in his sports car and speeding up that hill." Brendan pointed to the steep stone hill dividing the island. They both stared at the hill for a moment before Brendan added, "I was afraid he was leaving me behind."

"I was afraid he had come to take you home," Myles responded immediately. "I was about to tell you not to follow the light." Myles chuckled and patted his friend on the back. There was a moment of silence as the two men stared at one another, neither wanting to admit how close they had felt to death.

"Ahoy," came a voice from behind the raft.

Brendan and Myles turned and looked in the direction of the voice, both happy to be done with the previous conversation. Twenty feet behind the raft, Captain Kleinman stood at the front of his raft and waved both hands over his head to get their attention. One of the fraternity brothers stood next to him and pulled at the yellow nylon rope that connected the two rafts, bringing them closer together. The other two men had grown tired of paddling and returned to the shade of the canopy.

"What does he want?" Ashley asked as she and the others also turned to see who was calling.

"Ahoy," Captain Kleinman called again. The fraternity brother continued to pull, and the distance slowly closed between the two rafts.

"What is it?" Brendan asked in a disgusted tone when the two rafts were only a few feet apart.

"We've been talking," Captain Kleinman said. He turned and waved his left hand across the raft to indicate the other three men before returning his attention to Brendan and Myles. From the frowns on their faces, Captain Kleinman guessed they were still upset with him about the whole water sharing incident.

"Look…" Captain Kleinman started, "Why don't we put that previous incident behind us so that we can focus on more important matters?" he stated. "We can be adults, can't we?" he asked.

"Such as?" Myles asked. He and Brendan both ignored the comment about being adults.

"Such as what needs to be done once we reach the island," Captain Kleinman answered.

Brendan wouldn't admit it, but he thought that was a good idea, as he had also started to think about some of the things they would need to do once they reached the island, such as finding shelter and determining if the area was safe.

"I don't trust him," Ethan whispered from behind Brendan.

"What do you have in mind?" Brendan asked Captain Kleinman.

"Okay, well, there are eleven of us," Captain Kleinman stated. He waved his hand back and forth between the two rafts to emphasize his point. "So, we can break up into teams to accomplish the tasks we need to get done once we are on the island…tasks that will improve our chances of being rescued, ensure our safety, and make us more comfortable before the sun sets."

"Go on," Brendan said. He hated to admit it, but the captain was making sense.

"Well, we identified some tasks…and would like your input, so that we all know our goals once we reach the island." Brendan thought Captain Kleinman's smile looked forced when he announced he would like their input.

Brendan turned his back on Captain Kleinman to talk with his group in private. "What do you think?" he asked the group.

"I think he's going to stab us in the back as soon as he gets a chance," Myles said in a low growl.

"He does make sense," Ethan said softly. "I can think of a few things we need to do once we get on the island, and breaking up into teams would make them go faster." Madison and Spencer both nodded in concurrence with Ethan's statement.

"I don't trust the guy either, but if we work together, we might just make it home alive," Brendan said to Myles before spinning around to face Captain Kleinman.

"Okay," Brendan said to Captain Kleinman. "Let's talk about those tasks."

Captain Kleinman's smirk made Brendan think he might have just let the fox into the henhouse. "Before anyone does anything on the island, I think we need to ensure the area is safe," Captain Kleinman said. "It wouldn't make sense to survive what we have, only to be killed by something dangerous on that island."

Brendan looked around at his group and replied, "Agreed," when no one objected to the first task.

"I think the perfect team for security would be Brett and Kade," Captain Kleinman announced.

"Who?" Myles asked.

"Sorry," Captain Kleinman said. "Brett Alexander and Kade Stevenson." The two fraternity brothers rose and stood next to each other when Captain Kleinman called their names. The larger fraternity brother raised his hand at the name Brett, and the shorter brother did the same when the captain announced the name Kade.

"I think they are both well suited to manage any danger that may arise...don't you?" Captain Kleinman asked. Brendan looked at Myles, who simply shrugged, before responding, "Sure."

"Your turn," Captain Kleinman said. He held out his right palm as if actually offering Brendan something tangible.

"Okay, well, I think we need to build a bonfire before nightfall to have the best chance at rescue," Brendan said. He was about to announce his picks for the bonfire team when Captain Kleinman cut him off.

"We were thinking a large S.O.S.," Captain Kleinman interrupted. "Sorry, but a fire is only good at night, and the S.O.S. would only have to be built once."

"If I may," Ethan interjected. "A fire at night would be seen one hundred times further than the S.O.S...even a small candle flame can be seen over thirty miles away on a dark night."

"Myles and I will be on the bonfire team," Brendan announced. "We can make the S.O.S. the next day...unless you want to create another team and do it today?" Brendan smiled when Captain Kleinman sneered at the displeasure of having his judgment questioned. "Your turn," Brendan said, turning the tasks back over to the captain.

"We will need to find food and water before the sun sets," said Captain Kleinman. "Dwayne here..." Captain Kleinman turned and grabbed the arm of the Jamaican man, bringing him to the front of the raft, "is from the islands and is probably best qualified to know what is edible and what is not."

"I'd like to volunteer for the food team," Spencer said as he raised his hand and came to the front of the raft.

"Good, Dwayne and…" Captain Kleinman paused, waiting for the man's name.

"Spencer," Spencer said. "Spencer Collins," he said again and waved to the men in the other raft.

"We also need a shelter team," Brendan said after Spencer returned to his seat at the back of the raft. "To find the best spot that protects against the elements and shelter in the event of a storm."

"Agreed," Captain Kleinman said, nodding his head.

"Ethan here…" Brendan invited Ethan to the front of the raft, "and…the three women will be on the shelter team."

"Does the shelter team require four individuals?" Captain Kleinman asked. "I was thinking we could use a beach combing team to search the beach for any useful items that may have washed ashore from passing boats."

Brendan paused for a minute, considering the beach combing idea and how to split the women. He trusted his daughter and Madison but wasn't so sure about Helen. He also didn't think it would be a good idea to have a woman alone on a team with one of the men, especially Captain Kleinman.

"How about you and Ethan on the shelter team, and the three women on the beach combing team?" Brendan asked.

"Me?" Captain Kleinman asked as if he had been slapped in the face. "No, no, that won't work," he said while shaking his head emphatically.

"Why not?" asked Myles.

"Well, because I'm the one in charge," Captain Kleinman huffed. "Who else is better suited to organize and manage all the tasks?"

Ethan rolled his eyes. "Should have seen that one coming."

"Unbelievable," Myles groaned.

"So, you're going to sit around while the rest of us do all the work?" Brendan asked accusingly.

"It's not like that," retorted Captain Kleinman. "I was going to offer for you to join me as a co-manager, but you're the one who put yourself on one of the teams."

"The only thing we need less than a manager is a co-manager," Myles spat.

"Hey," Brett interjected from behind Captain Kleinman. "It was the captain's idea to come over and offer a plan for when we got to the island. I didn't see any of you stepping up."

"Don't even…" Myles pointed his finger at Brett and moved to the front of the raft as if he were going to try to leap across. Ethan grabbed his friend from behind and wrapped his arms around Myles to prevent him from going any further.

"Wait!" Brendan shouted. He continued when everyone calmed down and quit speaking. "Ethan and the three women will be the shelter team, and you can comb the beach in between your management duties."

Captain Kleinman glanced around the raft and debated whether to push the issue. "Fine," he finally said. "We'll organize on the beach once we've reached the island." He turned and crawled into the canopy with the three other men on his raft.

Everyone began pointing to various features on the island as the raft drifted closer. The excitement of finally leaving their confined space was evident on the weathered faces of the eleven survivors, and some had already forgotten the gnawing hunger in their stomachs. The rafts were only two hundred meters from the island when Ethan pointed out a stream of fresh water coming from the valley formed between the steep stone hill and the plateau at the base of the volcanic mountain. The river formed from countless years of rainwater collecting in the volcano's crater and then spilling through a fissure in the crater wall, dividing the island into two as it made its way to the sea. The river was about ten feet wide and flowed quickly from its steep descent down the volcano.

The right side of the island was void of trees or plants, and only the occasional barren shrub dotted the rocky terrain. The stone hill tapered steeply for about 500 meters to the smoother, more flattened rocky terrain, where flattened boulders dotted the landscape for another 400 meters before turning to a sandy beach for the remaining 200 meters. The left side of the island stood in stark contrast to its barren counterpart, with tropical trees, plants, shrubs, and grasses forming a lush landscape in the area between the river and the base of the volcano. A thin, 200-meter strip of semi-forested land ran to the left around the volcano to a yet unseen part of the island. This strip of land was connected to the ocean by a rocky cliff wall, dotted with small caves formed by the erosion of ocean waves. A large boulder was thrust from the water 100 meters from the beach and provided steeper cliffs for the nesting sea birds circling overhead. Upon closer inspection, it was revealed that the small volcano may have once had two separate shafts, each forming a small volcano in close proximity to one another. The area between the two volcanoes created a steep ravine, making it an ideal location for the formation of a sheltered tropical paradise. The two rafts carrying the eleven survivors drifted towards a pristine beach that ran 100 meters from the ocean to a row of palm trees lining the shore.

Brendan sat gaping at the beauty of the tropical island. He wondered if it was divine intervention, pure luck, or some other force that had guided them past the barren rocks on the right of the island and directly to the soft white sands of the tropical paradise. A nagging conversation tugged at his memory as the nylon raft slid onto the white sandy beach.

He recalled Helen's words as he cast her grandson's body into the ocean, "That's how he comes...looking wonderful."

Robert Anthony

Welcome to the Jungle

Spencer was the first to exit the raft, and he tripped and fell after his sea legs protested the firm terrain of the sandy beach. He was rolling in the sand when the others exited the rafts and plopped down to enjoy the warm, firm surface. Ethan buried his face in the sand after discovering the cooler, moist sand a few inches under the dry top layer. He emerged with a mask of sand sticking to his face, and his smile made him look like a circus clown with a painted-on smile. Spencer was also the first to notice the small brown balls dotting the beachy area under the palm trees. The laughter and joy of reaching land was pierced by the shrill cry of Spencer yelling, "coconuts!" and coming to his feet before attempting to race across the sand. He was two steps into his quest for coconuts when a large hand grabbed him by the shoulder and threw him forcefully to the ground.

Spencer groaned as he lay on the sand and looked up into the face of the muscular Brett Alexander. "What the hell, man," Spencer groaned.

"The area hasn't been cleared," Brett replied as he stared down at the smaller man.

Brendan rose from the sand and rushed to Spencer's side when he witnessed the incident. "Back up!" He yelled at the taller, muscle-bound man. "Who do you think you are?"

"We haven't cleared the area," Brett explained slowly. He clenched his fists and took a step in Brendan's direction. "Now, why don't you return to the beach where it's safe?"

"What? You gonna throw me to the ground now?" Brendan said. He wasn't about to back down from this bully.

Captain Kleinman had also witnessed the incident and was just in time to reach the big man before the situation escalated into a physical confrontation. "Gentlemen," he yelled. "This isn't necessary." He placed himself between Brett and Brendan, holding his hands out to separate the two men.

"What's not necessary is putting your hands on another person," Brendan fired back.

"He was about to run off…" Brett argued before Captain Kleinman held up his index finger and shushed the larger man.

"Now…" Captain Kleinman started as he looked back and forth between the two men, "We all agreed that no one would go anywhere, or do anything, until the area was safe. Brett here was only trying to do his job."

"Yeah!" Brett blurted and pointed his finger at Brendan. He was immediately hushed again by Captain Kleinman after the outburst.

"He didn't have to throw him to the ground," Brendan said. "That was totally uncalled for."

"That was a bit heavy-handed," Captain Kleinman said as he pointed at Brett.

"But…" Brett attempted to argue.

"Ah-ah-ah," Captain Kleinman interrupted. "Now, let's let Brett and Kade secure the area so that we can all get started on our tasks and hopefully find something to eat…" Captain Kleinman turned to Brendan and the others who had gathered around, "Shall we?" he asked.

Brendan offered his right hand to Spencer, who was watching the scene unfold from his back. He pulled Spencer from the ground, and they began walking back towards the beach as Spencer rubbed his sore back. Madison placed her arm around Spencer's waist and helped him back to the beach while Captain Kleinman turned to the two fraternity brothers and directed them to their task with a single word, "go!".

Brett and Kade raced into the first row of trees as sand kicked up from their heels. Kade stopped just inside the first row of trees and grabbed a coconut from the ground. He tossed the brown ball high into the air, and it landed only feet from the group. He held up his right hand and gave a *hang loose* sign before turning and disappearing into the trees. Captain Kleinman turned to the group and placed his hands on his hips.

"Listen up," Captain Kleinman called. "Go ahead and break up into your teams to start discussing where and how you'll accomplish your tasks. Does each team have someone with a watch?" he asked.

Brendan, Myles, and Ethan all held up their hands wearing the identical Garmin Fenix 7 watch.

"I have one too," Spencer said and then held up his arm to reveal his watch. The inexpensive, military-style Timex watch featured a black face with white numbers and hands, and an olive-green band. Despite the low cost, the watch had remained functional throughout their ordeal.

"Let's synchronize our watches and set the timer for two hours once we begin our tasks," Captain Kleinman said.

"Once *we* begin our tasks," Myles commented under his breath, emphasizing the word "we."

Spencer raised his hand before Captain Kleinman could continue. "Yes?" Captain Kleinman asked when he noticed Spencer's hand.

"I don't have a timer or alarm on my watch," Spencer said.

"Okay, well, I guess you'll just have to keep track of the time manually…just do the best you can," Captain Kleinman added when Spencer had raised his hand again. "As soon as they return, you can start…oh, and if anyone needs me, I'll be sitting over there," he turned and pointed to a large rock shaded by a palm tree at the edge of the beach. "One more thing," he said before climbing down from the rock. He paused and ran his hand over his head. "It was right there on the tip of my tongue," he mumbled to himself. "Never mind, guess it couldn't be that important." He sat on the rock for another moment, trying to remember what he wanted to say. With a shake of his head, he got up and walked back to his shaded spot under the tree.

As instructed, the group broke up into their teams and began discussing how they would carry out their tasks. Brendan and Myles thought it would be fairly simple to find wood to burn after seeing all the palm trees. The hardest part would be breaking the branches into the proper size and figuring out how to start a fire. Spencer and Dwayne didn't put too much effort into their plan and decided they'd just start by going straight for the birds. They spent the rest of their time trying to break into the coconut Kade had tossed to them. After biting it and stepping on it, they decided to look for something to beat it with. The three women gathered around Ethan and peppered him with questions as they discussed their task. Ethan ping-ponged between the women, trying to keep up with their inquiries.

It was about forty-five minutes later when the two brothers returned from their scouting. Brendan watched the two men as they spoke with Captain Kleinman under the palm tree, pointing in various directions. Ten minutes later, Captain Kleinman whistled and waved for everyone to gather around the large rock.

"Do you hear that?" Ashley asked the group as they assembled in front of the rock. She tilted her head as if listening to something far away.

Brendan and Myles looked at each other before looking back at Ashley and shaking their heads.

"It's like a low murmur. Almost like the rumble of your air conditioning unit when it kicks on outside the house," Ashley explained.

"I hear it also," Ethan said. "I thought I had water in my ears or that it was just from high blood pressure, but I do hear it."

The others listened in silence for a moment before shaking their heads. "Nothing," Madison said.

Captain Kleinman climbed onto the large rock and then addressed the group.

"Brett and Kade have just returned and briefed me on what they have found," Captain Kleinman said loudly. "They weren't able to cover the entire island, but they got a pretty good view from a low hill just through these trees. What we've seen of the island so far seems to be about all there is. The other side is much the same as this side, and there doesn't appear to be much across the river. That being said," Captain Kleinman continued. "No one is to travel more than thirty minutes out from this location until we have a better idea of what we're dealing with."

"Are there any dangerous animals on the island?" Ashley asked.

"Yes, I was just getting to that..." Captain Kleinman said, sounding annoyed. "They didn't see any signs of dangerous animals, but I would caution you to avoid any insects, amphibians, or plants that you don't recognize."

"That would be just about all of them," Ashley replied.

"Are there any other questions?" Captain Kleinman asked. He tried pretending he didn't see Spencer's hand until Spencer started to jump up and down. "Yes, young man," he asked finally.

"What should we do if we get hurt while we're out there?" Spencer asked.

Captain Kleinman paused, considering his response. "Just lie there quietly until you're found," he finally responded.

"Really?" Spencer asked. He looked around at the others to see if they thought that was a good idea. "That doesn't sound like a good..."

"Unless there are any other questions," Captain Kleinman continued. "Let's synchronize our watches...I have 1:32 pm," he said after checking his watch. "Let's meet back here at 3:30." He looked up from his watch to see if everyone was ready. "Let's go," he announced and made a waving motion with his hands.

Brendan and Myles headed towards the middle of the island in search of the tree Ethan had called the Pigeon Pea. Although technically a large shrub, the Pigeon Pea was capable of growing into a small tree in the right environment. The smaller tree would provide better branches for a bonfire than the bountiful coconut palm with its feathery leaves. They each stopped and collected branches as they followed the sandy trails that led through the plush forest.

"We should have been on the food team," Myles said. He pointed to a group of trees with green and yellow bananas growing skyward no more than six feet off the ground. They each picked a banana and ate it before continuing to look for wood.

A small rodent leaped from a brush pile and scampered up the leaning trunk of a coconut tree, where it scared a pair of nesting birds. The two yellow-breasted kiskadees fluttered into the air with a high-pitched screech, "Bee-tee-Wee!"

Brendan watched the birds fly towards the small volcano and, for the first time since the dream with his father, noticed the large dark hole on the side of the twin volcano.

"Hey, look at that," Brendan called to Myles.

Myles looked towards the volcano and squinted his eyes, trying to get a better view. "Looks like a cave or something," Myles commented. As he stared into the cave's dark center, he began to hear the low mechanical drone Ashley had described earlier. He felt mesmerized by the continuous murmur. A snapping twig nearby snapped Myles out of his trance. He looked around, wondering what had made the noise, and then checked his watch. "Hey," he called to Brendan. "What time do you have?"

Brendan checked his watch; the digital numbers read 2:14 pm. "A little over…" Brendan began to answer when he was distracted by a high-pitched scream coming from the beach. He and Myles looked at each other for a moment before Myles began to speak.

"That sounds like…" Myles said.

"Ashley!" Brendan yelled and then threw the wood he was carrying to the ground.

Myles and Brendan retraced their steps as they made their way back towards the beach.

"I knew I shouldn't have left her," Brendan said as he looked for signs of their passing in the loose sand.

"She's…with…Ethan," Myles huffed between breaths. "I'm sure he…wouldn't let anything happen to her," he added.

They made their way back to the beach and noticed that the screaming wasn't coming directly from that area of the beach, but rather just off to the right, where Ethan and the women had ventured when they left the beach in search of Shelter. When they reached the beach, they saw Captain Kleinman propped up on his left elbow as if he were just getting up from the ground. He rubbed his eyes and yawned before speaking.

"What is that racket?!" Captain Kleinman yelled when Brendan and Myles returned to their starting point.

"Have you been sleeping?" Myles asked when he saw Captain Kleinman.

"Over there," Brendan said. He grabbed Myles' arm, and they continued in the direction of the screams.

The closer they came to the screaming, the more they began to make out words between the yells.

"HEY! Everybody…HEY!" Ashley screamed. "We found…" She stopped yelling when she saw her dad and Myles enter a sandy area between a group of trees.

"Ash!" Brendan shouted. "Are you hurt…are you okay…what…" Brendan was yelling as he and Myles approached Ashley.

"Where are Ethan and the rest of the women?" Myles asked when they reached Ashley. Ashley had taken the opportunity to catch her breath and was leaning over when her father grabbed her by both shoulders and began looking her over for any signs of injury.

"No, I'm fine," Ashley answered. "Ethan is with the others down by the water," she replied to Myles. "We found a boat!" She blurted.

"A what?" Brendan asked in disbelief. He was so happy to find his daughter unharmed that he barely understood what she was saying.

"Did she say they found a boat?" Came a voice from behind Brendan. Brendan and Myles turned to see Captain Kleinman and the two fraternity brothers enter the sandy clearing.

"Yes!" Ashley yelled. "A big boat!"

At the same time, Ashley was answering Captain Kleinman's question, Spencer and Dwayne also entered the sandy clearing.

"Where is Madison?" Spencer yelled. "Is she okay?"

"Everyone's fine," Ashley answered. Spencer looked relieved and released his clenched fist, which had been holding a brownish-colored reptile he had found for dinner. The lizard fell to the sand with its tongue hanging out and its two eyes bulging from its head due to Spencer's tight grip.

"The boat, woman…get back to the part about the boat," Captain Kleinman insisted as he pushed past Myles and came between Ashley and her father.

"Hey!" Brendan protested before he was detained from behind by four large, meaty hands. "What the…" he started to say, before being cut off by Captain Kleinman.

"This is important," Captain Kleinman said as he turned to Brendan. "Now, about this boat, is it a Coast Guard boat? Are there people with the boat?" He shook Ashley's shoulders as he stared into her eyes.

Myles grabbed Captain Kleinman by the collar and jerked him backwards as the scene erupted into a scuffle in the sand. Spencer jumped on Kade's back, causing him to release his clutch on Brendan. Brendan, in turn, was able to spin around and tackle the surprised Brett to the ground while Captain Kleinman sputtered in Myles' chokehold. Dwayne simply stood back and watched the show.

"STOP!" Ashley yelled. The six men stopped their struggle and looked up at Ahsley in surprise. "I don't know what kind of boat it is…it's a big one, and no, there are no people with it, it looks abandoned."

Dwayne bent down and helped Spencer off the ground while the other men came to their feet.

"I'm supposed to come and get you all so I can show you where it is," Ashley continued. She turned and headed back in the direction she had come. "Come on," she called over her shoulder.

Spencer was the first to race after Ashley, and the other men followed after exchanging irate glances. Dwayne slowly followed the group after retrieving the smashed lizard and placing it in his pocket…just in case.

"This isn't over," Captain Kleinman complained while he rubbed his sore neck and followed after Spencer and Ashley.

The eight people wound through a sandy trail, crossed a small clearing, and entered the thin wooded area at the base of the small volcano, where the wooded area curved around the left side of the island. After a slow fifteen minutes of pushing through thick brush, the group found themselves in an area where the forest gave way to another sandy beach, which ran about 100 meters to the ocean. The beach bent 200 meters along the island until meeting the rocky cliff walls on the island's eastern side.

There, beached halfway on the sand between the rocky cliffs and the wooded forest, sat a 64-foot Riviera Sports luxury yacht. The large two-story seagoing vessel was sleek and white, with chrome handrails that ran from the back of the ship to a narrow, pointed bow. Wood trim accented the ship's interior, and the large single-paned windows were tinted black. A small cockpit rested on top of the yacht where Ethan stood, waving to his friends.

The name, FIRST RING, was written in large black letters at the tip of the yacht's bow and again across the flat portion of the ship's rear.

The First Ring

"We're saved!" Spencer yelled as he raced towards the beached yacht. Sand flew from his bare feet, and his toes dug into the loose sand, leaving a trail of footprints as he ran.

Ashley, her father, and the other five men tried to contain their enthusiasm as they walked briskly following Spencer. A set of folding stairs twisted down the side of the yacht, and Ethan climbed down to meet the group on the beach. Madison and Helen emerged from the other side of the yacht, where they had helped Ethan scale the rear swim platform to get inside.

"When do we sail, skipper?" Myles asked Ethan when the group had come within earshot. He saluted Ethan as he came to a stop a few feet from where Ethan stood.

Ethan was silent as the remaining group closed the distance and stopped in front of the yacht, staring up in amazement at the vessel's majestic size.

"Nice find," Captain Kleinman said with a smile. "How do we get it off the beach and back into the water?" He asked Ethan.

"Would you like the bad news first, or the good news?"

Captain Kleinman looked nervously at Ethan before speaking again, "Don't tell me it's not functional."

"It's not functional," Ethan repeated.

"Aw F-CK!" Brett shouted and threw his hands in the air.

The others began to moan and complain in disappointment before Captain Kleinman quieted them. "Wait, wait," Captain Kleinman said above the bickering. "You said you have good news…like it's not functional now, but you can repair it, right?" he asked.

"No," Ethan replied, shaking his head. "This thing isn't going anywhere. Aside from being beached on the wrong side of the shallow reef out there…" he pointed about 200 meters into the water, "it's also had one of its diesel engines ripped out before it was beached here. There is a large hole in the hull where the engine used to be. I'm guessing both happened during the storm when the water swells were much higher."

"What if we all went out there and were able to retrieve this diesel engine? Could it be fixed?" Captain Kleinman asked.

"First…" Ethan announced, "that one engine weighs over one thousand pounds…" he held up one finger as he counted, "two, it's submerged in fifteen feet of water…" he held up another finger, "and most importantly…I'm a scientist, not…" he was about to put of his third finger when Captain Kleinman cut him off.

"I know, a mechanic," Captain Kleinman interjected.

"I was going to say engineer," Ethan replied. "But you get the point."

"What about the radio?" asked Brendan. "I'm sure this thing probably has a satellite that could make a call to the moon."

"That's the strange part," Ethan answered. "Apparently, whoever owned the yacht smashed the radio before they left."

"That doesn't make any sense," said Brett. "Why would you smash your only contact with the outside world if you became shipwrecked?"

Ethan shrugged. "That's a good question, but you can go see for yourself; someone smashed the radio into a million pieces inside."

"So, who owns the ship?" Madison asked. "Where'd they go?"

Again, Ethan shrugged. "That's another strange part," he said. "There is no information anywhere on the ship that indicates who it belongs to. There are no bodies onboard and no footprints leading away from here." He pointed up and down the beach to indicate the lack of footprints. "There is no flag to indicate where the ship came from or even any personal effects of anyone who might have been on board."

"Could it have come untied while docked and drifted here?" Kade asked.

"That's what I thought," Ethan answered. "But the engine was on, and the throttle set to full ahead. It's like this ship had to fight the weather in order to make it here."

"Someone took the time to name her," Helen chimed in for the first time. She pointed to the name overhead, "First Ring. Any idea what that means?" she asked.

"Probably a young professional athlete who bought it after winning his first World Series or Super Bowl," Myles offered.

"No-no, I bet it was a young woman who married some old rich dude and then later divorced him and got his yacht," Madison said.

"This seems all wrong," Ashley warned. "There could be someone on this island with us, or worse yet, several people…watching us…waiting…"

"Stop it," Brendan said. "There's no one out there watching us."

Everyone nodded their heads in agreement as they nervously scanned the trees around them.

"You said there was good news," Brendan changed the subject. Everyone returned their attention to Ethan.

"Oh, right, plenty of good news," Ethan said with a smile. "Let's see," he turned towards the ship as he started speaking. "First of all, this thing is loaded; it has three double bedrooms and four singles…that doesn't include the captain's quarters that has its own on suite. It features three full-sized bathrooms, a kitchen with an eat-in area, and a formal dining room. It has a stocked bar, a lounge with plush couches, and an outside dinette and shuffleboard deck. It features a laundry room equipped with a full-sized washer and dryer, as well as a full outdoor kitchen located in the rear bulkhead. The foredeck has a sunbathing area complete with chaise lounge chairs and two hammocks."

"Oh my God," Helen breathed. "This thing is nicer than my Lakehouse on Lake Tahoe."

"But wait, there's more…" Ethan said in his best television commercial sales voice, "there is a stocked freezer in the ship's hull with steak, chicken, vegetables, juice, water…you name it."

Spencer gasped when he heard the large assortment of food.

"Is this where you tell us there's no gas, so none of the electric works?" Captain Kleinman called from the rear of the group.

"That's the best part," Ethan replied. He pointed to the top helm station, "It has solar panels on top!"

"Are you telling me I get to take a hot bath!?" Madison squealed. She leaped up and kissed Ethan before turning and running for the hanging stairs.

"I call dibs on the hammock!" Kade shouted as he also ran for the stairs.

"I'm making a steak," Spencer yelled. "Not even sure I'm going to cook it first," he added on second thought.

"No one touch the captain's quarters…that's mine," Captain Kleinman shouted as he ran to the ladder and tried to pull the others down so that he could board first.

Ethan was the last to climb aboard since he had already combed over all the ship's amenities. The others hooted and hollered as they ran through the ship and discovered the accommodations Ethan had just described. The yacht was much nicer than they had imagined when he was describing it. The Flooring, furniture, and accents were made of a rich, red-toned mahogany wood, while much of the yacht's trim was made of polished steel with gold highlights. The kitchen had marble counters and stainless-steel appliances that appeared brand new. The interior couches and seating were a plush, soft white fabric, while the exterior benches and seating were made of a more durable gray fabric with a woven texture. A mixture of modern chandeliers hung in each room of the yacht, with the largest being a glass waterfall-style chandelier hanging over the dining room table. The flooring of the cabin rooms and their connecting hallways was carpeted with a warm, beige-colored, durable nylon.

"This room's mine!" A voice called from below deck, where Myles had claimed one of the single rooms with two sliding windows that overlooked the water on the ship's port side. The room was equipped with a single bed against the left wall and a wooden desk against the right wall that wrapped around the far wall, providing a nightstand for the bed. The desk was made of the same, red-toned mahogany as the rest of the yacht's interior and had upper cabinets for storage as well as a black, leather captain's swivel chair for seating. Just inside the doorway, on the right-hand side, was a wooden closet with interior drawers for clothes and equipment.

The others, hearing Myles downstairs claiming a room, decided they had better get downstairs and find their own. Madison and Ashley were next to enter the lower deck cabin hallway and began opening the doors to each room. Ashley was just inside the doorway to another single cabin next to Myles' claimed room when her father called her.

"Ash…" Brendan called from down the hall. "I think we should share one of the double rooms."

"Why? I want my own room," Ashley protested as she stuck her head into the hallway.

"There are only four single rooms, so somebody is going to have to share a room," Brendan replied. "Plus, I think it's safer if we stay together. There is plenty of room," he added when Ashley began skulking towards the double room Brendan had chosen.

Ashley's eyes widened when she stood in the doorway of the double room and glanced inside. The room was easily twice the size of the single cabin and had a spacious queen bed against the right wall. The bed rested against a white, pleather-padded wall that ran from floor to ceiling and also contained a wall-mounted lamp on either side of the bed. A row of five windows ran along the rear wall, with a plush couch and armchair positioned underneath them. A long, wooden dresser lay across from the bed, with a 50-inch flat-screen TV mounted over it. Three rows of hidden can lights ran across the cabin's ceiling.

Myles had already emerged from his single cabin and was writing his name on the cabin door with a permanent pen he had found in the desk when Ethan occupied the single room next to him, and Helen the one across the hall. Dwayne claimed the last single room, which had a floating bed perched under two porthole windows and a plush couch under the bed. Madison claimed the double room across the hall from Brendan and Ashley, leaving the fraternity brothers to share the double room next door. The captain's quarters, at the end of the hall, was the largest room complete with a king bed, wrap-around desk, couches, an en-suite bathroom, and a small dining nook. No one bothered to challenge Captain Kleinman's claim to the larger room, as they were simply happy to have any bed at all. Myles passed the black marker around to the others to mark their rooms, and Madison was the last to receive the pen. She wrote *Mr. & Mrs. Collins* on the door and circled it with a heart.

"You okay?" Myles asked Brendan as he walked into the yacht's large living area, where Brendan slumped into the oversized couch. Myles held his nose high in front as he walked towards the smell of the rear deck, where Spencer used the outdoor grill to cook. He stopped and looked out the rear window, eyeing the sizzling steaks.

"Yeah," Brendan replied. "I just have this strange feeling like I'm forgetting something that I need to do…know what I mean?" he asked.

Myles turned away from the steaks and faced his friend. "You're probably just tired. You'll feel better after eating and getting a good night's sleep."

"Yeah, you're probably right," Brendan agreed. He was about to ask Myles if he thought they should be worried if the ship's owner returned when he recoiled at the yacht's interior door being kicked open.

"Smoke 'em if you got 'em!" Brett called as he came through the door he had just kicked open. He held a lit cigar in his right hand between his index and middle finger and a twelve-pack of Corona beer in the other hand. He had also found an oversized pair of women's sunglasses that shaded his eyes and were adorned with silver costume jewels along each ear frame. "Smell those steaks," he said as he joined Myles by the rear window.

"Are you sure that's a good idea?" Brendan asked Brett and pointed to the lit cigar.

"Now you're afraid you're going to die of secondhand smoke?" Brett laughed. "It's time to live a little." He took a long drag of the cigar and tilted his head to blow the smoke towards the ceiling.

"Now the party's started," Spencer yelled when he saw Brett with the beer and cigar. Spencer stood in front of the outdoor grill, his torn jeans and dirty T-shirt lying on the floor next to him. He wore only his boxer shorts and a white apron that ran from his chest to his knees. The caption on the apron read; *If You're Reading This, Bring Me A Beer.*

"We're just getting started," Brett yelled back to Spencer. "Maestro, cue the music!" he yelled in the opposite direction towards the door he had just come through. Almost on cue, the overhead speakers crackled to life, and the unmistakable drum beat from the song *Paint It Black* by the Rolling Stones began to play. The yacht's interior lights dimmed, and the outside running lights illuminated as the song's guitar chords began to play. Kade entered the room, smiling and pointing at the overhead speakers, happy with himself that he was able to figure out the ship's entertainment system. He carried a case of the same Corona beer Brett had found in the bar area and wore a red bandana around his head. "Beer?" he asked and lifted the case in his right hand towards Myles.

"What do I look like, some snot-nosed punk?" Myles asked. He curled his lip in disgust and then walked to the side of the living area and opened the glass-lined cupboard, where he pulled out a honey-colored bottle of whiskey and a heavy tumbler. He had a large grin on his face when he turned to Kade and said, "Now this is a real man's drink."

"Wooo!" Brett howled.

"Fair enough," Kade replied. "Beer?" he held out the case for Brendan.

"I'll pass, thanks," Brendan responded with a wave of his hand. It wasn't that he wouldn't like a drink, but he worried anytime alcohol and his sixteen-year-old daughter were in the same room.

"I'll take one of those," came a voice from the open door. Everyone turned to see Madison enter the room wearing pink sweatpants, a white T-shirt, and wrapped in a long white bathrobe. Her hair was still wet from her recent shower, and she wore a white pair of house slippers. She held out her right hand as she danced across the living room floor towards Kade, holding the beer.

"Hey!" Spencer yelled from the rear deck. He pointed to the caption on his apron when the others turned in his direction.

"Coming up," Madison replied. She took one beer from Kade for herself and carried another to her husband on the rear deck. "Nice outfit," she said. She winked and handed Spencer his beer.

Dwayne and Helen were the next to join the party. The Jamaican entered the room in a smooth stroll while snapping his fingers and bobbing his head to the music. He looked so calm and relaxed that you never would have guessed he had spent the past week in such desperate conditions. Helen came in behind Dwayne and couldn't have appeared more different. She had taken the opportunity to shower and change, but her constant scowl, deep-set eyes, and flat gray hair hanging over her face made Brendan wonder if she might actually be trying to look unhappy.

Ting, ting, ting. Spencer rapped the metal spatula against the steel grill and announced that the first round of steaks was ready. "Come and get 'em," he called.

Madison carried a plate of steaks through the room and into the adjacent dining area, where she laid the plate on the table. The others gathered around and began taking seats while she returned to grab a plate of frozen vegetables that Spencer had also thrown on the grill.

"Dang, that looks good!" Brett yelled. He downed the can of beer he held in his hand and then crushed the empty can with one hand on his muscular pectoral muscle. With a toss of his hand, the beer can flew across the room and out onto the rear deck. Brendan exchanged a nervous glance with Myles before finding a seat at the table.

"Thanks," Spencer yelled in sarcasm from the rear deck.

Ashley leaned her head into the open doorway and yelled into the dining room, "Hey, first loads going in if anyone has anything they want washed." Her hair was rolled in a large white bath towel, and she wore a yellow and white sundress she found in the bedroom closet.

"Wait," Madison called to Ashley as she went to the back deck to retrieve Spencer's jeans and T-shirt.

Brett had his dirty swim trunks halfway down to his knees, standing at the dinner table, before Myles blurted, "dude! Not here." Brett smiled and winked a bloodshot eye before pulling his shorts back up. Ashley disappeared with a handful of dirty clothes and returned a moment later to join the group for dinner.

"Beer?" Kade asked Ashley as she took her seat. He held up a can of Corona and twisted it back and forth over his head. Ashley looked from Kade to her father sitting across the table.

"Come on, pops," Kade joked.

"Just one," Brendan replied before Kade rolled the can across the table to Ashley. "Better wait…" he started to warn her before she grabbed the can and opened it, spewing beer all over the table. Brett nearly rolled out of his seat laughing.

"Dat be alcohol abuse, mon," Dwayne joked from his seat.

"Dig in," Madison announced when she laid the last plate of steaks on the table. Manners were thrown out the window as the group reached for meats and vegetables with their bare hands.

"Has…anyone…seen…the captain…or your smart boy?" Brett asked the group between mouthfuls of food.

"Yeah, where is Eth…" Myles began just as Ethan walked into the room. He carried a large manual in one hand and a stack of books in the other.

"Miss me?" Ethan asked as he entered the room.

"Whatcha been up to, Uncle Ethan?" Ashley asked.

"This thing has an amazing library," Ethan answered. "I was looking for this…" he held up the thick owner's manual for the yacht, "but also found these for some light reading." He laid the books that were under his arm on the dining table and took a seat next to Ashley.

Kade leaned across the table and read the title, "The Inferno," aloud. "By Dante Alighieri. Looks like something I might like," he commented as he gazed at the picture on the cover of a man walking through demons in hell.

"Oh, it's a classic," Ethan said enthusiastically. "It's actually a poem from a fourteenth-century poet about his journey through, what he refers to as the nine circles of…" he was suddenly interrupted by Brett.

"Stop!" Brett yelled. "You're making me lose my buzz."

"Oh, anyway, I can let you read when I'm done," Ethan said to Kade.

"It's a poem, you say?" asked Kade. Ethan nodded. "Yeah, you can keep it, I'm not into poems," Kade said.

"I wonna mind reading it when you're done," Dwayne called across the table.

"Sure thing," Ethan replied with a smile.

"So that you know," Helen said, surprising everyone at the table. No one was used to hearing her talk. "I marked the bathroom downstairs on the left as the girls' room…the men's is on the right, and the one in the middle is open to whomever needs it."

"Thanks, Mom," Brett said jokingly. Helen glared at him menacingly and lifted her lip in a snarl behind her hanging hair.

The room was silent as Brett glanced around the table. "What'd I say?" he said through a mouth full of steak.

"Forget it, long story," said Brendan across the table. He changed the subject by asking the group a question: "Hey, does anyone else think maybe we shouldn't be using so much energy?" he asked, referencing the music, lighting, washing machine, grill, and other similar items.

"Jesus man, do you ever give it a rest?" Kade responded. "Can't you just let us enjoy one day?"

"He's right, man," Myles said. He sat back in his chair and swirled the whiskey in his glass before continuing, "We've earned this."

"I think we'll be fine." Ethan patted Brendan on the shoulder. "It's a good point, but I don't think we've even touched the solar battery capability yet…not if I read the manual correctly," he said, tapping the manual on the table.

Over the next hour, the group sat around the table and mostly chatted since few were able to eat more than a couple of bites of the steak after a long period of fasting.

"I am so looking forward to sleeping in an actual bed." Myles rubbed his full stomach and then yawned, his hands stretched high above his head.

"Me too, mmm-hmm, yep," the others around the table agreed.

"Dad, you better not snore," Ashley said. She frowned at her father sitting across the table. Brett laughed and then held up his right hand, pointing his thumb at Kade sitting next to him.

"No promises," Brendan chuckled. "Sorry, honey," he added when he saw the displeasure in Ashley's face.

"Looks like leftovers tomorrow," Spencer said as he collected the uneaten food and returned it to the kitchen. When he returned, he grabbed Madison's hand and escorted her onto the wooden floor where they laughed and danced. The others took turns dancing, except Helen, before finding a comfortable spot to relax and have another drink. Brendan, Myles, and Ethan stayed in the living area while Brett and Kade made their way to the front deck where the hammocks hung between the yacht rafting. The two finished their case of beer and could later be heard breaking into the liquor cabinets under the bar. Dwayne and Helen both turned in after dinner while Ashley and Madison watched Spencer clean the grill on the back deck before sitting at a table and chatting in silence. No one even realized that Captain Kleinman had not joined them for dinner or any of the after-dinner celebrations.

The moon hung low on the horizon and cast a silent reflection in the calm island bay when Brendan stuck his head out the back deck window and called for Ashley.

"Hey Ash...we're heading to bed," Brendan said. He nodded his head to indicate Myles and Ethan were also leaving, and then waited for Ashley.

"Go ahead, Dad, I'll be down shortly."

Brendan hesitated, looking back and forth between his friends.

"She'll be fine," Ethan said.

"Yeah," Myles agreed. "They seem like pretty good kids," he added of Madison and Spencer.

"They're not the ones I'm worried about," Brendan responded. They all glanced towards the front deck, where it sounded like Kade and Brett were in a wrestling match. "Thirty minutes," Brendan called back to Ashley through the window.

"Ugh, dad...fine," Ashley groaned. "I swear he still treats me like a baby," Ashley complained to Madison and Spencer.

"Good night," Brendan called as he turned to leave. "I'll tuck you in and finish reading you your story when you come down." Brendan, Ethan, and Myles chuckled as they left the three on the rear deck.

"Your dad's kind of cool," Spencer said when he saw how embarrassed Ashley was.

"I guess," Ashley shrugged.

Madison cleared the empty beer cans from the table and asked Ashley and Spencer if they were ready for another.

"Sure," Spencer said. He and Madison looked at Ashley.

"I guess it'll be okay," Ashley replied sheepishly.

"Want me to come along?" Spencer asked his wife, knowing she was heading to the bar on the front deck where Brett and Kade were hanging out.

"I can handle those drunk clowns," Madison replied. She turned and walked into the yacht's living area, leaving the two at the table.

Spencer glanced nervously into the yacht after checking his watch. It shouldn't have taken Madison this long to get more beer. He was just about to get up and check on her when he saw her appear across the room. She was carrying three tall glass drinks and slowly sauntered to the slower country and western music that was now playing on the ship's playlist.

"I was getting worried," Spencer said when his wife entered the rear deck.

"Those apes drank all the beer, so I made these," Madison explained while she set a tall glass in front of Ashley and Spencer.

"What is it?" Ashley asked. She held her nose over the drink and recoiled at the bitter smell.

"I call it a Madison surprise," Madison replied. She winked at Ashley and then lifted her glass in a toast.

Ashley toasted with her glass but waited for Spencer and Madison to try the drink before taking a sip herself.

"Whoa," Spencer said. He wiped the back of his hand across his lips before adding, "I'd say you found the grenadine, simple syrup, and about four different bottles of alcohol."

The three sat and chatted into the early morning, discussing the music, the island, the weather, and life in general. Madison tipped her head and gulped the last of her drink before setting the empty glass on the table.

"I hav'ta pee," she slurred her words as she spoke. She rose from the table and stumbled back into the yacht, adding, "Be…right back." She leaned against the wooden stair rails and slowly made her way to the girls' room, where she proceeded to heave the contents of her stomach down the toilet. After rinsing her mouth in the sink, she made her way to her cabin, where she told herself she just needed to rest for a moment. She felt the bed spinning as she closed her eyes and drifted off to sleep.

Spencer glanced at his watch again and rose from the table. He lifted his half-empty glass and peered at it as if checking the water level in a rain gauge. "We should finish up and head to bed," he said to Ashley. The two stumbled into the living area and sat on the plush couch to finish their drinks.

"Hey," Ashley called softly to Spencer, sitting across the couch, when there was a lull in the music.

"Yeah?" Spencer answered. His bloodshot eyes were half closed as he spoke.

"I don't think I ever thanked you," Ashley said.

"For what?"

"You know, the situation on the raft with the dead boy," Ashley answered. "I felt so terrible...I just wanted to jump into the water...run away...to..." she choked back a sob.

"Hey-hey," Spencer said. He moved across the couch and placed Ashley's head against his chest. "It's okay, really," he said as he rocked her slowly back and forth. "That's all behind us...shhhhh." He stroked her hair and sat comforting her as she cried quietly in his arms.

Overhead, a guitar strummed lightly, and a deep country accent sang the words, "holding you in my arms tonight..."

At the top of the stairs, just inside the middle stairway, Madison stood and stared at her husband and Ashley on the living room couch. She had awakened from her sleep and returned to see if the other two were still finishing their drinks. A low guttural noise, almost like a growl, escaped her clenched teeth as she turned and headed back down the stairs. Before entering her room, she rubbed her hand back and forth across the heart she had drawn on the door.

The Council

Brendan yawned loudly and stretched on the queen bed in his double room before jerking his hand back when it encountered Ashley sleeping next to him. She twitched at his touch and took a sudden breath, but remained asleep. Her face was smashed against her pillow, and her hair fell all around her, looking as if she were probably asleep before her head ever touched the pillow.

"Ugh." Brendan wrinkled his nose at the strong smell of whisky coming from his daughter.

He quietly searched the closet and dresser for clothes he could change into and was pleased when he also found an overnight bag with toiletries for showering and shaving. The door creaked as he exited the double room and ambled down the carpeted hallway to the bathrooms. The men's door was locked, and he was pretty sure it was Myles singing in the shower inside. He entered the middle bathroom to shower and shave, then sneaked back into his room to return the overnight bag. The heavy smell of hot coffee beans floated down the cabin stairs as he rushed to find the source. The trash and debris from the previous night's party still littered the floor, and the once immaculate yacht was now a mess.

"Good morning," Brendan said when he reached the kitchen and saw Ethan sitting at the nook with a cup of coffee. Ethan was dressed in a long pair of blue Bermuda shorts and a white T-shirt with a picture of a marlin fish on the front.

"Morning," Ethan replied. He tipped his coffee mug in a toast before taking a sip. He laid the yacht manual he was reading on the table and pushed a seat out from under the table for his friend.

"I thought I was dreaming when I smelled the coffee." Brendan took a large white coffee mug from the bottom shelf and poured a cup. He held it in front of his nose and took a long breath before joining Ethan at the table.

"Looks like we missed the party," Ethan said. They both glanced out the bay windows at the mess on the front and rear decks. Empty beer cans were strewn across the floor, and broken glass bottles lay on the counters. Cigar ashes covered the living room from an empty ashtray that lay on the floor.

"I think the kids must have joined in after we went to bed…I doubt Ashley's going to be up before noon," Brendan replied.

"What time did she make it back?" Ethan asked.

"Not sure. I was out as soon as I hit the bed."

"Got room for a third?" came a voice from the hall. Brendan pulled out the third chair at the table for Myles as he entered the kitchen.

Myles paused before sitting and studied the mess around the yacht, "Looks like I missed the party."

Ethan rose from the table and returned with the coffee pot and another mug. He poured a cup for Myles and then pointed to the back deck. "Did you notice?" Brendan and Myles both turned and studied the back deck for a moment before realizing Captain Kleinman was sitting back there, huddled in conversation with another person.

"Who's he with?" Myles asked.

"Helen," Ethan answered. "They've been out there all morning."

"I just realized I didn't see the captain all evening, did you?" Brendan asked his friends. Myles sipped his coffee and shook his head.

"He's been busy," Ethan said. His friends gave him a puzzled look before he continued, "he didn't know I was in the library reading while he used the rear stairs to go back and forth between the hull and his room."

"What was he doing?" Myles asked.

"Stocking up on supplies, apparently," Ethan answered. "He was carrying cases of water and boxes of canned food to his room." He took another sip of coffee and continued, "I followed him to his room to ask if he needed any help, but he just shooed me away."

"That guy's weird," Brendan said.

"He's hoarding the food like he did on the raft," Myles scoffed.

"It looked like he was also building something to barricade the door," Ethan added.

"Should we say something to him about it?" Brendan asked.

Ethan shrugged. "Seems pretty harmless considering how much food is onboard...not to mention the abundance of food and water on the island."

The three turned their attention to the front deck when they heard moans coming from the floor. Brett rose from the ground and peered into the window. "You didn't happen to find any aspirin, did you?" he asked the men at the table.

"Check the medicine cabinet in the bathroom," Myles answered. "I think I saw a bottle when I was looking for a toothbrush."

Brett moaned and rose to his feet while holding his head. "Get up," he grunted and kicked at something on the floor. Kade moaned from the floor and soon stood, following his friend into the hallway and down the stairs. The three men at the table chuckled and continued their conversation while sipping coffee. Dwayne's whistling was heard long before any of the men saw him climb aboard the boat and walk along the side deck. He wore his camouflage cut-off shorts, a long-sleeved, moisture-wicking shirt, and flip-flops. The light blue shirt had the word Billabong written down each sleeve. A half-eaten banana was in his left hand, and he flipped a large silver coin with the other. He stopped whistling and sang a few words from the popular song *Don't Worry Be Happy* by Bobby McFerrin as he made his way around the ship.

"Morning, Dwayne," Brendan called when he approached the kitchen.

"Ain't it doe," Dwayne responded.

"What'd you got there?" Ethan asked when Dwayne flipped the coin again.

"A bit o' coin," Dwayne answered. He flipped the coin high into the air, then caught it and covered it with his left hand. He opened the left palm and revealed the large coin to the men, saying, "Found it on the beach."

"Nice," replied Ethan. Dwayne closed his hand over the coin and sauntered back onto the deck, returning to his whistling.

"I swear that man's stress is so low he would fall asleep if he stopped moving," Myles commented as he watched Dwayne cross the front deck and make his way to the other side of the yacht.

Myles went downstairs and retrieved a handful of fruit from the hull's storage while Brendan washed the coffee pot and mugs. He removed three small plates from the cupboard and a small paring knife when a group appeared from the stairs.

"Breakfast?" Brendan offered an extra plate to the group.

"Sure," Spencer commented. Dark rings formed under his eyes, and his hair looked like he had just rolled out of bed.

"Got a blender?" Kade asked as he examined the fruit, and Brett searched the refrigerator for milk.

"Now we know who had the party," Myles laughed when he saw the hungover group enter the kitchen. Madison turned and stormed out of the kitchen, making Myles reply, "It was just a joke." He looked at the others and shrugged before returning to the table.

"Sounds like Ashley's up," Ethan said when he heard a door downstairs. Brendan grabbed an apple from the basket, sliced it with the paring knife, and then set it aside for his daughter.

"Good morning," several people called when Ashley appeared at the top of the steps.

"Morning," Ashley replied. She ran her fingers through her hair and then took a seat next to her father at the kitchen table. She nibbled a piece of apple before asking, "Is there any yogurt?"

"How far we've come," Brett said. He reopened the refrigerator and pulled a small plastic tub from the first shelf. "Catch," he called to Ashley as he tossed her the yogurt.

"So, what plans do we have today?" Spencer asked the group.

"Day?" Myles laughed. "It's almost night again, party boy."

"Don't remind me," Spencer groaned.

"I'm going to finish reading this," replied Ethan. He held the yacht manual up and then flopped it back down on the table.

"I was thinking about going back to the beach where we landed," Brendan answered. "I keep feeling like I've forgotten something there. Want to come?" he asked Myles.

"Well…" Myles said as he pretended to think about it, "I need to check my calendar first." The two men chuckled.

"No one's going anywhere until we recheck the area," Brett said matter-of-factly. "It might not be safe."

"What?" Brendan asked. "You're joking, right?"

"No, you need to clear it with the captain first," Brett said. The room grew quiet as the others stopped and listened to the conversation between the two men.

"I don't need to ask anyone what I'm allowed to do with my own time," Brendan shot back. "Your little job you had when we got here isn't a permanent position." Brendan stood toe to toe with the bigger man, with his head only coming to Brett's chin. "You two need to get over yourselves," he said when Kade joined his friend in front of Brendan. Myles took a position next to Brendan, and the four men stood in silence as the others watched in anticipation.

"What's going on here?" Captain Kleinman shouted from the hallway when he saw the tense situation in the kitchen. He entered the kitchen with Helen following behind.

The room was silent for a moment before Brendan responded, "Your boy here thinks I need permission from someone before I decide what I'm going to do with my time."

"What's this about? Brett?" Captain Kleinman asked.

"I told him he needs to clear it with you before traipsing all over the island…it might not be safe," Brett said coldly.

"Good god," Captain Kleinman huffed. "Would everybody just calm down," he said as he squeezed between Brett and Brendan and pushed the two men apart. "Now…" he continued, "he brings up a good point," Captain Kleinman said as he turned to Brendan.

"Oh, do tell," Brendan retorted sarcastically.

Captain Kleinman rolled his eyes at the childish behavior before continuing, "Like it or not, we're eleven people living and sharing in the same area. We can't just believe we can do whatever we want, whenever we want, without considering how it might impact the others."

Spencer nodded his head.

"We need to establish some common rules for the good of the group…it's how people function in a civilized society," Captain Kleinman continued.

"Is that what you call this?" Brendan waved his hand at the beer cans and trash lining the floors. "A civilized society?"

"That's exactly my point, man," stated Captain Kleinman. "We need rules about parties, and drinking, and…well, whatever else went on up here. We should have a cleaning schedule, a cooking schedule, a curfew…" Captain Kleinman was just getting started when Brendan held out his hand and cut him off.

"I get it," Brendan said. "And I'm not disagreeing, I think having some ground rules would be a good thing, but nobody put you or the meatheads in charge." Kade and Brett both bristled at the name-calling. It was easy to see the two men would prefer to settle the matter with their fists than with words.

"Okay, then let's settle this like adults," Captain Kleinman said. "We'll take a vote for anyone who would like to be in charge."

Myles took a step forward to address the group, "Why can't we just govern by unanimous decision?"

"What?" Captain Kleinman asked.

"I mean, why can't we just take a vote on the rules and the chores and stuff?" Myles said. "That way we all have a say about everything."

"Because that's inefficient and ineffective," Captain Kleinman replied. "Can you imagine having to come together and vote every minute on who is cooking dinner, doing the dishes, and allowed to do anything?"

"I agree," Helen said from the far wall. "Having one person in charge would be a lot easier…plus we all get to vote on who that person is."

"Sounds about right," Spencer added.

Brendan looked back and forth between Ethan and Myles. Ethan appeared ready to agree with the captain, and Myles was counting the people in the room to see how he thought the votes might fall.

"Anyone who wants to volunteer for group leader, raise your hand," Captain Kleinman said. He looked around the room and then stepped to the middle with his right hand raised over his head.

Myles and Brendan looked at each other, knowing it was probably going to be one of them who had to volunteer for the job. Neither necessarily wanted it, but neither wanted Captain Kleinman to have the job either.

"I'll do it," Brendan said. He joined Captain Kleinman in the center of the room and looked around at the others to see if anyone else might like to volunteer.

The others looked around the room in silence, and a few shook their heads and took a step backwards. No one else stepped forward.

"No one…" the captain called to the group, "Ethan? Spencer? Helen?" He pointed as he named each person, and they all shook their heads no, one by one. "So be it," Captain Kleinman announced. "We'll take a short break to gather everyone and then reconvene in five minutes on the rear deck. There, we will take a vote on who will lead our group."

"Where's Madison?" Ashley asked Spencer. Spencer shrugged his shoulders and didn't even return her look.

"What about Dwayne?" Ethan asked. He walked onto the front deck in search of the Jamaican.

"I don't like this," Brendan said to Myles when the room had cleared.

Myles was counting with his fingers and then stopped and turned to Brendan. "I don't know, man, I kind of like our chances." He continued when Brendan didn't respond. "I think you got three votes locked up for sure…Me, Ethan, and Ash."

"But so does he," Brendan said quickly, making Myles believe Brendan was probably also counting the votes. "He has the meatheads and most likely Helen." Myles nodded in agreement after hearing Helen's name.

"That leaves Spence, Madison, and Dwayne," Myles continued. "You need two of the three...and I like those odds."

"Yeah?" Brendan asked.

"Of course, Spence and Madison were with us on the boat and know what a dick the captain was with the water," Myles said. "And I don't think Dwayne likes the man all that much either," he added. "You got this." Myles smiled and clapped Brendan on the back as they made their way to the rear deck.

Ethan and Dwayne were the last to join the others on the rear deck. "Found him," Ethan called as he and Dwayne rounded the corner.

"Okay, now that we're all gathered...if you would like to join me up front," Captain Kleinman said to Brendan. Brendan walked to the front of the crowd and stood next to Captain Kleinman. "As previously discussed, we, as a group..." he waved both hands across the rear deck at everyone gathered around, "have decided to vote on which of us..." he glanced at Brendan, "should lead this group."

Spencer clapped his hands rapidly at the announcement and then slowly stopped clapping when no one else joined in. "Sorry, not sure why I did that," he said.

"As I was saying..." Captain Kleinman continued, "Everyone here gets an equal vote..."

"Not that you have to vote," Ethan raised his hand when he chimed in.

"Of course," Captain Kleinman said dryly. "Now, you should know that the person you elect is not a dictator, not a king, or in any way trying to rule over you. We just want to elect someone to speak for the group, approve rules for all of us, and act in the best interests of us all."

"All of us will continue to have a voice on how things are done," Brendan added. "We can meet regularly to discuss how things are going and what needs to change."

Captain Kleinman forced a smile and continued, "so now, if everyone is ready…" he looked around to see if there were any questions, "I am going to ask all of you to move to one side of the deck or the other. Stand on the right side, next to me…" he pointed to his right, "if you vote for me, CAPTAIN Kleinman," he emphasized the word captain. "Or stand to the left deck, next to Brendan…" he pointed to the left deck, "if you vote for him. Where you are standing when we count the vote is how your vote will be recorded, understand?"

The group nodded their heads and looked around at the others before looking back to Captain Kleinman in acknowledgement.

"On three," Captain Kleinman announced. "One, two, three."

People began moving immediately, and as expected, each side had three votes within the first few seconds. Myles, Ethan, and Ashley went to the left side of the deck and voted for Brendan, while Brett, Kade, and Helen walked to the right side and cast their vote for Captain Kleinman. Brendan wondered if the conversation between Captain Kleinman and Helen earlier that morning had anything to do with her vote, or if she was still just upset about her grandson. Dwayne, Spencer, and Madison remained in the middle of the deck and stared back and forth between the two candidates.

"What are you doing, man?" Kade said under his breath to Dwayne.

"Hey, no interfering," Brendan shouted. "Everyone is free to make their own vote."

Dwayne continued to smile, looking back and forth between the two men. He flipped his coin and counted the heads and tails as if deciding who should be heads. Spencer shared a smile with Brendan and took his wife by the hand. He started to walk towards the left deck when Madison jerked her hand free and walked to the right deck, casting her vote with Captain Kleinman. She turned and glared at Ashley. Ashley looked shocked and watched as Spencer looked painfully back and forth between Brendan and his wife. Madison never said a word; she continued to stare at Ashley as a slow smile spread across the captain's lips. Spencer hung his head and joined his wife on the right side of the deck.

"Yes!" Captain Kleinman hissed. He raised his fist in triumph while Brett and Kade gave each other a chest bump. "It's settled," announced the captain. "Now, I have a few thoughts, and, as your newly elected leader..." he turned and smiled at Brendan and the group on the left of the yacht, "I would like for everyone to meet in the living area in two hours. I have some initial thoughts on what needs to be done and will share them with the group at that time."

"That didn't take long," Myles whispered from behind Brendan.

The group dispersed to finish getting ready for the day. Brendan held the rear deck door open as they filtered back into the yacht.

"What happened?" Brendan whispered to Spencer when Spencer walked through the door. Spencer hung his head and silently followed his wife down the middle stairs and back to their room.

"See you in a bit," Ethan called to Brendan. He returned to the kitchen, picked up the yacht manual, and made his way to the library to finish reading.

Brendan and Myles walked to the front deck and leaned over the yacht rail to speak in private. They stared at the distant volcano for a minute, thinking about what had just unfolded. The island's low hum also seemed to have intensified. Brendan was the first to break the silence. "That didn't go as planned," he said to Myles.

"Didn't see that coming...Madison siding with the captain," Myles replied.

"I don't think Spencer did either." The two men looked at each other and shrugged.

"So, what now?" Asked Myles.

"Doesn't look like we have much of a choice," Brendan answered. He was about to add something when Ashley called from behind.

"Hey, Dad." She continued when Brendan turned to face her, "Was there something you needed me for?"

Brendan thought for a moment before responding, "No, I don't think so. Is everything okay?"

"Yeah, I just had this feeling that I'm forgetting something, and thought maybe it was something you needed. No worries," she added as she turned to leave.

"Hey Ash…" Brendan called before she could leave, "Did anything happen last night with Madison?"

Ashley thought for a moment and then shook her head and shrugged at the same time. "No, we just had a few drinks, chatted, and went to bed. Why?"

"Nothing, just asking," Brendan said.

"Okay, well, I'm going to finish the laundry and find something else to wear," Ashley said and then turned and re-entered the yacht.

Brendan and Myles returned to their conversation and spent the next hour guessing what sort of rules the captain might have come up with. They made their way to the library, found Ethan, and then stopped by the kitchen for a bottle of water before taking a seat in the yacht's living area. Dwayne and Helen were already seated when they arrived, and Dwayne was showing his newfound coin to Helen. Madison and Spencer were next to join and moved silently to the far side of the room, where they sat in two low-back chairs. Ashley joined a minute later and sat next to her father. Brendan raised his watch to check the time just as the last three entered the room. They filed into the room in a single file with Brett in front, Kade in the rear, and Captain Kleinman in the middle. Captain Kleinman was wearing a new outfit that he had apparently found in his quarters. He wore a white pair of trousers, a blue sports coat over a white turtleneck, and a white captain's hat with a black brim. Dwayne chuckled when he saw the captain enter the room.

"You've got to be kidding me," Brendan said under his breath.

Kade retrieved a chair from the dining table for the captain to sit in and placed it to form a circle with the others in the room. He and Brett stood on each side of the captain when the captain was seated. Brendan, Ethan, and Myles exchanged a nervous glance before the captain began to speak.

"First…" Captain Kleinman said, "I'd like to thank you all for being here and for your trust in electing me as your new leader."

"Hmph," Myles snorted.

"I know you're all wondering why I asked you to be here, so I'll get right to it," Captain Kleinman continued. "I've been thinking about the best way to manage this group and decided it would be to form a council…a group of advisors to assist me in my duties. I was, after all, elected to this position and not appointed."

"Oh boy," Myles said quietly to his friends on the couch.

"Questions?" Captain Kleinman asked Myles after hearing his comment. "Okay, good," he went on when Myles didn't respond. "The first person and position I am appointing to the council is Brett here…" he turned and faced Brett on his right, "as security and policing." There were a couple of gasps from the group at the word *policing*.

"Policing?" Brendan asked.

"Yes," Captain Kleinman replied sharply. He appeared annoyed at the interruption. "If we are going to have rules, then we have to have some way to enforce them."

"Shouldn't something major like that be something the group votes on?" Brendan asked.

"Like I said…" the captain went on, "I am appointing these people…you voted for me, and this is how I have chosen to govern."

"Seems fair," Helen commented in support of the captain's idea.

"Whatever," Brendan replied before sitting further back on the couch.

"Shall I continue?" Captain Kleinman sneered. "The second person I am appointing is Ethan." He pointed at Ethan sitting next to Myles on the couch and smiled cunningly when he heard the group gasp again.

"Me?" Ethan asked. He held his right hand to his chest and looked around the room at the others. He was just as surprised as the rest.

"Yes, I need an advisor to help make decisions…someone who thinks logically and not out of emotion," said Captain Kleinman.

"That's Uncle Ethan, alright," Ashley said flatly.

"Uh…okay, I guess," Ethan stammered. "Couldn't hurt, right?" he turned to his friends and asked.

"Sure," said Brendan.

"I thought you would appreciate that one," Captain Kleinman said before continuing. "Third, and lastly…I am appointing a judge, someone to resolve disputes and determine punishment…I mean consequences…" Captain Kleinman corrected himself, "for anyone who breaks the laws…rules," he quickly added.

The others looked around the room and wondered who might be chosen to fill this position. "Dwayne might be good for that," Brendan thought as he surveyed the others.

"For this position, I choose you…Helen." Captain Kleinman smiled and pointed at Helen sitting across the room.

Brendan didn't think Helen looked at all surprised at the announcement.

"Really?" Ashley asked as she looked from Helen to her father.

"I accept," Helen said with a nod.

"Good," Captain Kleinman said. "Now that that's settled, I have a few rules to start us with. Rule number one is the boundaries. Nobody goes anywhere alone, no one climbs the volcano, and no one crosses the river to the other side of the island."

"Why not?" Myles asked. "We don't even know what's over there yet."

"There is nothing over there," Captain Kleinman shot back. "It's barren, rocky, and dangerous," he added. "Number two: curfew is thirty minutes after sunset. No one is to be outside the yacht after that time, and quiet hours will start at twenty-two hundred hours…ten for you civilians."

"Are you going to tuck us in too?" Brendan joked. A chuckle escaped Spencer, but he quickly quieted when Captain Kleinman turned his attention to him.

Captain Kleinman glared at Brendan before continuing. "Three, everyone will pull their weight and be appointed to a team. The teams will rotate and be assigned tasks that need to be completed for the day. Four, the council will meet once a week to discuss new rules or amendments. Everyone is free to attend the meetings, but only to observe. Any questions so far?" he asked the group.

"What about the consequences, drinking, and all that other stuff you mentioned before?" Spencer asked.

"Yes-yes," Captain Kleinman started. "The council will meet and come up with all those details over the next week. We'll reconvene with all those details and have a list of rules that we'll post here in the main living area. Any other questions?" he asked.

Everyone stared blankly around the room at each other and shook their heads.

"Good, one last thing then…" Captain Kleinman said as he came to his feet. "The first order of business for today is cleaning up this mess." He looked in disgust at the mess on the floor. "Everyone not on the council will begin clean-up as soon as we break. I'll let you figure out who cleans what area, but Kade will oversee the cleaning detail and will release you when he finds the area satisfactorily cleaned."

"Great, the two who made the biggest mess don't have to clean it," Myles whispered into Brendan's ear.

"Council," Captain Kleinman called. "Meet me in my quarters in five minutes." He turned and walked out of the room, followed by Brett and Helen.

"Guess that's me," Ethan said to his two friends before following after the captain.

"Have fun," Brendan called as Ethan disappeared down the stairs.

"At least we have him on the council," Myles said, looking towards the stairs.

"Maybe," replied Brendan. "I'm not sure that man will listen to anyone but himself."

Dwayne was already picking up empty beer cans in the living area when Spencer announced he and Madison would start on the rear deck. Ashley jumped up to join her new friends, but quickly stopped when Spencer gave her a blank stare and shook his head back and forth quietly.

"Why don't you help Dwayne in here, Ash," Brendan said. "Myles and I will start on the big mess on the front deck."

The cleaning detail lasted well into the night with only a short break for dinner. The council came upstairs from the captain's quarters just long enough to make a plate of leftovers before heading back downstairs. Kade roamed back and forth across the yacht, stopping occasionally to give orders about where to clean next. The yacht was once again spotless when the night ended, and the group made their way to bed. The captain's council adjourned just after midnight, and Brett posted something to the living room wall before heading to bed. The last thing Brendan remembered hearing before drifting off to sleep was Dwayne whistling his "be happy" tune from his cabin.

The next morning, Brendan again found Ethan sitting at the kitchen nook, drinking coffee. They spoke briefly about the council's activities the previous night before going to see the updated rules posted in the living room. Brendan found his name and scrolled his finger across the board to the task section.

"KP duty?" he asked Ethan.

"It's military lingo for kitchen work," Ethan informed him. "Preparing the food, cleaning dishes, you know."

"Great, and I see I'm working with Ashley all day," Brendan said after locating his daughter's name on the list.

"Could be worse," Ethan said, pointing to Myles' name. Today's task for Myles would be to clear and clean the yacht's septic system.

"I'll let you tell him," Brendan said when they heard Myles come up the stairs and go into the kitchen for coffee.

The group spent the day adjusting to their routine, attending to their duties, and socializing within their preferred cliques. Brendan noticed that Madison and Spencer spent most of their free time in their cabin, while the fraternity brothers preferred to spend their time exercising and working out. The two could often be heard grunting and huffing on the beach in the early morning hours and doing push-ups on the deck after lunch.

The following day's schedule was much like the first, except Brendan was assigned to laundry duty, and Myles and Ashley spent the day cooking breakfast, lunch, and dinner. Everyone now also realized that the council was exempt from the chores list, and Kade seemed to always be on some supervisory task. After dinner, Brendan and Myles sat on the rear deck drinking a can of beer and watched the sun set on the horizon. Light danced on the rolling waves and appeared to spread from the entrance of the bay all the way to the setting sun.

"Tomorrow," Brendan said quietly to Myles.

Myles turned and waited for his friend to continue. "Tomorrow?" He finally asked when Brendan didn't continue.

"Yeah, tomorrow I'm going to head to the beach where we landed," Brendan replied.

"What for?" Myles asked.

"I don't know…I feel like I've forgotten something, and that's as good a place as any to start."

How Could We Forget

Brendan tossed his quilted, lightweight blanket to the floor and then fluffed his pillow for the third time in the past two minutes. He had spent the night tossing, turning, and checking the time every fifteen minutes. He opened one eye and read the small digital numbers on the desk clock next to the bed: 05:15. Yep, fifteen minutes since he last checked.

"THUD!" A heavy sound traveled through the yacht.

Brendan stared into the darkness for a moment to try to determine what had made the sound. He sat on the edge of the bed and moved his eyes back and forth across the dark room in an attempt to discover where the noise had originated. Nothing. "Someone probably tripped in the dark," he thought as he tiptoed across the floor. The feel of loose sand on his bare feet as he made his way to the bathroom made him hope he wasn't assigned to cleaning detail today. No matter how many times you sweep the floors, someone was constantly tracking fresh sand across the yacht. Yesterday, Kade made Dwayne do a final sweep right after everyone had gone to bed.

"Mrmurmrn." Brendan heard a low tone when he was halfway up the steps on his way to the kitchen. He paused on the middle step and cocked his head to listen to what now appeared to be muffled conversation.

"Thud...screech..." The sounds appeared to be coming from somewhere around the yacht's outside deck.

"Probably Brett and Kade exercising," Brendan thought. He continued quietly up the stairs and peered around from the top of the stairs, trying to determine where the noise was coming from.

"CRASH!" A loud noise from the front deck startled Brendan and made him take one step back down the stairs in case he needed to flee. He could now clearly hear voices coming from the front deck and recognized the deep husky tone of Brett and Kade.

"Wait," he breathed under his breath when he realized there was a third voice coming from the deck.

Brendan moved quickly down the narrow hallway and stepped onto the front deck. The outside air was heavy with salt and humidity and felt warm on his skin. The morning sky was already fading to a lighter shade of blue, and Brendan's vision was perfect in the low light, having just come from the darkened hall. Across the deck, lying next to an overturned lounge chair, Dwayne was on his back with both hands held out in front of him. Brett stood over Dwayne with his finger pointed at him while Kade stood next to him with his hands on his hips.

"Hey, what's going on?!" Brendan demanded. He moved quickly towards the group and stopped when Kade turned and blocked his path. The muscle-bound man crossed both arms over his chest before speaking.

"You should mind your own business," Kade said. He held out his right hand to prevent Brendan from trying to help Dwayne.

"Don't tell me..." Brendan said as he tried to push Kade's arm aside.

"I was just helping Dwayne get up...he tripped," Brett said, ignoring Brendan. He held out the hand that he had been using to point at Dwayne and offered to help him up.

Dwayne looked at Brett's hand and then at Brendan before sliding back against the side of the yacht and coming to his feet. He stood there quietly and just stared at Brett. Dwayne's lower lip was swollen on the left side of his mouth, and a small drop of blood dripped from his left nostril.

"You okay?" Brendan called to Dwayne. Dwayne turned for a moment to look at Brendan but then returned his attention to the bigger man in front of him.

Brett turned to face Brendan. "He's fine." He turned back to Dwayne and added, "Isn't that right?"

Dwayne remained silent and glanced back and forth between the two men. A broad grin crossed Brett's face as he forcibly patted Dwayne's shoulder. He turned and walked towards the kitchen, grabbing Kade by the arm as he passed by. Kade simply grunted and bumped Brendan with his massive shoulder on their way to the kitchen.

Brendan watched the two enter the yacht and then turned back to Dwayne. "What happened?" he tried again.

"Nuttin," Dwayne replied. He wiped the blood from his nose with his right hand and stared at it for a moment before turning to leave.

"Wait," Brendan called. "You don't have to put up with that."

"It's okay," Dwayne replied. His smile looked awkward with the swelling in his lip.

"No, it's not okay...we can't let them treat people that way. We need to take this to the group and tell them what happened. I will be your witness." Brendan grabbed Dwayne by the arm as he tried to convince him to report what had happened.

"There be more important dings ta worry about, mon," Dwayne replied. He looked down at Brendan's hand around his arm and waited for Brendan to release his grip. "Their time be com'n…" he nodded his head in the direction the two large men had left in. "Trust me," he called back to Brendan before disappearing into the yacht.

Brendan stood on the front deck and contemplated going to the council on his own. He wondered if the captain would do anything about it or just brush it off like he did when Brett threw Spencer to the ground on the beach. He also wasn't sure if Helen could be trusted to act reasonably, given the situation on the raft with her grandson. He contemplated demanding a re-vote and was wondering what had caused Madison to vote the way she had when he heard someone call his name.

"Brendan, hey!" Myles strolled across the front deck with a cup of coffee in each hand. He continued when Brendan finally turned and acknowledged him, "You okay?"

Brendan checked his watch and realized he must have been lost in his thoughts. "Sorry, just…" he didn't finish his thought.

"Must have been something really important," Myles said as he handed Brendan a cup. "I tried calling you three times from the window." Myles took a long sip from his cup and watched Brendan just stand there holding his coffee. "Are you sure you're okay?" he asked. "You look like you've seen a ghost."

"I'm fine." Brendan smiled and took a long drink from his cup. "Ergh," Brendan spat the cold liquid onto the deck floor.

"Sorry, it's instant," Myles explained. "Someone must have taken the coffee pot."

Brendan furrowed his brow and took a smaller sip before continuing, "There is something I want to talk to you about, though," he said.

"Yeah?" Myles asked. He raised both eyebrows as he took another drink.

"Not here, maybe somewhere a little more private."

"Well, we have plenty of time," Myles replied.

"What?" Brendan asked. He wasn't sure what his friend was referring to.

"You haven't seen the schedule for today?" Myles asked. Brendan shook his head and waited for Myles to elaborate. "Either there are no chores for today, or somebody forgot to update the schedule," Myles said.

The two men walked back into the yacht and made their way to the main living area, where Madison and Spencer were gathered around the schedule. Spencer turned his attention to the two men as they entered the room.

"What's a... electronics-free day?" Spencer asked after rereading the schedule board.

Brendan and Myles looked at each other and then shrugged. "No idea," Myles said. Madison and Spencer stepped aside to allow the two men to read the schedule.

"E.F.D." was written in large red letters across the top of the schedule, with a brief explanation underneath. No chores today, as it's an electronics-free day. There were no chores listed next to any names.

"That's probably why I couldn't find the coffee pot," Myles commented.

"But why?" Spencer asked.

"That was my idea," came a voice from the hall. The group turned and watched Ethan walk into the room with his own cup of the instant coffee. He took a sip and continued when he guessed everyone was waiting for him to elaborate. "I thought everyone could use a break. Everyone's been working hard." Brendan rechecked his watch when Ethan mentioned taking a break.

"So why not just call it a day off?" Madison asked. Spencer nodded in agreement.

"The captain thinks there is already enough time off. He's worried about what people might do with too much time on their hands," Ethan replied.

"Idle hands…" Myles started.

"Are the Devil's tools," Brendan finished.

Ethan pointed his finger at Brendan, "Exactly," he said. "So, I was able to convince him that we needed a day to let the solar panels recharge…a day in which none of the ship's electronics could be used."

"An electronics-free day, E-F-D," Spencer said. He nodded his head slowly as if he had just figured out a complicated riddle.

"Perfect," Madison smiled. "I've been wanting to spend the day lying on the beach and swimming in the bay."

"Nice," Spencer added. "Maybe we can bring a bottle of wine."

Spencer held Madison's hand as they left the room, discussing what they needed to pack for their beach day adventure.

"Doesn't sound like a bad idea," Myles said as he watched the young couple leave. "Maybe we should have our own little luau." He was smiling as he looked back and forth between his two friends, hoping they would agree with the relaxing idea.

"Can't," Ethan replied first. "I'm working on rewiring the ship's electric system, so we don't lose power to things we don't need…like the engine sensors and NAVI," he explained when his friends stared at him blankly.

"I was hoping we could talk today," Brendan said. "Just the three of us, in private."

"Can it wait?" Ethan asked. "I promised the captain I would get the wiring taken care of if he agreed to the day off."

"Sure," Brendan agreed. "And thanks, by the way…for looking out for us."

"Oh yeah, no worries," Ethan said. "I know everyone could use a break."

"I don't know about everyone," Myles replied. He wrinkled his nose as if he smelled something foul.

"I agree," Brendan added. "I'm worried about this arrangement with the captain and his two henchmen."

"Mmmm, Hmmm," Myles agreed.

"What do you make of him?" Brendan asked Ethan.

"Well..." Ethan scratched his head as he began to talk, "he's definitely one of the most self-centered and selfish men I have ever met, but he's not dumb, and he does seem somewhat reasonable."

"Do you think he's dangerous?" Brendan asked.

Ethan thought for a moment before answering, "No...I don't think so." He pushed his glasses further up his nose before continuing. "Like I said, if it were between saving his own life or the life of others, he's going to save his first, but I think he does have good intentions when it comes to leading the group."

"I don't know if I believe that," Myles grumbled. "I don't trust that snake in the grass."

"I don't either," Brendan added, shaking his head. "But I guess we'll have to for now. Ethan..." he said, turning to face his tall friend, "keep an eye on him and let me know if you see or hear anything suspicious."

"Like what?" Ethan asked.

"Just...well, anything not normal," Brendan replied.

"Not normal," Ethan repeated.

"You realize he has no idea what that means, right?" Myles asked Brendan.

Brendan and Myles both looked at Ethan, who simply stared back at them. "Right," Brendan said. "Listen, Ethan, just keep your eyes open and let me know if anything comes up that you think I should know about."

"Sure," Ethan responded before finishing his coffee in one gulp and returning to the kitchen.

"What do you have in mind?" Myles asked once they were alone.

"I'd like to head back to the beach," Brendan replied. "The one we landed on."

"What's there? I mean, what are you looking for?" Myles asked.

"I'm not sure." Brendan turned his gaze to the ocean just over the couch in the living room and was lost in thought for a moment before turning back to Myles. "I just have a nagging feeling…" he trailed off again and then checked his watch before speaking. "Meet back here in one hour?" It was more of a statement than a question.

The two men walked into the hall and then down the main staircase in silence, each returning to his room to prepare for the day. Brendan turned the small wooden knob of his room closet and studied the multiple shelves and drawers inside. He ran his hand along the top shelf and then lifted the hanging clothes to search the rear closet. There, against the rear closet wall, were the shoes he figured were in here somewhere. He had noticed each of the others wearing new shoes they had found in their room, but he had been content with the brown casual sneaker he was wearing on the plane. Now, however, going on a hike into the jungle, he was hoping to find something a little more rugged. He reached for a pair of brown, woven nylon shoes with a thick, knobby tread and retrieved the new hiking shoes.

"Perfect," he thought of the leather and mesh upper body. The black rubber sole was thick at the heel and narrower around the arch. The sole was streaked with yellow rubber markings and had the word *VIBRAM* in bold yellow lettering on both sides of the shoes.

He pulled the speed laces tight and stood to feel the shoes support his weight. He was surprised at how comfortable the shoes were and thought he couldn't have found a better-fitting pair of shoes anywhere in the world, even in the largest shoe stores.

"What were the chances of that?" He thought. That he would find the perfect pair of shoes, that also fit perfectly, in the random closet of a shipwrecked yacht.

"Whatcha doing, Dad?" Ashley asked when she came into the room. Her wet hair was wrapped in a beige towel, and she wore an oversized white bathrobe with the initials FR on the breast pocket.

"Oh, hey, hon," Brendan replied. "Just trying on some shoes." He lifted his right foot and twisted the shoe back and forth for Ashley to see.

Ashley studied the shoes for a second before replying, "Nice. Going for a hike?" she asked.

"Yeah, Myles and I are going to explore the island. Want to come? It's a no-chore day."

"Yeah, Uncle Ethan told me, and he already asked me to help him with some project he's working on." Ashley moved to the closet, picked up a pair of gray sweatpants and a white T-shirt, and then opened the door to head back to the bathroom. "Oh," she said before the door closed. "No hot water, in case you haven't showered yet."

Brendan followed his daughter out of the room and took the stairs to the main hallway. He went into the kitchen and took two bananas from the fruit basket that someone had set out earlier that morning. The temperature was already uncomfortable and was sure to rise as the day went on. He grabbed two bottles of water from the refrigerator and took a seat in a lounge chair shaded by the overhead cockpit. He checked his watch for the fourth time this morning as his uneasy feeling returned.

"Got a hot date?" Myles asked as he joined him on the front deck.

"What? Oh," Brendan said. "I just have this weird feeling like I'm forgetting something."

"Whoa, nice shoes," Myles changed the subject when he noticed the new hikers Brendan was wearing.

Brendan sat back in his chair and raised both feet. "They fit like a glove," he said. "Don't you think it's kind of strange that all the shoes and clothes on this yacht fit everyone perfectly?" he asked Myles.

"Speak for yourself." Myles lifted his left foot to show Brendan. The pearl-white sneakers featured three black stripes running diagonally down each side, with a thin black strip separating the leather upper from the sole. "Twelve and a half," he added.

"You're what, size eleven?" Brendan asked.

"Exactly," replied Myles. "Not that I'm complaining… It's better than wearing the one shoe I had on when we got here."

The two continued the conversation as they walked to the right side of the yacht and scaled the hanging ladder to the beach.

"Don't you ever wonder whose clothes we're wearing…or food we're eating?" Brendan asked when Myles dropped to the beach in front of him.

"Not really." Myles shrugged as he steadied himself and began to walk along the beach. "I mean, I'm sure they'd understand."

"You're probably right," Brendan agreed.

The two walked along the flat, partially wet area of the beach that marked the high-tide point. They stepped into the loose, uneven sand whenever a large wave pushed water further up the beach. Their conversation was briefly interrupted by the splashing of feet running in the shallow water behind them. They both turned and realized it was Brett and Kade on their afternoon run. The two shirtless men ran a few hundred feet further up the beach before turning and heading back to the yacht. They came to a slow trot just twenty feet from Brendan and Myles and then stopped when they were only a few feet away.

"Where are you going?" Kade asked. He placed his hands on his hips and waited for a response.

"What, seriously?" Myles asked.

"I said…where are you going?" Kade repeated.

"We're heading over to Nunya," Brendan responded before Myles could say anything.

Kade was silent and looked confused for a moment before asking, "Where is that?"

"It's right next to bizniz," Brendan replied and then turned and smiled at Myles.

"Where?" Kade asked. His look changed from confusion to anger when he realized the joke. "Oh, I get it…none of your business. That's very funny. You two are a real clown show." He took a step closer to Brendan as he spoke.

"Hey," Myles said. He held up his right hand to indicate that Kade should stop. "It was just a joke. Why don't you just relax?"

Brett came closer and stood next to his friend before addressing Myles, "You two have been nothing but trouble since we arrived. You're lucky the captain likes your goofy friend."

"Whoa," Brendan said while holding both hands out in front of him. "We know the rules, and there is no rule that says we need to let anyone know where we're going."

"It would be a shame if you got hurt out there and no one knew where you were," Kade said. He raised his eyebrows and pursed his lips in a feigned look of concern.

"Who would be around to look after that pretty little daughter of yours?" Brett added with a huge smile.

Brendan took a step forward but was cut off by Myles, who stepped between the two men.

"What are you going to do, old man?" Brett spread his arms, inviting Brendan to come at him.

"FWWEEET!" A high-pitched whistle caused the four men to turn their attention towards the yacht. The captain stood in the yacht's cockpit, the highest point on the yacht, and was blowing into a whistle to get their attention. He waved his hand over his head when he saw the four men on the beach turn and face him.

"FWEEET!" The whistle sounded again as the captain continued to wave his hand over his head.

Brendan turned back to Brett and Kade, smiling. "Master's calling, better run along now," he said.

Brett and Kade glared at Brendan before Brett stuck his finger in Brendan's face. "You're lucky little man," he said and then turned and began walking towards the yacht.

"Better hurry," Myles called after them. "Your mirror is missing you…it's been more than ten minutes since you last looked at yourself."

Kade stuck his middle finger in the air as the two men walked away.

Brendan and Myles continued their walk along the water's edge until they came to a large rock wall that separated the bay from the rest of the island.

"Nunya bizniz? I haven't heard that one since the eighth grade," Myles said. They both laughed as they left the sandy beach for a sturdier rock path.

They turned and followed the rocks to an opening in the trees and then found the small trail that led back towards the island's river.

"Can you believe those guys?" Myles asked as they walked.

"That's one of the things I wanted to talk to you about," Brendan replied. "You should have seen the number they did on Dwayne earlier this morning."

Myles used his left hand to move a hanging branch when they entered a narrow part of the trail. "Are you serious? What happened?" Myles asked as he followed Brendan along the soft dirt trail.

"I'm not sure," Brendan replied. "I came in on the tail end, but I'm wondering if the captain was sending a message to Dwayne for not voting for him."

"You think it was the captain?" Myles' voice sounded surprised.

"I don't know…I mean, why would the meatheads care about Dwayne? The guy doesn't bother anyone."

"That's true," Myles said. "He's a bit too nonchalant. He gives me the creeps."

"I think he's harmless," Brendan said over his shoulder. "And did you catch what Brett said about us being lucky the captain likes Ethan?"

"Yeah, I caught that," Myles said. "Do you think they've been talking about us?"

Brendan stopped and turned to Myles. "I'm almost sure of it." The two men stood staring at each other for a moment before Brendan turned and continued along the trail.

"So, what should we do about it?" Myles asked as they continued to walk.

"I'm not sure, but I'm worried about what plotting this little council has been up to."

"Yeah, I think Helen is still pretty angry with you," Myles said.

"It's more than anger," Brendan replied. "I think she wants revenge…" he was about to explain his thoughts when he tripped on something in the grass and fell headfirst into the sand.

"Are you okay?" Myles asked as he ran to his friend and knelt beside him.

Brendan rolled over and placed his hands behind him, propping himself up in a seated position. He looked back at a pile of large branches lying in the grass and rubbed his shin. "I'm fine, just a scratch." He reached up and grabbed Myles' outstretched hand and pulled himself to his feet. "This place looks familiar," he said as he looked around.

They had come to a grassy clearing with dense trees on their left, a sloping hill with clumps of bunched grass leading down to a sandy beach on the right, and the barren landscape of the other half of the island to their front. The small volcano jutted like a large black rock over the tops of the dense trees on the left.

"There." Brendan pointed down the hill to the sandy beach where the group had come ashore. His eyes focused on the barren rocks on the far side of the river that cut the island in half and carved a trench in the sand where it emptied into the ocean. He felt dizzy and found it difficult to concentrate with a constant hum in his head. There was something there, just on the tip of his memory that nagged at him like an itch that can't be scratched. He shook his head, trying to jog the memory free, but the harder he tried to focus on the memory, the louder the droning hum became.

"Are you alright?" Myles asked after observing his friend shaking his head vigorously. He placed his hand on Brendan's shoulder to help steady him.

Brendan focused on Myles and let the dizziness and droning hum fade before speaking. "I'm fine, just a little dehydrated, I think." He sipped from the bottle of water Myles offered him before continuing. "I think that's the beach down there," he said as he pointed down the hill. Myles followed his gaze to the area where the clumpy white sand gave way to a smooth, glass-like surface before reaching the clear, turquoise water. Rolling waves formed thin white caps where they met the receding water, and then splashed onto the shore.

"Are you sure?" Myles asked.

"I'm pretty sure this is it," Brendan said, nodding his head slowly. "You don't remember?" he turned to Myles and asked.

Myles studied the beach and shook his head. "I just remember being happy to be on land...I remember sand, but it all looks the same to me."

"Let's go," Brendan said. He started down the hill and wound his way between the clumps of grass until reaching the uneven white sandy beach.

The two strolled along the beach and then stopped, turning in a circle to study the area before continuing.

"What are we looking for?" Myles asked after the second stop.

Brendan didn't answer but continued to walk and study the area intently. After the fifth stop and circle, Brendan focused his attention on the volcano looming over the trees. From the current position, closer to the freshwater river dividing the island, he could now also discern the second volcano tube and the large gaping hole on its side. He felt drawn into the dark hole, and his knees weakened as the droning hum intensified. The hole was so dark...so frightening. The humming increased until it was all he could hear. A thought crept into his memory of something coming out of the hole...no, something going into the hole...someone...dad!

"Dad, don't go!" Brendan shouted. The sudden disruption of silence made Myles jump, as he had worriedly been watching his friend in silence. Brendan shook his head and looked around as if it was the first time he had seen the island. "That's it," he whispered and checked his watch.

"You're scaring me, man," Myles said slowly. He thought maybe his friend had cracked in the heat.

"Don't you see?" Brendan's eyes were wide as he held his friend by the shoulders.

Myles looked around again. "I see the same beach we've been on for the past hour," he replied.

"What's missing?" Brendan asked. He spoke quickly, almost manically, as he jerked his head around, studying the area.

"A McDonalds…my couch…" Myles answered sarcastically and was worried when his friend only nodded his head. "Maybe you should sit down and rest," he said to Brendan.

"The rafts!" Brendan practically shouted.

Myles looked at his friend for a moment and then turned to gaze out at the beach, before looking back in the other direction. No rafts. "They probably washed away," Myles said finally. "I don't remember us tying them down."

"Do you remember just before we got off the rafts? The plan we agreed to with the captain?" Brendan asked.

Myles stared out into the water and tried to recall the day they landed on the beach. Something poked at his memory, but he found it difficult to concentrate. He covered his face with his hands and then ran his fingers over his head. "What is that? That droning noise that seems to be crowding out my thoughts," he thought.

"Think," Brendan said. "You and I had a task…"

A thought was bubbling up in Myles' consciousness—a word formed on his lips. An image was there in the fog…but that damned humming. Myles shook his head; his knees felt weak.

"Where is Shanice?" Brendan asked.

"What?" Myles asked. He looked like he had just been slapped in the face. Brendan watched as the memories flooded back to Myles, and his facial expression changed from confused to horrified. Myles looked around the beach as if seeing it for the first time. "The fire, the S.O.S," Myles said.

"Yes!" Brendan threw his hands in the air.

"Oh God, we haven't done anything to try and get off this island." Myles covered his mouth with his left hand.

"How long would you guess we've been on the island?" Brendan asked.

Myles scratched his head and looked around for a second before responding, "Two…maybe three days?" he guessed.

"Try seven," Brendan said.

"What? No-no, that's not possible," Myles gasped. He shook his head and looked at Brendan as if waiting to hear the punch line to a joke.

"Seriously, check your watch," Brendan replied.

Myles pressed the small silver button on the left of his watch and stared at the information: 17 Sept 2024.

"We left on the tenth of September," Brendan said to Myles. He watched as Myles tried to process the information. "Thomas' wedding was on the twelfth, remember?" he added.

"How is that possible?" Myles asked. "I remember we were collecting wood to build a fire, and then…"

"Then we found the yacht and forgot all about trying to get off the island," Brendan finished his thought for him.

"The party…could the alcohol have affected us? Maybe something we ate?" Myles asked. He continued when Brendan didn't answer. "Do you think the owners of the yacht could have drugged us for some reason?"

"For seven days? Why not do whatever they were going to do after the first day?" Brendan asked.

"Good point," replied Myles. "Ethan would probably know. We need to warn the others."

"I'd like to check the other side of the island before we head back," Brendan said. He looked over his shoulder at the barren rocks before continuing, "We have plenty of time to check it out and still get a fire built by this evening."

"We're not supposed to go over there," Myles warned.

"Things have changed, Myles," Brendan said. "There might be something over there that can help us get off this island."

"I don't know," Myles said slowly as he studied the barren landscape across the river.

"Isn't it weird?" Brendan asked. He continued when Myles didn't respond, "We remember the rules the captain came up with when we got here, but we couldn't remember to build the fire."

"I suppose," Myles answered. "Look, I think we need to get back and inform the others what's going on. We can come back and explore the other side once everyone is working to get off the island."

Brendan shook his head while Myles was speaking. "Why don't you go back and tell the others what's going on," Brendan said. "I'll check the other side for our rafts. It won't take long, I promise."

"Split up? That's not a good idea," Myles said.

"I'll be thirty minutes behind you," Brendan said before Myles could protest anymore.

"Okay, thirty minutes…and if you're not back by then, I'm coming back looking for you." Myles turned and began a slow jog along the beach.

***

Brendan walked to the area of rushing water where the island river emptied into the sea. The current was swift, but Brendan gauged the river to be only ten feet across and no more than waist deep here at the estuary. He stepped carefully into the current and felt his new hikers sink into the loose sand. The current was stronger than he anticipated, but the sandy bottom helped him remain anchored and on his feet. After three steps, he was already chest deep and regretting his decision. On his fourth step, he almost lost his footing and felt the strong current tug him towards the open ocean. He was sure this would be where Ethan would tell him about how sharks patrol this part of the island, hoping to catch fish and other animals washed into the ocean by the strong currents. The current decreased after crossing the midpoint, and he took a chance and dove diagonally to the bank for the remaining three feet. His fingers dug into the muddy bank and finally found one of the large rocks characteristic of the other side. He pulled himself onto shore and lay on the bank to catch his breath.

"That's strange, no humming," he thought. He sat up and tilted his head, listening for the low, droning hum that was almost constant on the other side. Nothing.

He emptied the sand and water from his shoes before standing up and surveying the area. His first thought was how different this side felt from the other. He couldn't explain exactly how it felt different, but even the air he breathed seemed lighter and fresher. A light breeze blew uninterrupted across the barren rocks, drying his cargo shorts, hiking shoes, and T-shirt within a few minutes. He climbed the sloping stone hill, he dreamed his father had driven up, and surveyed the other half of the island. The stone hill tapered to the end of the island, where large boulders dotted the narrow beach, creating hidden alcoves as the ocean eroded the stone. A few dried bushes sprang up between the rocks, providing only minimal protection from the elements. Across the island, a large flat rock met the stone hill, creating a barren, open plateau that dropped abruptly into the ocean after about 300 feet. The stone hill rose towards the volcano but was cut, almost with precision, by the river that flowed from the volcano crater. A few deep crevasses in the stone hill provided walking access to the river, but the drop from the top of the hill to the river below was almost two hundred feet down.

A reflection from the narrow beach caught Brendan's attention, and he wondered if it might be from one of the rafts. He made his way down the stone hill and dropped to the narrow rocky beach to make his way between the boulders.

"What do we have here?" He said to himself when he came across a stack of stones in the shape of a horseshoe just feet from the water. The structure was made with thick, squared stones around the base and then large, flat stones that extended to the mid-waist. The area between the rocks was filled with a hard, clay-like substance, and a few wooden poles were used to keep the structure level in the rocky sand.

Brendan was sure the structure was man-made, but he had no idea what it was used for. He wondered if it was perhaps some sort of trap to catch fish during high tide, or maybe a defense against something in the water. He ran his hands across the stones and tried to remember what it looked like so he could explain it to Ethan when he returned to the yacht.

He continued along the rocky beach and made his way to the most immense boulder he could see. When he turned the corner, on the far side of the boulder, he stood amazed at the sight before him. A large alcove was carved into the rock wall along the beach. Pictures and words from different languages were painted and etched onto the rock wall, and a large cross was drawn over the entrance to the alcove. The word *SANCTUARY* was written in dried oil below the cross. It was clear to Brendan that people had lived in this area for many centuries. A series of smaller caves inside the alcove were furnished with rudimentary tables and chairs, and various articles of clothing were scattered in piles throughout the area. A rusted Spanish sword lay on the ground with a rounded handguard and a thin piece of metal that ran from the sword's hilt to the handguard. The blade was broken halfway up the sword, and the leather grip had withered away.

"Ethan would love this," Brendan said to himself as he kicked a small pile of books on the floor.

An old leather boot with a pointed toe, reminiscent of a time before shoes became mass-produced, rested on the ground next to a modern baseball cap featuring the thick stitching of the New York Yankees logo.

Brendan lifted a small wooden gate that probably served as a door to what appeared to be an office of some sort. Various books were stacked on a small, makeshift table, and an old oil lantern rested next to them. A small leather-bound journal lay open on the table, and it appeared someone had been journaling their time on the island with the dates written in the upper right-hand corner of the page. Brendan took the journal and placed it in the left cargo pocket of his shorts, then checked the time.

"Better get going," he said to himself.

As much as he wanted to stay and explore the area, he knew the others would soon be looking for him. He continued following the rocky beach and noticed several more signs that people had lived on the island. Plastic bottles, wooden planks from an old ship, colored glass, and old pottery littered the beach. He climbed onto the rocks and walked along the open rock plateau when the rocky beach ended at high cliff walls. A carved stone cross at the edge of the plateau caught his attention, and he went to investigate. Looking down from the edge of the plateau, he saw a rudimentary set of steps leading down to a narrow beach. The beach was covered in makeshift wooden crosses and what he was sure were probably headstones.

"Good God," he whispered. "That's a graveyard."

Brendan felt uneasy, and his pace increased as he made his way across the rock plateau back towards the river. He debated climbing the sloping stone hill back to the other side of the island, but decided against it when he found an entrance to one of the fissures that appeared to be well-traveled. The fissure cut a ravine in the hill that twisted and turned for a quarter of a mile before ending at the river. The floor was mostly sand but was also dotted with large rocks that had calved from the high stone walls. The ravine was shaded, but well-lit enough to see the rocks in the path. A thin strip of blue sky snaked overhead, pointing the way like a route on a digital map.

Brendan could hear the rushing water of the volcanic river before he saw it. The ravine path ended abruptly at the bank of the river, where the water flowed much faster and looked much deeper than where he had crossed at the estuary. A large tree trunk crossed from one side of the river to the other and appeared to have been intentionally placed. The top of the tree trunk was worn flat, and grooves were carved into the wood to provide traction. An old wooden sign lay on the rocks in front of the bridge. KEEP OUT, the sign warned. Brendan walked to the edge of the river and gaped in awe at the lush forest on the other side. The thick vegetation and colorful flowers stood in stark contrast to the rock and sand on his side of the river. He placed his foot on the tree trunk and pushed to see if the bridge was sturdy. When the trunk didn't move, he climbed on and bounced with both feet to again test the sturdiness. Comfortable with the bridge, he placed one foot in front of the other and made his way slowly across. When he reached the middle of the bridge, he noticed the low, droning hum had returned. He glanced around and found his gaze drawn to the volcano and the large, dark cave on its side. He had the distinct impression that the humming originated from that hole.

"I wonder," he thought. "Can I reach the cave and inspect the inside?" The entrance to the dark cave appeared to be no more than five or six feet across from a narrow ledge on the adjacent volcano. The cave was three to four hundred feet above the volcano floor, so the only way to access it would be to find a path up the adjacent volcano and then across the ledge.

Brendan checked his watch. "Sh-t" he breathed. It had been forty-two minutes since he left Myles on the beach, and he was sure his friend would be worried.

A sandy trail led him back towards the forested area where he and Myles had initially looked for wood to build a bonfire. He passed a shallow freshwater pool where he stopped for a moment to rest and gain his bearings. He thought the small pool would come in handy if they ever needed another source of fresh water, and made a mental note to find his way back. He rechecked his watch and had the odd sensation that there was something he was forgetting…something he needed to do before returning to the group.

"Must not be important," he said to himself and continued along the trail.

Just past the pool, the ground sloped gently downward towards the beach, and Brendan's pace doubled as he began a slow jog. He was starting to recognize the area when he heard a voice calling in the distance.

"BRENNDAANN!" The long call extended his name. "BRENNDAANN!" the calling continued.

"Here!" Brendan called out as he hurried towards the voice. He felt guilty that he had been gone longer than he promised and told himself he would apologize to Myles for making him worry.

He continued to try to get the caller's attention as he came into a clearing that opened to the clumpy grass dunes leading to the beach. At the bottom of the sandy dunes, just before the beach, Myles stood facing the beach and yelling with his hands around his mouth to amplify his voice.

"BRENNDAANN!" Myles yelled.

"Here!" Brendan yelled. "I'm over here!" He waved both hands over his head as he yelled.

Myles lowered his hands and looked around as if he had just heard something. He continued to search for the sound when Brendan called again from behind.

"Over here!" Brendan yelled. He saw Myles turn in his direction and then begin running towards him.

Brendan ran down the hill, and the two men ran towards each other until they were only a few feet apart.

"You won't believe what I found!" Brendan called as he grew close to his friend.

"I'm...so glad...I...found you," Myles said as he tried to catch his breath. "We..." Myles placed his hands on his knees to catch his breath.

"Did you tell the others? What did Ethan say?" Brendan said excitedly when Myles paused to catch his breath.

"We have to get back." Myles appeared almost in a panic. He grabbed Brendan by the arm and pointed back up the hill.

"Are the others already starting to build the…" Brendan started to ask a question.

"Listen!" Myles huffed and jerked Brendan's arm. "We need to get back to the yacht, RIGHT NOW!" he yelled.

"What's wrong with you?" Brendan asked. He rubbed his arm where Myles still held a tight grip.

"It's…Ashley," Myles said.

The panicked look in Myles' eyes made the hair on the back of Brendan's neck stand straight up. "What?" Brendan asked. "What's wrong with Ashley?"

"Go!" Myles jerked Brendan's arm again and began moving back up the hill. "NOW!"

Brendan's lip quivered as he spoke, "Is she…hurt?" he asked. He began to follow Myles up the hill, but then stopped and pulled his arm back in frustration. "What's wrong with Ash!" he demanded.

Myles stopped and turned back to face Brendan before responding, "She's been arrested." He paused to let the information sink in before adding, "We have to get back before the trial starts…NOW!" He yelled and then turned and started running up the hill.

Brendan stood dumbfounded, watching his friend run up the hill before coming to his senses and following behind.

"What happened?" Brendan called to Myles when he had caught up.

"Don't know…" Myles called back over his shoulder. "Wasn't there…when it…happened," he said between breaths. "Now shut up and run."

The First Ring

Ashley's Trial

The living room door burst open as Brendan and Myles ran into the yacht's main living area. The sudden commotion caused the others in the room to stop and stare in surprise at the two men.

"Where is Ashley!" Brendan demanded when he didn't immediately see her in the room.

Brett stood from his chair and started to move towards Brendan, but was stopped by the captain, who placed his hand on Brett's shoulder.

"Mr. Clark," the captain said. "We were wondering where you'd gone off to."

Spencer and Madison sat on the main couch and faced the captain while Helen and Ethan sat at the dining table across the room. Dwayne sat alone in the corner of the room and flipped the large silver coin he had found on the beach. Brendan thought he saw Dwayne smile as he came into the room and briefly wondered why he always seemed so aloof before turning his attention back to the captain.

"Where is Ashley!" Brendan repeated. "I swear, if you've..." he was saying as he moved across the room to confront the captain.

"Mr. Clark, please calm down," the captain interrupted and held his right hand out, gesturing for Brendan to stop.

Brendan pushed the captain's hand aside with his left hand and grabbed him by the collar with his right. "Don't tell me to calm down," he barked. He pulled the captain's face towards him. "Where is Ashley?" he snarled in the captain's face.

Brendan had forgotten about the others in the room and focused his attention solely on the captain. He was about to give the captain an ultimatum when he felt massive arms wrap around his arms and chest and squeeze. The immense pressure forced the air from his lungs and left him gasping for air. He immediately released the captain and struggled to free himself from Brett's vice-like grip. Brett thrust his knee into the back of Brendan's legs, and Brendan immediately fell to his knees. Brett instantly changed his grasp to a choke hold around Brendan's neck. Brendan's head was cradled in Brett's left elbow, and Brett's right hand was placed behind Brendan's head, where he pushed with crushing force. Brendan sputtered to breathe and saw spots in his eyes as he pulled desperately against Brett's forearms with both hands. He knew he was about to pass out.

"YARRGH!" Myles yelled and jumped on Brett's back, joining the melee. The three men crashed to the floor with fists and feet flailing in all directions. Despite being outnumbered, the larger Brett was holding his own against the two smaller men.

"STOP IT!" The captain commanded. No use, the three men continued their struggle. Captain Kleinman stood over the men and tried again, "I said stop it...RIGHT NOW!" Brett immediately stopped fighting and released his grip on Brendan, placing both hands over his head. Myles continued to struggle and attempted to put Brett in an arm-lock, but slowly eased up when he realized the big man was no longer fighting.

"Look at yourselves," Captain Kleinman scolded the men. "You can't even have a civilized conversation without resorting to violence…and you wonder why I appointed a police force."

Brendan knelt on both knees and rubbed his neck with his right hand. "What have you done to Ashley?" he demanded. His voice was hoarse and barely audible due to the choke hold.

"Good God, man," the captain huffed. "If you would just give me one second, I'd be happy to tell you about your daughter."

"She's fine, Brendan," Ethan said. He had left the table when the melee started and was now standing next to Captain Kleinman. "She's in your room." He stepped in front of Brendan and offered his hand to help him to his feet. "Myles," he said as he offered his hand to his friend. Myles didn't accept the offer and came to his feet on his own. He eyed Brett suspiciously when Brett got up and stood next to him.

"Why didn't you just say so when I asked?" Brendan asked.

"Well, you really didn't give us the opportunity, did you?" stated Captain Kleinman. He continued, "Now, if you would like to have a seat and talk civilly, I can explain what's going on." Captain Kleinman held out his right hand and gestured for Brendan to have a seat at the dining table.

Brendan looked at Captain Kleinman, and then at Helen sitting at the table before turning to Ethan. Their eyes met, and they shared an unspoken moment before Ethan nodded, indicating that everything was okay. Brendan walked to the table and sat in a chair next to Helen while Ethan took the seat across from him. Captain Kleinman walked to the far chair and took a seat at the symbolic head of the table. He offered Myles a seat before starting.

"I'll stand," Myles refused the offer. He didn't like the idea of sitting with Brett looming over them.

"Fine." Captain Kleinman rolled his eyes. "Now isn't this much better?" He asked sarcastically and smiled.

"Get to the point," Brendan replied.

"Of course," Captain Kleinman continued. "Mr. Clark…"

"Cut the bullsh-t…it's Brendan," Brendan interrupted.

Captain Kleinman nodded. "Right, Brendan…" he continued, "well, Brendan, your daughter has been confined to her room…"

"Confined how?" Brendan interrupted again.

"She's been asked not to leave the room, and Kade is posted downstairs in the hallway to see that she doesn't." Captain Kleinman held up his hand and continued when he saw Brendan about to interrupt again. "It's just temporary…just until we have the trial."

"What trial? Why does she have to go to trial?" Brendan demanded.

"I was about to get to that," Captain Kleinman replied. "Ashley has been accused of an…offense," he said, choosing his words carefully.

"What offense?" Brendan asked.

"Accused by whom?" Myles asked almost simultaneously.

Captain Kleinman looked back and forth between the two men before answering, "That's not important right now." He held up his hand again when he saw Brendan about to interrupt. "What's important right now is that we understand the process. When someone is accused of an offense, they have the right to a fair trial…" he paused when Myles interrupted.

"Fair my as-," Myles huffed.

"As I was saying," the captain continued. "The accused will have a fair trial in front of Helen, who will act as the mediator or judge, depending on the offense. Once she makes her decision, the defendant can appeal to the council if they think the ruling is unfair."

"What happened to a jury of your peers?" Brendan asked.

"Take a look around, Brendan." Captain Kleinman waved his hand around the room. "Who do you think would serve on this unbiased jury?

You? Your best friend? I'm pretty sure everyone here knows how you would vote, and you don't even know the offense yet."

Brendan looked around the room and knew the captain had a fair point. Everyone on the yacht would likely have a biased opinion. Even Ethan raised his eyebrows and tilted his head slightly as if suggesting the captain was right.

"She's a sixteen-year-old child," Myles interjected. "Are you even listening to yourself? You're going to have a trial for a kid?"

"Fair point," Captain Kleinman acknowledged. He nodded his head for a moment and then looked down at the table before continuing. "That is something the council took into consideration." He looked back up and turned to Ethan so that Ethan could acknowledge to his friends that that was indeed something the council had considered.

Ethan looked back and forth between his friends and then back to the captain. "We did," he said.

Captain Kleinman continued. "There is a concept in law called the age of majority…that is, the age at which a minor can assume legal control over their own person and make their own decisions…thereby terminating the control of their parents."

"I'm pretty sure the age of majority in the U.S. is still 18," Brendan argued.

"Not necessarily," Helen said, finally breaking her silence.

"In some states, the age of majority is 16," the captain added. "Those states allow the minor to do things such as get a driver's license, get married, or even…vote." He looked at Brendan to see if Brendan understood what he had just implied.

Brendan looked around the table, waiting for someone to explain something he apparently wasn't understanding.

"We all voted on who should be the group leader," Helen said. She continued when Brendan just stared blankly at her. "Ashley voted, you let her vote, and we all accepted her vote as an equal member of the group."

"Oh horsesh-t," Brendan said once he understood the implication. "You agreed to this nonsense?" he asked Ethan.

Ethan shrugged. "I'm a scientist, Brendan, not a lawyer."

"Jesus, Ethan," Myles moaned.

"If you think about it rationally, you know it makes sense," Captain Kleinman said. "We have treated your daughter equally in everything we have done; equal say, equal work, equal share of food and water…"

"Don't even go there," Brendan spat.

"We gave it fair consideration and agreed on it in a unanimous vote. Your daughter was granted the age of majority when we all agreed to accept her vote. You can't cry about the outcome every time it doesn't go your way," Helen interjected.

Brendan sat quietly for a moment to collect his thoughts. He needed a new angle to argue since he didn't seem to be winning the age debate.

"Don't you remember your own words?" Helen asked. "I do," she continued. "You said a vote was the fairest way to settle things."

Brendan remembered the conversation from the boat and hated that Helen was using his own words against him.

"You said it wasn't like that when I complained…you asked that I listen to reason…you wanted me to trust that you were doing the right thing…and now, when I ask the same of you, you don't want to…"

"Fine!" Brendan yelled and slammed his fist on the table. A slight grin spread across Helen's lips.

"You can have your little trial," Brendan said. "But I'm going to be there to ensure it's fair."

"Of course, we wouldn't have it any other way," Captain Kleinman said. "But remember that you are only an observer...you must let the system work."

"So when do we find out about the so-called offense?" Brendan asked.

"In due time," replied the captain. He lifted his sleeve and checked the time. "This has gone on longer than I had anticipated. I move that we conduct the trial tomorrow morning once everyone has had an opportunity to rest."

"Agreed," said Helen. Brett nodded his head from his position behind Helen.

The captain turned his attention to Ethan. Ethan looked at Brendan and then at the captain before saying, "Agreed."

"Good, we're all agreed. We'll reconvene for the trial tomorrow morning at ten o'clock. Until then, I wish everyone a good evening...Oh, one more thing," Captain Kleinman said as he turned to Brendan. "I don't think it's a good idea for you to stay in your cabin tonight."

"You don't want me to see my daughter?" Brendan asked.

"No-no, you can see her, but I don't think you should stay the night. It sort of defeats the purpose of pre-trial confinement."

"You think I'm going to bust her out and flee the country?"

"It's already been a long evening, let's not make it any longer than it has to be, shall we?"

"Whatever," Brendan said and then turned to Myles. "Looks like we're bunking together."

Captain Kleinman rose from his seat and crossed the living room until he eventually disappeared down the main hallway. Brett hurried after him as the others in the room slowly dispersed.

Ethan rose from his seat and moved to the other side of the table once the last person had left the room. "Are you okay?" he asked Brendan. The three friends were the only ones left in the room.

"What the hell happened?" Brendan asked. "I thought Ashley was going to be with you and you would look after her."

"She was with me all day," Ethan replied. "This isn't even about today," he added.

Brendan looked at Ethan and waited for him to explain. "You know what the offense is, don't you?" he asked.

Ethan twisted uncomfortably in his seat and then looked around the room to see if anyone else was in earshot. "I'm not supposed to tell you," he whispered.

"Spill it," Myles said

"I can't," Ethan hissed. "Look, if the captain finds out I told you, he will kick me off the council. He listens to me, and I can help you as long as I have his trust."

Brendan stared at Ethan for a moment before replying, "Can you at least tell me whose accusing her?"

Ethan looked around the room again before shaking his head. "I better not," he finally said. "But listen…the whole thing is really kind of ridiculous. I think once you realize what it's about, you won't be so concerned."

"That's not very reassuring," Brendan replied.

Ethan placed his hand on Brendan's knee. "Trust me," he said. "If I thought it was something serious, I'd be the first to stand up for Ashley." He could see that his friend was still unsure and wanted to ask more questions. "Rat Pack forever, right?" he asked.

Brendan put his hand over Ethan's and looked up at Myles. "Rat Pack forever," the two men repeated.

"I better get going," Ethan said as he rose to his feet. "The captain will be wondering what we're talking about."

Ethan was halfway across the room when Brendan called out to him, "Tell him we were talking about nunya." Ethan turned and was about to ask what that meant when he suddenly remembered. "Just like the eighth grade," he smiled. "Speaking of…" he said as if just remembering, "where were you today?"

Brendan stood and put his hand to his chin. With all the commotion, he had forgotten what he wanted to tell his friends. He tried to concentrate, but the low, droning hum of the island was distracting. "I was…" he started to say.

"DAD!" Ashley called from downstairs.

"Ashley?" Brendan called and then sprinted across the room and down the center staircase.

"You're not allowed to leave your room," Kade said as he stood with his arms crossed in front of the cabin door.

"I haven't left the room," Ashley argued. The cabin door was partially cracked, and Ashley stuck her head around the door and called again, "DAD!"

Brendan leaped down the last three stairs and sprinted across the hallway to his cabin. "Move aside," he said to Kade.

"Dad!" Ashley said and flung the door wide open.

"She's not allowed to leave," Kade insisted. He stuck his hand out to prevent Ashley from leaving the room.

"She's not going anywhere, you ape," Brendan yelled. "I'm going inside."

Helen's door opened across the hall, and Helen watched the commotion from her doorway.

Kade stood between Brendan and his daughter, holding his hand out towards both. "The captain told me…" Kade started to say.

"It's fine, Kade," Helen said from her doorway. "You can let him in for a few minutes." Kade stepped to the side and let Brendan enter his room.

"I'm so happy to see you," Ashley sobbed. She threw her arms around her father's waist and rested her head against his chest.

"It's okay, kitten," Brendan said as he stroked her hair.

"What's happening, Dad?" Ashley cried. "Why wouldn't he let me out of my room?"

Brendan guided his daughter slowly towards the bed, and they both sat while Ashley continued to hold onto her father.

"I'm not exactly sure what happened," Brendan said quietly while continuing to stroke her hair. "Apparently, someone has accused you of some offense."

Ashley pushed away from her father and sat upright. She held her right hand to her chest, "Me?" she exclaimed. "What did I do?"

"I don't know, they wouldn't tell me," Brendan replied. "There is going to be some sort of kangaroo court tomorrow where they're supposed to tell you what you're accused of and ask you to state your defense."

"My defense? What does that mean? I'm going to jail?" she began to sob again.

Brendan pulled his daughter close and hugged her until she stopped sobbing. "You're not going to jail," he reassured her. "Ethan says it's just something silly and nothing to worry about."

"What if he's wrong?" Ashley whined.

"Shhhh, I won't let anything happen to you." He rocked Ashley in his arms for a few minutes and then held her chin up with his right hand. "Do you have any idea what this is about?" he asked her. Ashley thought for a moment and then shrugged her shoulders and shook her head. "You can't think of anyone you've upset or hurt in the past couple of days?"

Ashley bit her lip as she thought. "I threw a banana peel at Uncle Myles when he fell asleep during our kitchen duty yesterday," Ashley said.

"Well, that would be ridiculous, but I doubt that's it," Brendan said. "I doubt it's Helen, she probably wouldn't be allowed to hear the case," he thought out loud. "Or Dwayne…that's just not him." He pointed his index finger at Ashley and asked, "What about Spencer or Madison? Could one of them be upset at you about something?"

Ashley shook her head. "No, we get along good, and we haven't even talked much lately since they've been doing a lot of couples stuff."

"I wonder…" Brendan started to say when he was interrupted by a loud banging at the door.

"Two minutes," yelled Kade from the other side of the door.

"No, can't you stay tonight?" Ashley pleaded. She hugged her father tightly and buried her head in his chest.

"I wish I could, kitten," Brendan replied. He held her tight and added, "But I'll be right next door with Uncle Myles if you need anything, okay?"

"Sniff…okay," Ashley sobbed.

"Don't worry, Ash, everything's going to be just fine," Brendan said. "I'll be back tomorrow morning with some breakfast. The trial isn't until ten, so we can talk a little more before then." He rose from the bed and searched the dresser for a fresh pair of clothes before turning and heading for the door. "Try to get some sleep, okay?"

Ashley sprang from the bed and hugged her father tightly before letting him go. She wiped a tear from her eye and nodded her head. Brendan leaned over and kissed her forehead before opening the door and stepping into the hall. He took a deep breath and felt his stomach turn as he walked away from the cabin and knocked on Myles' door.

"Come in," Myles called from inside the cabin.

Brendan opened the door and looked around the room. "Where did that come from?" he asked while pointing to a single bed on the opposite side of the room.

"It's the bed from the empty single room across the hall," Myles replied. "I figured I'd make myself useful while you went to see Ashley…how is she doing?"

Brendan crossed the room, placed his fresh clothes on the bed, and then sat facing Myles. "She's scared," he said softly.

"I don't blame her," Myles replied. He moved around his bed and sat down to face his friend. "Poor thing was taken by that goon without any explanation. Does she know who filed the complaint?" Myles asked.

Brendan shook his head, "No, she has no idea. I can't imagine who would go to the council before just talking with her," he added.

"I bet it's one of those meatheads," Myles said. "They probably made a pass at Ashley, and she turned them down."

"Yeah," Brendan agreed. "Hey, thanks for the help earlier."

"Oh, that? No problem, but I'm not sure how much help I was. I felt like I was wrestling with a small car."

"Ha," Brendan chuckled. "At least you got him to the ground. I just got manhandled and thrown around like a ragdoll."

"You did scream like a little girl," Myles joked.

Brendan reached behind him and grabbed the feather pillow on the bed. "I'm not the one who got beat up by Jamika Jones in the sixth grade," he said as he threw the pillow across the room at Myles.

"Don't pretend you weren't afraid of Jamika the Freak-a," Myles laughed.

"We better get some sleep," Brendan said when Myles tossed the pillow back at him. "Tomorrow's going to be a long day."

Brendan lay in bed with his eyes open, staring at the ceiling. He wondered if Ashley was able to sleep and wished he had some way to let her know he was thinking about her. For the next several hours, he tossed and turned, thinking about who had filed the complaint. He kept coming back to Dwayne since none of the others made any sense. There was something about Dwayne that didn't feel right, something that Brendan couldn't quite put his finger on. He fell asleep, realizing he never really said more than a couple of words to Dwayne.

***

Brendan awoke the next morning convinced that it must be Dwayne who filed the complaint. Who else could it be? He checked his watch and then rolled quietly out of bed. He reached for the fresh set of clothes that he had placed next to the bed and crept towards the cabin door with his hand held out in front of him.

"Couldn't sleep?" Myles' voice called in the dark room.

Brendan stopped and turned towards the voice just as the bedside lamp came on. "Whoa," Brendan complained, shielding his eyes. "Sorry, didn't mean to wake you," he said when his eyes adjusted, and he saw Myles propped up on his elbow.

"Nah, I couldn't sleep either," Myles replied.

"I'm going to shower and change and then take Ash some breakfast," Brendan said.

"I'll go get some coffee started," Myles replied. "Extra strong," he added as he sat up in bed and yawned.

"Thanks, see you soon." Brendan opened the door and peered to the left and right before walking slowly towards the bathrooms. At the base of the stairs, sitting on the last step and leaning against the wall, Kade slept with his head tilted back and drool dripping from his chin. Brendan thought about going in to see his daughter while Kade was asleep, but didn't want to wake Ashley in case she was actually able to get some rest. He continued to the bathroom where he showered and changed, and then went back to Myles' room to drop off his dirty clothes before heading upstairs to the kitchen.

"Coffee will be ready in about five minutes," Myles replied when Brendan entered the kitchen.

"Thanks, what do we have for breakfast?" Brendan asked. He opened the refrigerator and studied the contents.

"Ashley's been on a yogurt kick the last three or four days," Myles said as he watched Brendan search the fridge.

"Good idea…" Brendan was about to continue when he heard a noise. He stopped and listened for a moment before turning towards the rear of the ship. He could barely make out the soft tune of a light whistle.

"That would be Dwayne," Myles said. "He came inside for a banana and then headed right back out before you came up…I don't think he really likes people all that much."

Brendan placed the yogurt on the kitchen table and turned to his friend. "What do you make of him?" he asked.

"Dwayne?" Myles replied. "Seems like a decent guy. Why?" he asked.

"No reason," Brendan answered. "I just don't know anything about him."

"He's shipwrecked on this island like the rest of us. What more do you need to know?"

Brendan looked from his friend to the rear deck. "I don't know…I'm going to go talk to him." Brendan replied.

"Coffee's almost ready," Myles reminded Brendan.

"It'll just be a second," Brendan responded and then walked through the yacht to the rear deck.

"Good morning, Dwayne," Brendan said when he opened the door to the rear deck.

Dwayne was leaning on the yacht's handrail and peering out over the water, watching the sun rise. He turned when he heard Brendan open the door and greet him, and then turned back to study the sky.

"Yes sir, dat it is," Dwayne said when he turned back to Brendan.

"Sorry, I didn't mean to bother you, but I realized I never got a chance to get to know you since we first met." Brendan walked across the rear deck and joined Dwayne, looking over the rail at the water.

"No bother, mon," Dwayne replied. "But der init much to know."

"Every man has a story. What's your last name?" Brendan asked.

Dwayne smiled. "My dad be called Ferraman," Dwayne answered.

Brendan wasn't sure if the name was Ferraman or just Ferra, since Dwayne always seemed to put mon at the end of his sentences. "Ferra..man? Dwayne Ferraman?" Brendan asked to be sure.

"Dat's it," Dwayne smiled.

"Does Dwayne Ferraman have any family?" Brendan asked.

"No, jus me," Dwayne replied.

"And where are you from, Dwayne?"

Dwayne spread his hands out over the water. "All over, I go where da money takes me," Dwayne replied.

"Your accent sounds Jamaican," Brendan said.

"Been der too," Dwayne answered.

"Okay, so what do you do for the money?"

Dwayne smiled again and flipped his silver coin. "Dwayne Ferraman," he said.

"Right, I know your name…never mind," Brendan said. He could see he wasn't getting much out of Dwayne. He decided to switch tactics and see what Dwayne thought about the others on the yacht. "What about the captain? And the others?" he asked.

Dwayne shrugged, "What about em?" he asked.

"They haven't been very kind to you." Brendan wasn't trying to bait Dwayne into an opinion, but he figured Dwayne couldn't be pleased with the way things were going.

"My dad once tol me da story of da frog and scorpion, do you know dis one?" Dwayne asked.

"Yeah, I think," Brendan replied. "Something about the frog helping the scorpion cross the river and the scorpion stings the frog midway across, killing them both?"

"Dat be it," Dwayne laughed. He clapped his hands together and then rubbed them vigorously. "Da scorpion can only be who he is…him will do what scorpions do. The cap'n can only be who he is, to expect otherwise would be foolish."

"I guess you're right," Brendan said after thinking about it for a moment. "But doesn't it make you mad the way he treats others?"

"Not my place to judge, Mr. Brendan," Dwayne replied.

"What is your place?" Brendan thought he had cornered him now.

Dwayne smiled broadly and patted Brendan on the back. "Dwayne Ferraman," he said as he left Brendan standing on the rear deck.

"Figures," Brendan groaned. He walked back into the kitchen, where Myles had his coffee ready for him.

"So, what did you learn?" Myles asked as he handed Brendan a cup. The light blue ceramic mug was warm to the touch and had a large number 1 on both sides of the handle.

"Nothing," Brendan shrugged. "Other than his last name, which is Ferraman, and he has a dad."

"I could have told you half of that before you went out there, and I've never really talked to the man," Myles stated.

Brendan grabbed the yogurt and an apple and headed down the stairs to see Ashley. He saw Kade standing next to the cabin door and noticed a large red whelp on the man's forehead. He guessed correctly that someone must have caught him sleeping on the job.

"I'm just going to be a minute," Brendan said when Kade sneered at him.

Brendan knocked on the door and entered when he heard his daughter yell to come inside.

"Breakfast?" Brendan asked. He held up the small plastic container of yogurt and a spoon in his right hand, and the apple in his left, along with his coffee cup.

"I'm not really feeling hungry," Ashley said. She sat at the end of the bed with large bags under both eyes. She was wearing a pair of khaki cotton twill shorts and a white t-shirt with a caption on the front that read "Bee Good, Do Good" in cursive letters. The picture of a black and yellow bumble bee was above the caption. Her hair was pulled back from the bangs, over the ears, and into a short ponytail in back.

"I really think you need to eat something; it's going to be a long day." Brendan sat next to her on the bed and opened the cup of yogurt.

Ashley dabbed at the creamy white yogurt and swirled the spoon to mix the honey that was at the bottom of the cup. "I've been trying to think of what to say to Helen when it's my turn to speak," she said.

"I wouldn't worry too much about that," Brendan replied. "Just be honest and tell her exactly what happened."

"Do you think she's still mad at me for casting the deciding vote on her grandson?"

"No," Brendan lied. "If she's mad at anyone, it would be me, and I don't think she would hold that against you."

Ashley took a bite of the yogurt and then turned to her dad, "Every time I see her, she gives me a dirty look like she's mad at me."

"That's how she looks at everyone," Brendan said. "I think she's just a grumpy, unhappy woman."

"I guess I would be too if I were in her shoes," Ashley said softly. She finished the yogurt in two spoonfuls and then tossed the apple in the air with her left hand. "I'll save this for later," she said. "Am I supposed to come up with you and wait for the trial to begin?" she asked.

"I think you're supposed to stay here in the room until they come and get you."

Ashley stood up and paced nervously to the other side of the bed and then back again. "I think I'm going to go crazy in this place," she said when she returned to her father's side of the bed.

"Don't worry, this will all be over soon, and we can take a long walk on the beach afterwards," Brendan said.

Ashley walked to the cabin window and looked out over the beach. "That would be nice..." Her words trailed off as she became lost in thought. "Oh, and thanks, Dad...for everything," she added. She turned and walked to her father and hugged him tightly for several minutes.

"I love you, kitten," Brendan said and kissed her on the top of her head. When Ashley released her grasp, he walked back towards the door. "I better get going before Tweedle-dum outside has a fit." He pointed his right thumb at the door and rolled his eyes, making Ashley smile.

"Thanks for breakfast," Ashley called as Brendan opened the door and walked into the hallway.

By the time Brendan returned to the main floor, the rest of the group had already gathered. The living area had been rearranged so that the dining table ran longways in the room, with one large chair placed in the middle of the table. The chair rested on a six-inch wooden platform that made it sit higher than the other chairs in the room. Across from the table, two chairs were placed six feet apart and facing the dining room table. Three dining room chairs were placed to the left of the dining table and angled to face the two chairs in front of the table. In the rear of the room, the couch and two love-chairs were placed against the far wall.

"What's all this?" Spencer asked as soon as he entered the room. "Can I sit here?" he said and then took a seat in the chair on the platform.

"This isn't a game, you idiot," a voice called from the hallway. Everyone turned to see Helen enter the room, wearing a long, black dress with flared sleeves and a collar that came to mid-neck. The dress was made of a heavier, cotton-like material, and Brendan guessed it was some sort of cold-weather evening gown. Her hair appeared wet and was combed back behind her ears. She carried a long wooden spoon in her right hand that she had just found in the kitchen, and a black leather-bound book in her left. She walked to the dining table and placed both objects on either side of the chair. "This is the courtroom, and this is my seat," she said to Spencer once she had placed the spoon and book on the table.

"Are we having soup?" Spencer asked.

Helen shot him a nasty look and pointed to the rear of the room. "Those are the spectator seats," she said, pointing to the couch and chairs. She turned and was about to leave the room when Ethan pointed to the book she had just placed on the table.

"Is that my Great Gatsby novel?" Ethan asked Helen.

Helen looked from the book and then at Ethan. "Oh, sorry, I was going to let you know that I borrowed it," she said. "It was the only official-looking book in the library," she explained.

"Oh, okay," Ethan exclaimed. "Don't lose my page," he said.

Helen turned and left the room just as Brett was entering. He carried a stack of papers and a roll of clear tape. He taped the top sheet of paper to the dining table and then moved to stand in front of the two chairs facing the table. The sign he had just taped to the table read *JUDGE*. One of the chairs in front of the table was labeled *DEFENDANT*, and the other *ACCUSER*. He taped signs on the three chairs to the side of the table and then placed the last one in the rear of the room. The first chair next to the table read *CAPTAIN*, *ADVISOR* on the second, and *SECURITY* on the third. The last sign in the rear of the room read *SPECTATORS*.

When he was finished placing the signs, Brett checked his watch and then announced, "Everyone, find your seats. We will begin in five minutes." He moved to stand in front of the chair labeled "Security" and indicated to Ethan that his seat was the one labeled "Advisor."

Brendan stood in front of the couch at the rear of the room, with Myles to his left and Dwayne sitting to his right. Madison and Spencer stood in front of the two love chairs, and Kade stood next to the door at the front of the room. At exactly noon, Brett called for everyone to rise for the entry of the official party, and music began to play on the ship's overhead speakers. Brendan was sure he remembered the tune from a Fourth of July celebration hosted by the local VFW, recalling it as a military march for the entry of the flag detail bearing the U.S. flag, the Army flag, and the state flag. As the trumpets grew louder, Captain Kleinman and Helen walked through the door. Captain Kleinman was first, wearing his white slacks and blue jacket, while Helen followed behind in her black dress.

"If this wasn't a kangaroo court already, it is now," Brendan leaned over to Myles and whispered.

Captain Kleinman walked to the chair labeled "Captain", and Helen stopped in front of the chair sitting on the platform.

"You may be seated," Brett announced once the music had stopped.

Everyone took their assigned seats while the two chairs facing the table remained unoccupied. Once Helen was seated, she called to the group, "Will the accuser please take your seat." She pointed to the seat labeled accuser on her left.

Everyone looked around the room, wondering who would get up and take the seat. Brendan turned to Dwayne when he felt him move on the couch. Dwayne leaned back on the sofa and smiled his broad grin when Brendan turned to him. Brendan heard the commotion coming from his left and turned to see Madison rise from her seat and walk to the accuser's chair.

"Madison…what, why?" Brendan said, looking from Madison to Spencer, who was still sitting in the rear of the room. Madison never turned around but sat quietly, her eyes fixed on Helen.

"WHACK!" A loud sound came from the dining table where Helen had struck the table with the wooden spoon.

"QUIET!" Helen yelled. "Quiet or you will be asked to leave this courtroom," she added.

The murmuring quieted, but Brendan still stared intently at Spencer, who wouldn't return his gaze and just stared at the floor.

"Bailiff, you may bring in the defendant," Helen called once the room was silent. She turned in her chair and looked at Kade standing near the door. "That would be you," she said to Kade and then rolled her eyes when he scurried down the stairs.

It only took a moment for Kade to return, followed by Ashley. Kade stepped to the side and pointed to the seat labeled defendant. Ashley looked wide-eyed around the room as she walked to her seat.

Brendan nodded his head and mouthed the words, "it's okay," to Ashley when she noticed him in the rear of the room.

"Raise your right hands," Helen said once Ashley was seated. She raised her own right hand and continued when both women had raised their hands. "I promise to tell the truth and will not make statements which evade or conceal the truth and do so willingly. I promise to abide by this court's decision and follow the rules set forth by the judge." She paused and waited for the two women to respond.

"I do," stated Madison.

Ashley looked around the room and then at Madison, who was staring straight ahead. "Yes," Ashley replied once her gaze returned to Helen.

"Good," Helen stated. She returned her right hand to the table and turned to Madison. "Now, Mrs. Collins, you have a grievance against Miss Clark. Please state your grievance."

Brendan leaned forward on the couch and listened intently to what Madison was about to say.

"Well," Madison started. She shifted uncomfortably in her seat and then looked back at Spencer before returning her attention to Helen. "Ashley..." she said and then paused, "I mean, Miss Clark has made unwanted advances on my husband and has tried several times to seduce him." She paused when a loud murmur erupted in the room.

Ashley turned to Madison and exclaimed, "I did not!"

"What!?" Myles exclaimed.

"What kind of nonsense is this!?" Brendan yelled at Spencer. He threw his arms in the air and looked around the room with indignation, much the same way professional basketball players do when they are trying to draw a foul.

"Told you," Ethan mouthed to Brendan.

"WHACK-WHACK-WHACK!" Helen rapped the wooden spoon vigorously against the table. "SILENCE!" She yelled. "Silence or you will be removed from this court." She stood and pointed the wooden spoon at Brendan. "This is your last warning, Mr. Clark." She turned her attention to Ashley when Brendan nodded his head. "Miss Clark, you do not speak directly to Mrs. Collins and will only speak when it is your turn. Do you understand?" she asked.

"Yes," Ashley said as she nodded her head.

Helen sat in her chair and turned to Madison. "Now, Mrs. Collins," she started. "Those are serious accusations; can you please elaborate?"

"Yes," Madison replied. "It started when we were on the raft and I noticed that Ash...I mean, Miss Clark," she corrected herself, "was trying to sleep next to my husband. I heard her whispering to him when she thought everyone else was asleep. Then, when we got to the island, she started wearing clothes that were too small and revealing and tried to hang around with me and Spencer."

Ashley turned to Madison with her mouth agape and eyes wide.

Madison continued, "The night we found the yacht, I caught her on the couch, cuddled up with my husband. She was taking advantage of him because he had had too much to drink."

"I see," Helen said when Madison was finished. "I have a couple of questions for you. What were Miss Clark and your husband doing on the raft? What were they talking about?" she asked.

Madison shrugged, "I'm not sure, my back was turned to them...but I heard her say something about Spencer being brave and thanking him."

"And did you ever say anything to Miss Clark or your husband about this behavior?" Helen asked.

"Yes," Madison replied. "I told Spencer that I thought it was inappropriate and that I didn't appreciate it. He let Miss Clark know that she was no longer welcome to hang out with us."

"Is that true, Mr. Collins?" Helen asked Spencer.

Spencer stood and looked around the room. It was clear he was uncomfortable being called to testify against Ashley. He looked sideways at Brendan before responding, "Yes." He continued when Helen just stared at him, waiting for more. "Madison told me she thought Ashley was being inappropriate and told me I needed to ensure I let Ashley know that she wasn't welcome to hang out with us."

"And you let her know?" Helen asked.

"Yes," Spencer replied. "She wanted to join Madison and me cleaning the rear deck the day we cleaned up the mess from the party…that was the first time I let her know she wasn't welcome to join us."

"Thank you, you may sit back down," Helen said to Spencer. She turned back to Madison and asked, "Mrs. Collins, did anyone witness this event on the couch that you allege?"

"I wasn't sure at the time…" Madison replied, "but later I learned that Mr. Kade also witnessed it."

"Kade," Helen called. "Can you confirm Mrs. Collins' story?"

Kade walked to the front of the table to address Helen. "Oh, sure…I saw everything," Kade said. He looked down at the floor and shuffled his feet as he spoke.

"He's lying," Myles whispered to Brendan. "He was drunker than a skunk when we went to bed."

"What exactly did you see?" Helen asked Kade.

Kade was still looking down at the floor when he responded, "I saw Ashley and Spencer on the couch…Ashley was on top of him…" Kade said.

"She was on top of him?" Helen interjected.

"Well, she was kind of leaning on him…with her head on his chest," Kade explained.

Captain Kleinman raised his hand and interjected, "May I?" he asked.

"Of course," Helen replied.

"You were with Brett at the front of the yacht. How could you see what was happening on the couch?" Captain Kleinman asked Kade.

"How does he know where Kade and Brett were?" Brendan whispered to Myles. "He never came upstairs during the party."

"I uh…oh yeah, I had to go to the bathroom and saw them from the hallway," Kade responded.

"I smell a setup," Myles whispered back to Brendan.

"Thank you, that's all I have," Captain Kleinman said to Helen and then sat back down.

Helen turned to Ashley after dismissing Kade. "So, Miss Clark, how do you respond to these accusations?"

"Well, they're not true," Ashley said after a moment of thinking about a response.

"None of it's true? You didn't talk to Mr. Collins or sleep next to him on the raft?" Helen asked.

"Well…I mean…" Ashley started to say.

"You didn't wear tight clothing and attempt to join Mr. and Mrs. Collins in their activities?" Helen interrupted before Ashley could finish.

"I…uh…thought we were friends…" Ashley stammered.

"And you weren't alone with Mr. Collins on the couch?" Helen cut her off again.

Brendan had had enough and sprang from the couch, "You're not even letting her answer," he shouted at Helen. "This is a sham…" he started to say.

"WHACK-WHACK-WHACK!" Helen slammed the wooden spoon on the table. She stood and yelled at Brendan, "You are out of order!"

"This whole court is out of order," Brendan shouted back. "Some stupid accusations due to petty jealousy and a whole lot of lying are all I see," he added.

"WHACK-WHACK-WHACK-WHACK!" Helen continued to pound the spoon on the table. "Bailiff, escort this man from the courtroom!" Helen called to Kade. Kade ran to Brendan and grabbed him by the arm. He used both hands when Brendan tried to pull away.

"Mr. Clark, you agreed to this," Captain Kleinman shouted when Myles stood to help his friend.

"Fine, fine!" Brendan yelled. He threw his hands in the air to stop the situation from escalating. "I'll go," he said to Kade. Kade stepped aside and let Brendan walk out of the room on his own.

"Now, where were we?" Helen asked when Brendan and Kade left the room.

Ethan raised his hand as Captain Kleinman had done and asked, "May I?"

Helen looked to Captain Kleinman and then back to Ethan before responding, "Please."

"It is coming across as badgering the defendant," Ethan said. "I think we need to give Miss Clark the opportunity to explain."

Helen scowled at Ethan for a brief second before putting on a fake smile. "Of course," she replied. She turned to Ashley, maintaining her phony smile, and said, "Miss Clark, please continue."

"Well...on the raft, it was Spencer who lay next to me, and I only talked to him because he spoke to me first."

"Is that true, Mr. Collins?" Ethan asked Spencer.

"Um," Spencer looked at Madison and then to Helen before replying. "Yes, but…" Spencer started to say.

"Thank you, that's all you needed to confirm," Ethan said, cutting Spencer off. "Go on, Ashley," he said.

"As for the clothes, I only wore what I could find in the room. The sundress I found is actually a size larger than I wear, and I've also been wearing sweatpants to do my chores."

"I can confirm that!" Myles interjected. He stood up and held his hand in the air.

"WHACK!" Helen slammed the spoon on the desk. "You are only a spectator," she scolded Myles.

"Myles, can you confirm any of what Ashley is saying?" Ethan asked.

Helen glared at Ethan and then looked at Captain Kleinman, who only gave a brief shrug of his shoulders.

"Oh yes, I pulled several work shifts with Ashley and can confirm that she has been wearing sweats during work," Myles answered. "Thank you, Ashley, go on," Ethan said.

"As for the night on the couch…" Ashley continued, "I was crying, so Spencer moved next to me on the couch to comfort me."

"That's not what I saw," Madison interrupted.

"I'll let the judge remind you not to speak until it's your turn," Ethan said to Madison.

"Wait your turn," Helen said quickly and then turned back to Ethan.

"Can you tell me, Ashley…" Ethan began, "What were you drinking the night of the party?"

"Uh, I had a couple of beers…and then some drink Madison made," Ashley replied.

"And can you tell me what was in this drink Madison made?" Ethan asked.

"I'm not sure," Ashley answered. "She called it a Madison surprise, and it smelled really strong. I think Spencer said it had about four different kinds of alcohol."

"Thank you," Ethan said to Ashley. "Mrs. Collins, can you tell me why you made a drink for Ashley and your husband, that had four different kinds of alcohol, and then left them alone if you had been so worried about Ashley's previous behavior?"

"I…I uh…I trust my husband," Madison said.

"But wasn't it your husband who initiated the conversation with Ashley on the raft, and the one who initiated the contact on the couch?" Ethan asked.

Madison didn't answer the question and glared at Ethan.

"Is that all, Mr. Advisor?" Helen asked as she tried to move on with the trial.

"Just one more thing," Ethan said. "Kade, the night of the party, I went to the bar to get more drinks and noticed you and Brett had broken into the liquor cabinet."

"Yeah, so," Kade said.

"How much alcohol would you say you drank after you finished the case of beer?" Ethan asked.

"I don't remember," Kade answered.

"But you specifically remember seeing Ashley and Spencer on the couch?" Ethan asked.

"Yes," Kade lied.

"And I thought I saw you urinating off the side of the yacht earlier in the evening. Why would you need to go downstairs to use the bathroom later?" Ethan asked.

"That wasn't me," Kade replied. "That was Brett."

"Oh, so Brett urinated over the side, but you had to go downstairs? Do I have that right?" Ethan asked.

"Yeah, so what?" Kade answered.

"No further questions, your honor," Ethan said to Helen. He then sat back down and crossed his arms over his chest.

"That's my boy," Myles said quietly to himself.

"Is there anything either of you would like to add?" Helen asked while turning back and forth from Madison to Ashley.

"No," both women replied in unison.

"I will now go to my quarters to consider what both of you have said. When I return, I shall give you my verdict. Are there any questions?" she asked. Both women shook their heads.

"All rise," Brett announced when Helen rose from her seat to leave. "We will have a short recess until the judge returns," he continued once Helen had entered the hallway.

The others in the room began to mill around and discuss the case with each other when the captain turned to Ethan. "Nice defense," he said with a wry smile.

"Not at all," Ethan replied. "I just needed to clarify some things in case either side decides to appeal the verdict…as I'm sure you were doing when you asked about Kade witnessing the couch incident."

"Of course," the captain sneered.

Brendan returned to the room when he saw people entering the kitchen to get a drink. He walked straight to his daughter and gave her a tight hug.

233

"You did good, girl," Myles said as he approached the two.

"Thanks," Ashley said. "I was so nervous."

"I'm starting to wonder if this trial is just a formality. It seems like this whole thing was just a setup," Brendan said.

"We've still got Ethan on our side," Myles said. "You should have seen him mop the floor with those weak accusations."

"Yeah, Dad, I think Madison was about to cry when Uncle Ethan was done with her," Ashley said.

The group sat around and discussed what had happened when Brett made an announcement for everyone to take their seats. It had been about an hour since Helen had departed, but the time had flown by quickly.

"All rise," Brett announced as Helen returned to her seat.

"Please be seated," Helen said. She looked around the room and contemplated her words before beginning. "I would like to take a moment to share some thoughts before I announce the verdict," she said. She laid a piece of paper on the table where she had written a few notes. "As you know, this is not a murder case, so the burden of proof I had to decide was not beyond a reasonable doubt, but rather if it was more than likely that the defendant committed the offense."

"I don't like where this is going," Brendan whispered to Myles.

"The other things I had to consider," Helen continued. "Was even if these things did happen, was any rule or law even broken…and if so, what should the punishment be." She paused and looked at both women before her to see if they understood what she was saying. "After listening to both parties, I find that it is more than likely that these events did happen," she said. There was a gasp from somewhere in the room. Helen put her hand in the air and continued when things quieted. "I find it reasonable to assume that there were times in which the defendant and Mr. Collins shared an intimate moment."

Madison turned to Ashley and smirked.

"Now, I am not so sure who initiated the intimacy…and it is fair to consider that Mr. Collins may have been the primary instigator. However, I firmly believe that in these situations it takes two to tango, as the saying goes," Helen said. She continued, "It should be noted that Mr. Collins is not on trial. Therefore, I can only make a ruling on the defendant before me. To that point, I find Miss Ashley Clark to be guilty of the inappropriate behavior of which she is accused."

"What!?" Ashley gasped. She fell silent when Helen glared at her.

"As to whether or not this is even a crime," Helen continued once Ashley had quieted. "I know some of you here in the room are very familiar with infidelity and how damaging it can be." She paused and looked up at Brendan before returning to her notes. "Let me be clear that emotional infidelity is just as bad, if not more so, than the physical kind. This sort of betrayal erodes the trust and respect we need to function as a civilized society, no matter how small it may be. Infidelity is only a crime in a handful of states, but it is a cornerstone of moral standing and, therefore, important to this group. I understand that we do not have a written rule against infidelity, but I believe none of us would argue that something like murder would naturally be against the rules. Murder and infidelity are, after all, two of the ten commandments." She paused and looked around the room before continuing. "I therefore find that a rule has been violated."

A wide grin spread across Madison's face when she realized that Ashley would now be punished for breaking the rules.

"Next is the punishment," Helen continued. "I want to emphasize that I believe Mr. Collins is just as guilty of these crimes and perhaps even more so since he is the older adult."

Spencer covered his face with both hands and hung his head at Helen's announcement.

"However…" Helen went on, "It doesn't alleviate Miss Clark from her responsibility in the matter, and she will therefore be punished for breaking the rules. To begin with, Miss Clark will offer a public apology to Mrs.

Collins for the pain and suffering she has caused. Miss Clark will also serve an additional month of extra duties, which will begin tomorrow. And, she will have no contact, spoken or otherwise, with Mr. Collins for six months unless accompanied by another adult." Helen rose from her seat and looked at Ashley. "Do you understand these punishments?" she asked.

"Yes," Ashley nodded.

"That wasn't so bad," Myles whispered to Brendan.

Brendan was still upset about the whole situation, but had to admit the punishment wasn't so bad. He was looking forward to hugging Ashley and taking her for a walk on the beach when Helen began to speak again.

"Good," Helen said to Ashley. "Lastly, I sentence you to one month's confinement to the box."

"The what!?" Brendan gasped.

Ashley looked back at her father and then at Ethan before returning her attention to Helen. "What is the box?" she asked.

A quick smile crossed Helen's lips before she explained. "The box is the closest thing we have to a jail cell. A place where we confine people who break the rules."

"A jail cell!" Brendan yelled. He rose from his seat and was about to head to the table to confront Helen when Myles restrained him.

"Calm down, calm down…we still have a chance to appeal this. Let's not escalate this until we absolutely have to," Myles said calmly. He wrapped both of his arms around Brendan and held him tightly.

Helen lifted the wooden spoon and prepared to start striking it on the table while Brett stood up from his seat in anticipation of having to constrain Brendan. Brendan glared at Helen and then turned his gaze to Ethan. Ethan only briefly met Brendan's gaze and then looked down at the floor, shaking his head slowly.

"We want an appeal!" Brendan shouted at Helen.

Helen smiled before replying, "Take it up with the council." She turned her attention to Ashley and Madison. "I have made my decision," she said before turning and walking out of the room. She briefly paused halfway across the floor and turned to stare at Brett.

"Oh yeah," Brett said. "All rise for the departure of the judge."

Helen rolled her eyes before turning and leaving the room.

"If I can have your attention," Captain Kleinman addressed the group. He walked to the center of the room and stood on the platform where Helen had just departed. "This was our first attempt at a trial here on the island, and although we need to improve in some areas, I think that it was an overall success."

"A sham is what it was," Brendan shouted from the rear of the room where Myles was still restraining him.

"Yes, well, regardless of whether you liked the outcome or not, you have to admit that Judge Helen provided sound reasoning for her decisions and fairly executed the case," Captain Kleinman said. "Now I know you're going to ask about the appeal, so let's just get that out of the way…would either of you like to appeal the ruling?" he said to Ashley and Madison.

"I would!" Madison blurted.

"YOU!" Ashley exclaimed. "You're the one who won," she added.

Captain Kleinman raised his hand to quiet Ashley before asking, "On what grounds would you like to appeal, Mrs. Collins?"

"I don't think the punishment was severe enough," Madison responded.

"Severe enough!" Ashley cried. She placed her right palm on her forehead and closed her eyes.

"Interesting," Captain Kleinman mumbled before turning to Ashley. "And you, do you wish to appeal?" he asked.

"YES!" Ashley shouted. She didn't wait for Captain Kleinman to ask about what grounds before explaining. "The intimacy Helen referred to is nothing more than compassion, and if compassion is a crime, then everyone here in this room is guilty. Also, if there was any emotional infidelity, it was only on the part of Spencer. I never had any feelings for him other than as a friend, and no evidence given today showed otherwise. If there is anything I might be guilty of, it would be that I was too naive to see the jealousy in her heart!" Ashley pointed directly at Madison when she spoke the last part.

"How dare you!" Madison yelled. "You little tramp," she said and then rushed at Ashley with her arms flailing.

There was a brief commotion as Captain Kleinman grabbed Ashley by the arm and tried stepping between the two women. Acting out of anger, Ashley pushed the small man to the ground and had a handful of Madison's hair in her left hand when Brett lifted her off the ground with one hand.

"Let her go!" Brendan yelled and ran towards his daughter.

"STOP!" Ethan yelled. He stood between Brendan and Brett, holding his hand out towards Brendan. "Let her go," he turned to Brett and said.

The big man returned Ashley to the ground and held his hand out to stop Madison from starting in again.

"Take Ashley and go to your room," Ethan said to Brendan. He then found Spencer still sitting at the rear of the room. "And you," he said, pointing at Spencer. "Take your wife to your room and wait there until the council has decided on your appeal."

"My daughter isn't going in any box!" Brendan shouted and pointed at Captain Kleinman.

"Brendan…" Ethan said as he stepped between Brendan and Captain Kleinman. "You're not helping…please just go to your room," he said quietly to Brendan. He looked at Myles for support.

"He's right, man," Myles said quietly. "Let's go to the room and let Ethan do his thing."

Brendan, Ashley, and Myles went to Brendan's room and waited while Spencer and Madison waited in their room. Ethan, the captain, and Brett went to the captain's room to consider the appeals. It was just over two hours before Brendan heard a knock at the door.

"It's about time!" Brendan exclaimed when he opened the cabin door and saw Ethan.

"Give us the good news," Myles said as Ethan walked into the room and sat in the desk chair across the room.

Ashley and Myles sat on the bed facing Ethan while Brendan stood next to him.

"Well?" Brendan asked once Ethan was seated.

"You need to understand…" Ethan began.

"AW SH-T!" Brendan shouted. He slapped his hands on his thighs, turned around, and started walking towards the door.

"Listen, listen…" Ethan pleaded.

"Ash is not going in some box…period," Brendan said as he turned and pointed at Ethan.

"Would you listen to me for just a minute?" Ethan pleaded.

"Let him talk, Dad," Ashley pleaded with her father.

Ethan continued when Brendan calmed down. "Captain Kleinman is between a rock and a hard place," Ethan said. "He doesn't want to go against Helen's decision, and he has Madison pushing hard for a harsher sentence."

"What is wrong with that woman?" Myles spat.

Ethan shook his head before continuing, "Look, you didn't hear it from me, but I think there was some sort of arrangement made between Madison and the captain before everyone voted for the group leader."

"I knew it," Brendan hissed. He clapped his hands and balled his fists before pointing at Myles and saying, "Right?"

"Well, now Madison is using that as leverage to try and sway the captain," Ethan said.

"So I have to spend a month in the box?" Ashley asked. Her voice quivered, and her eyes began to water as she spoke.

"No...no," Ethan was shaking his head as he spoke.

"I knew you wouldn't let us down!" Myles cheered while leaping off the bed.

"Wait-wait!" Ethan held out his right hand to prevent Myles from hugging him in the chair. "I did the best I could..."

"But?" Brendan asked.

"I could only get him down to three days," Ethan said quietly. "That's not too bad, right?" he asked.

"That's the best you could do?" Brendan glared at Ethan.

"That's a lot," Ethan protested. "You don't understand the pressure he is getting from Madison, Spencer, Helen...even Brett wanted a longer sentence." He held both hands out in front of him as he explained. "He does want something in return, though," he added.

"What?" Brendan asked suspiciously.

"He's worried about another election...that he might lose his leadership position if you run against him in the future..." Ethan clasped his hands as he talked.

"And?" Brendan asked.

"He wants your promise that you will never run against him in the future," Ethan said quietly.

"He can kiss my…" Brendan started to say.

"If you don't agree he's ready to give in to Madison and increase Ashley's sentence to two months," Ethan interrupted.

"That's not fair," Myles growled.

Ethan rose to his feet and turned to Brendan. "Three days isn't that long, it'll be over before you know it," he said. He placed his hand on Brendan's shoulder. "I'm sorry, but it was the best I could do."

Ashley rose from the bed and hugged her father. "Three days isn't so bad." She looked up into Brendan's eyes. "But I don't know if I can do two months."

Brendan hugged his daughter gently. "What is the box anyway?" he asked Ethan.

Ethan looked down at the floor as he answered, "It's a cave…Brett and Kade discovered it while exploring the volcano. They've built a cell door out of wood and found a way to secure it from the outside."

"Damn," Myles breathed.

"You'll be able to visit her every day, and she'll get the same meals we're getting each day," Ethan added.

"I can do it," Ashley said quietly.

Brendan was quiet for several minutes as he contemplated the offer. He hated the idea of Captain Kleinman staying in charge for the foreseeable future, but he hated the thought of Ashley spending two months in a cave even more.

"Are you sure you're okay with this, Ash?" he asked.

Ashley nodded her head while still in her father's embrace.

"Okay," Brendan replied. "I'll do it."

Ethan patted his friend on the back, "I think you're making the right decision." He put his right hand on Ashley's shoulder and squeezed it gently before turning and heading for the door. "I'll let the captain know," he said as he left the room.

"Can you believe that guy?" Myles asked about the captain. "We're talking about putting a sixteen-year-old kid in a cave for two months, and all that man cares about is making sure he stays in power." Myles shook his head as he walked towards the door. "I'll see you two tomorrow," he said as he opened the door. "And don't worry, Ash, we're going to be there with you and make sure you're okay in that cave."

Brendan closed his eyes and rested his chin on his daughter's head. He heard Myles' footsteps echo in the hall and then the sound of him opening and closing the door to his room. "He's right, we'll be there as much as we can...now let's find a bag so we can pack some things you'll need while you're gone."

The two spent the next thirty minutes packing items into a large beach tote bag they found in one of the dresser drawers. The tote was beige with large horizontal green stripes and had two twisted rope handles.

"You should probably go with long pants," Brendan said when Ashley laid a pair of shorts on the bed. "The cave probably won't be as nice as this yacht," he explained.

Ashley found a pair of sweats and two pairs of jeans and put them in the bag with a few t-shirts that she had packed earlier. Brendan went to the bathroom to get ready for the night and found Ashley already in bed by the time he returned. "It's going to be alright," he whispered and turned off his light next to the bed. He had only just closed his eyes when he heard a door slam in the hall, followed by another door slamming seconds later. He then heard the muffled sound of yelling coming from one of the rooms.

"She always gets her way," Madison shouted. "It's not fair!" The shouting was followed by heavy stomping and something being thrown to the floor.

Brendan guessed that the other door was likely slammed by Helen after learning Ashley's sentence would be reduced.

PART III

The Journal of Walter Tobias

The next morning, Brendan lay in bed and watched his daughter sleep. He decided to spend as much time with her before she was taken to the box. She had tossed and turned most of the night, and he thought it must have been around three in the morning before she finally fell asleep.

"Ugh," Ashley groaned. She opened one eye and turned her head towards her father's side of the bed. "Tell me yesterday was all just a bad nightmare," she said when she saw her father staring back at her.

"Sorry, kitten," Brendan replied and then ruffled her hair.

Ashley yawned and stretched across the bed. "I'm guessing they're not going to let me come back here for showers," she grumbled.

Brendan smiled. "Ask Uncle Myles to tell you about the time we decided to join JROTC in the ninth grade and spent a week in the woods with no bathrooms."

"Eww, I don't think I want to know," Ashley groaned.

"Come on," Brendan said, rising out of bed. "I'll make you an omelet and toast this morning."

"Great, my last meal."

Ashley rolled out of bed and followed her father to the kitchen. She wore a pair of beige flannel pants and a long blue nightshirt that read "Let Me Sleep" on the front. Brendan was wearing a cut-off pair of gray sweatpants and a black t-shirt. The two walked into the kitchen and were greeted by Myles and Ethan, who sat at the kitchen table sipping coffee.

"Morning," Myles called when he saw Brendan and Ashley enter the kitchen.

"Early bird gets the worm," Ethan said and raised his coffee mug in a toast.

Ashley retrieved a bottle of orange juice from the refrigerator and poured a glass before joining Myles and Ethan at the table. "Worms are gross," she said when she sat in her seat.

Ethan took a sip of coffee and then turned to face Ashley. "It's not really about getting a worm," he explained. "It's about getting up in the morning to get an advantage over others who sleep in."

Ashley stared at Ethan over the rim of her cup for a moment before responding, "Mornings are gross."

Ethan furrowed his brow. "I don't think you're understanding the idiom," he said.

"I don't think you're understanding the teenage sarcasm," Myles laughed.

"Omelets, anyone?" Brendan called from his position in front of the stove. A carton of eggs lay on the counter next to a freshly cut tomato and a half-frozen package of sliced ham. Brendan held a medium-sized skillet in his right hand and swirled the melting butter around in the pan.

"I'll take one," answered Myles.

"Ethan?" Brendan asked when he didn't hear his friend respond.

Ethan finished the last of his coffee and then set the mug on the table and stood from his chair. "No thanks," he said. "I need to get a couple of things done before noon."

"What's going on at noon?" Brendan asked.

"Oh, sorry, forgot to tell you…" Ethan paused and glanced at Ashley before turning back to Brendan. "That's when we're…uh…taking Ashley…to, you know."

"This reminds me of when we took Cookie to the vet to be put to sleep," Ashley said.

"I plan on going, will that be okay?" Brendan asked. "I don't want to break any rules that no one knows about," he said sarcastically.

"I'm going too," Myles added after finishing a gulp of coffee.

"I'm sure it'll be fine," Ethan replied. "I'll let the captain know," he said and then exited the kitchen through the hallway leading to the center stairs.

"Did you hear the shouting last night?" Myles asked when Brendan brought the omelets to the table.

Brendan raised his eyebrows and nodded his head while drinking from his coffee.

"Ethan said Helen's face was so red he thought her head was going to pop." The two men chuckled and then began discussing the conversation Ethan had shared with Myles before Brendan and Ashley came upstairs.

"I'm going downstairs to take a shower," Ashley said after taking a couple of bites from her omelet. She twirled the orange juice in her cup and took a sip before getting up from the table. "Sorry, I just don't have much of an appetite right now," she explained.

Brendan placed his hand on her arm. "It's okay, honey," he said. "It'll be over soon."

Ashley walked across the room and stopped before entering the hallway. She turned back to her father and said, "A long, hot shower."

"I understand," Brendan replied. He and Myles finished their breakfast before going back downstairs to get ready for the day.

It was noon when everyone assembled in the living room and waited for Captain Kleinman to address the group. Ashley was escorted into the room by Kade and carried the green-striped beach tote in her left hand.

"Miss Clark," Captain Kleinman said when Ashley arrived. "You will now be escorted to the box where you will spend the next three days. Do you have the supplies you will need during that time?" he asked.

Ashley looked down at the bag she carried and nodded her head. Her knees felt weak, and she had an overwhelming desire to turn and run. She closed her eyes and focused on standing straight.

"You got this," Myles said from behind Ashley.

"Take her away," Captain Kleinman ordered.

Kade stepped forward and grabbed Ashley by the arm. "This way," he said. He led Ashley onto the rear deck and towards the hanging ladder on the side of the yacht. Brett, Ethan, Brendan, and Myles followed them.

Kade led the group along the beach and then turned north into the tree line, where a narrow dirt trail cut through the trees. The winding path twisted and turned among the palms and pigeon pea shrubs. The volcano loomed in the distance and appeared to grow taller the longer they walked.

"There," Kade shouted and pointed to the base of the volcano where the trees thinned and gave way to a series of large rocks around the volcano's base.

A thin worn trail angled upwards around the volcano and then cut back sharply as the path continued up the slope. The criss-cross pattern allowed for a gentle rise in elevation but made the trip much longer to navigate. Halfway up the volcano, the trail climbed steeply and turned towards the far side of the hill, casting a shadow over the entire trail. A combination of wooden and stone steps was constructed on the trail to assist climbers in maintaining their footing on the steep incline.

"Looks like we're not the first to find this cave," Brendan called back to Ethan and Myles behind him.

Ethan paused and studied the steps. "They've been here a long time," he called back up to Brendan.

"How long?" Myles asked.

Ethan studied the steps again and ran his right hand through his hair. "Hard to say," he said. "The wood looks like it's been carved with sharpened stone. Hundreds of years, maybe," he added.

As the climbers turned the last bend, they could see the cave up ahead in the distance. The trail narrowed and wound up towards the cave entrance, forming a narrow ledge the last fifty yards before reaching the cave. The cave was nestled in a crevasse and featured a wide platform at its entrance. The narrow ledge continued to the right of the cave and ended another one hundred yards up the volcano, where the first volcano met the second.

"Are we sure this is safe?" Brendan asked as they approached the narrow ledge.

Kade took the lead and stepped onto the ledge. "Just walk slowly and keep your back to the mountain."

Brendan took Ashley's hand and the two stepped onto the ledge. Brendan peered over the side of the ledge and then quickly backed away, placing his back against the volcano wall. He guessed the ledge must be at least 250 feet above the forest floor, but it was impossible to see the bottom since the dark shadows covered the ground in total darkness. Brendan held Ashley's hand tightly as the two slid along the ledge. Halfway across, Brendan could make out the dark outline of the large dark hole in the second volcano. It was the same hole he remembered seeing from the raft as they approached the island. The dark hole was even darker than the deep shadows cast over the crevasse where the two volcanoes merged.

Brendan paused, staring into the darkness. He would swear the island's low, droning noise intensified as they moved towards the hole. He took another step and then froze in place. He had the intense sensation that he was forgetting something…something about that hole. A memory of observing the hole from a different spot emerged just on the tip of his consciousness. He couldn't pinpoint the place; it was somewhere further away but shrouded in haziness.

"Hey, keep moving!" Kade shouted from further up the ledge.

Brendan looked at Kade and then back at the dark hole. He shook his head as if shaking off a bad dream and continued sliding towards the cave.

"Are you alright, Dad?" Ashley asked. She stared at her father with a puzzled look and added, "You look like you've seen a ghost."

"I'm fine," Brendan replied. He turned his head to face his daughter and smiled. "I just…never mind," he said and turned back to the trail in front of him.

Brendan and Ashley side-stepped slowly until they reached the large platform with Kade, then waited for the others. Myles, Ethan, and then Brett joined them on the platform, where Brett and Kade unlocked the wooden door to the cave. The cave entrance was about eight feet tall and broader at the bottom than at the top. The cave was three feet wide at the base and tapered to a point eight feet up. The wooden door was only about seven feet tall, but the small gap at the top was too narrow for even a small child to fit through. The vertical bars of the gate were made from small palm trees and tied to the horizontal pigeon pea branches with a thick grassy fiber where the two pieces of wood came together. The gate was sturdy and anchored to two thick palm trees on either side of the cave entrance.

"Home sweet home," Kade said as he held the gate open for Ashley to step inside. "Who's the comedian now?" he said quietly to Brendan as Brendan approached the entrance.

"Two minutes and then we're locking the gate," Brett announced.

Ashley walked into the cave, followed by Brendan, Myles, and then Ethan. The inside of the cave was dark, as the gray volcanic rock appeared to suck in the daylight. The cave floor was a combination of rock and sand, approximately fifteen feet wide. The ceiling varied in places from as high as ten feet in the front to as low as four feet at the rear of the cave. A single mattress had been brought from the yacht and placed against the far wall, accompanied by a set of white sheets and a blue and green comforter. A wooden chair was placed next to the mattress.

"Please tell me that's not the toilet," Ashley said. She pointed at a large blue bucket with a white recycling symbol on its side.

"Hope you brought toilet paper," Kade laughed. "Otherwise, there are a few palm leaves in the corner." Brett joined the laughter and slapped his friend on the back.

Ashley placed her beach tote on the mattress and sorted through the items she had brought, while Brendan, Myles, and Ethan continued to study the cave.

"Times up," Brett called. He held the gate open, indicating it was time for the three men to leave.

"Only three days," Brendan said. He kissed Ashley on the forehead and left the cave.

Myles clenched his fist and held it out to Ashley for a fist bump and said, "Too easy," once Ashley had punched his fist.

Ethan hugged Ashley and then slipped something into the left pocket of her sweatpants. "Found them in the library," he said of the shareable-sized bag of M&Ms. He joined Brendan and Myles just outside the gate and waited as Brett secured the door with a small lock and chain from the yacht.

"We're going to stay awhile," Brendan said to Brett and Kade after they locked the gate.

"Don't miss curfew," Kade warned.

"And don't forget you still have chores that need to be done before bed," Brett added.

The two large men stepped onto the ledge and made their way slowly back to the trail.

"Don't slip," Myles called to the two men when they were halfway across. Kade lifted his left hand and gave Myles the middle finger.

Ashley carried the wooden chair from the rear of the cave and placed it next to the gate. "Guess this would be a good time to hear that story about JROTC," she said.

"The one where your Uncle Ethan passed out on the field during the homecoming ceremony?" Myles asked.

"No," Ashley replied. "The one where there were no bathrooms for a week," she said, shaking her head. "But I guess we have time for both," she added.

"Oh my God!" Myles threw his head back and laughed. "I totally forgot about that...your dad was soooo embarrassed," he said, drawing out the word so.

Brendan turned to Ethan while Myles told Ashley the story. "Hey, I was going to ask you something," he said to Ethan.

"Yeah?" Ethan replied.

"Did you notice the dark hole across the ravine?" He continued when Ethan nodded. "Do you think that humming noise we are hearing could be coming from there?"

Ethan walked to the edge of the wide platform and stared across the ravine. "Yeah, I suppose."

"What do you think could be causing it?"

Ethan thought for a moment before responding. "It could be an indication the volcano is still active." He continued when Brendan didn't say anything and simply continued to stare at him. "The inside of the volcano is probably hollow, with a layer of rock across the bottom. If there is still flowing lava underneath, it is likely causing the rock layer to shift."

"That would cause the noise?" Brendan asked skeptically.

"Sure," Ethan replied flatly. "The rock would be constantly grinding against itself, and the empty volcano caldron would amplify that noise…not to mention these high rock walls," he added while pointing to the area where the two volcanoes came together.

The two men continued to stare at the volcanoes for a moment before Ethan asked, "Why do you ask?"

"I don't know, there is just something about that hole that…" he was saying when he heard Ashley yell from across the platform.

"Eww, dad!"

Myles had his right hand on his stomach and was bent over in laughter.

Brendan and Ethan returned to the cave and watched Myles continue to laugh before Brendan spoke. "You didn't tell her all the gory details, did you?" he asked. Myles nodded his head as he continued to laugh.

The three men spent the next couple of hours with Ashley before noticing the sun was setting lower on the horizon, sending the cave area into a darker shadow.

"I'm sorry, but it looks like it's about time for us to head back," Brendan said.

"Thanks for staying and keeping me company," Ashley replied.

"We'll be back tomorrow morning with breakfast," Ethan said.

"Wait until I tell you the story about what happened after we got back home," Myles added.

"The poor girl isn't going to eat her breakfast!" Ethan laughed and shook his head at Myles.

Brendan, Myles, and Ethan made their way across the ledge and then back along the trail, arriving at the yacht just before sunset.

"Meet you for dinner after I get the laundry started," Myles called and then went downstairs to start his chores.

"Save me a plate," Ethan said. He followed Myles downstairs and went to his room to clean up.

Brendan walked into the kitchen and prepared three plates of the baked chicken and roasted vegetables Dwayne had prepared for the evening meal. He carried the plates through the living area where Helen sat by herself eating dinner, and then onto the rear deck. He set the plates on the outside table and returned to the kitchen for flatware.

"How is the little princess liking her new accommodations?" Helen sneered when Brendan re-entered the living area.

Brendan paused in the middle of the room and glared at Helen. Helen returned the glare and then smirked.

"If you have a problem with me, you can take it up with me…leave my daughter out of it," Brendan said.

"You have clean-up today, don't you?" Helen asked. She lifted her glass and emptied its contents onto the table, watching as the ice and red liquid flowed across the surface and then spilled onto the floor below. She rose from the table and pushed her plate of leftovers off the table. The silverware made a metallic clank when they hit the plate and bounced across the floor.

"You gotta let that hatred go, Helen, it's going to eat at you until you're consumed by it," Brendan said while shaking his head.

Helen walked past him as she crossed the room to return to her cabin. She stopped in the doorway and turned her head to look back at Brendan. "This isn't over," she said. "Not by a long shot." She walked into the hallway and then disappeared down the stairs.

Myles passed Helen on the stairs and stopped in the living room, observing the mess around the table. "What happened?" he asked.

Brendan looked at Myles and simply shook his head. "Foods out back," he said, and the two men walked onto the rear deck and sat at the small outside table. Ethan joined the two after five minutes and carried three cans of beer from the bar. The men ate dinner while Brendan filled the other two in on what had transpired with Helen in the living room.

Myles was the first to finish his dinner and said, "I need to get back to the laundry," before rising from his seat and heading towards the living room. "Oh, and I put your book in your room," he called back over his shoulder as he passed through the back door and into the yacht.

Brendan and Ethan looked at each other for a moment. "Why does everyone keep taking my books? Ethan asked.

"Since when does he read?" Brendan asked. "The last time he bought anything to read was when we were still using fantasy football magazines to draft our teams."

Brendan and Ethan stayed on the rear deck and drank another beer before calling it a night and heading back to their rooms. Brendan opened his cabin door and immediately missed Ashley. He wished he could take her place and hoped the comforter was enough to keep her warm in the cool, dank cave. He changed into his nightshirt and shorts and then was about to pull back the blanket when he saw a small leather-bound book on his pillow. His first thought was that Myles had accidentally put Ethan's book in his room. He placed the book on the nightstand and then stared at it. There was something familiar about the book. He got into bed and then reached for the book, turning it over in his hands as he ran his fingers over the soft leather cover.

"Where have I seen you before?" he asked himself.

Brendan opened the book's cover. *W. Tobias* was handwritten in large cursive letters on the first page. Aside from the name, the page was blank.

He flipped to the next page and continued to read. The same handwriting from the first page appeared on the next page and read:

WARNING: Your life and very soul are in danger. If this is the first time you are reading this journal, heed this warning:

- If you are currently on the barren, lifeless side of the island, keep reading.

- If you are on the island's lush green side, STOP READING. Go immediately to the barren rocky coast and continue reading once your mind is clear.

READ NO MORE; You must heed this warning

A rocky coast came to Brendan's memory along with some sort of stone structure built on the beach. He tried to focus on the memories, but only a brief series of images crossed his mind. He saw an old Spanish sword, a large cross painted on a rock with the word sanctuary written underneath, and then a wide-open rock plateau that dropped into the ocean. He recalled walking along the plateau to a large, stone-carved cross at its edge. Something told him not to look over the edge. He was afraid of something at the bottom of the cliff. "Somebody is dead down there," he thought. "Who?" Could it be…dad? No! He didn't want to look, didn't want to know what was down there. His memory continued to the edge of the plateau, and he peered down.

"Dad!" He yelled. His stomach churned, and he had a sensation of falling.

No…it wasn't his dad. It was…a graveyard. So many crosses and headstones. What was this place? Who is buried down there? The memories came like a flood and washed over him like a giant wave crashing on the coast. He remembered crossing to the other side of the island, the alcove where people lived, the bridge crossing the river, and…the journal he had found and placed in his shorts. He closed the journal and studied again as if seeing it for the first time.

"Jesus," Brendan whispered.

"What is going on?" he thought. "How did I forget about the other side?" He recalled the events that occurred after crossing the bridge and realized that during the drama of Ashley's trial, he had completely forgotten about what he had found across the river.

Brendan opened the journal and reread the name. "Who are you, Mister Tobias?" he asked himself. He turned the page and re-read the warning. He couldn't explain why, but he believed the message and knew he needed to stop reading until he made it back to the other side. "But when? How?" he thought to himself. "Would Myles come along knowing they were already on the captain's bad side? Is it even fair to put Myles in that position?" He laid the journal back on the nightstand and stared at the ceiling. He tried to sleep, but the words from the journal kept coming to mind…your life is in danger, go to the other side.

"Once your mind is clear," Brendan said as his eyes shot open. "Now, while everyone is asleep," he whispered.

Brendan got out of bed and removed his sleep clothes. He retrieved the jeans and t-shirt he had worn earlier from the pile of clothes in the corner of the room, where he kept his dirty laundry. He tied the new hiking shoes and then slowly opened the door. He listened for a moment before deciding the coast was clear and making his way to the central stairs. He paused once again before entering the kitchen and then crept to the side of the yacht with the hanging stairs. It briefly crossed his mind that he shouldn't be doing this…that Helen would throw the book at him if he were caught.

"I have to know," he thought, and then gently climbed down from the yacht. He paused and listened to the gentle lapping waves, trying to discern if anyone had seen or heard his escape.

He chose to walk on the loose, uneven sand to avoid splashing in the water and made his way to the trail on the far side of the alcove. He walked briskly up the sloping grass-clumped clearing and then back into the thick island forest before turning to the right in the direction of the river. He was happy he had stopped at the clear water pool and forced himself to remember the trail that led to the river and the makeshift bridge. The dark outline of the large tree trunk stood in stark contrast to the river flowing underneath and the light stone on the other side. Brendan glanced up and was pleased that the moon and stars shone brightly on this night. He searched the sky for the constellations Ethan had pointed out when they were on the raft, but was unable to identify any. In fact, the entire constellation of stars overhead was like nothing he had ever seen before. He made a mental note to ask Ethan about it when he saw him next.

"Whoa," Brendan exclaimed when he was halfway across the bridge. The sudden cessation of the low, droning hum took him by surprise. He found it odd that after a while, you no longer realize the humming is there…until it's gone.

He sat on the first large boulder he came to on the barren trail and opened the leather-bound journal. He illuminated a small pocket flashlight he found on the yacht and then looked around to see if anyone had seen the sudden flash of light. When he was satisfied that no one had seen the light, he opened to the journal's third page. The page was a bit water-damaged, but still readable. He continued to read:

Travel Journal: Walter Tobias

Page 1

12 August 1929 - Today, we set sail from Charleston to La Rochelle, France. Lilly is worried that Tommie and Margaret may become seasick on the Transatlantic voyage. The cabin is splendid. The RMS Empress of Scotland is one of the finest steamships I have ever seen, and we will make the transatlantic voyage in seven days.

13 August – At breakfast, Lilly met a young mother from Toronto, and they spent the afternoon playing deck tennis with the woman and her children. I think that I would enjoy an afternoon of Bridge while Lilly and the kids are occupied. We are excited to learn of the captain's dinner tomorrow night.

14 August – A pod of whales was spotted crossing the ship's bow just before lunch. The animals are so large and majestic when seen in their natural habitat. The captain's dinner was marvelous. Lilly was beautiful in her long gray skirt and white blouse. The long bow around her neck matched her hair clip perfectly. We will not likely have a fine dinner like that again until our return trip. We dined with Father Benedict, a Priest on his return trip to the Vatican. Father Benedict gives a morning sermon in the ship's chapel each day after breakfast.

Page 2

15 Au...

The entire second page was completely damaged by water, leaving it barely readable. Brendan was able to gather a few minor details about the lunch menu, someone getting seasick, a "fancy dress" ball that turned out to be a costume party, and a beautiful evening under the stars with champagne.

Page 3

17 August – The fog has gotten thicker. You can barely see the two steam stacks from the front deck. The sea has become much more turbulent, and we have been advised against resting on the ship's outer rails. The nighttime is the worst…the large waves seem to rise out of the dark night and come crashing against the port windows. We can see lightning in the distance and know we are approaching a storm.

18 August – We are lost. The ship has lost all power during the night, and we are at the mercy of the sea. The ship lists with each wave, throwing furniture across the deck. We have been confined to our cabins until help arrives. I am sure this ship cannot stay afloat in these conditions. God save us.

20? August – We have come aground on some island after several days adrift. I'm not sure how long we've been at sea. The captain and a few crew members are taking a lifeboat to explore the island. Father Benedict has been very comforting during this time.

21 August – I am unsure of the exact date. The captain has returned with good news. Other people inhabit the island, and there is fresh water and food on the island. We have begun evacuating the ship. There is a large hole where the ship came ashore, and the ship is sinking.

Page 4

Day 1 – Our first day on the island. I do not know the date. My ankle was broken when jumping from the lifeboat onto the rocky coast. Tommie and Margaret are sick with a fever. There is no doctor. This part of the island is bleak and lifeless. Several people have crossed to the other side of the island, where it is beautiful and lush...like Eden. I hope to visit Eden soon and leave this God-forsaken side of the island.

Day 3 – Something is wrong. Those who travel to Eden do not return as promised. Margaret has passed away, and Tommie's condition continues to worsen. Lilly has offered to travel to Eden to bring back fresh food and water. Father Benedict has been a godsend, caring for the sick and injured. We continue to pray for rescue every day.

Day 5 – A handful of survivors remain on the rocky, barren coast. Lilly has not returned. The RMS Empress of Scotland has disappeared...perhaps it has sunk below the waters? We must find food and water before we all die. Where are the others? Why do they not return and bring us to Eden?

Day 6 – Tommie has passed. We found a place just across the rock plateau to bury the dead. I have made a cross and carried it down to a small sand beach where Tommie and Margaret are now laid to rest. Where is Lilly? We have taken refuge in a hollow alcove...it appears others were here long before us.

Day 8 – Lilly has returned! She tells of a crazed society of survivors living in Eden. The captain and crew are alive but refuse to return to the rocky beach. The leader of Eden has placed this side of the island off limits, claiming it is cursed. There are survivors in Eden who Lilly says have been there for years. Are we cursed?

Brendan flipped the page and discovered that the following several pages were unreadable due to the water damage. Pages 5 and 6 were stuck together and began to tear when he tried to pull them apart.

"Snap." The sound of wood snapping came from the other side of the river.

Brendan shined the flashlight in the direction the sound had come and looked for any movement. The flashlight illuminated the lush trees and bushes on the other side, scaring a small animal from a nearby tree. Several small orbs glowed when the light passed over them, but nothing moved. The eyes of the woodland creatures watched and waited for Brendan to leave their home.

"Probably just an animal," Brendan said quietly. He shined the light back on the journal and continued reading:

Page 8

Day 11 – I was right! It is not this side of the island that is cursed; it is Eden! Something on the other side of the island lulls you into complacency, makes you forget about trying to escape the island. Once you cross into Eden, the complacency effect starts to take place in 30 to 45 minutes. By one hour, the mind has completely forgotten, and the person is lulled into complacency by the abundance of riches on the other side. What is this place?

Day 13 – We have learned that it is possible to break the spell of complacency, but only with the deepest, most shocking of memories...like the death of a loved one, or the strong sense of love for a lost child. These profound memories cut through the fog of complacency and slowly restore one's memory. Once restored, the complacency effect takes hold again unless intervened by another memory. We may yet escape this island.

Day 14 – We have tried several methods to counter the effects of Eden. We have sent men into Eden in pairs to remind each other, we have tied a rope to a man and then attempted to pull him back after 45 minutes, and we have even burned a man's arms so that he might never forget the pain and the memory of us on the other side. Some attempts were successful, but we have lost too many men to keep experimenting. I wish my ankle were better.

Day 16 – The people on the other side of the river have begun to set traps to try to capture us when we cross the river. Once caught, they hold you until the complacency takes over, and you then become part of them. They are devolving, becoming almost animal-like in their most basic human vices. They are angry and hateful, having overindulged in the abundance of Eden.

Day 19 – We are too few, and there is no hope left. Rescue is not coming. We are in Hell, and there is no way out. This will be my last journal entry. I leave this journal here in the alcove in the hope that it may help others shipwrecked on this island. I must ensure they understand the caution I have added to the beginning of the journal. Eden is cursed. I leave you with the words of Father Benedict's last sermon;

Brendan turned the page to read the sermon, but the page had been torn from the book. He closed the journal and took a deep breath before releasing it in a loud sigh.

"Can this be real?" he said quietly. "Maybe this is just some elaborate story by someone previously shipwrecked on the island," he thought. No, too much of it makes sense.

Brendan checked his watch and then looked overhead where clouds now covered much of the sky. He contemplated how long it would take to return to the yacht. On the one hand, it was only about half a mile, but on the other, it was dark, and he wasn't all that familiar with the route. He decided he would take the chance. He knew he needed to keep the memory of the journal on his mind until he got back to his room, where he could write himself some sort of note to keep the memory from fading. The Garmin watch beeped twice as he changed the watch's function to timer. He stepped lightly on the tree trunk and held his arms out wide to his sides to help keep his balance. He started the timer when he was halfway across the bridge and heard the low humming return. As he returned his arms out wide for balance, the toe of his shoe caught on a groove in the bridge, causing him to stumble forward.

"Splash." Brendan released the journal as his arms flailed, trying to keep himself balanced on the bridge. The journal splashed into the river and was gone before he could regain his footing. "No!" he hissed. He turned on the flashlight long enough to scan the water and then turned it back off when he didn't see any sign of the journal. The digital numbers continued to race on the timer, and he knew he didn't have time to stop and look for the book. The occasional tree branch appeared out of the darkness on the trail, causing him to stumble as he hurried back down the trail.

An accidental left turn on the trail wasted ten minutes, but he was still making good time and thought it wouldn't be a problem making it to his room with time to spare. He tripped three times in the open area with the grassy clumps but was soon on the final leg of his journey. He paused briefly in the tree line before the beach and studied the area around the yacht. He needed to make sure no early risers were taking a stroll on the beach. He was just about to dart into the open when he saw a slight movement on the yacht.

"Sh-t," he breathed when he saw the dark silhouette move back and forth on the front deck.

He checked his watch; 47 minutes read the timer as the seconds raced by, unreadable. He didn't have time to waste. It was still another five minutes across the beach and then two to three minutes until he was on the yacht and down the stairs to his room. If he were caught, he would most likely end up in the box, where he was sure to forget everything he learned tonight.

A familiar whistle and humming came from the yacht, and Brendan was sure it was Dwayne who was on the front deck. "Would Dwayne turn me in?" he wondered. He had to chance it.

Brendan sprinted into the open and darted for the yacht. He was focused on keeping his balance in the loose sand but was also very aware that Dwayne had stopped whistling and had moved to the side of the yacht to watch his return. He paused briefly on the top step to check the timer before jumping onto the deck and sprinting through the kitchen and down the steps to his room. With only minutes remaining, he didn't have the time to try to plead with Dwayne not to turn him in. The cabin door swung open as he ran to the desk and opened several drawers before finding a pen and paper. Just under one minute remained...what to write? He scribbled something before wadding up the paper and throwing it in the corner. He thought for a second and began writing frantically.

Shocking Memories

The morning sun cast shadows across the cabin and sent sunrays bouncing off the mirror on the other side of the room. Brendan groaned and held his hand over his eyes to block the sunlight before rolling over to check the time.

"Already?" he moaned. He sat up in bed and tried to recall the events from the previous night. A vague memory of reading a book came to mind, but he couldn't remember anything past that. He glanced at the nightstand where he thought he had placed the book and was surprised to see only a single sheet of paper instead. The jagged edge of the paper showed that it had been aggressively torn from the notepad sitting across the room on the desk. He lifted the page and recognized his handwriting.

"Was I drinking?" he thought when he saw the sloppy penmanship written hastily across the paper.

He read the message.

Read the following message slowly and repeat it five times.

Julia is in danger and needs your help. You must escape the island.

Brendan

"What kind of sick joke is this?" he thought. A flicker of a memory flashed in the back of his mind. Julia. He felt lightheaded and warm when he was suddenly interrupted by a knock at the door.

"Hey, you up yet?" came the familiar voice of Myles from the other side of the door.

"Yeah, be up in a minute after I shower," Brendan called back. He folded the paper and set it back on the nightstand, then checked the time and rushed to the shower.

With the bathroom door locked, Brendan removed his clothes and turned on the shower. He ran his towel over the mirror and stared at the reflection as the water warmed. "What is that?" he asked himself when his reflection showed black markings on his stomach. He stared down and noticed three-inch letters written in a black permanent marker. The letters on his chest were a message he had apparently left for himself. It read: Read the paper.

He ran back to his cabin and retrieved the paper from the nightstand. After staring at the message for a minute, he followed the directions and read the message slowly.

"Julia is in danger and needs your help. You must escape the island...Julia is in danger and needs your help. You must escape the island..." he read the message five times. Julia...the memory of seeing his wife in the airport after a long separation came to his mind. He sat on the bed when his knees became weak, and the memories flooded back.

"It worked," Brendan whispered. He dropped the paper to the ground and quickly dressed, knowing that he didn't have much time.

The cabin door swung open and slammed behind him as Brendan made his way up the stairs and into the kitchen.

"Look what…" Myles started.

"Where's Ethan!" Brendan shouted. He continued when Myles looked at him in shock, "Sorry, I just need to find Ethan."

"Library," Myles said quietly. He pointed to the front staircase that led one level down to the ship's lower deck. "Everything okay?" he asked and then stared after Brendan as he darted across the kitchen floor and across the front deck.

The library door was closed when Brendan reached the second deck. He twisted the small silver latch and pushed the door open. The ship's library was a large room with floor-to-ceiling bookshelves on three walls and an electric fireplace on the fourth. A large oil painting of a ship sailing into a thunderstorm hung over the fireplace, and a wooden coffee table with a glass top was placed in front of the fireplace. There was a small, plush couch and two high-backed armchairs on either side of it. The wood in the library was made of a dark colored walnut. Music played softly from two recessed speakers placed above the couch.

Ethan sat in one of the high-backed chairs, holding a book in one hand and a cup of coffee in the other. His right leg was crossed over his left knee, and his foot swayed to the rhythm of My Girl by the Temptations. "There you are," he said when Brendan entered the room. "I've been looking for you."

"What?"

"I came by your room to see if you wanted to go with me to take Ashley breakfast."

"Ashley? Oh my…how is she?" Brendan asked. He had totally forgotten about Ashley being in the cave.

"She's…" Ethan started to answer.

"Wait!" Brendan interrupted. He threw out his right hand to stop Ethan from continuing. "Before we get to that, there is something I need to ask you."

The urgency in Brendan's voice took Ethan aback, and he froze with his coffee cup halfway to his lips.

"I've been forgetting things lately..." Brendan started to explain.

Ethan raised his eyebrows and returned his cup to the coffee table.

"I was wondering if you had any way to help me remember?"

Ethan continued to stare at his friend with a puzzled look on his face. "That's more important than hearing about how your daughter's doing?" he asked.

Brendan sat on the couch next to Ethan before responding, "Sorry, I just don't want to get distracted and forget."

"I really don't understand people," Ethan exclaimed and set the book he was reading on his lap.

"Please, it's important." Brendan leaned forward on the couch and waited.

Ethan eyed his friend skeptically, "Are you feeling okay?" he asked.

"I'm fine, I just feel like I can't remember things lately."

Ethan reached for his coffee cup and held the drink in both hands before replying, "You're probably just tired and need a little rest."

Brendan sat upright and shook his head. "No, I don't think that's it."

"There are many studies that show mental decline due to a lack of sleep. Some studies suggest that lack of sleep can have a greater impact than alcohol..." Ethan began to explain the studies. He paused and then started wagging his index finger. "You know, it's probably all this stuff going on with Ashley," he explained. "All this worrying has probably affected your sleep."

"No...stop! that's not it," Brendan said as he rose from the couch. "Aside from sleep, what else can I do to help myself remember?" He paced in front of the coffee table and checked his watch repeatedly.

"How about just setting your alarm?" Ethan stated flatly.

Brendan lifted his arm and stared at his watch. He was lost in thought for a moment before speaking, "I don't know...I need a constant reminder, something like tying a string around my finger that makes me remember."

"That's more of an old wives' tale than a scientific theory," Ethan said skeptically. "It could be effective for short-term memory recall, but over time, you're going to become used to having it there and then forget why you put it there in the first place."

"There has to be some way..." Brendan continued to pace.

"Classical conditioning might work," Ethan said to himself while strumming his fingers on his lips.

"What was that?" Brendan asked.

"Oh," Ethan exclaimed after realizing he had spoken out loud. "I said classical conditioning might help you remember whatever it is you're trying to remember."

"Right...what's that?" Brendan asked.

"Classical conditioning...you remember studying Ivan Pavlov's theory."

Brendan stared at Ethan and shook his head slowly.

"Pavlov's dog?" Ethan asked.

"Oh yeah, something about the dogs getting hungry when they heard a bell?" Brendan asked.

"Erm, not exactly," Ethan replied, looking at Brendan over the rim of his glasses. He pushed the glasses higher on his nose and continued, "Dr. Pavlov was studying the digestive system in dogs and discovered the dogs would salivate at the sound of the dinner bell, even when he didn't serve them any food. The dogs associated the sound of the bell with eating and therefore became conditioned to salivate when they heard the bell."

"I see…" Brendan said slowly. "And how exactly does this help me?" he asked.

"Whatever it is you are trying to remember," Ethan started to explain. "You just need to associate that memory with a sound or particular word…something like that."

"So, think of the thing I want to remember, and then play the alarm? That's it?"

Ethan shrugged. "In theory. The dogs associated the bell with food, which is a basic survival need…and they were conditioned over several weeks. But I suppose you could try to associate whatever you're trying to remember with a strong emotion…and after a while it should stick. Is there something you want to tell me?" he asked.

Brendan glanced at his watch again. "I don't have a while," he said under his breath. It was worth a try, though, right? "I need to get going," he said suddenly.

"Wait," Ethan called as Brendan turned to leave. "Don't you want to hear about Ashley?" he asked.

Brendan didn't bother turning to answer. He was already out of the library door when he replied, "I'll catch up with you later!"

"Nope, I'm never going to understand," Ethan said to himself as he returned to his book.

Brendan hurried back to his cabin and fumbled with his watch once he was seated at the desk. He pressed the small center button on the left and scrolled through the watch menu. Alerts…notifications…Alarm, there. "Set alarm," he said to himself as he began scrolling through the alarm features. Time, one hour. Reset, Automatic. When the duration was set, the option for alarm notification popped up.

"I'm going to draw a lot of attention if my watch is going off every hour," he said to himself. He continued to scroll through the options until…there! He set the alarm notification for vibrate and held the watch against his wrist to test it.

"Bzzzzttt – Bzzzzttt," The vibration felt like ants crawling on his skin. He adjusted the intensity to "high" and tried again. "BZZZZTTT – BZZZZTTT!" This time, it felt more like a minor shock. "Kind of like placing your tongue on the positive and negative contacts of a 9-volt battery at the same time," he thought.

Now he needed a strong emotional event to associate with the alarm. His first thought was to use the plane crash and the loss of Julia, as he had done with the message he had left himself the night before. "No, that was something I came up with on short notice…and it didn't seem all that effective unless I read it five times slowly," he thought. He needed something with a stronger emotional response. "I need your help, Julia," he said while staring at his wedding ring.

"No," he whispered. His thoughts went to the night Julia had told him about sleeping with her boss. The fight ensued, which led her to stay with her mother. He felt his heart sink to the pit of his stomach, and he knew that was the memory that he needed to tie to the alarm.

"I have something I need to tell you." He remembered Julia saying while he worked at the computer in the home office. He remembered being annoyed when he was interrupted while working. "I'm sorry," Julia said. She hung her head and sobbed. "I love you and I want to be honest with you…"

Brendan remembered sitting silently, not knowing what his wife was talking about. Why was she crying?

"I don't know how else to say it…I…slept…with Eric," Julia whispered.

Brendan felt the room spinning. He tried to hold onto the office chair, but the whole world seemed to be falling.

"I'm so sorry," was all he remembered Julia saying.

Brendan felt like throwing up just hearing the man's name, Eric. He held the watch against his arm and repeated Julia's words, "I slept with Eric." He repeated the phrase over and over again. Each time, feeling the shocking notification on his wrist.

"I slept with Eric." Bzzzzttt! "I slept with Eric." Bzzzzttt. "I slept with Eric." Bzzzzttt.

He repeated the process until tears ran down his face and his stomach was in knots. He strapped the watch to his wrist and set the alarm. "Not sure I really want this to work, but here goes nothing," he said, and then left his cabin to find Myles.

The smell of bacon cooking on the stove made Brendan realize he hadn't had anything to eat since yesterday's dinner. When he arrived at the kitchen, he saw Spencer spreading mayonnaise on toast. A plate of leftover fruit was sitting on the kitchen table, and Brendan decided to have an apple instead of asking Spencer about the bacon.

"There you are," Myles called from the front deck. He waved for Brendan to come outside and then waited by the kitchen door. "You gotta see this," he said when Brendan stepped through the door. Myles led Brendan to the side deck and then pointed at someone standing on the rear deck, talking to Kade.

"Is that…Madison?" Brendan asked.

Madison was wearing the yellow and white sundress that Ashley had previously worn, and her hair was dyed blonde. It was also recently cut, and she wore it tied back in a short ponytail.

"Remind you of anyone?" Myles asked.

"She looks like Ashley," Brendan replied while shaking his head.

"There is something seriously wrong with that girl," Myles said.

"Speaking of Ashley," Brendan said. "Do you want to come with me to see her?"

"Of course," Myles answered. "I was actually afraid you had gone without me when I couldn't find you earlier."

"Oh, I slept in and then had to go see Ethan about something," Brendan replied.

"Is everything okay?" Myles asked.

"It's fine," Brendan said as he turned and walked to the hanging stairs.

The two men were about to climb down from the yacht when they heard Ethan calling from the front deck.

"Brendan! Hold up," Ethan shouted. He ran to the side deck to meet his friends by the hanging stairs.

"Want to come with us to go see Ash?" Myles asked when Ethan stopped and stood in front of Brendan. Ethan shook his head.

"What's up?" Brendan asked.

Ethan looked at Myles and then back to Brendan before asking, "Why were you so tired this morning?" He explained when Brendan gave him a puzzled look. "I mean, you didn't even answer the door when I knocked."

Brendan shrugged his shoulders and replied, "Just tired, I guess…like you said, from not being able to sleep."

Ethan stared at his friend for a moment before speaking, "So you didn't go anywhere early this morning?" he asked.

There was an awkward moment of silence before Myles spoke up. "What's this about?"

Ethan continued to stare at Brendan and didn't acknowledge Myles' question. "And?" he asked Brendan.

"No," Brendan replied. He looked Ethan in the eyes and shook his head.

"What's going on, Ethan? Why all the questions?" Myles asked.

Ethan turned to Myles. "There's a rumor that someone saw Brendan out early this morning...by himself."

Myles looked at Brendan and then back to Ethan. "So? He just told you it wasn't him."

"The captain thinks you probably went to see Ashley last night and tried to make it back before anyone was up," Ethan said, turning back to Brendan.

Brendan continued to shake his head. "Nope," he said. "I didn't go see Ashley."

Ethan didn't respond and simply continued staring at Brendan.

"You can ask her yourself, you know she wouldn't lie to you," Brendan said.

"You'd know anyway," Myles added. "Her neck gets all splotchy red when she lies."

"You know it's against the rules to go out past curfew...and to go alone," Ethan replied. "No one would blame you for being worried about your daughter," he added.

"So you're here to interrogate me and report back to the captain so they can put me on trial and lock me up with Ash?" Brendan asked. He didn't appreciate being questioned by his friend, and his anger was apparent in his tone.

Ethan was quiet for a moment. "I'm trying to help you," he said in frustration. "I'm your friend, and if you haven't noticed, you don't have many of those left around here."

"Are you?" Brendan asked. "Every time I see you lately, it's the captain this and the captain that."

Myles looked nervously back and forth between his two friends.

"You've had a chip on your shoulder about the captain ever since you met him," Ethan said. "It's almost like you're trying to get into trouble so you can have some sort of showdown with the man."

"Maybe that's what we need to help everyone see the man is a self-centered fraud who only cares about himself," Brendan spat.

Ethan shook his head. "Just remember that you're not just hurting yourself. Others are going to get hurt in your little turf war." He looked at Myles and then turned and walked away.

"Let's go," Brendan said to Myles. The two climbed down from the yacht and walked in silence across the beach to the far tree line.

"What were you doing out this morning?" Myles asked once they had made their way into the thick trees.

Brendan shuffled his feet in the sand and considered continuing to deny that it was him. He stopped on the sandy trail and hung his head. "How did you know?" he asked quietly.

"Hrmmph," Myles smirked. "I've known you for a long time, Brendan Clark. I know you almost better than I know myself."

Brendan nodded in agreement. "There's something I need to talk to you about."

"Okay, out with it," Myles said.

Brendan was about to start telling Myles about the journal when he was distracted by a shocking vibration on his arm. He grimaced when an image of Julia came to his memory. "I slept with Eric," he recalled her saying, and then the memory passed, and he lifted his watch to check the time. One hour. It worked. Myles stared at his friend, wondering what was going on, when Brendan suddenly smiled and took off along the trail.

"What just happened?" Myles asked as he hurried to catch up with Brendan.

"I'll tell you after we see Ashley," Brendan called back to his friend. "I want to show you something also," he added.

"Now I'm really worried," Myles replied.

The two men continued up the trail, walking in silence as their breathing grew heavier due to the rising altitude. They reached the narrow ledge and crossed slowly with their backs against the volcano wall. Brendan paused when he was halfway across and stared at the dark hole across the ravine. "What are you hiding?" he asked himself quietly.

"You talking to me?" Myles asked.

Brendan glanced back at his friend. "No, just taking a break," he said before continuing across the ledge.

"Dad!" Ashley called when she saw her father.

"How ya doing kiddo?" Myles asked as he and Brendan approached the gate.

"Better," Ashley answered. "Something was creeping around up here last night…Uncle Ethan thinks it was probably just a squirrel or possum smelling the dinner from last night," she added when she saw the worried look on her father's face. "He brought me some books and a flashlight," she smiled and held up a book she was reading.

The three sat and talked for the next couple of hours. Myles told Ashley about Madison changing her hair and how they thought she was trying to look like Ashley. That led to a conversation about the trial and speculation that Madison must be a very insecure person.

"It could mean she doesn't trust Spencer," Myles offered. "Maybe he's done something in the past that makes her not trust him around other women."

"Could be," Brendan agreed. "Or maybe she's just an envious and jealous person."

The conversation turned to Spencer and then to the others on the yacht before ending with all of them agreeing Dwayne was perhaps the biggest enigma of them all.

Brendan checked his watch and frowned. "Sorry, kitten, we have to get back early today," he said.

"We do?" Myles asked.

"Yeah, I don't want to get into any more trouble if I don't finish my chores," Brendan groaned. Myles nodded his head. "True," he agreed.

"Last day tomorrow!" Brendan said when he kissed his daughter goodbye.

"I'm so ready for my own bed!" Ashley replied.

"We'll see you in the morning with breakfast, and then we can have a celebration once we get back," Myles said.

"No alcohol this time," Brendan laughed. Ashley smiled and then waved as the two men crossed the narrow ledge and disappeared back down the trail.

"We're not really going back early to do chores, are we?" Myles asked when Brendan turned left at a fork in the trail that led towards the river.

"I told you I wanted to show you something," Brendan replied. He searched the area for the trail that led to the freshwater pool as he walked. "Hey," he called to Myles, who was following on the trail behind him. "Do you remember Pavlov's dog from school?" he asked.

Myles was silent for a moment as he walked, trying to recall the name. "Oh yeah, the German kid who lived down the road with that giant rottweiler," he finally answered.

"Who?" Brendan called from up ahead on the trail.

"You remember…in the sixth grade when you jumped over the kid's fence to get our ball back and got attacked by the crazy rottweiler," Myles explained.

Brendan stopped walking and turned back to face Myles. "No! I'm not talking about Pascal Schumacher and his crazy dog...I'm talking about the Russian scientist who discovered the theory of classical conditioning!"

Myles continued walking until he had caught up to Brendan. "I don't know about a Russian scientist, but I remember you had a scar on your behind for three years where that dog took a bite out of your butt!" Myles laughed. "You remember you told everyone you got the scar from playing football."

"Ugh," Brendan groaned. He turned around and continued walking for another five minutes before reaching the clearwater pool.

"Nice," Myles exclaimed when he saw the pool of water. "Is this what you wanted to show me?" he asked.

"Have a seat," Brendan pointed to a large rock at the edge of the water. He continued when Myles was seated, "I want to tell you about a dream I had."

"Is it the one where your dad is flying through the air in his orange car?" Myles asked.

Brendan smiled. "No, this one is about a fishing trip," he said.

Myles clapped his hands together and rubbed them back and forth. "Whoo, I love a good fishing story," he said.

"I had a dream I went fishing with my dad..." Brendan started but then paused when Myles interrupted.

"I thought your dad didn't like fishing?"

Brendan continued, "It was just a dream. Anyway, we were riding in an old Volkswagen van when we came to a river with a deep ravine...the banks of the river were steep, and there was an old railroad track that crossed the ravine from one bank to the other. It was one of those railroad tracks like you see in old movies..."

"Wait," Myles said. He shook his head and was quiet for a moment. "Have you told me this one before?" he asked.

"No," Brendan replied and then continued telling the story. "I was so happy to be fishing that I took off across the tracks. When I was halfway across, it occurred to me that my dad might have difficulty keeping his balance on the tracks. When I looked back…"

"He fell," Myles whispered. "Dad…no," he added a moment later.

Brendan watched his friend as his memories began to return. Tears formed in Myles' eyes, and he placed his hands on his head as if he had a massive headache. "What are you doing?" he asked Brendan. "Why would you bring up that memory?"

Brendan placed his hand on his friend's shoulder. "Let that pain guide you. Your memory is trying to awaken from a long sleep."

Myles began rocking back and forth with his hands over his face. He stopped after several minutes and took a deep breath. "What happened?" he asked after placing his hands back down to his side.

"We've been on the island for two weeks," Brendan said calmly.

Myles shook his head. "That's not possible."

"I need to tell you something that you're going to find hard to believe," Brendan said.

Myles looked up at his friend. "Harder to believe than we've been here for two weeks?"

Brendan knew his friend was trying to process a lot of difficult information. "Maybe I should show you something first." Brendan led Myles a short distance up the trail until they came to the felled tree trunk crossing the river.

"I don't know…" Myles hesitated when he saw the bridge. "We're not supposed to cross over."

Brendan nodded. "I know, but you'll find it easier to accept what I have to tell you if you see for yourself what's on the other side."

Myles continued to look skeptically at Brendan. "You know they're looking for any excuse to lock you away."

"I know," Brendan acknowledged. "But if there is any chance of making it off this island, it's going to be by understanding what's over there." He pointed to the other side of the bridge.

Myles took a deep breath and nodded. "Let's do it," he said. He stepped onto the bridge and followed Brendan to the other side.

"Do you feel it?" Brendan asked once they had both crossed over the bridge.

Myles closed his eyes for several seconds and then opened them, looking around. "It feels…strange…I can't put my finger on it, but something feels different."

"That constant hum you've heard since we arrived on the island is gone," Brendan said.

Myles closed his eyes again and listened to the sound of the island all around him. He heard the rushing water of the river, the wind blowing in the trees, a distant bird call, and the far-off sound of waves crashing against the rocks. "You're right," he said softly. "It's like I can think clearly," he added.

"Exactly," Brendan replied. "Look," Brendan said, pointing to the old wooden sign by the bridge.

Myles walked over to the sign and read it, "Keep Out," he read out loud. "Makes sense," he said, turning back to Brendan. "This side is supposed to be dangerous."

"So why put the sign on this side of the river?" Brendan asked. "If you were trying to keep people out of this side, wouldn't you put the sign on the other side, before they crossed to this side?"

Myles read the sign again and then looked back over to the other side of the river. "Maybe a storm or something blew it across? I mean, why would you want people to avoid the side of the island with all the food and water? That doesn't make any sense."

"No, it doesn't," Brendan agreed. "Follow me," he said and led Myles through the narrow crevasse and onto the large rock plateau. They crossed the plateau and then scaled the rocks to the rocky beach below.

"This place seems so dead," Myles said, studying the rocky coast. "I'm not sure what it is you wanted me to see here." After another five minutes of walking, Myles began to notice the broken pottery and other debris from people previously shipwrecked on the island. When they finally arrived at the hidden alcove, Myles let out a long whistle. "Looks like we found where everyone's been living."

"Don't you think that's odd?" Brendan asked.

Myles studied the alcove before turning to Brendan. "Not really, this place seems to provide good protection from the elements."

"But why this side? If you were going to set up camp, wouldn't you want to be on the side with the food and water?"

Myles looked around the alcove as he pondered the question. He kicked at the rusting sword lying on the ground. "Maybe they lived here before the other side had trees and all."

"Even the guy with the New York Yankees cap?" Brendan asked. He pointed to the almost new baseball cap lying in the corner of the alcove.

"I don't know," Myles shrugged. "Is this what you wanted to show me? A baseball cap and a bunch of old garbage."

"You tell me where the same old garbage exists on the other side of the island? Where is there any sign of people having actually lived anywhere over there?" Brendan argued.

"What is it you're trying to say?" Myles asked.

Brendan paused and looked around the alcove. Even he wasn't entirely convinced of what he was trying to say. "I...found a journal, in one of the rooms, the last time I was here," he said.

"Okay?" Myles replied.

Brendan wasn't sure he wanted to continue. "It was a journal of someone who was shipwrecked here a long time ago. He wrote..." he paused and considered how his words were going to sound to Myles.

"He wrote...what?" Myles asked.

"He wrote...that the other side of the island is cursed," Brendan blurted and then crossed his arms defensively over his chest.

Myles looked at Brendan and then around the room before returning to Brendan. "Cursed," he said skeptically.

"Yes," Brendan answered. "He said that there was something about the other side that made people forget about trying to escape the island. He said that once you crossed the river, you would only have an hour before you fell under the island's curse."

"Is that so?" Myles nodded.

"Yes, he called it complacency," Brendan answered.

Myles approached Brendan slowly, his face filled with concern. "And you believe this?" he asked.

Brendan stood defiantly. "I do."

"Can I read this journal?" Myles asked. "Maybe you just misinterpreted it."

Brendan's posture deflated, his body loosened, and he unfolded his arms. "I lost it," he said. His head hung for just a second before adding, "I know, I know...this doesn't look good, but I promise you I read it."

"I don't know, Brendan," Myles almost pleaded. "You know how this sounds, right?" he asked.

"How do you explain it? Why are there no signs of life on the other side? Why have we been on this island for two weeks and haven't lifted a finger to try and get off?"

"I want to believe you, I really do," Myles answered. He paced around the alcove for a minute before returning to Brendan. "Tell me…if you become…complacent…" he said, trying to remember the word Brendan had used, "once you cross the river, then how did you remember how to get back?"

"Pavlov's dog," Brendan said matter-of-factly. "Not the German kid," he added when he saw Myles about to ask about the rottweiler.

He spent the next twenty minutes explaining how the journal had described a way to recall your memories once you had become complacent. He described how he had written himself a note and how that almost didn't work if he hadn't also written the note on his stomach. He pulled up his shirt and showed Myles the fading traces of the black permanent marker. He went on to describe his conversation with Ethan and how he had successfully conditioned his memory to respond to the vibration of his watch alarm.

Myles' mouth hung open as he listened, and he even tried to read the writing on Brendan's stomach when he told him about the mirror. "So that's why you were out early this morning," he said to Brendan when he learned about the note.

Brendan nodded. "I think Dwayne saw me when I returned to the boat."

They were both quiet for a minute while Myles absorbed the information. "Okay, suppose everything you said is true," Myles said.

"It is," Brendan interrupted.

"Right…so what do we do about it?" Myles asked.

"I've been thinking about that," Brendan answered. "We haven't made any real attempts to get off the island, right?" he asked. "We haven't made an S.O.S, we haven't built a bonfire, and I don't think Ethan's really put his mind to trying to fix the boat or the radio." Myles was nodding his head in agreement as Brendan spoke. "I think the first thing we need to do is try to condition your memory...like I did with mine." Brendan paused to gauge Myles's response.

"I guess it couldn't hurt." Myles' reply sounded unenthusiastic. Brendan didn't think he was completely convinced, but it was a good start.

"Then..." Brendan continued, "We get Ethan on board." Myles was still nodding in agreement. "Then we make a serious attempt to get off this island...we build the bonfire, see if Ethan can fix the radio...whatever else we can think of," Brendan explained.

"What about the others?" Myles asked. "Shouldn't we try to get everyone's memory conditioned...or whatever you called it?"

"It's not a bad idea," Brendan agreed. "But let's take this one step at a time." He checked the time before adding, "We'd better get going, the others will start to wonder where we are."

The two men crossed the rocky beach and made their way onto the rock plateau. The afternoon sun had heated the rocks, making it feel like they were crossing the desert until they reached the shaded crevasse. Myles wiped his hand across his brow when he stepped into the shade. "When do I do the watch thing?" he asked, referring to the conditioning process with his memory.

"Up ahead," Brendan answered. "There's a spot to rest right before crossing the river." He began following the trail back to the river, and Myles followed behind.

"Here," Brendan said when they reached the river. He pointed to a large rock where Myles could rest and try to condition his memory. "Let me see your watch," he said to Myles and then proceeded to set the alarm to its highest intensity. He returned the watch to Myles, saying, "You need to think of an intense memory and then push the alarm button. After repeating the process several times, the alarm should trigger the memory and prevent you from becoming complacent."

Myles looked skeptical as he retrieved his watch and strapped it to his left wrist. "An intense memory? Like the dream with my father?" Myles asked.

"Sure," Brendan replied. "Or any other painful memories you think might be more intense. I'll let you have some privacy," Brendan said, recalling his own experience with remembering the painful memory of Julia cheating. "Meet you at the pond!" he called to Myles as he turned and crossed the bridge to the other side.

Myles closed his eyes and tried to think of his most painful memory. The dream was certainly an intense memory, but so was the phone call he received from his mother the day his dad had passed away. There was the painful memory when he learned he would never play football again and when the school rescinded his scholarship. Shanice had had a miscarriage…that was devastating news after the excitement of becoming a father.

"I guess I could try any one of those," Myles said to himself. He placed his right hand on his watch and was about to start the process when another memory came to mind. "No…" he whispered. He didn't even want to think about it. He had repressed the memory in order to deal with the pain it caused. A tear rolled down his cheek, and he looked down at his right hand. He could vividly remember the weight of the gun as he held it up to his head. He remembered crying because he felt scared to pull the trigger and end his life. "Do it!" he had screamed at himself for being a coward. As much as he hated it, this was the memory that he needed to use. He placed his hand over the watch and closed his eyes, saying, "Do it," and then pressed the alarm.

"Do it!" BZZZZTTT! "Do it!" BZZZZTTT! "Do it!" BZZZZTTT! "Do it!" BZZZZTTT!

He repeated the process over and over. He was unaware of how many times he pressed the alarm or how much time he had spent in the process.

He finally stopped when he was shaking and couldn't stand to dwell on the memory any longer. His whole body felt heavy as he rose from the rock and made his way back to the freshwater pond. The humming returned as soon as he was halfway across the bridge, and he almost lost his balance when he shook his head, forcibly trying to clear his mind. Brendan leapt off the large rock by the water when he saw his friend turn the bend in the trail. He saw his friend's bloodshot eyes and the faraway look that told him Myles had spent time remembering a memory he'd rather forget.

"You okay?" Brendan asked when Myles approached the pool. Myles didn't respond but simply nodded his head.

They walked back down the trail, only saying a few words to each other along the way. "How will I know if it worked?" Myles asked.

Brendan barely heard him ask the question from ahead on the trail. He slowed his pace and then answered when Myles was closer, "You won't notice that the complacency has started to set in," he started to explain. "But, in an hour, when you feel the alarm, your memories will come rushing back, and you'll get that sensation you felt when you crossed the bridge. It's kind of like a fog is lifted."

They were leaving the forested part of the island when Myles stopped and peered down the hill across the clumped-grass clearing. He held his right hand up to shield his eyes from the sun and pointed down the hill with his left. "See 'em?" he asked.

Brendan followed Myles' finger to the bottom of the clearing, where the outline of two large men stood out against the beach. "What do they want?" He asked. The question was rhetorical; he knew Myles had no idea why Brett and Kade were waiting at the bottom of the clearing.

"Whatever it is, it can't be good." Myles shrugged and continued across the clearing.

Brendan and Myles slowed their pace when they were about ten feet from the two men. Both wore oversized dark aviator sunglasses and a white tank top that stretched over their broad chests. Brett wore a camouflaged pair of cut-off shorts, while Kade wore a thin, red pair of stretchy nylon swim trunks. Both also wore a black pair of hiking shoes that Brendan thought looked more like combat boots.

"I guess they missed us and sent out the welcoming party," Brendan joked as they approached the two men. He stopped only a few feet from Brett when Brett stepped in the middle of the trail and crossed his arms. Kade joined him and placed his hands on his hips.

"Where've you been?" Brett asked Brendan when he had come to a stop. Myles stopped just behind Brendan's left shoulder.

Brendan thought about replying with the *NUNYA* joke again, but figured it wasn't worth the effort. "Just went for a walk," he replied. He continued when the two large men didn't respond. "That's not against the rules now, is it?"

The two men continued to stare at Brendan, making him wonder if they knew he was lying and had somehow seen him and Myles cross to the other side. Kade finally broke the silence, "The captain wants a word with you."

Brendan shrugged and curled his lips while turning to face Myles. "Guess the captain knows where to find me," he said as he turned back to face Brett and Kade. His head had barely returned to face forward when he felt a massive fist smash into the right side of his face.

The big man moved with such surprising speed and agility that Brendan's brain barely had time to register what had just happened. He saw stars in his eyes and felt warm blood spurt into his mouth as he fell backwards onto the ground. The entire right side of his face was numb from the hit, and he was still wondering what had happened when he saw Myles kneel beside him.

"What the f-ck is wrong with you!" Myles shouted at Brett.

Brett stood over Brendan and crossed his arms back over his chest. "We're tired of your sh-t," he replied. "And your goofy friend isn't here to save you."

Kade took a step forward. "Let me put this another way," he said. "We're taking you to see the captain. We can do it the easy way, or we can do it the hard way." He looked down at Brendan and smiled. "Personally, I'm hoping you choose the hard way," he added.

Myles clenched his fist and considered his options. He didn't think Brendan would be much help for another few minutes and wondered how long he would last against the two larger men. He was considering punching Kade in his skimpy nylon swim trunks when he felt Brendan's hand grab his arm. Brendan was slowly shaking his head when Myles turned to look at him.

"Smart move," Brett sneered.

Myles helped Brendan to his feet and held onto him as Brendan regained his bearings.

"After you, ladies," Kade said and stepped aside to let Myles and Brendan pass.

Myles placed Brendan's right arm around his shoulder and supported Brendan as the two slowly made their way down the trail. Brett and Kade followed only a few feet behind to ensure the two men didn't decide to take a detour. When they reached the ladder, Myles went behind Brendan to make sure he didn't fall.

"I barely hit him," Brett laughed.

Spencer and Madison were on the front deck, watching Brendan struggle to board the yacht. A wry smile crossed Madison's lips when she saw the large red welt on the side of Brendan's face.

"The captains in the main living area," Kade directed Brendan.

Brendan exchanged a worried glance with Myles and wondered if he was about to leave the frying pan and enter the fire.

Under Suspicion

Captain Kleinman sat at the head of the dining table and swirled a honey-colored liquid in a heavy glass tumbler in his right hand. An overfilled plate of cooked meats and vegetables sat in front of the captain, and he had a large white cloth napkin tucked into the front of his shirt as he ate. Helen and Ethan sat in twin armchairs behind the captain. Captain Kleinman pulled the napkin from his shirt and placed it on the table when Brendan and Myles entered the room.

"Thank you for coming to see me," he said with false gratitude.

Brendan walked to the table and then stood with his arms folded over his chest. "I wasn't aware I had a choice," he said and returned the captain's fake smile. The right side of his face appeared to be swollen, making it look as if he was trying to squint.

"Yes, well…" Captain Kleinman shrugged. "You really shouldn't antagonize them," he said, turning to Brett and Kade, who were standing by the door.

Brendan rolled his eyes. "Was there something you wanted?" he asked.

"Please have a seat," Captain Kleinman said and gestured to the chair on the other side of the table.

Brendan looked across the table at the chair Captain Kleinman pointed at and then back to Captain Kleinman.

"Please," Captain Kleinman said again. He kept his hand outstretched, pointing at the chair, and his fake smile broadened even more.

Brendan moved slowly to the opposite side of the table and sat in the chair. Myles followed but remained standing behind his friend.

"Can I offer you something to eat? Drink?" Captain Kleinman asked. He held up his glass of whiskey when offering the drink.

"I'm assuming you didn't go through all this trouble to invite me to lunch," Brendan replied.

"There's no reason we can't..." Captain Kleinman started to reply.

"Spit it out or we're leaving," Brendan interrupted. "Goons or not," he added, and then turned towards Brett and Kade. The two big men stepped towards the table but stopped when the captain held out his hand.

"Well trained," Myles said. The two men glared at him and then turned to the captain as if to say, "See."

"Fine," Captain Kleinman said to Brendan. "Right to the point...I like that. Where'd you go this morning?" he asked. He placed his glass on the table and his eyes narrowed, waiting for Brendan's reply.

Brendan glanced at Helen sitting behind Captain Kleinman before responding, "Am I on trial? Is that what this is?"

"No," Captain Kleinman replied. He sat back in his chair and continued to stare at Brendan. "Not yet anyway," he added. "Being out by yourself after curfew is against the rules, though."

"And who is saying I was out by myself past curfew?" Brendan asked. He quickly glanced around the room, hoping Dwayne wasn't waiting somewhere to turn him in.

"So you deny being out early this morning? Maybe to go see your daughter?" Captain Kleinman asked.

Brendan glanced over at Ethan, sitting next to Helen. "I've already answered that question," he said, returning his gaze to the captain.

Captain Kleinman turned around in his chair to look at Ethan. When he turned back to face Brendan, he replied, "Your friend is only trying to help you, Brendan. "May I call you Brendan?" he asked.

Brendan turned to face Ethan again and ignored the captain's question. "Was it my friend who was asking? Or your advisor?" he asked while continuing to look at Ethan. Ethan pursed his lips and slowly shook his head in silence.

"What about this afternoon?" The captain asked. "Where were you before coming here?"

Brendan returned his attention to the captain. "We went to see my daughter," he answered.

Brett stepped forward. "We checked there first," he said to the captain. He turned to face Brendan before continuing, "We found them coming down from the forest trail that leads to the river."

Captain Kleinman raised his eyebrows. "And?" he asked Brendan.

"We were checking out a freshwater pool we found," Myles said before Brendan could respond.

Brendan looked back at his friend and then turned back to face the captain. "We went to see Ashley and decided we would have a little party when she gets out tomorrow. We thought the pond would be a good setting for a pool party and decided to check it out before heading back to the yacht."

"We went up there and didn't see them," Kade said as he stepped forward to address the captain. "There is a bridge that crosses the river just past the pond," he added.

Brendan shrugged his shoulders and shook his head while looking back at Myles. "Is there?" he asked. Myles also shrugged and shook his head in reply.

"Crossing to the other side of the island is also against the rules," Captain Kleinman said.

"Why would we want to go to the other side of the island?" Brendan asked. "There's nothing over there and…"

"Stop," the captain interrupted and held out his right hand. He looked back and forth between Myles and Brendan before continuing. "I can't prove that you went to see your daughter this morning, and quite frankly, I don't believe a word about the pool party…so you can stop with all that nonsense." Brendan was about to respond when the captain held up his hand further and stopped him. "What have you been up to? What's your game, hmmm?" he asked.

"Our game?" Myles asked. "What about your game?" He glanced at Brett and Kade to make sure they weren't going to try to stop him from speaking. Captain Kleinman turned his attention to Myles and clasped his hands in front of him, waiting for Myles to continue. "You were elected to be in charge of this group, and you haven't lifted a finger to do anything to help us off this island. Do you even know how many days we've been here already? Thirteen!"

Everyone in the room fell silent, and the captain appeared confused as he lifted his watch to check the date. Brendan heard Kade whisper, "can't be," and realized Myles was going to try to bring the whole group out of their fog. "Remember our chores when we arrived on the island?" Brendan asked the captain. He looked around the room and watched the others wrestling with their memories. "After the plane crash, all we could think about was being rescued."

Myles saw the dazed look on the others' faces and pressed even harder. "We were going to build a bonfire, make a large S.O.S. on the beach…" he stopped mid-sentence when Helen stood from her chair and interrupted.

"Liars!" Shouted Helen. She walked over to the table and stood beside the captain. "Don't listen to them…" she pointed her index finger back and forth between Brendan and Myles. "They're trying to confuse you so that they can take over and make rules that favor their own little clique."

Brendan watched the confusion fade from the captain's face and knew that the complacency had set back in. In only a few short seconds, the captain's demeanor went from confused to complacent to angry. "That's ridiculous!" Brendan argued. He slapped both hands on the table and shook his head.

"It's not," Helen retorted. "I heard them earlier this morning when they thought they were alone. He…" she pointed to Brendan, "said he was intentionally making trouble so that he could have a showdown with you…to get you out of the way."

Captain Kleinman's eyes narrowed. His face was flushed and his brow furrowed when he turned to Brendan and hissed, "I knew it."

Brendan shook his head and wagged his index finger at Helen. "That is not what I said."

"It is!" Helen shouted. She turned and pointed at Ethan. "Ask him," she said to Captain Kleinman.

Captain Kleinman turned in his chair to look at Ethan sitting behind him. Ethan looked back and forth between Captain Kleinman and Brendan before answering, "Yes…he did…but…" Ethan stammered. Myles stared at Ethan and shook his head slowly from side to side.

"SEE!" Helen turned to Captain Kleinman and shouted. Captain Kleinman's lips curled in a snarl as he returned his attention to Brendan.

Brendan rubbed his hand across his forehead and squeezed his eyes before responding, "It wasn't like that…that conversation is being way misrepresented."

Helen continued when she saw Brendan trying to backtrack from his comments. "He said you were self-centered and only cared about yourself!"

Brendan clenched his teeth in anger and felt his rage take control. He jumped out of his chair and pointed at Helen. "You miserable B-tch!" he yelled. "You're so filled with rage and hate because of what happened on the raft...if your son was even a halfway decent father, he wouldn't have left his son with you to take care of, and I wouldn't have had to do what I did!"

Helen's eyes were wide with shock, and her mouth hung open as she listened to Brendan. "How dare you!" she breathed. "You're one to talk...that little daughter of yours is locked up because she's a cheating whore like her mother!"

"You miserable..." Brendan shouted and charged at Helen.

"ARRGHH!" Helen screeched and lunged at Brendan.

The two met in the middle of the table, where the melee intensified. Brendan held Helen by the collar as she kicked and clawed at him with everything she had. He was about to pin her to the table when he felt arms grab him around the waist and neck. He struggled but couldn't free himself from the firm grip.

"ENOUGH!" Captain Kleinman yelled.

Brendan released his grip on Helen and was pulled back to his chair by Myles. Helen was dragged by Kade from her position next to the table back to her seat behind the captain.

"Everyone out!" Captain Kleinman yelled. He pointed his finger at Brett and Kade and then turned to look at Helen and Ethan. "Out!" he repeated. The four hurried out of the living area, and Captain Kleinman turned to Brendan and Myles. "I'd like to speak with you in private," he said across the table to Brendan.

Brendan turned to Myles. "Can you give us a minute?" he asked. Myles looked at Brendan and then at Captain Kleinman before turning and leaving the room.

Captain Kleinman sat in his chair and glared across the table at Brendan. "Let's cut the sh-t, shall we," he said. He continued when Brendan didn't respond. "What is it that you want?" he demanded. Brendan looked confused and remained silent. "Oh, come on," Captain Kleinman continued. "Everybody wants something."

"You think you can buy me?" Brendan spat. He couldn't believe what he was hearing.

"I help get you what you want, and you help me get what I want. That's how the game's played," Captain Kleinman growled.

"I see," Brendan said. "And what did Madison want? And Helen?" Brendan asked. He now understood how Captain Kleinman had manipulated the others to get their votes.

"Come on," Captain Kleinman replied. "You know exactly what they wanted."

"So you get Madison's vote and Ashley gets locked up in a cage." Brendan felt his rage returning.

"Oh, please," Captain Kleinman scoffed. "It was only three days. You want revenge? I can help you get it." A sly grin spread across his face.

"You're sick," Brendan muttered.

"Don't look down your nose at me!" Captain Kleinman barked. "They might be petty, but at least they were honest. Everybody has their price, and you're no better than any of them."

"I don't need anything from you," Brendan sneered.

Captain Kleinman's eyes narrowed. "You will, trust me, you will. One day you're going to slip up…tomorrow, next week, next month maybe…and when you do, I'm going to be there to make you pay."

Brendan leaned forward in his chair. "Is that a threat?" he demanded.

"Yes," Captain Kleinman shot back. "And you'd be wise to heed it." He slid his chair back and swallowed the last of his whiskey before rising from his seat and leaving the room.

Brendan watched him go and contemplated his threat. He knew Captain Kleinman was right about slipping up. It was only a matter of time before they trumped up some charge to punish him for. It all felt very helpless. He placed his hands over his face and thought about giving in to the captain when his alarm buzzed.

"Bzzzzttt!"

He glanced at his watch. "What do I do, Julia?" he asked himself. He leaned back in the chair and watched the sun set through the yacht's rear window. Sunlight shimmered on the blue water, and for just a moment, it looked like the sun was setting into a pool of fire.

"And?" a voice called from the doorway.

Brendan turned away from the fiery scene to see Myles re-enter the living area carrying a plate in one hand and two cans of beer in the other. Myles set the plate on the table and turned to face the rear of the cabin to see what it was that had captured his friend's attention. "Kind of makes you wonder how a place so beautiful can be so wicked," he said. He turned to Brendan and offered him one of the beers he carried in his hand. "What did Captain Kangaroo want?" he asked as he took a seat at the table.

Brendan shook his head, "I'm not even sure. I seriously think the man has lost his mind…he's convinced that everything I do is some sort of plot to overthrow him. He's obsessed with his own delusion."

"You think it has something to do with the island?" Myles asked.

Brendan shrugged and sat back in his chair. He popped the lid of the beer and took a long drink before saying, "He's going to be watching us…they all are. They're looking for any excuse to put us on trial."

"Hmmph," Myles nodded in agreement. "Do we need to lay low for a while? Maybe give it some time to blow over before we start our rescue efforts?" he asked.

"I don't know," Brendan replied. "Time's not on our side. I think it's only a matter of time before we slip up and end up in trouble or somehow forget again."

Myles turned his wrist and stared at his watch when he felt the alarm. "It feels like I'm going through Hell all over again," he whispered as he recalled the memory of his attempted suicide. He looked from the watch on his left hand to the imaginary gun in his right.

Brendan saw the pain in his friend's face and wished he didn't know what he was thinking about. "I think we're going to need some help," he said. "Someone who can be a lookout and provide information on what's going on here at the yacht while we're on the other side."

"Are we still going to try to get Ethan to remember?" Myles asked.

A dubious look crossed Brendan's face as he stared at his friend. "What do you think? Can he be trusted?"

"Good question," Myles muttered under his breath. "I mean, it's Ethan, right? But every day that goes by on this island, he seems less and less like the man I know."

"I know what you mean," Brendan replied. "I sometimes wonder what deal the captain offered him."

"Who else can we trust…Ashley?" Myles asked.

"No!" Brendan snapped. "I'm not getting Ashley involved in this. I…can't…" he choked up, "I can't have her locked up again."

Myles knew how much it hurt Brendan having his daughter locked up in the cave and wasn't going to push the issue, even though he thought she was the only one they could really trust at this point. "Maybe we need to reconsider our options in the morning," he said. He grasped his friend's arm and squeezed it before rising from the table and returning the plate to the kitchen. "See you in the morning," Myles called from the stairs. He waited for Brendan to acknowledge him before walking down the steps and disappearing into his room.

Brendan lifted his beer from the table and crossed the room to the rear door leading to the back deck. He walked to the rail and stared over the water while occasionally sipping from the can of beer. Tomorrow was a big day. Ashley had only been gone for three days, but it felt like an eternity. Despite the terror of the plane crash and of being shipwrecked, he had actually grown closer to Ashley over the past two weeks. After Julia moved out, Ashley became distant and spent most of the time hidden away in her bedroom. He tried to talk to her about the situation with her mother, but Ashley had always found a reason why she was too busy to speak at that moment. Since the shipwreck, she now confided in him again and seemed to enjoy spending time with him. It reminded him of the backyard camping adventures they shared before Ashley started high school, and those things weren't considered cool anymore. He was lost in the memory of telling Ashley ghost stories in their sleeping bags when a sound surprised him from behind.

"Oh, sorry," Spencer said. He had tripped on one of the deck chairs while making his way to the rear deck.

"You!" Brendan growled. "You have some nerve."

"Wait, wait," Spencer pleaded. He held out both hands in front of him in case Brendan attacked. "I just wanted to say I'm sorry."

"A bit late for that now, isn't it?" Brendan spat. "Give me one good reason why I shouldn't break you in half right now, you lying little..." Brendan clenched both fists and took a step towards Spencer.

Spencer covered his face with both hands and braced for the assault. He peeked between his fingers when nothing happened. "Go ahead, I deserve it," he said when he saw Brendan just standing there, clenching his fists.

"Is this some sort of trick to get me put on trial for breaking the rules?" Brendan asked. He looked around to see if anyone was watching from inside the yacht.

"No trick," Spencer said between his fingers. "I just want to tell you that I'm sorry. I never meant to get Ashley in trouble…she didn't deserve that."

Brendan almost felt sorry for the pathetic kid standing in front of him. "So why'd you do it?" he asked.

"I didn't…" Spencer started and then paused, "I had no idea of what was happening until just before the trial." He dropped his hands to his side and let out a huge sigh as his shoulders slumped forward. "I know this must seem hard to believe," he continued. "But I was just as surprised as everyone else when I learned it was Maddi who was bringing the charges against Ashley."

"Why didn't you just say the truth then…during the trial," Brendan asked.

Spencer lifted his gaze from the floor to Brendan. "She's my wife," he pleaded. "I wanted to support her…to stand with her and show her…" his voice trailed off. "I didn't think it would be a big deal; I thought they would just make her apologize…I had no idea they would…" Spencer paused when he recalled Ashley being sentenced to the cave. "I'm so sorry," he whispered.

Brendan dropped his hands to his side. He was starting to feel sorry for the young man. "Why didn't you guys just come talk to me…or Ash?" he asked.

Spencer hung his head again and stared at the ground. "I don't know…she's changed. Ever since arriving on this island, I've watched her change into this green-eyed monster."

"Madison?" Brendan asked.

Spencer nodded. "Yes, I don't know what happened, but it's almost like she's becoming a different person." He looked up and took a step towards Brendan as if pleading with him to do something. "She was always a little jealous, but this is different...I feel like I don't even know her anymore. And the captain..."

"What about the captain?!" Brendan interrupted.

Spencer looked around the yacht. His voice was almost a whisper as he spoke, "he's been talking to Maddi...telling her stuff..."

"What kind of stuff?" Brendan asked. He stepped closer to Spencer and grabbed the young man by his shoulders.

"I'm not sure..." Spencer said, wide-eyed. "She doesn't tell me, and they stop talking if I get too close. I think he talked her into making the accusations."

Brendan shook Spencer by the shoulders. "And what did the captain tell you?"

"He said if I want to keep my wife, then I need to support her."

Brendan released Spencer and turned back to look over the water. The trial, and the vote for that matter, were starting to make a lot more sense. This was all about the captain's need for control.

"I'm sorry," Spencer sobbed. "I didn't mean for it to go that far...I...I don't know what to do."

Brendan turned around to face Spencer. "What do you mean?"

"I need to get Maddi away from the captain before she...we need to get away from here."

"You mean escape the island?"

"Yes!" Spencer blurted. "Like you said to the captain earlier, no one's even tried to get us off this island."

Brendan eyed Spencer suspiciously. "You'll be in big trouble if the captain hears you talking like that."

"I don't care!" Spencer cried. "I remember what happened when we were on the raft. I don't trust him…I need to get Maddi out of here before it's too late."

Brendan continued to eye Spencer suspiciously for several seconds. He was still angry with him, but was beginning to wonder if the young man had been duped like the rest of them. "Listen," he said. "You need to get some rest and forget about this conversation. I understand what happened, and I forgive you." He patted Spencer on the back and then walked into the yacht and made his way to the stairs. He looked back and saw Spencer still standing with his head hung on the rear deck. He walked slowly down the steps and then across the padded hall to his cabin.

Brendan lay on his bed and thought about his conversation with Spencer. He still wasn't sure he trusted the young man, but he was beginning to believe Spencer was being manipulated through his wife. He couldn't really blame him; he knew how important it was to support the one you love, even when you think they might be wrong. His memories went to Julia and their conversation at the airport. He wanted so much to go back in time and tell Julia he forgave her; tell her he remembered…everything he couldn't put into words because of his selfish anger. Julia, shaking her head to show off her new haircut at the airport, was the last thing Brendan remembered before he fell asleep.

The dream was familiar. He stared around the crowd, wondering who the people were, while his mother held his hand and prevented him from finding a spot to play with the toy car in his pocket. A man patted his head and spoke softly with his mother. The man wore black pants and a black long-sleeved collared shirt. Brendan had seen him somewhere before. Where? The man was thin and balding, with gray hair, and he wore black-framed glasses that made his eyes appear to bulge when he bent over to speak with him. Brendan remembered the man being kind. He liked the man, but didn't like the stuffy clothes he always wore when he saw the man. The man was carrying something in his right hand — a book. He said something before leaving to mingle with the others in the room. Brendan couldn't recall the exact words, but remembered it didn't make sense. What did he say?

Who Can You Trust

When he woke up the next morning, Brendan felt better than he had in a long time. He still had all the same problems he went to bed with the night before, but today he was being reunited with his daughter. He felt ten feet tall when he rose out of bed and stretched his arms over his head. He felt energized even before the smell of coffee and bacon began to fill the ship. He showered and bounded up the stairs two at a time as he made his way to the kitchen. Not even Helen's scowl as he entered the kitchen dampened his mood.

"Good morning." He smiled and walked past Helen to pour himself a cup of coffee. He glanced around the yacht and found Myles sitting on the front deck speaking to Dwayne.

"Good morning, mind if I join you?" Brendan asked before taking a seat on one of the deck's outdoor chairs.

Dwayne smiled at Brendan and replied, "Yes, it just might be."

"I was just telling Dwayne how I got this limp from playing ball," Myles said. He placed his right hand under his knee and rotated his ankle in the air.

Brendan let out a low whistle, "Whew, the man was one of the best players in the country before that accident."

"One stupid step," Myles murmured. "Who knows what I could have become…" he said under his breath.

Dwayne rose from his seat and looked back and forth across the sky before turning his attention back to Myles. "Der be an old saying where I come from…don't pay the ferryman before he gets ya to da other side." He winked at Brendan and then retrieved the silver coin from his pocket. He began whistling his favorite tune as he crossed the deck and disappeared around the side.

"That's one strange man," Brendan said to Myles as he listened to Dwayne's song fade in the distance. Myles nodded in agreement. "Learn anything useful?" Brendan asked.

"I think he's a taxi driver…he kept talking about taking people where they need to go," Myles answered.

"I mean that might be useful to us getting off the island," Brendan said. "Do you think he can be trusted?"

Myles shrugged. "I tried asking his opinion about the others, but he just said…"

"It's not my place," Brendan finished his sentence.

"Exactly," Myles replied. Myles looked around the yacht before moving in closer to Brendan and asking, "Any thoughts about our discussion last night?"

Brendan also peered around the yacht before answering, "What do you think about Spencer?"

Myles sat back in his seat and raised his eyebrows. "The Spencer who got Ashley sent to the cave?"

"I had a chat with him last night."

"And you didn't wring his scrawny little neck?"

"Oh, I thought about it, trust me. But I think the captain has been using his wife to manipulate him. I think he might be getting tired of it, and he's looking for a way out."

Myles shook his head slowly. "I don't know, man…you sure you can trust him?" he asked.

"It's not like we have a lot of options," Brendan answered.

"You'd trust him over Ethan?"

In truth, Brendan didn't really trust anyone but Myles…and Ashley, but he wasn't about to get Ashley in trouble and have her sent back to the cave. Dwayne was odd, but he hadn't turned Brendan in, and Brendan felt like there might be an opportunity to get him on their side. After all, he hadn't voted for the captain and clearly wasn't a big fan of Brett and Kade. On the other hand, he really never went out of his way to help anyone. He just seemed to be a guy who tried to walk the middle of the road and not get on anyone's bad side. Spencer was afraid to stand up to his wife and just seemed to need someone to follow. He may have been a coward, but he took a big chance opening up to Brendan last night about wanting to escape the island. Had he been pushed too far? Had he found some courage?

"Then there's Ethan," Brendan thought to himself.

Ethan, the friend he's known for over forty years. The friend who's always had his back and has always been there through thick and thin. But was he still that person? Brendan recalled his argument with Ethan the previous day. Had he made a deal with the captain? He spent so much time with the captain and his council that Brendan wondered if he was beginning to believe the crap they were coming up with. Still, it's Ethan…right?

Brendan slowly nodded his head. "I'll go talk to Ethan."

"Want me to come?" Myles asked.

"No," Brendan answered. "That might look suspicious to the captain." He finished his coffee and then brought the cup back to the kitchen before heading towards the front staircase that led to the library. He paused at the top of the stairs when he heard a voice coming from below.

"We had a deal!" the voice bellowed. Brendan was sure it was the captain. It was followed by the sound of a door being slammed.

Brendan made his way slowly down the stairs towards the library. He paused on each step to try and determine who was in the library and whether the captain might return after storming off towards his cabin. He listened at the library door before knocking.

"Knock-knock," he rapped on the thin door.

"I said I would do it!" shouted a voice from inside.

Brendan turned the silver handle and pressed the door open. The familiar song *My Girl* by the Temptations played softly on the overhead speakers. Ethan stood on the far side of the room with his back to the door. He held what Brendan thought looked like one of the ship's instruction manuals in his left hand. "Hey…" Brendan called. "Is this a bad time?" he asked.

Ethan spun around and was surprised to see his friend at the door. He leaned his head to the side, trying to peer into the hall behind Brendan before speaking, "Uh, no…it's fine. What's up?"

Brendan had an uneasy feeling in his stomach and wondered what deal his friend had made with the captain as he walked slowly into the room, debating his next step. "I…" Brendan started, "I just wanted to…" he turned and looked into the hallway behind him before turning to Ethan and continuing, "Thank you for the help the other day."

"With the memory?" Ethan asked. He walked slowly towards Brendan when he didn't answer. "What…exactly, were you trying to remember?" he asked as he crossed the room and stood in front of his friend.

Brendan took a step back. "Oh, it was…uh…" he stammered.

Ethan placed his hand on Brendan's shoulder. "You can tell me," he said softly. His eyes bored into Brendan's.

"And one more thing!" A voice shouted from the hallway. Captain Kleinman rushed into the room, waving his finger before seeing Brendan and immediately falling silent.

The three men stared at each other for several seconds before Brendan spoke, "I'd better get going." He turned and walked to the door, then paused and called back to Ethan, "Thanks again, it was very helpful," he said, and then disappeared up the stairs. He stopped at the top of the stairs and tried eavesdropping on the conversation in the library. He could only make out bits and pieces of a muffled argument and decided to begin his chores. There was no way he was going to miss bringing his daughter back to the yacht.

This was the third time this week he had been assigned to the sanitation detail. The smell was horrible, but hauling the yacht's 40-liter holding tank to the waste burial point was the most challenging part of the task. He was also required to flush the toilet lines with seawater and then refill the yacht's freshwater tank with water from the river. Traveling back and forth carrying the water was time-consuming, but he didn't mind the chore since the time walking to and from the river gave him time to think. The smell of something cooking caught his attention as he returned from his final trip to the river. He was surprised since lunch was typically a cold meal. The person assigned to the cooking detail usually saved the hot meal for either breakfast or dinner and used lunchtime to prepare vegetables and other sides for the main meal. Brendan followed his nose into the kitchen and called to Myles when he saw him in front of the stove.

"Hot lunch today?"

Myles turned and smiled at his friend. "No, a surprise for Ashley," he said. He turned back to the stove and lifted a large plate with a tall stack of pancakes. "Closest thing we had to a cake," he said as he showed Brendan the makeshift cake he had made.

"She'll love it," Brendan said.

Myles opened the stove and placed the plate on the lower metal rack. "Shall we?" he asked. The two men left the yacht and waited on the beach for Brett and Kade. Brendan looked back up onto the yacht as they waited for the two large men and noticed a crowd had gathered on the front deck. Madison and Spencer leaned over the side rail while Helen took a seat in the outdoor chair that Brendan had used earlier that morning. Dwayne sat with his feet hanging over the yacht and his arms resting on the lower rung of the railing. Brendan wondered if they were hoping to see more fireworks when Ashley returned. At precisely noon, Brett and Kade made their way down the stairs and walked across the beach to the far trail leading to the volcano. Brett led the way, carrying the cell key on a black cord tied around his neck.

The two-hour journey to the cave and back was uneventful aside from the brief celebration when Ashley was released from the cage. Brendan had told Myles about his earlier meeting with Ethan, and the two took turns speculating what deal the captain could have made with Ethan. They both agreed that it probably wasn't a good time to try to get Ethan on their side and spent a good portion of the trip debating who they could trust. In the end, they decided to give Spencer a chance and also decided they should start their rescue ideas as soon as possible.

On the return trip, Brendan carried a laundry bag filled with Ashley's dirty clothes while Myles filled Ashley in on the big dinner he had prepared for her return. Ashley spent a good deal of time explaining a book Ethan had brought to her on her first day in the cell. The book was titled *"The Path to Heaven"* and described a man's journey through seven concentric circles to the center ring, called enlightenment. She said she found the book uplifting and credited it with helping her through the long, dark nights.

"I never thought I'd miss this place," Ashley said when they left the rocky trail and entered the sandy beach. Her smile quickly faded, and she stopped in her tracks when she saw Spencer and Madison on the front deck.

"It's okay," Brendan said when he noticed what Ashley was looking at. "Just hold your head high and ignore them."

Ashley began walking again and turned to her father, "In the book, the second ring on the path to Heaven is called forgiveness. The whole chapter is about the man forgiving a drunk driver who killed his son in a car crash…you can't get to the next level until you learn to forgive."

"And did you learn to forgive?" Brendan asked. He put his arm around his daughter's neck and the two strolled along the beach.

"I thought I had," Ashley answered after a moment. "Then I saw them up there on the yacht, and now I'm not so sure."

"Forgiveness can be a difficult thing," Brendan said softly. He rested his head against hers as they made their way to the stairs.

"Welcome back, kiddo," Ethan said when Ashley climbed aboard the yacht. He hugged her and ruffled her hair. "You should probably take a shower before dinner," he added as he took a step back from her.

"Well, it's good to see some things haven't changed," Ashley said and then hurried down the stairs to her cabin.

Ashley was gone for several hours and returned well after dinner had already started. After a long shower and a fresh change of clothes, she felt like a new person and didn't mind the stares from some of the others when she entered the dining room. Brendan, Myles, and Dwayne sat on one side of the dining table with an empty chair between Brendan and Myles. Ethan sat on the other side of the table, across from the empty chair, with Brett and Kade seated on the same side of the table. Captain Kleinman sat at his usual position at the head of the table, and there were three empty chairs where Helen, Spencer, and Madison usually sat.

"Sorry, I'm late," Ashley said when she entered the room. She wore a navy blue, sleeveless blouse tucked into a loose-fitting pair of white casual slacks and a brown belt with a large gold buckle. Her bangs were trimmed neatly above her brows, and her hair was cut and curled to outline her face and hang in a bob just above her shoulders.

"Whewwt wheew!" Myles whistled and stood from his chair. He pulled out the empty seat next to him and offered it to Ashley.

Ashley crossed the living area and paused when the rear door swung open, and Madison and Spencer entered. Spencer stared dumbfounded while Madison stomped her foot on the floor and immediately turned and left the room. Spencer followed quickly after her.

"It's nice to have you back," Captain Kleinman said when Ashley took her seat between Myles and her father. The sides of his mouth lifted in what could only be an attempt at a smile before he added, "See, that wasn't so bad, was it?"

Ashley offered a faint-hearted smile and then turned her attention to the meal Myles had prepared. A large plate of pork chops was placed in the center of the table, accompanied by a rectangular baking dish filled with scalloped potatoes. There were two smaller bowls filled with green beans, one at each end of the table. The bowls were white on the outside but had a colorful pattern on the inside. She speared two pieces of pork chops with her fork and then pulled the dish of potatoes close to her plate, digging out two large spoonfuls.

"This smells so good!" she said before asking her father to pass the bowl of green beans.

The others returned to their dinner conversations as Ashley filled her plate with food. Dwayne and Myles were discussing whether American football or European soccer was a more athletic sport. At the same time, Brett and Kade debated which type of push-ups was better for strengthening their pectoral muscles. Brendan was listening to the discussion between Dwayne and Myles when he felt the familiar vibration on his arm. He looked down at his watch and became lost in memory of his conversation with Julia. A clip of Julia walking out the front door with her suitcase played over and over in his mind. He wished he had had the strength to stop her, to ask her not to go. He was pulled from the memory when Ashley spoke.

"Mmm…" she gulped, "wow!" she said with a mouth full of potatoes. "Sho…gud…Unle Myles." Her cheeks bulged with the potatoes when she turned and smiled at Myles.

Brendan looked up from his watch and noticed Ethan had been watching him intently. Ethan's eyes narrowed when he saw Brendan move his left hand off the table and place it on his lap.

"Ashley tells me you took her a book to read," Brendan said to Ethan. He hoped he could change the subject before Ethan realized he was responding to his silent alarm. Ethan continued to stare at him until Ashley interrupted.

"Oh yeah, thanks, Uncle Ethan. The book was awesome," Ashley said after swallowing her potatoes.

Ethan turned his attention to Ashley, and Brendan was relieved when the two began discussing the book. They were comparing their favorite chapters when Ashley asked about how Ethan gained his appreciation for poems and other literature that weren't related to science. Ethan explained how he was forced to take an English literature course in his first year at Yale, when Brendan saw the opportunity to leave the table. He excused himself and carried his plate into the kitchen, where he scraped the pork chop bones into a biodegradable bin before rinsing them and placing them in the bottom of the sink. Brett and Kade had also finished their dinner and followed Brendan into the kitchen, where they simply put their plates on the kitchen counter without disposing of the bones or rinsing them.

"Nice," Brendan commented before clearing the plates and placing them in the sink. It probably wouldn't have bothered him as much if Myles weren't on kitchen duty. He stepped through the kitchen door and entered the bar area, where he retrieved a six-pack of beer from the small refrigerator and then returned to the dining area. Dwayne and Myles had joined the conversation about the book, and Dwayne was explaining his theory about the scorpion and the frog, as well as whether people could truly change their nature. Captain Kleinman said he didn't really believe in Heaven and became bored when the conversation dragged on after Myles and Dwayne joined in. He left the table and returned to his cabin before Brendan returned with his beer.

"I'll be on the back deck," Brendan called to the group and lifted the six-pack of beer to invite the others if they cared to join him.

Myles rose from the table with his plate and began walking to the kitchen. "I was just about to bring out the cake," he said when he passed Brendan. "Sure, you don't want to wait?"

Brendan shook his head, "No thanks," he said. "You guys enjoy. Join me whenever you're done in here," he added and then continued across the living room to the rear deck. He paused at the door and turned back to face the table when he heard Ashley laughing. Dwayne was standing and making a gesture as if he were rowing a boat. Brendan wasn't sure what they were talking about, but he was happy to see Ashley smiling and enjoying herself. He opened the rear door and walked into the warm darkness. The sun had set, and a thick blanket of clouds covered the moon and stars. It was quiet except for the rhythmic lapping of waves against the rear hull. Deck chairs and a small outdoor table stood out against the gray sky. The clop-clop-clop of Brendan's flip flops moved across the deck to the small table where Brendan placed the beer and pulled a chair to sit in.

"Not enjoying the party?" A voice came from out of the dark.

"Jesus!" Brendan breathed. He glanced towards the rear railing, where he barely made out the outline of a person slouched in one of the deck chairs.

"Sorry," said a familiar voice. "Did it again, didn't I?" Spencer said.

Brendan pulled two beers from their plastic carrier and walked to the rear of the yacht. He held out a beer to Spencer when he stopped in front of the chair.

"No thanks." Spencer waved his hand to dismiss the offer.

"You don't need anyone's permission to go in and have a piece of cake," Brendan said. He popped the lid of the beer and then held it away from his body as a small amount spurted over the side and ran down the can.

"Thanks," Spencer replied. He looked over his shoulder at the group gathered at the dining table and then returned to facing the water. "Not really in the mood," he added and then slumped back into the chair.

"My mom used to make a healthy version of pancakes with wheat and no baking soda," Brendan said. "They tasted like a fluffy sourdough bread. What's your excuse?" he asked.

Spencer was silent for a moment and then began to shake his head. "No matter what I do, I can't ever seem to do anything right." He paused and looked out over the water as if remembering something. "I find myself saying I'm sorry all the time, and half the time I don't even know what I'm apologizing for."

"Ah," Brendan remarked. He walked to the yacht railing and leaned back with his elbows resting on the top rail. "Sounds like you have the curse..." Spencer raised his head and looked at Brendan, waiting for him to explain. "Of the married man," Brendan continued.

"I'm serious," Spencer said and let out a sigh.

"Every man who's ever been married has said those exact same words at some point in his marriage. The young, the old, the educated, the wise...doesn't matter, we've all been there," Brendan said.

"Even you?" Spencer asked.

Brendan laughed. "Especially me."

Spencer placed his hands over his face and massaged his forehead with his fingers. "I was hoping you were going to say it goes away as you get older."

"I'd be lying if I did," Brendan replied. He tipped his beer back and took a long drink. "Marriage can be a wonderful thing…but it's hard and you have to work at it constantly."

Spencer groaned and sank deeper into his chair.

The two men were quiet for several minutes. Brendan was trying to determine the best way to approach Spencer about helping him and Myles while Spencer simply sulked in his misery.

"I was thinking about our conversation yesterday," Brendan started. He waited for Spencer's response, but Spencer only grunted and continued staring at the water. Brendan continued, "If you're serious about helping Madison and getting her out of here…" he paused when Spencer turned to face him. Spencer's eyes were wide.

"You found a way off the island?" Spencer asked. He was no longer moping, and his voice was filled with enthusiasm.

"Kind of," Brendan answered. He turned to face the water so that Spencer couldn't see his face. He still wasn't sure how much he could trust the young man. "Myles and I…" he hesitated, "need to spend some time on the other side of the island."

"We're not allowed on the other side," Spencer said. The enthusiasm had left his voice.

Brendan turned back to face Spencer. "Which is why we need some help."

"Right!" Spencer uttered suddenly. He leaned forward in his chair and continued, "The captain wouldn't expect me…" he began nodding his head as if contemplating a plan. "I can go over there and…" he paused and looked up at Brendan. "What exactly would I be doing over there?" he asked.

"Nothing," Brendan replied. "We need your help back here on the yacht."

"Oh," Spencer mumbled. He reclined in his chair and waited for Brendan to continue.

"We just need someone back here to provide a little cover, let us know if anyone is looking for us, and be our eyes and ears around the yacht."

Spencer didn't seem so enthusiastic about the idea anymore and just sat there silently. "Wait," he said. A little of the enthusiasm had returned to his voice. "I have an idea." He rose from his seat and walked around the yacht to ensure no one else was around. He returned and placed both elbows on the rail next to Brendan before continuing, "Madison and I found a place on the back side of the volcano. It's through the thin stretch of trees before reaching the steep cliffs on this side of the island." He pointed back across Brendan's shoulder at the side of the island opposite the barren rocks. "There is a small area where mangoes grow in a clearing before reaching the cliffs…"

"We're not trying to hide," Brendan interrupted.

"No-no, listen," Spencer protested. "Maddi and I always bring back a sack of mangoes when we visit the area. You can take the sack with you when you're away from the yacht, and if anyone asks, I'll say I asked you to bring back some mangoes while you were out for a walk."

Brendan nodded his head. "And we come back to the yacht carrying the mangoes after having been gone for a couple of hours…everyone will just think we went to pick some fruit."

"Yes!" Spencer exclaimed.

Brendan turned and leaned his back on the rail. "That's actually not a bad idea."

Spencer turned and leaned his back on the rail just like Brendan, and was about to continue with the idea when the rear deck door swung open, and Ashley and Myles came onto the rear deck. Spencer looked back and forth between Ashley and Brendan and shuffled his feet.

"I…uh…should be going," Spencer said. He hung his head and scurried across the rear deck towards the door.

"Wait!" Brendan called. Spencer paused halfway across the deck and turned back to Brendan. "Thank you for all of your help," Brendan said. He smiled and raised his beer in a toast.

Spencer returned a half-hearted smile and turned nervously towards Ashley and Myles. "I'm…sorry…I mean I'm happy…that you're back, that is." He was flustered, and his tongue seemed to have a mind of its own as he tried to express his thoughts. "Never mind," he said before Ashley could respond, and then hurried through the open door.

"What was that about?" Myles asked as he and Ashley crossed the deck and joined Brendan against the rail.

"Tell you later," Brendan answered. "So, what did you two determine about getting to Heaven?" he asked to change the subject.

"I think I agree with Uncle Ethan," Ashley answered immediately. The conversation was still fresh on her mind, and she had enjoyed having others around to converse with. "He says that there are some things that science just can't explain."

"Ethan said that?" Brendan asked in disbelief.

"I learned that Dwayne is even stranger than I originally thought," Myles added. Ashley nodded her head in agreement.

The three spent the next hour discussing their dinner conversation and guessing at what they thought Dwayne did for a living. Myles stuck to his theory that Dwayne was a taxi driver, while Ashley told them about listening to Dwayne play the ukulele and speculating that he could be a musician. As much as Ashley was enjoying her freedom and the open air, she yawned and stretched her arms high overhead, announcing she was ready for bed. Brendan insisted on escorting her to the cabin despite her repeated claims that she was well capable of going on her own. She was trying hard to regain her independence in light of the trial, but in truth, was happy with her father's insistence.

"Tomorrow's the day," Brendan said to Myles as they parted on the lower deck. Myles gave him a knowing nod and entered his room.

"What's tomorrow?" Ashley asked when she and Brendan entered their cabin.

Brendan smiled. "We're picking mangoes."

Caught

Brendan's leg bounced nervously as he sat and had his morning coffee with Ethan on the front deck. Ethan appeared distracted and sat quietly, occasionally humming the song *My Girl* that he was constantly listening to in the library.

"Is that your new favorite song?" Brendan asked after listening to Ethan hum the same verse over and over.

Ethan turned to Brendan as if he had just come out of a dream. "Hmm?" he asked.

"The song," Brendan replied. "You've been singing it almost constantly for the last week."

Ethan smiled and then nodded his head. "The playlist in the library is pretty short," he said.

Brendan was about to ask why it was that he spent so much time in the library when Myles joined them with a hot cup of coffee cradled in his palms. "Sanitation today," he said when he took a seat in one of the deck chairs.

"Lucky you," Brendan replied. "I had it three times last week, so I'm just glad somebody else gets a turn."

"That should leave you plenty of time to do something else today," Ethan stated. "Any other plans?" he asked.

Myles pretended to take a long sip of his coffee. He briefly glanced over the rim of the cup at Brendan, who was also staring back at him. "Not really," Myles replied when he pulled the cup from his lips. "I found some fishing line and some hooks in the hull…" he lied, "maybe you'd like to come fishing with me?" he asked, knowing Ethan would likely decline.

Ethan offered a weak smile and shook his head, "No thanks." He turned to Brendan and said, "Maybe Brendan would like to go."

Brendan thought Ethan was the one doing the fishing. "I have laundry," Brendan said. "And if I get any free time, I'd like to spend it with Ash now that she's back," he lied.

"What about you? What are you up to today?" Myles asked Ethan.

Ethan finished his coffee and stared into the bottom of the cup for a second before turning to Myles and replying, "Doing a little reading on Pavlov."

"That kid's lucky his rottweiler didn't eat our ball," Myles said.

Ethan stood silent for a moment and furrowed his brow before stating matter-of-factly, "That was Paschal." He shrugged and began humming *My Girl* as he walked back into the yacht.

"Has he been acting strange to you lately?" Myles asked Brendan. "I mean stranger than usual."

Brendan watched Ethan disappear into the yacht. "There is definitely something on his mind. Do you remember when his dad didn't want him hanging around with us because he thought we somehow forced Ethan to choose basketball over taking another university prep course?" he asked.

"Yeah, he avoided us for weeks because he didn't want to tell us the truth," Myles replied.

"It would probably be best to avoid him until after we're done with the bonfire and S.O.S," Brendan said.

Myles agreed. "So, what's the plan?" he asked.

Brendan explained the idea Spencer came up with, and they both agreed it sounded like a great idea.

"I'll pick up the bag of mangoes from Spencer this morning after breakfast," Brendan explained in a hushed tone. "We should head to the river during lunch since Brett and Kade will be out on the beach exercising after lunch."

"What if someone sees us leaving?" Myles asked.

"Spencer is going to ask us to get mangoes while we're out. He'll do it in the kitchen to make it public. If anyone follows us past the tree line, we'll head east and go pick mangoes…if no one follows, then we'll turn west past the clearing and head to the river."

Myles nodded. "And how long does it take to pick mangoes?"

"I think we'll have about three hours before anyone gets suspicious," Brendan replied. "That should be enough time to collect some wood for the bonfire, get to the other side, and make the S.O.S on the beach. Depending on how it goes, we'll either return the next day to finish the bonfire or lay low and finish it when we can."

"Sounds like a plan," Myles said. He rose from his seat and stretched. "See you shortly." He walked back into the yacht and began collecting the supplies he would need to start his chores.

Brendan walked back to his cabin and changed into a pair of black gym shorts and a short-sleeved Hawaiian shirt with a tropical drinks pattern. He chose the hiking shoes instead of his usual flip-flops and then retrieved the folding laundry baskets from each of the bathrooms. Brett and Kade's musky gym shorts almost made him wish he were back on sanitation detail.

He emptied the laundry baskets onto the laundry room floor and began sorting the clothes by color.

"Need help?" Ashley called from the hall when she saw her father sorting the laundry.

"No thanks, got it," Brendan called back. "Where are you today?" he asked.

Ashley rolled her eyes. "KP…with Spencer," she replied.

"Oh," Brendan said. "I'm surprised they're letting you two work together."

"I'm mainly preparing the sides and cleaning," Ashley answered. She waved and headed upstairs to begin her day.

Brendan returned to sorting and then put in the first load. He liked doing the towels and sheets first so he could hang them outside to dry and still use the dryer for the cotton and blended fabrics in the following loads. This method cut the time for the laundry chore in half, and he would need the extra time today. He turned the white temperature dial to hot and started the washing machine. By late morning, most of the laundry was washed, and he had separated the clothes by item, allowing the others to drop by the laundry room and pick up their own clothes for folding. He would need to fold the towels and sheets once they were dry, but it wouldn't take long since only two people had decided to change their sheets on this day. He made his way through the living area and onto the rear deck, where a metal-framed foldable drying rack held the towels and sheets.

"Nice sunny day for laundry," Spencer called from behind Brendan. He walked to the drying rack and pretended to test the dryness of the kitchen towels before whispering, "I put the sack of mangoes on your bed." He then yanked one of the kitchen towels from the rack and headed back into the yacht. Brendan fluffed the sheets and then headed back downstairs to retrieve the sack of mangoes. He checked his watch; it was 11:27. Lunch would start in 3 minutes, and he knew Myles was likely already upstairs, around the kitchen, waiting for him. He opened the cabin door and headed for the center stairs.

Almost on cue, a voice sounded from the dining room, "Lunch!" He recognized Ashley's voice and figured she had probably just laid out a platter of sandwiches of some sort. When he reached the top of the stairs, Ashley was returning to the kitchen.

"Sandwiches on the table if you're hungry," Ashley said as she passed her father. She returned to the kitchen and began peeling the vegetables they would be having with dinner.

Brendan entered the dining room and retrieved two sandwiches from a large plate on the table. He grabbed two more when he heard Ashley in the kitchen telling Myles about the sandwiches.

"Ham and cheese again," he said to himself after lifting the bread and inspecting the contents.

Brendan walked into the kitchen and held up the sandwiches so that Myles knew he had already grabbed him two for the road. "We decided it's too nice of a day to be inside," he said to Ashley. She was washing potatoes in the sink and turned to listen to what her father was saying. "We're going to go for a walk if you want to join us."

Ashley glanced out of the port window. "I wish I could," she said. She turned to her father and pouted her lips. "I have to finish the potatoes and then peel the carrots and cucumber. By the way, we only have one box of cucumbers left," she added.

Brendan counted on it being unlikely that Ashley would join them for a walk since KP was one of the duties that kept you busy all day long. He also knew they were not only getting low on cucumbers, but almost every other fruit and vegetable they had in storage. There were still plenty of canned goods, and they still had the fruit from the island, but it was only a matter of time before they would need to start rationing. He was wondering how much food and water the captain had squirreled away in his room when a voice called from the hall.

"Hey, did I hear someone say they are going somewhere?" Spencer asked. He spoke loud enough for Brett and Kade to hear in the dining room.

"We're just going for a short walk, to enjoy some sun…want to come?" Brendan asked, knowing Spencer would refuse.

"Aw, can't," Spencer replied. "Would you mind getting a few mangoes while you're out? I can tell you where to find em."

"Ummmm…" Brendan replied as if he were giving it thought.

"Please," Spencer added. "I need them for the chicken recipe I am making for dinner."

Dwayne entered the kitchen and opened the refrigerator. He pulled a bottle of mustard from the bottom shelf and added a squirt to the sandwich he held in his other hand. "No one make a betta jerk chicken wit mango salsa than my Auntie Sharon," he said. "Da secret is da marinade, you know."

"Please," Spencer begged. "For Auntie Sharon."

"Okay-okay," Brendan agreed.

Spencer spent the next two minutes explaining how to get to the mango orchard he and Madison had found on the island. He left out a few steps just in case anyone was paying attention and might try to find the place on their own. So far, everything was going to plan. Brett, Kade, Ashley, and Dwayne had all overheard the conversation and expected Brendan and Myles to be away from the yacht for the next couple of hours. Having the mango for dinner this evening was a perfect setup for making everyone believe that was where they had gone. Brendan and Myles left the yacht and hurried along the beach to the trail just inside the tree line. They stopped and listened several times for any signs of followers before turning west and heading for the river. Their pace slowed once they reached the thicker trees on the other side of the clumpy-grass clearing to start collecting branches for the bonfire.

"I'm almost full," Myles said with an arm full of the thickest branches he could carry.

"Me too," Brendan said. He carried the pieces of wood across his arms, and the blue sack of mangoes hung from his left shoulder. He checked his watch. "Forty minutes, not bad," he said to Myles.

They hurried along the forest trail, taking several right turns as they made their way west to the river. Brendan found it much easier to remember the way to the clearwater pool with a clear head.

"There," Brendan said. He pointed to the clearwater pool ahead in the distance. He set the wood on the large rock next to the water and removed the sack of mangoes from his shoulder. "Don't let me forget these," he said to Myles and then placed the sack on the other side of the rock where it wasn't visible from the trail.

The two men carried their wood across the river and made their way along the rocky crevasse trail. They crossed the large rock plateau and were about to climb down to the beach when Brendan dropped the wood he was carrying.

"This looks like a good spot for the bonfire," Brendan said.

Myles surveyed the area and held up his hand to gauge the wind. "There is nothing to block the wind. Are you sure the fire will stay lit?" He walked to the pile of wood Brendan had placed on the ground and added his wood to the pile.

Brendan turned and faced the wind. The steady breeze felt cool against his face, and he stood silent, enjoying the moment. "It's the best place," he said after a moment of silence. "It's still visible for miles around, and not quite as windy as it is further up the rocky hill."

Myles turned and glanced up the hill. He was happy he wouldn't have to haul wood up the gradual slope. "We'll need more wood," he said after kicking the pile of wood at his feet.

"Let's start on the S.O.S.," Brendan said. He pointed to a wide-open area on the beach below. "There," he said. He walked to the edge of the plateau and began the thirty-foot descent to the beach. He placed one hand on a large boulder and hopped to the next rock below. Using this process, they managed to make it down the cliff in about ten minutes.

Brendan studied the beach as they made their way to the clearing. He stopped when he was in an area with less debris than the surrounding area. "We'll put the message here," he said and pointed to an area of the beach about fifty feet in diameter. "I think there are enough rocks in the area to make each letter about thirty feet long. Start by finding the largest rocks you can carry and put them in three piles about ten feet apart." He pointed to three places on the beach that would serve as the rock pile for each letter.

Myles checked the time. "Two hours," he called to Brendan and then began collecting rocks.

The larger rocks were located at the top of the beach where the beach met the cliff wall. Over the years, several boulders had calved from the cliff and broken into smaller pieces as they tumbled to the beach below. The rocks almost seemed to migrate towards the ocean, becoming smaller the closer they approached the water. Brendan and Myles removed their shirts and began the process of moving rocks across the beach. Myles picked up a few pieces of driftwood he found along the way and added them to the pile of stones. The rocky beach provided plenty of suitably sized boulders, and the process of collecting the rocks in piles went faster than anticipated. A few of the larger boulders required both men to lift, but the majority of the time was spent with the two men moving back and forth on their own with a large boulder cradled in their hands. The heavy rocks hung low in their arms, making them look like crabs scurrying along the beach.

"What do you think?" Brendan asked after surveying the three piles.

Myles tossed the rock he was carrying into the third pile and reached for a long piece of driftwood. "I'll spell out the letters," he said. He walked to the first pile and began carving the letter *S* into the sand with the piece of wood. He looked at the letter after making the first curve and then kicked at the sand, redrawing it. "Good enough," he said when the first S was complete.

The two men placed the first pile of rocks along the outline of the letter that Myles had drawn. They began with the largest rocks to ensure they were evenly spaced across the outline, and then filled in the rest with smaller rocks from the pile. They repeated this process for the second and third piles of rocks before stepping back to assess their handiwork.

Brendan slapped his hands and rubbed them together to knock off the loose sand. "That'll work," he said of the thirty-foot S.O.S sign they had just built on the beach. He followed Myles to the water to wash his hands and rinse the sweat and sand from his chest and legs.

"Not bad for two old men," Myles said.

"And with time to spare," Brendan added.

They walked back to the beach with their arms straight out to the side to dry, and then put on their shirts and sat on the beach for a minute's rest. They were tired, but happy with their progress.

***

Ashley peeled the last cucumber and diced it into cubes before adding it to the large bowl sitting next to the sink. She mixed the cucumbers with the chopped tomatoes and onions and then sprinkled the mixture with a light dressing. Despite being frozen, the vegetables were still firm, and she was pleased with the taste of the mixed salad she had prepared. She enjoyed a second forkful of salad before covering the bowl and sliding it into the refrigerator. She rinsed the prep bowls and placed them in the sink to wash later.

"Hey kiddo," came a voice from behind. Ashley wiped her hands on the kitchen towel hanging on the oven handle and turned to see who had called.

"Oh, hey, Uncle Ethan," Ashley replied. "Would you like to try the cucumber salad I made for dinner?"

"No thanks," Ethan replied. "I was just looking for your dad. Have you seen him?"

Ashley looked out the kitchen's port windows and then through the window to the front deck before turning back to Ethan. "I don't think they're back yet?" she answered.

"Uncle Myles and your dad?" Ethan asked.

"Yes, they went out about two hours ago to get some mangoes."

"Mangoes? Hmmm…"

"Spencer needed some for his dinner recipe, so he asked Dad to bring some back while they were out."

"Sh-t," Ethan cursed under his breath.

"I can check with Spencer to see if they've come back. I was just about to go see if he needed help with the chicken."

Ethan shook his head and rushed back down the stairs to his cabin. Ashley heard his door slam as she walked through the main hall towards the rear deck where Spencer was preparing the chicken. She paused before opening the rear door and looked around to see if Madison might be somewhere nearby.

"Hey," she called when she opened the door.

Spencer looked up from the small table where he was dusting the chicken with a dry rub Dwayne had helped him prepare. He wore the white cooking apron with the caption, *If you're reading this, bring me a beer*, over a white t-shirt and a khaki pair of cargo shorts. The chicken was cut into chunks and placed in evenly spaced rows on a cutting board in the center of the table.

"Have you seen my dad?" Ashley asked from the doorway.

Spencer shook his head and then checked his watch. "He went to get mangoes for dinner."

"Yeah, I was just wondering if they had made it back yet."

Spencer shrugged and shook his head again.

"I'm finished with the sides; do you need any help out here?" Ashley was hoping he would say no. KP duty was a team effort, and you were expected to help the other person, so she felt compelled to ask.

Spencer was quiet for a moment as if contemplating his answer. "Erm…not really." He looked down at his feet and then quickly blurted, "But there is something I'd like to talk to you about."

"I still have some dishes to finish," Ashley replied. She so did not want to be doing this right now.

"It'll just take a second," Spencer said. "I promise."

Ashley crossed the rear deck and stopped in front of the small outdoor table.

"Well…it's just that…" Spencer struggled for the right words as Ashley waited for him to collect his thoughts.

"Yeah?" Ashley replied. She really wanted to tell him to just hurry up and spit it out so she could leave.

Spencer took a deep breath. "I just want you to know that I'm here for you," he blurted.

A puzzled look crossed Ashley's face. "What?" she asked.

"Just in case," Spencer added.

Ashley wasn't sure what he was trying to say and stared blankly at him while he shuffled his feet and stuttered.

Spencer placed his left hand on his hip and held his right hand out as if literally offering an explanation. "You know, in case anything was to ever happen to your father…I would take care of you."

Ashley was shocked and took a step back. "What does that mean?" she demanded.

Spencer immediately began to backpedal. "No-no, I'm just saying…you know."

"No, I don't think I do," Ashley bristled. "Did you send my dad somewhere dangerous?"

"No! Of course not," Spencer quickly answered. "Maddi and I have been to the mango orchard many times…it's not dangerous at all."

Ashley knew her stare was making Spencer uncomfortable. He smiled feebly and waited for her to say something. She was sure the conversation didn't end the way he had envisioned, and she guessed he was hoping she would be thankful for his generosity.

"Whatever," Ashley quipped and then turned and walked back into the yacht.

Spencer breathed a sigh of relief and returned to seasoning the chicken.

Ashley was halfway through the living room, wondering what Spencer had meant by his remarks, when she saw Captain Kleinman, Brett, and Kade come up the stairs and then exit the yacht through the front deck. Captain Kleinman wore a khaki pair of hiking pants and a white t-shirt. Ashley thought he didn't look comfortable without his white and blue sailor's outfit. Brett and Kade were dressed in their traditional shorts and tank tops, but carried some sort of wooden poles and a black sack.

"Wonder what they're up to," Ashley thought as she returned to the kitchen and began washing the dishes.

***

"I'd like to check out the alcove again before we head back to the yacht," Brendan said.

Myles glanced at the time and nodded. He followed Brendan further up the beach until they came to the large formation of rocks on the beach and the hollowed alcove littered with debris. Brendan entered the large cave and began sifting through the items covering the floor.

"What are we looking for?" Myles asked as he watched Brendan lift a rusting circular item from the ground.

Brendan opened the item's cover of broken glass and tipped it over, emptying a metal dial and thin arrow on the floor. He tossed the old ship compass aside and replied, "Anything that might help us get off this island."

Myles kicked at an old wooden suitcase with two leather straps tied around it and muttered, "These people wouldn't have been stuck here if they had anything to help them get off the island."

Brendan ignored the remark and continued digging through the debris. He entered a smaller cave inside the alcove and immediately ran back out holding his nose. "Not sure what they used that area for, but I wouldn't go in there if I were you," he said to Myles as he moved on to the next small cave.

One of the caves was littered with rusting silverware and broken pottery, leading Brendan to believe it had been used as a kitchen. He tested a couple of knives, but they were all either too rusted or too dull to be of any use.

"We should probably get going," Myles called to Brendan from across the cave. He pointed at his watch when Brendan looked in his direction, but didn't answer.

"One more," Brendan replied, referring to the last cave in this part of the alcove.

Brendan entered the familiar cave and recognized the oil lantern resting on a small table. He walked to the makeshift bookshelf and began pulling books from it, inspecting each one. The first book was severely water-damaged and written in a foreign language that Brendan didn't recognize. "Latin, maybe?" Brendan said to himself. He returned the book to the shelf and examined the rest of them. There was a hard cover version of the King James Bible, an instruction manual for a board game he didn't recognize, a couple of novels by Agatha Christie, and an old western comic that was sold for 10 cents in 1937. He replaced the books and turned his attention to the oil lamp, which was resting on the table. A thin wire handle connected to both sides of the lamp's metal frame, and a round glass bulb rested on a metal base in the center. Brendan lifted the lamp and shook it, listening for fluid in the base. It was empty, and the rusted metal crumbled when handled. He returned the lamp and picked through a pile of torn and crumpled paper under the table.

"Let's go," Myles called from the alcove.

"Coming," Brendan replied. He quickly sorted through the discarded paper and then paused when he came across some familiar writing. The torn page from Walter Tobias' journal was water-damaged, but still readable. He read the first line; *These words are from Father Benedict's final sermon*. He folded the paper and placed it in his pocket before exiting the cave and joining Myles in the alcove.

"Find anything?" Myles asked.

"Nothing useful," Brendan replied.

The two men left the alcove and made their way across the beach and back to the rocky plateau. They paused at the top of the cliff long enough to survey their handywork on the beach below, and although slightly lopsided, it was still very readable.

"We should probably fill in a few more rocks," Myles said. He pointed to a few areas of the sign with fewer rocks than the others.

"Yeah," Brendan agreed. "After we finish the bonfire."

They passed by the pile of wood they had carried from the other side and headed to the narrow crevasse across the plateau. They moved quickly across the weathered rock but then slowed as they entered the narrow trail leading to the river. The loose sand and occasional rocks falling from above were a sure way to twist an ankle if they weren't careful. The narrow path twisted for two hundred meters before ending in a clearing where the river cut its way to the ocean.

"Ready?" Brendan asked before taking a step on the fallen tree bridge.

"It might sound crazy, but I'll feel better once we're back on the other side," Myles replied.

"You think they noticed we've been gone?" Brendan asked. He was already halfway across the bridge when Myles stepped onto the bridge and balanced himself before placing one foot in front of the other. Myles was concentrating on his footing and didn't say anything else until he was on the other side.

"I'm never going to get used to the feeling you get when you cross over to this side," Myles said.

Brendan nodded in agreement and then turned, leading the way back towards the yacht.

The small trail leading back to the Clearwater Pool was overgrown with grass and small bushes, causing them to slow their pace until they reached a wider part of the trail. Brendan thought the overgrown trail would conceal their footprints and wasn't worried about leaving any signs that they had traveled through the area. Once they reached the wider trail, they walked along the outside path where the loose sand was bordered by rock.

They were careful not to leave unmistakable traces of their movement and sometimes moved off the trail, walking through the thicker forest to remain undetected. Brendan picked up the pace when he recognized the area and knew they were only minutes from the pool. It felt like they had been gone for longer than two hours, but he didn't need to be reminded about the mangoes. He was confident about the plan and started contemplating coming back over the next couple of days to finish the bonfire and improve the S.O.S. He was wondering what else they could do to improve their chance of rescue when he entered the clearing leading to the pool and approached the bend just before the large rock.

Just around the bend, Brendan came to a sudden stop and placed his arms at his side to warn Myles of the abrupt halt. The two men stood silently, staring in disbelief. There, on the rock, sitting with his arms folded over his knees, Captain Kleinman waited, a grin that looked both disturbing and ominous on his face.

Leap of Faith

Brendan and Myles approached the captain slowly. They scanned the area, wondering if he had come alone or if someone else was waiting somewhere out of sight. On cue, Brett and Kade appeared from behind a clump of trees just off the trail. Brendan eyed their wooden clubs cautiously and continued his slow approach to the large rock where the captain sat waiting. Brett brandished a four-foot, teak flagpole with a large wooden knob on top. The pole had previously rested in a socket above the captain's cockpit, where it was meant to fly the flag of the ship's nationality. Kade's pole was a bit shorter and made of a lighter colored wood. It looked like it may have been a wooden oar, but it was broken off where the flat piece met the pole.

"We…" cough, "we were…" Brendan cleared his throat to try to sound more confident.

"Wait-wait," the captain interjected. "Let me guess, you got lost while looking for the mango orchard." His ominous smile grew even wider as he reached behind him and pulled the sack from behind the rock.

Brendan and Myles stared at the captain in disbelief. Both tried to make sense of what was happening.

"I knew we couldn't trust that little punk," Myles growled.

Captain Kleinman lowered the sack of mangoes onto the rock. His wicked smile was replaced with an almost wild-eyed anger. "I told you…" He hissed between clenched teeth. "Everybody has a price."

"And what deal did you make him for his betrayal?" Brendan asked.

The coldness in the captain's voice was chilling. "Let's just say…" the captain began, "his needs are somewhat more…primitive." He stared at Brendan, wondering if he would understand the inference. Brendan's furrowed brow, clenched teeth, and snarl told the captain he did.

Brett and Kade immediately stepped in front of the rock where the captain sat to block the way. Brett held the pole in his right hand and slowly tapped the large wooden knob in his left.

"I'm curious," the captain said. His voice dripped with suspicion. He stood on the rock and peered over the two large men. "What's over there on the other side that makes you so willing to risk your life for?"

Myles placed his hand on Brendan's shoulder to try to calm him. "It's a way off this island," Myles said. He was hoping his friend would understand what he was trying to do.

Brett and Kade looked at each other and then turned to the captain.

"It's true," Brendan blurted. "We can show you… it's right over the bridge, just ten minutes up the trail."

The captain's eyes narrowed.

"What could it hurt to check it out?" Myles shrugged with both hands out to his side.

"LIES!" Captain Kleinman shouted.

"No-no," Brendan protested while shaking his head vigorously. "We'll show you."

"I'm sure you would," the captain scoffed sarcastically. "And what? Lead me into a trap? Maybe some rocks fall on my head…get pushed off a cliff? Fall into a hole, Hmm? I don't think so!" He pointed accusingly at Brendan.

Brendan felt his anger rise. "Listen to yourself!" he shouted at the captain. "I'm telling you we found a way for everybody to get off this island, and all you can think about is yourself!"

"YOU JUST WANT WHAT I HAVE!" Captain Kleinman shouted. "I'M THE CAPTAIN!" he continued ranting. "I'M THE ONE IN CHARGE! ME!" Spit flew from his lips as he jumped up and down on the rock and pointed at himself with both hands.

"You've gone mad!" Myles shouted in astonishment.

"YOU CAN'T TALK TO ME LIKE THAT!" Captain Kleinman howled. "GET THEM!" he ordered! He stomped his feet and pointed at Brendan and Myles.

Brendan and Myles knew there was no use running. They had spent the afternoon hauling heavy boulders and were too tired to run from the more athletic and younger men. They were going to have to fight. In truth, Brendan knew it would come to this eventually. As long as the captain wielded the threat of unleashing his two attack dogs, he was never going to listen to anything anybody else had to say. Brendan and Myles widened their stance and braced for the fight.

"Remember Kyle Morris from tenth grade?" Myles asked Brendan as the two large men approached.

Kyle Morris was a high school senior when Brendan and Myles were both sophomores. He was the captain of the football team and didn't think underclassmen should be allowed on the varsity team. Myles was promoted to varsity and became the lead running back during fall camp of his sophomore year. Kyle had gone out of his way to make Myles feel unwelcome and bullied him at every opportunity. Brendan thought it was better just to avoid Kyle, but Myles was never one to back down from a fight. On the last day of Fall camp, Kyle and two of his friends approached Myles in the locker room after practice. Kyle held a dirty jock strap in his right hand and his two friends were snickering as they came. Myles was a firm believer in the old saying, "the bigger they are, the harder they fall", and the boys had spent the previous Saturday afternoon watching the hit classic Karate Kid.

Myles bent low as Kyle approached and performed a perfect "leg sweep". The swift kick to Kyle's left calf sent him sprawling to the ground. He gripped his leg in pain as Myles ripped the jock strap from his grasp and wrapped it over Kyle's head. Myles was eventually tackled by the other two boys and stuffed into his own locker, but Kyle left the locker room limping and never bothered Myles again.

"I remember," Brendan said. He bent his left knee and rested his weight on his left leg and waited for the perfect time to strike.

Brett came for Brendan while Kade went to Brett's right and approached Myles.

Brett raised the teak pole above his head, and Brendan saw his opportunity. He bent his left knee and lowered himself towards the ground while simultaneously swinging his right leg out wide and whipping it towards Brett's left calf muscle. The arch of Brendan's foot swung into Brett's leg, and Brendan yelped in pain. He felt like he had just kicked a rock wall. Brett's left leg buckled slightly, but he immediately regained his footing. Brendan felt the solid teak ball smash into the left side of his head. He saw stars and almost lost consciousness. After falling to the ground, Brendan braced himself on his left arm. He was about to try to get to his feet when he felt the wooden pole crash down on his forehead. Blood sprayed over Brett's legs, and Brendan felt warm fluid flow over his face and into his right eye. The blow hit him so hard he felt his teeth compress, and he wondered if any had cracked. He held up his right hand to prevent further blows to his head and almost immediately felt Brett's boot crushing into his chest. He remembered being kicked again and then struck with the wooden pole several times before losing consciousness.

Brendan felt like he was floating. He bobbed up and down and, for a second, almost believed he was asleep on the raft, still floating out at sea. He tried to open his left eye, but his eyelid wasn't cooperating. He would later realize that the eye was swollen shut. His right eye squeezed open but was blurred by the combination of blood and sweat pooling around the eye socket. He realized he was being carried over someone's shoulder and guessed it was Brett from the broadness of the man's back. He became dizzy when he tried to lift his head to look around, but was able to catch a glimpse of Myles walking a few feet behind. Myles was bleeding from his nose, and both eyes appeared bruised and swollen. His shirt was ripped from the collar down to mid-stomach, and his hands were bound behind his back. A silver piece of duct tape was placed over his mouth, and a rope was wrapped around his neck and held by Kade, who walked beside him. Myles was severely beaten, but it was apparent he didn't go down easily. A large black and purple bruise covered Kade's right eye, and his lower lip was split from top to bottom. Myles hung his head as he walked and occasionally looked up to gauge the trail in front of him. He turned towards Brendan a few times, but Brendan wasn't sure if he could see him.

"It's too bad you're not half the fighter he is," the nasally sound of Captain Kleinman's voice came from Brendan's left. Brendan turned his head and saw the captain walking a short distance away. The captain looked back and forth between Myles and Kade. "If Brett wasn't there to help, I think your friend may have won."

Brendan spat a mouthful of blood towards the captain. The red spital splashed in the dirt at the captain's feet. He was too weak even to take another breath and say anything to the captain. Blood rushed to his head, and he became lightheaded. His head bounced off Brett's back with each step the large man took. The world spun, and he slipped into unconsciousness.

"Brendan," a voice called in the distance. "Brendan, honey…" he heard someone calling…someone familiar.

"Mom?" Brendan moaned.

In his dream, he was surrounded by many people. It was so stuffy in here, and he just wanted to go…play. The dream was hazier than usual, and he felt so tired.

"Would you please stop fidgeting," his mother said. She yanked his hand and pulled him closer to her.

Brendan wrapped an arm around his mother's leg and peered up at the man she was speaking with. "It's the nice man," Brendan thought. He smiled at the man. The man leaned over until his face was even with Brendan's, and Brendan thought the man looked very tired. His eyes appeared magnified through his thick glasses, accentuating their weariness. The man's lips were moving. He was saying something. Brendan focused on his lips. "I'm…" I'm what, Brendan wondered. "So…" Yes, the man is saying I'm so…so what? "For your loss…" the man finished. Brendan's four-year-old brain was struggling to understand. He mulled it over and over until the light came on. "I'm so sorry for your loss." That's what the man was saying. But why? Four-year-old Brendan reached into his pocket to make sure his car was still there. Yep. The man patted him on the head and then walked towards the front of the room. There was something up there, something large. Brendan wasn't quite sure what it was; he had never seen anything like it. The large, polished wooden box had long handles along its sides and a padded white interior when the lid was raised open. The people in the room occasionally walked by and looked into the box…some cried. Whatever was in there must have been very bad.

"Urrgh," Brendan groaned when he hit the ground. He opened his eyes and stared into the face of Brett, who had just tossed him to the ground like a sack of potatoes. The loose sand on the beach had softened the fall, but not by much.

Brendan rolled his head to the left and saw Myles standing next to him. His eyes were still swollen, but Brendan knew he could see him. He turned his head to the right and saw the yacht's stairs hanging over the side. Someone was peering over the yacht's rail and seemed excited.

"Get up!" Brett commanded. He kicked Brendan in the lower back when Brendan didn't immediately start moving.

Brendan moaned again and pushed himself onto his knees, where he rested for a second before Brett placed his meaty hand around Brendan's upper arm and pulled him to a standing position. He realized his hands were also bound behind his back like Myles's.

Captain Kleinman climbed the stairs and then peered over the rail. "Up," he called down.

Brendan felt a push at his back, and he stumbled towards the stairs. He was lifted onto the stairs by Brett and managed to climb to the top without losing his balance. Myles was brought aboard in the same fashion, and then the two men were escorted into the yacht. As they passed through the central hallway, Brendan could hear voices coming from the main living room. Captain Kleinman entered the room first, followed by Brett, then Brendan, Myles, and lastly Kade. Helen sat in a dining chair to the left of the room, and Dwayne sat behind her against the wall. Ethan stood by the entrance with Ashley while Spencer and Madison sat on the couch.

"AYYYYYGHHHH!" Ashley screamed when she saw her father enter the room. Ethan immediately grabbed her by the waist to hold her back. "Dad!" She continued to cry. "What happened! Dad!" She struggled against Ethan's grasp and tried to reach her father.

"It's okay, Ashley, I'm fine," Brendan tried to reassure her. He could imagine what he must look like after seeing Myles and knew his daughter must be terrified.

"It's not okay...what did they do to you!" Ashley screamed. "Uncle Ethan...you have to do something, please," she pleaded. Ethan hung his head and continued to hold her back from running to her father's side.

Brendan and Myles were pushed into the middle of the room, where they were turned to face Helen sitting on the other side. Brett kneed Brendan and Myles in their hamstrings, forcing them to their knees.

Spencer and Madison moved off the couch and walked to the side of the room next to Ethan and Ashley to get a better view.

"Will somebody…please…shut her up!" Helen yelled. She turned and stared at Ashley.

Madison was now standing close to Ashley and took the opportunity she had been waiting for. She reached her right hand across her chest and then swung it wide. The back of her hand caught Ashley across the left side of her face and sent her head snapping rearwards.

"Hey!" Ethan yelled. He still held Ashley around the waist and turned her away from Madison so that she couldn't be hit again.

Ashley quit screaming. A large red handprint formed on the left side of her face, and she began to sob with large heaves of her chest.

"I swear…" Brendan started to say. He fell forward when Brett kicked him in the back. He groaned and then slowly made his way back onto his knees. "I guess this is my trial, then?" A mixture of blood and saliva dripped from his mouth, and he peered around the room with his one unswollen eye.

"Ha-ha-ha, haaaa-ha-haaaa-ha!" The captain laughed hysterically. "Trial?" he said between laughs. "No, Mr. Clark, that would be a waste of time since you have already admitted your guilt." He crossed the room to stand in front of Brendan and stood over him with his hands on his hips. "This…" he said, waving his hand around the room, "this is the sentencing."

"Figures," Brendan spat the blood dripping from his lip at the captain's feet.

"Before I pass judgment," Helen said from behind the captain. "I just want you to know that we settled this in the fairest way possible…" She paused and let a malicious grin spread across her face. "You remember, don't you?" she asked Brendan.

Brendan glared at Helen with his one eye. "Is that what this is about? You finally getting your vengeance?" he said. His voice was raspy, but calm.

Helen rose from her seat and walked across the room to stand next to Captain Kleinman. "I thought you were a fan of votes. No?" She leaned over in front of Brendan and growled, "Or is it only when they go your way?" The question was rhetorical since she didn't really care about his response.

"Please, listen to me…" Brendan pleaded. "There is something wrong with this place…something is wrong with all of us, but if you just let me take you to the other side…" he choked on blood running down the back of his throat and coughed several times, trying to catch his breath.

"What!?" Ethan asked. His interjection from across the room startled everyone listening to the conversation. "What's on the other side, Brendan?" He took a step forward and peered intently at his friend. "You can tell me," he added. There was a long pause before the captain broke the silence.

"NOTHING!" Captain Kleinman shouted. He continued, "There is nothing on the other side…we all know that…" he looked around the living room at the others, and his voice took a more pleading tone. "We all saw the other side when we were on the raft. There is nothing over there, nothing but rock, sand, and…death."

Madison, Spencer, and Kade all murmured in agreement.

Captain Kleinman pointed at Brendan. "For weeks, we have put up with his lies. Put up with his insubordination and refusal to follow the rules that we all helped come up with…"

"Bmmshhnnttt," Myles shouted through the tape covering his mouth. He was immediately kicked in the back and went sprawling to the floor.

Captain Kleinman continued, "I gave him every opportunity! I was reasonable and fair, and he took advantage of that kindness. He has been sneaking out at night and plotting against me…" he immediately tried to backpedal, "us…he has plotted against us. He is sick with whatever delusion he thinks is on the other side and is putting us all in danger…"

"That's not true!" Ashley shouted. She pulled against Ethan's grip. "My dad has done nothing but try to keep us all alive…"

"SILENCE!" Captain Kleinman yelled and pointed at Ashley. "Or you will be joining your father."

"Hey," Spencer interrupted. He turned to the captain, "You said I get to have…"

"SHUT UP!" Captain Kleinman screamed and moved his hand from Ashley to Spencer. Spencer immediately fell silent. "Enough," Captain Kleinman said and turned to Helen. "Sentence them!" he ordered.

Helen bent over again to speak privately with Brendan. "You're going to like this," she smirked. "It's exactly what you've been wanting." She rose back to a standing position and announced to the group, "Brendan Clark, you and your friend here…" she pointed to Myles still lying on the floor, "will be exiled from this island."

Brendan looked puzzled. He was trying to understand what she meant when she continued.

"That's right," Helen said. "Tomorrow afternoon, the two of you will be set adrift in a raft…"

"You can thank your friend for that," Captain Kleinman interjected gleefully. He looked at Ethan and continued, "he found the ship's life raft compartment while reading those manuals."

Brendan turned his head and glared at Ethan.

"It's too bad the raft is only a small two-person model," he added in feigned sadness.

"You're going to put us in a small raft and set us adrift at sea?" Brendan's voice was low as he voiced his understanding of the situation.

"That would…" he mumbled. "We'll die for sure," he said more loudly. His eye was wide with shock.

"NO!" Ashley screamed. "You can't do that, they'll die…Uncle Ethan, tell them they can't do that!"

Captain Kleinman spun around to face Ashley. "Oh, don't be so dramatic." He rolled his eyes. "He's already survived being adrift at sea, and there's no telling how many other islands there are in this area." He turned back to face Brendan. "And the best part is that we're giving each of you your own bottle of water…you know, to be fair. Each of you gets the same number of bottles." He grinned at Brendan and then looked at Brett, still standing behind Brendan. "They'll spend the night in the cave."

Brett glanced out of the window at the setting sun and then bent over and rubbed his left calf. A large dark bruise ran from his knee to just above his ankle, where Brendan had kicked him. The leg sweep didn't knock him off his feet as intended, but did cause him to walk with a limp.

"Oh, what is it?" The captain asked. He sounded very annoyed.

"There's a narrow ledge just before the cave," Kade answered for the larger man. "It wouldn't be safe to walk across at night in that condition."

"Fine," Captain Kleinman huffed and waved his hand as if shooing a fly. "You can manage by yourself…or take Spencer with you."

"I think you should send the girl as well," Ethan said from across the room.

"What!?" Ashley said in surprise.

Ethan continued when the captain gave him a puzzled look. "She's not going to just sit quietly in her room. She'll try to sneak out and free them. Someone will have to stand guard all night on her room."

"Why Uncle Ethan…" Ashley cried.

"You son of a…" Brendan growled and sprang to his feet. He was halfway to Ethan when he felt the heavy wooden ball smash into the back of his head. He was out before he hit the ground.

"Damn it, Brett," Kade complained. "Now I'm going to have to carry him."

"I'll come with you to bring the girl," Ethan told Kade.

"Parties over people," Captain Kleinman announced and headed for his cabin.

Spencer walked quickly to the captain's side and whispered as they walked, "I thought we agreed that I get the girl."

Captain Kleinman turned to Spencer and wrinkled his nose. He sounded disgusted when he replied, "Tomorrow, after they're gone…that's what we agreed."

Brendan once again felt the floating sensation as his head bobbed rhythmically to Kade's steps. His eye burned from the sweat when he glanced around and saw Ethan and Ashley walking behind. Ashley's hands were now bound behind her, and she walked with her head hung, watching the trail in front of her. He couldn't see Myles but heard Kade call to him a few times to give directions to the cave. Myles could barely make out the rocky trail in the fading light and tripped on a few rocks along the way.

The last thing Brendan remembered before making it to the narrow ledge was Ashley sobbing as she walked. "Don't cry," he was thinking to himself when he lost consciousness.

He was dreaming again. This time, he was with his father riding in the orange sports car. He felt the seatbelt strapped tightly across his chest and the ridges of the soft leather seats on his back. He looked out the windows, but could only see the blue sky overhead, as he was too small to see anything else.

"One day she's going to be all yours," his father said. He turned and smiled at Brendan, sitting in the seat next to him. Brendan wasn't sure what that meant, but he was happy and smiled back.

Brendan pulled a toy car from his pocket and held it overhead. He moved the car across the air in his hand and made car sounds, "Vrooommmm....spweeewww."

His dad laughed. "That's right," he said. "It's in your blood, Champ." He revved the car's engine and laughed even louder.

"Errrrr...shhhh," Brendan continued, making car noises. He brought the car down low and then quickly jutted it into the air.

"You got it, boy!" His dad shouted above the revving engine. "Sometimes you just gotta press the gas...and jump!"

Brendan recalled sitting in the stands at a car rally where his dad was jumping over three buses. The long yellow buses were parked side by side, and a long wooden ramp was on both sides. The crowd was cheering so loudly when the orange sports car spun in circles one hundred yards from the ramp. The car straightened and shot off like a dart towards the ramp. People stood and cheered as the car raced closer to the ramp. Brendan couldn't see past the people in front of him. He heard a loud noise, and then people were screaming. He couldn't tell if they were happy or scared, but there seemed to be a lot of activity. He remembered his mother grabbing him and rushing out of the stands. Brendan couldn't remember ever seeing his father again, but as he got older, his mother told him that was about the time his father had left them.

"Whoa!" Brendan heard Kade call. He opened his eye and saw they had reached the narrow ledge leading to the cave.

"You're going to have to cross on your own," Kade said to Brendan as he set him on the ground.

Brendan rose to his feet and stumbled towards the ledge. "Can you at least free my hands?" he asked.

Kade looked suspiciously between Brendan and Myles. "Okay," he agreed. "But if you try anything, your girl's going over the side." He removed the duct tape holding their hands behind them and then walked to stand next to Ashley.

Brendan and Myles rubbed their wrists to get the blood flowing again. Myles also removed the tape from his mouth and spat blood that was draining from his nose.

"Why don't I go first?" Brendan said to Myles. "Hold onto my hand," he added when he set foot on the ledge.

Stars dotted the sky, and a full moon shone brightly overhead, but the deep shadow from the volcano made it almost impossible to see more than a foot or two ahead. The two men inched slowly onto the ledge and then began crossing one step at a time. Brendan slid his left foot forward and felt for the edge of the ledge before moving his foot back towards the volcano wall and then sliding his right foot behind his left. He kept his back to the wall and tugged Myles's hand gently when he was ready for Myles to follow.

"Hurry it up," Kade yelled impatiently from behind.

"Please, Uncle Ethan," Ashley continued to plead with Ethan in private. "Why are you doing this?"

Ethan didn't respond and wouldn't even look her in the eyes. He pushed her along until it was their turn to cross the ledge. He nudged Ashley onto the ledge and followed her closely the entire way across. The group stopped in front of the tall wooden gate and waited for Kade to unlock the chain that held the gate locked.

"Wait," Ethan called as Kade swung the gate open. "I don't remember all the forks and knives making it back to the yacht when she was up here." He nodded towards Ashley.

Kade looked into the cave and then back at Ethan.

"We better make sure there isn't anything in there that they can use to escape," Ethan continued.

"Why!?" Ashley moaned. Brendan glared at his friend.

"Sit," Ethan ordered Ashley and sat her against the volcano wall next to Myles and her father. He held the gate open while Kade went inside to search for anything that wasn't supposed to be there.

"What deal did you make with the captain, huh?" Brendan spat.

"Oh, now you want to talk to me?" Ethan replied. "I've been trying to get you to tell me what's been going on for a week."

"Nothing's in here," Kade called from inside the cave.

"Check in the back, under the bucket," Ethan called back.

"Traitor," Myles jeered.

Ethan knelt and faced the two men. "Do you remember what we used to always say?" he asked. "Huh?" he continued when both men just glared at him.

"Rat Pack forever," Ethan whispered and then stood, closed the gate, and locked it shut with Kade inside.

Brendan and Myles stared at each other in disbelief. "Wha…" Brendan breathed and was cut off when Kade realized he had been locked inside the cave.

"Hey!" Kade yelled and rushed to the gate. "What are you doing?" he demanded from Ethan. He pulled at the heavy wooden bars and then tried to break them down by throwing his weight against them. The cell was well built. The wooden gate buckled but remained standing. "Let me out!" he shouted at Ethan.

Ethan stood in front of the gate with his arms crossed over his chest. "I never did like you," he said to Kade.

Kade tried reaching Ethan through the gate, but his arms were just a few inches too short. He stuck his face through the bars. His cheeks squeezed together, making his lips pout and spit when he spoke. "The captain's going to make you pay," he screamed. "You'll be put on that raft with them!" He pointed to Brendan and Myles, who were sitting just outside the gate.

Ethan turned to his friends. "We'd better get going before they realize something's up."

"What just happened?" Myles asked. He looked over Ethan's shoulder at Kade trying to break the bars, and then back to Ethan.

"I'll tell you on the way," Ethan said.

"On the way to where?" Brendan asked.

"I was hoping you could tell me," Ethan replied. He looked back and forth between the puzzled faces of his friends before continuing, "No, seriously."

"So, you saved us…but didn't have any plan on where we were going to go after you rescued us?" Myles asked.

"Hey, this is your fault," Ethan answered defensively. "Why in the world would you hatch some stupid plan with that little rat without coming to talk to me first?"

Myles and Brendan were quiet for a moment. "I told you we should ask him first," Myles said to Brendan.

Brendan tilted his head back and took a deep breath. "Wait," he said, and turned to Ethan. "How come you're not affected by the island?"

"I'm going to kill you when I get out of here!" Kade yelled. He continued to throw his weight against the bars, attempting to break them.

"We'd better go," Ashley said. She grabbed her father by the arm and began pulling him back towards the ledge.

"You said we could all be saved on the other side of the island," Ethan said to Brendan. "What did you mean by that?"

"That was...erm...kind of a lie," Brendan answered.

"But it would be safer over there," Myles interrupted. "The other side doesn't affect you like this side does, so we'd be safe from the others...at least until we had a chance to recover."

"I guess..." Brendan said.

"Let's figure it out on the way." Ethan grabbed Brendan's other arm and headed towards the ledge.

The four made their way slowly back across the ledge and began the slow trek back down the volcano. Clouds had moved in, and the trail was now much darker than when they had made their way up. Brendan wrapped Myles' arm around his neck and helped his friend navigate the rocky trail while Ethan held Ashley's hand and followed behind the two men.

"So, tell us," Brendan called back to Ethan. "Why are you not affected by the island like the others?"

"My Girl," Ethan answered. "You know, the song."

"Right," Brendan answered. "The one you've been singing for the last week."

"That's it," Ethan nodded. "It's a song someone special taught me how to play on the guitar when I was younger..."

"Was it Amelia?" Ashley interrupted.

Ethan smiled. "Yeah, Amelia. Anyway, when I heard it in the library for the first time, it was like it brought me out of some spell. Suddenly, my mind was clear, and I could remember things clearly." He paused for a second. "I'm not really sure how to explain it."

"We know exactly what you mean," Brendan replied from up ahead.

Ethan continued, "I'm not sure what happened, but I was making plans to tell everyone…" he paused again, trying to remember the day it happened. "And I just forgot. Yeah, just like that…I can't explain it. I didn't even realize I had forgotten until I heard the song again two days later."

Brendan paused on the trail and waited for Ethan and his daughter to catch up. "That effect you're describing ceases when you cross the river. It's like your mind all becomes clear all of a sudden…and that humming also ceases."

"Fascinating," Ethan whispered. "I wonder if the noise affects a person's nervous system…"

Brendan held out his hand. "Whoa, now's not the time to develop theories."

"Right," Ethan muttered. "Still…never mind. So, when you came to the library asking about a way to remember things, I eventually realized you must have also stumbled across this phenomenon."

"Yes!" Brendan exclaimed.

Ethan continued, "It seemed to be working for you, so I started experimenting with Pavlov's theory, and well…here we are."

"Why didn't you just say something?" Brendan asked.

Ethan shrugged. "I wasn't sure how much you knew, and I wanted to take it slow, to try and understand what was happening, to try and fix it. I think maybe you somehow figured out a little more than I did…which is surprising."

Brendan ignored the last comment. "I found a journal on the other side…" he started to explain.

"Dad!" Ashley screamed. She pointed down the mountain to the base where the trail began. Small orange lights bounced in the night and moved in their direction. The line of fire moved like a snake along the trail leading up the volcano.

"Torches!" Brendan said to Myles, who still couldn't see very well, but had heard the fear in Ashley's voice.

"They must have realized something went wrong," Ethan muttered. "One, two, three, four, five..." he started counting the torches. "Looks like they've brought the whole cavalry."

Brendan's eyes followed the trail back down the hill for several seconds before turning to the group. "I don't think we're going to make it to the river trail before they do." He pointed at the base of the mountain and ran his finger along the path that was the trail leading to the river.

"Maybe we...we can make a shortcut and...cut across the volcano," Ashley offered. Her voice trembled with fear.

"Not even if we were in perfect health and in the middle of the day," Brendan said. He turned and looked across the volcano. "The terrain is very uneven and too steep without the proper equipment."

"What do we do?" Ashley wrapped her arms around her father and began to sob.

"We have two choices, and neither of them is very good," Ethan stated matter-of-factly. "We can continue down the trail and face the mob with torches, or we can go back up the hill and corner ourselves in a crevasse."

"What if we go back across the narrow ledge and then make our stand on the other side?" Brendan suggested. "We can pick them off one by one if they try to make it across."

"I say we meet them on the stairs," Myles said. He pointed to a steep part of the trail just a few feet away. "We have the high ground."

"Either way, they could just wait us out," Ethan stated. "We don't have any food or water. How long would it take for one of us to get desperate enough to try and scale the volcano or make it through their torches?"

"I'm scared, Dad," Ashley whimpered.

They were in deep trouble. Either way, they decided it was dangerous with little or no hope of escape. Brendan covered his ears with his hands. The droning hum seemed to be intensifying, and he found it difficult to concentrate. "What to do," he wondered as he slowly shook his head back and forth.

"Let's go, Champ." The words echoed distantly in Brendan's head. He clasped his ears and tried to concentrate, then turned and stared back up the hill.

"We go back," Brendan said and pointed back the way they had just come.

Myles followed Brenda's finger and then turned back to the steep steps just up the trail. "I still think this is our best chance," he said, pointing at the steps.

"No." Brendan shook his head. There was a new sense of determination in his voice. "I saw something from the other side." He turned to face the rocky hill across the river. "I think there is a way out up there." He pointed to an area high above them, where the two volcanoes converged.

"I'm with Brendan," Ethan said to Myles. "Not that your idea doesn't have merit," he continued, "but I'm not getting into a fight where I'm outnumbered and having to rely on two, near-dead old men."

"Fine," Myles relented.

The four started back up the trail. The incline made the going twice as slow as it was when they were walking in the other direction. Ashley glanced back over her shoulder when the trail leveled off and they started towards the narrow ledge. The torches had gained on them, and she could now see the massive outline of Brett in the lead, followed by Spencer and possibly Helen.

"They're gaining on us," Ashley cried. The three men turned and watched the first of the torches climb onto the trail they had just left, not ten minutes ago.

"We need to pick it up," Ethan said. He released Ashley's hand and went to Myles' side so he could take Brendan's place to help his friend. Their pace increased a little, but they could almost feel the pressure from the group on their heels.

"There they are!" Brett yelled. He pointed up the trail to where Brendan and Ashley followed behind Ethan and Myles.

Brendan turned and watched the fires get closer. The fire from the torches reflected in the eyes of the group chasing them, making it appear as if a band of demons was pursuing them. He could also now see that the group not only carried torches, but also wielded poles, rods, and large knives from the kitchen. The razor-sharp steel glinted in the night.

"Aww Aww, A-wooooo," Spencer began to howl like a wolf when he spotted Ashley ahead on the trail.

The four were hurrying so fast that Myles nearly slipped and fell from the narrow ledge. He was thankful Ethan was now helping him, since he doubted Brendan had the strength to prevent him from sliding. They hurried across the open plateau by the cave, trying to ignore the calls from Kade, still locked in the cell.

"Run, you little cowards!" Kade shouted between the bars. He doubled his efforts at trying to break out when he heard Spencer's howl.

"Where are we going?" Ethan shouted to Brendan when Brendan crossed the plateau and followed the narrow ledge past the cave.

"Just a little further up ahead," Brendan called back.

"The ledge ends just two hundred feet past the cave," Ethan tried to argue. It was no use; Brendan had disappeared around the bend.

Ethan, Myles, and Ashley followed Brendan along the ledge and had just turned the bend around the cave when Spencer cleared the narrow ledge. He ran to the wooden gate and began kicking it to help Kade. A loud cracking noise let Brendan know that Kade was about to be freed from the cell. Ethan, Myles, and Ashley hurried along the ledge and came to an abrupt halt when they came to Brendan, standing and staring out over the ledge. They turned their attention across the ravine to the large, dark hole on the other side. The hole was about ten feet wide and slightly lower in elevation from where they stood.

"What are you doing!!?" Ethan shouted at Brendan. "They'll be here in minutes."

Brendan quietly turned from the dark hole and looked at the others. "There," he said, and pointed at the hole.

"What!?" Ethan asked, looking back and forth from the hole to Brendan.

"We jump," Brendan said calmly.

"WHAT!" Ethan, Myles, and Ashley cried in unison.

"That's suicide!" Myles shouted. He walked to Brendan and grabbed his friend by the shoulders.

Ethan threw his hands in the air. "This was your plan?" he shouted. "We had a better chance back there, standing and fighting with Myles."

Brendan took Myles by the shoulders and looked him in the eyes. "This is it." His voice was calm and serene. "This is what my dad has been trying to tell me, remember?" he asked Myles.

Myles turned to Ethan and Ashley. "I think he's lost his mind."

Brendan shook his head, "No, you told me...my dad was trying to tell me something and I just needed to stop trying to figure it out and listen."

Myles stared wide-eyed at Brendan. "Your dad left you and your mom and is somewhere in Arizona getting drunk and watching NASCAR."

Brendan smiled. "My dad died; I know that now."

Myles' jaw dropped.

"What's he saying?" Ethan asked. "This doesn't make any sense."

"He thinks his dead father is telling him to jump across this ravine into that hole over there." Myles turned to look at the hole on the other side.

Ethan walked to the ledge and looked down into the darkness before turning back to Brendan and Myles. "That's at least a twelve-foot jump, and two hundred feet to the bottom."

"No," Brendan said. "It looks that way from here, but it's much closer. I saw it from the other side of the island, where your mind is clearer."

"Okay, let's say you're right; even if we make it to the other side, who's to say that volcano isn't hollow? We'll fall to our deaths once we make it into the hole." Ethan placed both hands on his head and pulled at his hair as he tried to reason with Brendan.

Brendan looked over Myles' shoulder and saw Brett, Kade, and Spencer turn the corner. They began yelling in rage and held the torches over their heads as they ran towards them.

"You have to trust me," Brendan said calmly. "It's the fourth quarter with only seconds left in the game, but we have the ball." He smiled at Myles and then turned to Ethan. "Do you trust me?"

Brendan grabbed Ashley's hand and walked back towards the volcano wall. They turned to face the ledge, and then Brendan turned to Ashley and smiled. "It's going to be okay, ready?" The two began running at a full sprint and leaped into the air when they reached the ledge. Ashley closed her eyes when her foot left the ground.

Myles and Ethan looked at each other for a second before sprinting towards the ledge. Myles gave everything he had for the last ten feet. "Rat Pack forever," they yelled and leaped off the ledge.

The Last Sermon of Father Benedict

Everything was dark. Brendan couldn't tell if his eyes were closed or if it was really just that dark inside the hole. He felt his hair and clothes flapping in the wind and knew he was falling at a rapid pace. He had somehow lost hold of Ashley's hand, and he wasn't sure if she had made the jump.

"Shhhhhhhhhhhhhhh," the rushing air grew louder and louder as he continued to fall.

The freefall was somehow comforting. He couldn't see anything, and the only thing he heard was the constant rushing of air and the low hum of the island. The sensation seemed to last forever. Then…a noise.

"Ding," the chime was penetrating…and familiar.

Brendan slowly opened his eyes. He was no longer falling, but he still had the sensation of moving. He looked up and immediately realized that his eye was no longer swollen. There was no burning sensation from the blood and sweat, and, in fact, he felt no pain at all. A bright light from above blinded him, and he squinted to try to make out the image floating next to the light. A thick straight line ran from left to right and ended in the shape of a large square. There was a smaller square inside the larger one. Next to the image was a red arrow pointing to another symbol. The following symbol resembled a small square adjacent to a larger square, followed by the same thick, straight line. The small square appeared to have a hollow center.

"Ding," the chime sounded again, and the entire symbol flashed three times.

Brendan became aware of movement next to him.

"Excuse me, sir," a woman's voice said softly. "The captain has turned on the seatbelt sign." The stewardess pointed to the image next to the reading light above the row of seats.

Brendan stared at the woman as if she were a three-headed alien from another planet.

"You'll have to fasten your seatbelt," she said when Brendan simply sat there and stared at her.

Brendan instinctively reached down and grabbed the two sides of the seatbelt, fastening it over his lap. "Thank you," the woman said. She smiled and continued down the aisle, checking the other passengers.

A beige airplane tray was folded open and rested just above Brendan's knees. The magazine he had purchased at the airport rested on the tray, illuminated by his overhead reading light. A small Styrofoam cup, half filled with cold coffee, sat in a small indentation next to the magazine. Brendan glanced to his right. Ashley lay asleep in her seat with her oversized black headphones wrapped around her head. Her head leaned to the other side of the seat, and her arms were curled under her chin.

"Ash," Brendan whispered as a tear ran down his cheek.

"Let her sleep," Julia called from her window seat. She gave Brendan a puzzled stare and continued, "Poor thing just fell asleep."

Brendan stared at Julia and began to weep. He rubbed his eyes with his left hand and reached the other across Ashley's seat to touch Julia's arm.

"Are you okay?" Julia said. Her voice was low, but Brendan could sense the concern in her voice.

"I remember," Brendan said softly. He clenched Julia's arm, and tears ran down his cheeks. He closed his eyes and felt a lump forming in his throat. The warm caress of Julia's hand over his made him smile. His eyes suddenly sprang open when he heard the constant hum of the plane's engines and the whooshing wind outside the window.

"Have I…" Brendan paused and wondered if it could be possible. "Have I been asleep?" he asked Julia.

"Yes, you fell asleep reading your magazine about forty-five minutes ago," Julia answered. "Are you sure you're okay?" she asked when she saw the confused look on his face.

Brendan turned his attention to the magazine resting on the food tray. He picked it up and flipped a few pages to the title of the article he was reading when he fell asleep. The Theory of Wormholes and the Fourth Spatial Dimension was the title. He shook his head slowly back and forth. He immediately snapped his head to the left and peered down the aisle. In the low light of a few seat monitors, he made out Ethan's silhouette. Ethan's eyes were closed, and his head rested against the plane's window. Myles and Shanice sat in the next row back. Shanice's head rested on Myles' shoulder, and Myles' head rested on Shanice's. Brendan turned his attention to the other side of the plane, where Spencer and Madison shared a row with Dwayne…the row was empty.

"What?" Brendan said softly and immediately turned to look for Helen, her grandson, or the captain, who was sitting in first class. Those seats were also empty.

"Is something wrong?" Julia asked when she observed Brendan's erratic behavior.

Brendan shook his head and turned to Julia. "I had the strangest dream," he said. Julia continued to stare concernedly. "Were there more people on the plane when we boarded?" he asked.

Julia lifted her head above the seat and peered around the plane. "No, I don't think so," she said while shaking her head. "You're starting to scare me," she added. "Would you like me to get you something to drink?" she asked and moved her finger towards the flight attendant call button on her handrest.

"No-no, that's okay," Brendan said. He waved his left hand in front of him to wave off Julia's offer. "I think I just need to rest." He sat back in his seat and reclined his head on the padded cushion. "A dream? Is it really possible?" He wondered. It made sense. The constant hum he thought he heard on the island was probably just the hum of the jet engines, and the mysterious dark hole was perhaps connected to the article he was reading about galactic wormholes. And the people? They were probably just images of the people he remembered seeing in the terminal. He sighed and slumped into his seat. He closed his eyes and rested his hands on his legs. When he opened his eyes, he noticed Julia watching his hands tremble. He smiled when she looked up at him and then slid his hands into his pockets. Something crumpled in his right hand. A wrapper? His ticket? He pulled out the crumpled piece of paper and unfolded it.

The paper was old and worn, and Brendan was wondering how it had gotten into his pocket when he began reading the first line. *These words are from Father Benedict's final sermon…*

∗∗∗

Children of God, be comforted, for all is not yet lost. In this time of evil, look to the Lord and practice his holiness while doing good whenever you can. Evil, she tempts you and beguiles you with her beauty. But remember, all that glitters is not gold. We have come to find ourselves in a place that is neither here nor there. It is not Heaven, and it is not Hell, but rather a place somewhere in between.

Some have called this place Gehenna, while others refer to it as Naraka; the Romans described it as the first of a series of rings leading to Hades. My faith teaches that this place is called…*Purgatory*.

There are those who have struggled and led a good life; pure, baptized, blessed—they who pass straight from here to Heaven. There are also those who are cursed, wicked, and evil, who are sent straight to Hell. But what if I were to tell you that some leave this valley of tears and find themselves waiting? Those who walk a razor's edge between salvation and damnation. This place is in limbo. The souls who find themselves here have not yet been condemned to punishment, but neither have they been offered the eternal joy of existence in Heaven. We await the final judgment.

Do not give in to earthly temptations.

This island will test you, and it will offer your heart's desire. The Bible teaches that there are cardinal sins —vices that will lead a person to ruin. That will close forever the gates of Heaven. These vices are counted as seven and are called Pride, Wrath, Envy, Lust, Gluttony, Sloth, and Greed. Seven are the deadly sins. A man who comes to Purgatory with any of these cancers in his soul will have that cancer magnified tenfold. He is a slave to his vice and will eventually succumb to it. Do not let your eyes be blinded; remember that Satan will reveal himself, appearing to be beautiful.

Walk through this place with a clean soul. Think good and generous thoughts and know that we are loved…a love that knows no limits, an infinite love. I pray that you are judged worthy of that love and come to know its blessing.

When judged worthy, you will be taken from this island to a place of ultimate peace and joy. There you will know the presence of God. An Angel will reveal to you and show you the way.

Wherever the Ferryman takes you, be it into Hell, across the river Styx, or to the pearly gates of Heaven, know that here, in this place, we were given a final opportunity.

May God have mercy on our souls.

***

"It can't be…it can't be…" Brendan muttered over and over as he read the torn page from Walter Tobias' journal. "No," he finally whispered and set the page down, taking another look around the airplane.

His heart raced, and the world seemed to be spinning out of control. "What does it all mean?" he thought to himself. He looked frantically between Ethan, Myles, and the empty row of seats where Spencer, Madison, and Dwayne once sat.

"Where are they!?" He wondered.

"Ding," the overhead indicator chimed.

Brendan looked up at the information panel, expecting to see that the captain had once again changed the seatbelt condition. The seatbelt indicator light remained unchanged from the previous notification, indicating "fasten." He then noticed that the stick figure representing bathroom occupation status had changed from red to green. *Now Available* illuminated under the green stick figure. The thin folding door of the plane's center bathroom slid open, and the interior bathroom light illuminated the aisle. Brendan heard the man inside the bathroom start humming a song before he exited.

"Hmm-hmm-hmm-hmm-hu-humm," came the familiar tune of Bobby McFerrin's song, Don't Worry, Be Happy.

Brendan stared in disbelief as Dwayne stepped into the aisle while snapping his fingers and bobbing his head. He strolled slowly down the aisle and reached into his pocket to retrieve a large silver coin. He flipped the coin three times, catching it in the same hand, before stopping at row 16. He looked down and smiled at Brendan.

Brendan's mouth was dry. He had so many questions, Where am I? Am I still dreaming? Where are the others? In the bathroom? Why do I still have the page from Walter Tobias's journal?

His mouth wasn't cooperating with his head, and he sat with his mouth wide open, staring at Dwayne for several seconds. "Wh…where…what…" he fumbled. "What's happening?" he finally muttered.

Dwayne stopped smiling and flipped his coin one final time. "Dwayne Ferraman," he said, and then returned to humming and strolled down the aisle past Brendan.

Brendan again thought about how strange a man Dwayne was. He remembered his last conversation with Myles. "I think he's a taxi driver," Myles said. "He kept talking about taking people where they need to go."

"Dwayne Ferraman," Brendan said softly to himself. He turned and watched Dwayne continue to his seat. "Dwayne…Ferra…man," he whispered. "Dwayne…is…Ferraman…" Brendan froze in shock. A horrified look crossed his face. He picked up Father Benedict's last sermon and reread the last part. He dropped the page and mouthed the words…

"Dwayne is…The Ferryman."

END

www.ingramcontent.com/pod-product-compliance
Lightning Source LLC
Chambersburg PA
CBHW070622260626

47161CB00007B/2542